"Say a prayer, boys," Sam said quietly. "This is it." Captain Baugh scrambled down the ladder and ran across the plaza to the room where Travis lay sleeping.

"Colonel Travis!" he shouted. "The Mexicans are coming."

Travis leaped up from his bed, grabbed his sword and shotgun, then raced across the plaza toward the ladder on the north wall.

Out of the morning darkness came the shadowy figures of hundreds and hundreds of Mexican soldiers. They were all shouting now. Some were issuing challenges; others were just shouting to keep up their own courage.

"We're loaded and ready, Colonel," one of the Texians said to Travis.

"Blast away," said Travis. "Then reload and fire again!"

*St. Martin's Paperbacks Titles
by Robert Vaughan*

YESTERDAY'S REVEILLE
TEXAS GLORY

TEXAS GLORY

Robert Vaughan

St. Martin's Paperbacks

TEXAS GLORY

Copyright © 1996 by Robert Vaughan.

ISBN: 0-312-95938-9

Printed in the United States of America

St. Martin's Paperbacks edition / September 1996

10 9 8 7 6 5 4 3 2 1

To Jim Harris

One

Like nearly all the buildings in the little town that lay along the east bank of the Guadalupe River, the Farmers and Merchants Bank of Gonzales was built of adobe brick. Most of the structures in town had straw-covered mud floors, but the bank, in keeping with its lofty status, had a fine, pine-plank floor. The inside walls were whitewashed and bounced back the sunlight which splashed in through the three large windows. The strong light pushed away the shadows even at the back of the room near the teller's cage.

Hunter Grant, a tall man with a rangy build that belied a solidly muscled body, stood at one of the windows, looking out onto the street, curious about what was going on outside. There were, by his count, at least thirty men gathered in front of the apothecary across the street from the bank, and every one of them was carrying a long rifle. In addition, there were more men joining them every minute.

At a table just behind Hunter, two men sat, studying the document he had just presented to them. The younger of the two, a tall, thin scarecrow of a man, was Jules Clay. The older man was John H. Moore, one of "The Old Three Hundred," meaning that he was one of the original settlers Stephen Austin had lured to Texas.

Moore looked up from the document. "Are you sure New Orleans can handle all the cotton we can produce, Mr. Grant?" he asked.

Hunter turned away from the window.

"Mr. Moore, my office is in New Orleans, that is true. But I have markets in Philadelphia, New York, Boston, London, Liverpool, and Paris. You get word to me when you have cotton ready to ship and I guarantee that within a fortnight, I'll have a vessel standing by, off the mouth of the Guadalupe, ready to take on as many bales as you can move down the river."

"There's only one thing I don't like about it," the younger man said.

"And what would that be, Mr. Clay?" Hunter asked.

Clay pointed to the contract. "The way I read this document, if we sign it, we will be agreeing to sell the cotton at the price you have here."

"You are reading it correctly," Hunter said.

"Well, now, suppose the price goes up between now and then? Do you expect us to sell our cotton to you for less than we might get for it somewhere else?"

"Oh, I will not only expect it, Mr. Clay, I will insist upon it," Hunter said. "But consider this. The price of cotton may also go down, in which case I will be buying from you at a price more dear than I would have to pay elsewhere. That, however, is the nature of my business. I am a cotton broker. You two gentlemen are cotton producers. In any producer-broker relationship, there is a degree of risk. But there must also be trust, if the system is going to work."

"Mr. Grant is right, Jules. He has offered us a fair price," Moore said. He stood up from the table, then walked over to extend his hand. "Mr. Grant, I shall be glad to let you handle our cotton."

"Thank you, Mr. Moore. Now, if you two would be so kind as to sign the contracts, we'll be in business."

Moore signed his name with a flourish, then handed the quill over to Jules Clay, who dipped it into the inkwell, preparatory to affixing his own signature.

"Mr. Moore," Hunter said, returning to the window. "May I call your attention to the street?"

Moore glanced through the window. "Yes, I see them," he said.

"Don't you find the gathering of so many armed men curious?"

"Not at all," Moore answered. "Considering the trouble we are having with Mexico."

"Trouble with Mexico? But I thought Texas was a part of Mexico."

"So it is, Mr. Grant, so it is," Moore said. "But, before the War of Independence, the thirteen colonies were a part of England, were they not?"

"What are you saying? That Texas is about to fight its own war of independence?"

Moore stroked his jaw as he gazed out into the street. The group of armed men was now twice as large as it had been when Hunter first noticed it, and it was still growing.

"There is going to be a war with Mexico, of that I am certain," Moore said. "But the unanswered question is, what will the war accomplish? There are some who would have the war do no more than force an agreement from Mexico City to separate Texas from Coahuila and make it a state equal to Mexico's other states. But as far as I'm concerned, in for a penny, in for a pound. If we are going to fight Mexico anyway, we may as well make the fight count for something much more substantial. I count myself in with those who are for severing all ties with Mexico."

"What about the Mexicans who live in Texas? Or is it only the Americans who want to sever ties with Mexico?" Hunter asked.

"Actually, we call ourselves Texians, Mr. Grant," Clay offered, bringing one copy of the signed document over to Hunter. "That includes the Americans and the Mexicans who live here. And you would be surprised by the amount of support we have from our local Mexicans."

Hunter held up the document. "Gentlemen, I was aware of none of this. Under the circumstances, I can't help but wonder if we might have been a bit premature in conducting our business? If you wish, I could take the document back to New Orleans with me and we can meet again, next year, after things have settled down."

"No, the instrument must stand!" Moore said quickly. "Commerce does not stop because of a war. Indeed, that is all the more reason for the conduct of business as usual, for if our enterprise is to be successful, we shall need to call upon all our resources. And cotton, as you well know, Mr. Grant, is one of Texas's most valuable commodities."

From outside, Hunter heard a loud shout: "*If you want this cannon, you Mexican bastards, come and take it!*"

"They seem to be getting a little more worked up out there," Hunter observed.

"They are getting anxious for the ball to be opened," Moore said. "Would you like to go outside and have a look around?"

"Yes, thank you."

As soon as Hunter, Clay, and Moore stepped out of the bank, one of the group of armed men saw them, and cupping his hand around his mouth, he shouted across the street.

"What do you think, Colonel Moore? Are we ready for the Mexicans?"

"I think we're ready for them, boys!" Moore shouted back.

"Three cheers for Colonel Moore!"

"*Hurrah! Hurrah! Hurrah!*"

"Are they calling you *Colonel* Moore?" Hunter questioned, looking with curiosity at the man with whom he had just been doing business.

"Yes, but I have no officially recognized commission as colonel," Moore said. "That's just what the boys are calling me."

"After we formed the Gonzales militia, we voted for John Moore to lead us," Clay explained. "It seemed only natural, he being one of the original three hundred and all. He may not have an official commission, but as far as we are concerned, he is our leader."

"Come down to the end of the street with me," Moore said to Hunter. "I have something I would like you to see."

Hunter followed Moore down to the far end of the street, to an oxcart that was parked under a cottonwood tree. A small brass cannon was loaded onto the oxcart, and hanging from the cannon was a large, hand-lettered banner which read COME AND TAKE IT! A tall, thin, young man was in the cart, polishing the barrel of the cannon, which was already glistening gold in the sun.

"You've got it looking good, Lieutenant," Moore said. "This is Almeron Dickerson, Lieutenant of Texas Artillery," he added. He pointed to the little cannon. "And that is our artillery."

"It's little," Hunter said.

"Aye, it's that, all right," Moore agreed. "This is the Gonzales cannon," he explained. "A couple of years ago the Mexican government gave us this cannon to use for defense against the Indians. But since Santa Anna has assumed power unto himself, all civil authority for Texas has been suspended, including our right to bear arms."

"Yeah, and the sons-of-bitches want their cannon back!" one of the men shouted.

"Which they can have over my dead body!" another insisted, and his challenge was greeted with a rousing cheer.

Moore put his hand on the shining brass barrel. "This cannon is what's behind this morning's demonstration," Moore said. "Colonel Domingo de Ugartechea demanded that we turn it over to the Mexican army. When we sent him our refusal, he swore to confiscate the cannon by force of arms. We are just as resolute that he will not."

"May I ask a question, Colonel?" Clay asked. "Why are you defending this cannon so ardently?" Clay took in the cannon with a wave of his hand. "Look at this thing! I've seen *signal* cannons that could do more damage. Why, any foundry in the United States could provide you with bigger and better cannons, and at very little cost. Lieutenant Dickerson, if you have a background in artillery, surely you know this already."

"You are quite correct," Dickerson answered. "The military value of the cannon is negligible. But what this cannon represents is important to us. It is a symbol of our defiance of the military authority, and our determination of the right to bear arms for our own defense. Because of that, it is vital that we keep this particular cannon away from the Mexicans."

"When do you think this Colonel Ugartchea will come for it?" Hunter asked.

Hunter had no sooner asked the question, when a rider came galloping down the street, shouting at the top of his lungs: *"They are coming, they are coming! The Mexicans are coming!"*

Moore smiled. "Well, Mr. Grant, it would appear that fate has guided your footsteps. You are going to be present for the opening scenes in an act which I predict will be of great historical significance. Come on, boys!" Moore shouted to the others. "Let's meet them at the ford!"

"Bring the cannon," Clay suggested. "Let the Mexican bastards see what it is they came for."

"Yeah, and what they are going to die for," Dickerson added.

With a loud cheer, Dickerson, and half-a-dozen others, started rolling the oxcart and cannon down the road toward the river. Hunter saw what Moore meant about the symbolism of the cannon. It was very obviously not going to be used.

"You'd better take this," Clay offered, handing his pistol to Hunter.

Hunter held up his hands and shook his head. "Thank you, but I won't be needing that, Mr. Clay. This isn't my fight."

"You're American, aren't you?"

"Yes, but—"

"As far as the Mexicans are concerned, there are no buts," Clay interrupted. "To them you are a Norteamericano and you are in Texas. That's all it takes to make you their enemy."

"I'm afraid Jules is right, my new friend," Moore said. "We are not asking you to join in the fight with us, but if things don't go well, you may need that pistol for your own self-protection."

Hunter held the pistol out and looked at it.

"It's loaded, but it isn't primed," Clay explained.

Hunter nodded. "All right," he said. "I'll carry it with me. And thanks."

Hunter headed toward the river with the others. As they passed the houses and buildings, women and young girls began appearing in the doorways and leaning out the windows to wave handkerchiefs and shout encouragement to their men.

Looking around at the other men with him, Hunter was struck by the wide range of ages in the militia. Some were very obviously in their seventies, while others may have been as young as thirteen. And even younger boys were running excitedly alongside, until they reached the river where, protesting, the youngest were retrieved by anxious mothers and dutiful older sisters.

By the time the militia reached the river the rider who had given them their initial warning was galloping back from his second scout. His horse's hooves drummed on the hard-packed road like the beating of timpani, and he forded the river with a silver splash of water. Jerking to a stop, he leaped down from the saddle, then slapped his horse on the rump to send it out of harm's way.

"They'll be along in just a few more minutes, boys!" the rider explained. "It's a company of mounted dragoons and they are just west of the Brubaker place."

"All right, we'd better spread out, men," Moore suggested. "Take up positions behind anything you can find."

With their long rifles loaded and primed, the Texians spread out on both sides of the road and along the eastern edge of the river, looking west as they waited for the Mexicans.

Priming the pistol Clay had given him, Hunter moved behind a fallen log, where he took up a position between Moore and Clay. He could scarcely believe what was happening to him. He had come to Texas to conclude a business deal with the cotton producers of Gonzales, and now he found himself thrust right into the middle of a war! Hunter's blood was racing and his heart was pounding, though whether it was from fear or excitement, he didn't know.

"Hold your fire, boys! Don't shoot until you can see the pretty brass buttons on their coats," Moore ordered his men.

Though the men had been very talkative all morning long, they now became very quiet, so quiet that Hunter was aware of the singing of birds. Then, as if sensing that something was about to happen, even the birds quit their chatter. It grew so still that the loudest sound to be heard was the whispering of wind in the alamo trees.

Hunter was startled by the sudden flapping and whirring of a hundred beating wings. As one, the birds all flew away.

The quiet stretched on for another long minute.

Jules Clay coughed.

Dickerson blew his nose on the ground.

Someone broke wind, and there was a twittering of nervous laughter.

More silence.

Hunter felt the vibrations of the approaching dragoons before he could hear them.

He heard them before he could see them.

Finally he saw them, a large body of men moving up the road en masse, with a flag bearer riding in front of the column. A little piece of red, white, and green fluttered from the top of the staff the flag bearer was carrying.

Hunter felt a slight thrill as he realized that what he was seeing was a battle flag. It was the first time he had ever seen such a sight, and even though it wasn't his country's flag, and it wasn't his country's battle, the scene was awe-inspiring.

When the dragoons saw the armed Texians spread out along the riverbank, their commander held his hand up to stop them.

"Whew, them is some kind of pretty uniforms, ain't they?" someone said, almost reverently.

The Mexican army was well-mounted and resplendently dressed in brass-covered uniforms of scarlet and green. The Gonzales militia was dismounted, and they had no sense of uniformity whatever.

"Hey! Mexicans! You want this here cannon?" one of the Texians shouted. He turned his backside to them, then patted himself on the rump. "Well, you can come get it, but how's about kissin' my rosy red arse while you're at it?"

The Gonzales militia roared in laughter at the taunt.

The two armies were close enough together that individual faces could be seen, and Hunter saw an intense anger reflected in the face of the Mexican commander at the mockery his men were receiving from the upstart Americans. Perhaps stirred into activity by the derision, the Mexican commander stood in his stirrups and turned to shout something to his men.

The commander's shout was followed by the loud bleat of a bugle. At the sound of the bugle the Mexican column spread out in both directions, forming a wide front. Now the two armies were facing each other across the Guadalupe River and, for a long moment, the Mexicans were perfectly still, horse and rider creating an eerie *tableau vivant.*

"Get ready, men," Moore called to his men. "Get ready!"

Looking around him, Hunter saw the Texians' faces tense, and their fingers move deliberately to the triggers.

There was another blast from the Mexican bugle, and then the scarlet and green army started toward them.

At first there was only the beat of the hooves, the jangle of the gear, and the rattle of sabers. But when they reached the edge of the river the Mexican soldiers began shouting and screaming at the top of their lungs.

The Gonzales militia had both the favored position and the superior numbers. But they were untrained farmers and merchants, whereas the attacking dragoons were seasoned soldiers, experienced in Mexico's many battles.

"Now, men, fire!" Moore shouted, shooting even as he gave the order.

There was a deafening roar of musketry as both Texians and Mexicans opened fire. Hunter could hear bullets whizzing by his ears and snapping through the tree limbs behind him.

Immediately after the first volley, a great cloud of gun smoke billowed up to cover the battlefield. The smoke was so thick that Hunter couldn't see more than a few feet in front of him. Several men continued to fire into the smoke, though it was obvious they also could see nothing.

Finally the shooting ceased, with only a few ragged and disjointed shots here and there to put a coda on the volley that had been fired. After that the field grew as quiet as it had been just before the battle commenced.

The men paused, staring out across the river, waiting for the cloud of smoke to roll away so they could see what was happening.

"Be on your toes, men," Moore cautioned. "They're likely to come bustin' out of that cloud, any minute now. Reload, and reprime!"

Hunter's nose and eyes were burning with the acrid tingle of expended powder. Up and down the line, Texians were in various stages of preparing for a second attack. Some were pouring in powder, others dropping in the balls, while still others, farther along, were already tamping their loads down. Hunter glanced down at his pistol. As he had not discharged it, it was still ready. He straightened out his arm and aimed at the billowing cloud of smoke.

Soon, all the weapons were loaded and ready, and Hunter and the Gonzales militia waited tensely for the smoke to roll away. Finally, it cleared enough to allow them to see the other side of the river.

"Glory be, boys! They're gone!" The artillery lieutenant shouted excitedly. "Look at that! The Mexicans has turned tail and run!"

"Yahoo!" another shouted.

"Hey, you Mexican fellas! What's the matter? Was we too much for you?"

Leaving their positions of cover, the Texians began laughing and celebrating their victory. They milled around on what had been the battlefield and pounded each other on the back, exchanging congratulations for "whuppin' the best ole Santy Anny could send after us!"

By the time the last vestige of gun smoke rolled away, John Moore was able to take stock of his situation. Not one of their number had been killed or even wounded. As thick as the bullets had been flying around him, Hunter was amazed by that bit of information.

"Boys, it don't do nothin' but prove that God was on our side, all along," someone suggested.

"Hey, look over there! They's a Mexican soldier, lyin' on the bank of the river!" someone shouted.

Hunter looked in the direction indicated and saw one of the green-and-red-uniformed men lying facedown, just at water's edge.

"Is he dead?"

"He is unless he's learned how to breathe underwater," someone noted, and Hunter saw that the man's face was, indeed, underwater.

Several of the militiamen waded across the shallow ford toward the body. The first one to reach him turned him over, then called back to the others.

"He's dead, all right. He's got a hole right through his heart!"

Almost immediately the dead Mexican soldier became an object of interest as scores of the Texians ran splashing across the ford to stand around and look down at him.

"I reckon, when you get right down to it, that pretty uniform didn't mean all that much," someone said, and several of the others laughed, nervously.

Ashamed of himself for giving in to his own morbid curiosity, Hunter also crossed the river to look down at the slain soldier. The Mexican's large brown eyes were dull and flat-looking in death. They stared out of a face that was already turning blue. Someone found a pipe on the soldier's body and he stuck it in the dead man's mouth.

"There," the soldier said. "I reckon ole Pancho will have hisself a smoke on his way to hell."

A few of the men laughed nervously.

"There's no need to be poking fun at him, boys," Moore said. "He was one of God's creatures, same as we are."

At Moore's gentle chastising, some of the men crossed themselves, including a few of the same ones who had earlier engaged in ridicule.

"Well, Mr. Grant," Moore said, putting his hand on Hunter's shoulder. "It wasn't much of a battle, I'll admit. But when word of this gets back to Mexico City, I do believe that Santa Anna is going to realize that we Texians are serious."

"What if he sends a larger army?" Hunter asked.

"Oh, I'm sure he will," Moore answered. "But the moment Santa Anna sets foot in Texas he'll be playing right into our hands. I believe that even those who now want to appease the Mexicans and negotiate statehood will be ready to declare independence. We will become an independent republic. You can mark my words."

"*Long live the Republic of Texas!*" someone shouted, and the shout was met with a universal chorus of cheers.

The next day, as Hunter was packing to return to his home in New Orleans, Almeron Dickerson came over to the boardinghouse where Hunter had been staying. He was carrying a small package.

"Lieutenant Dickerson, how are you today?" Hunter asked.

"Fine, thank you," Dickerson replied. He held out the little package. "This is for you. My wife put together some food for your trip back. There's some dried beef, salt, flour, and coffee beans. She also made some fried peach pies out of some peaches we dried last summer. You'll find 'em wrapped up in a cloth.''

"I'm much obliged," Hunter said.

"No, it is we, Mr. Grant, who are obliged to you," Dickerson replied. "According to Colonel Moore, your guarantee to buy our cotton will give us the wherewithal we are going to need to fight, and win, this war.''

"Maybe the war won't come to much," Hunter suggested. "If you think about it, the Mexican soldiers didn't stick around long yesterday.''

"No, they didn't," Dickerson agreed. "But they lacked a long shot, being Santa Anna's best.''

"Do you know Santa Anna?" Hunter asked.

"I don't know him personally, but Stephen Austin told me about him. Mr. Austin has met him.''

"What is he like?''

Dickerson filled his pipe and lit it, not speaking again until his head was encircled by pipe smoke. "*El Presidente*, General Antonio López de Santa Anna, is a very vain man. And the fact that his army was defeated by an untrained militia ... a bunch of merchants and farmers ... isn't going to sit well with him. When they come back for us, Santa Anna will be at its head.''

"Do you mean to tell me that the president of Mexico will actually fight in the field with his army?''

"I'm sure of it. Don't forget, before Santa Anna was president of Mexico, he was a general.''

"So was Andrew Jackson, but I can't see him leading an army in the field.''

"Well, that's the difference between Andy Jackson and Santa Anna.''

"What kind of soldier is Santa Anna?''

"According to Colonel Moore, he's a pretty good one, actually," Dickerson answered. "In 1829, on the east coast of Mexico, he defeated a large, and well-equipped Spanish invasion. Later, he led a military coup against Bustamante. The Mexican people have taken to calling him the 'hero of Tampico,' and Santa Anna has a few more glorious names and titles for himself, including, the 'Napoleon of the West.' "

"He does all that, and yet you say he is not a buffoon?"

"He is definitely not a buffoon. And the truth is, when he first became president, everyone in Texas was for him."

"Really? Why?"

"I believe it was a choice of the lesser of two evils. I guess we didn't know what Santa Anna would be like, but we did know that Bustamante was a tyrant. Also, Santa Anna promised to uphold the Constitution of 1824, which granted us Texians the right of full citizenship. So it is no wonder that most of us wished for his success. We thought that after Santa Anna took over we would be allowed to live our lives in peace, raise our families, grow our crops, and prosper. But when Santa Anna saw what we Americans could do with land that, for three hundred years, the Mexicans had thought was worthless, things changed. He was afraid that we were taking over Texas, so he decided to discourage any more of us from coming into Texas. He even tried to force out those of us who had already settled here. He passed laws, one after another, until, before we realized it, all civil authority in Texas had been suspended."

"I can see where you might have grievances," Hunter said. "But don't you think war is a pretty drastic step?"

"It's too late for second thoughts now," Dickerson concluded. "The fat is in the fire. The United States had its Bunker Hill, and now, Texas has its Gonzales."

Hunter picked up his bag, then reached for the little package Dickerson had brought to him. He lifted it to his nose and sniffed appreciatively. "Fried peach pies, huh?" He smiled. "It smells wonderful. I'm already looking forward to eating them."

Dickerson returned the smile. "Oh, I think you are going to enjoy them, all right. You just ask anyone. Susanna Dickerson is well-known for her fried pies. Some folks say that's why I married her."

Hunter stuck out his hand. "Almeron, I want you to know that whatever happens, I wish you and your fellow Texians all the luck in the world."

Dickerson shook Hunter's hand, then held up a finger, as if asking for a moment of attention.

"Before you leave, Mr. Grant, Colonel Moore has one more business proposal he wanted me to make on his behalf."

"What would that be?"

"That you move your business here."

Hunter laughed. "You mean just pull up stakes in Louisiana and come to Texas?"

"Why not? I left Tennessee that way. Fact is, most of us did that very thing. Think about it, Mr. Grant. When we get our independence, we will be ready to take our place among all the other nations of the world. And we are going to be a nation that produces a great deal of cotton. We did three thousand bales in 1833, ten thousand in 1834, and the indications are that there will be more than twenty thousand bales this year. Within less than ten years, I have no doubt that Texas will be producing a million bales of cotton a year.

"A million bales, Mr. Grant. At forty-five dollars a bale, that's forty-five million dollars! Now, if a smart, young cotton broker would come in early enough, that broker would be a very wealthy man someday."

"Almeron, you tell Colonel Moore that his offer does, indeed, sound tempting," Hunter said. "But what you don't realize is, there is something drawing me back to Louisiana that not even cotton can compete with."

Almeron smiled. "It has to be a woman," he said. "I can't think of anything else that would cause a man like you to turn his back on such an opportunity."

"It *is* a woman," Hunter conceded. "But not just any woman. Lucinda Meechum is the prettiest woman in Louisiana." He smiled as he thought about her. "She has hair the color of sunset and eyes the color of emeralds."

"Hair the color of sunset, eh? Well, I sure wouldn't want to be the one to pull you away from that," Dickerson said. He put the pipe back in his mouth and spoke through clamped teeth. "And, I guess when you stop to think about it, it might not be a bad idea for us to have a few friends in the outside world. We are going to need them, as we build our new nation. And Colonel Moore thought that might be your reaction, so he instructed me to tell you to just consider the offer open, for now. In the meantime, it has been a pleasure doing business with you, and I look forward to your return."

"So do I," Hunter said. "Only the next time I come here, I hope the entire Mexican army isn't trying to kill me."

"Was it you they were shooting at then?" Dickerson asked, laughing. "And all this time I thought it was me. *Adios*, my friend."

Two

SATURDAY, OCTOBER 24, 1835, TRAILBACK PLANTATION, LAFOURCHE PARISH, LOUISIANA

Every slave on the plantation had been up since before sunrise, preparing for the big day. In the backyard, beneath a spreading live oak tree, a fire burned under a huge vat. The vat was filled with water, to which had been added whole potatoes, onions, lemons, hot peppers, various spices, and one hundred pounds of crawfish. Two hogs and two goats were butchered, split open, coated liberally with salt and cayenne pepper, then placed on iron grills over a pit of glowing coals. Several loaves of bread were being baked in a stone oven, while jambalaya simmered in one big, black kettle, and rice and red beans in another. The aromas thus produced were so enticing that the invited guests would need no maps to guide them. All they would have to do is follow their noses.

The fit of cooking activity had been put into motion by Angus Meechum, owner of Trailback Plantation, who was, at this moment, standing in the entry foyer of the big house, looking through the latest issue of the *New Orleans Picayune*.

Diane saw him reading the newspaper when she came down the stairs. "Is there a story about our party in the newspaper?" she asked.

Angus looked up at his wife. "I don't know," he replied. "I haven't looked."

"You haven't looked? My gracious, why not? What have you found in the newspaper that is so interesting that you haven't even looked to see if there is a story about your own daughter's engagement party?"

"The people in Texas are holding a convention in San

Felipe to decide whether or not they are going to declare independence.''

"Oh, who cares about what is going on over in Texas?"

"You haven't forgotten, have you, that Hunter was nearly caught up in what is going on over there?"

"No, I haven't forgotten, though I am trying to. To think that our daughter was almost made a widow before she became a bride.''

Angus chuckled. "I don't think it was nearly as bad as all that," he said. "Actually, I think he rather enjoyed it. And I wouldn't be a bit surprised if Johnny didn't go to Texas to get a little taste of adventure himself. I know, if I were a young man, I would be tempted.''

Diane shivered. "Oh, for heaven's sake, Angus, don't even think that," she said. "Johnny is our only son. If he should go over there and something happened to him, I would never get over it.''

"My dear, Johnny is not a child. He is twenty-three years old," Angus said. "Now, I am obviously not going to encourage him to go to Texas, but you must know that he has been talking about it. And if he does decide to go, there is really nothing we can do about it.''

"Johnny has such a case of hero worship where Hunter is concerned. I could just throttle Hunter for coming back with all those stories about Texas," Diane said.

"Well, you know those two boys have always been close," Angus said. He turned the pages of the newspaper. "Ah, here is the story you were looking for.''

"Read it aloud.''

Angus cleared his throat, then began to read in a dramatic, stentorian voice: " 'The *Picayune* receives so many applications in various ways for notices in these columns, that it is only fair to state that we must certainly disappoint most of the applicants.

" 'For an item, purely of a social nature, to make it into these pages, then, is no matter of little note. And thus we are pleased to carry the announcement of a grand party to be given on the grounds of the elegant Trailback Manor, only four miles north of this city, on the twenty-fourth, instant.

" 'The purpose of this most important occasion is the initial publication of the intent of marriage between the beautiful daughter of Mr. and Mrs. Angus Meechum, Lucinda by name, and Hunter Grant, a cotton broker of this city, recently returned from an adventure in Texas, the details of which were carried in this same newspaper one week previous.

" 'Those who enjoy an acquaintance with the family Meechum sufficient to be invited, are assured of a wonderful time in the presence of the most delightful company our fair state has to offer.' "

"Oh," Diane said, her eyes beaming in excitement. "What a wonderful article to have appear."

"Yes, well, I suppose we should go outside and make certain that everything is proceeding according to plan. Thanks to the story in the newspaper, we now have much to live up to."

"Where is Johnny?" Diane asked. "I do hope he has made himself ready to help with the hosting."

"Right now he is attending to something even more important," Angus said. "He is helping with the barbecue."

"Maybe we had better go hurry him along," Diane suggested.

Outside, they found Johnny poking at the coals under the roasting meat. The glowing of the coals made his hair appear even redder than usual.

"Johnny, why don't you leave that now and hurry along to get dressed?" Diane asked.

Johnny looked at the coals, and satisfied they were as they should be, nodded. "All right," he said. "Though, I still don't understand why we even have to have this party in the first place. Don't get me wrong, I think it is going to be a great party. But having to announce that Hunter and Lucinda are going to get married, is a little like announcing that you have just discovered Spanish moss hanging from the trees. Everybody already knows that Hunter and Lucinda are going to get married."

"That may be true," Diane agreed. "But there are some things that etiquette dictates, and the formal announcement of an engagement is one of them. Otherwise, one may as well run off and be married by some civil authority."

"It would be just as legal, wouldn't it?" Johnny quipped.

He walked over to the big vat, then picked up a net and scooped a few crawfish out of the swirling, aromatic liquor. He started blowing on the little red crustaceans, to cool them.

"Recognized in the eyes of the law, perhaps, but not in the eyes of the Church. And certainly not in my eyes," Diane replied.

"I suggested to Hunter that he and Lucinda should just run off and get married, but he said no," Johnny said. He peeled one of the crawfish, then popped it into his mouth.

"I should certainly hope so," Diane replied. "Do run along and get dressed, now. And stop eating the food. I don't want to run short."

"Ha!" Johnny said. "As if my nibbling could cause us to run short. We've got enough food here to feed the entire state of Louisiana."

"Perhaps so, but don't forget that our people will have to eat as well," Diane reminded him. She was referring to the slaves, who, after the guests were served, would be given the rest of the food. That prospect made today as festive an occasion for the slaves as it was for the Meechums and their guests, and their excitement was reflected by the smiles, laughter, and singing as they worked.

"Where is Lucinda, anyway?" Johnny asked. "After all, it's her party. Why isn't she down here helping out?"

"She is getting dressed. As you should be."

"Getting dressed? For crying out loud, how long does it take her to get dressed?"

"Don't you go teasing her today, Johnny. This is a very special day for her," Diane said. "Oh, Doney, you have done a wonderful job! The bread looks beautiful," she called to one of the black women who was removing several pans.

"Yes'm, it turned out real nice," Doney said, smiling over the compliment.

Johnny started into the house, but on the way he made a quick detour to snatch off a piece of just-baked bread. The bread was so hot that he had to toss it from hand to hand to keep from burning himself.

About half an hour later, a white-haired, well-dressed black man called to Angus from the front of the house.

"Mr. Meechum, some of your guests be arrivin' now."

"Thank you, Troy."

"Oh, heavens, is it that time already?" Diane asked. "I am so nervous. I hope everything goes all right."

"Don't worry about a thing, dear. We're all ready and everything will be fine," Angus promised, patting his wife reassuringly on the hand. "Come, let us go greet our guests."

The party was already in full swing when a landaulet carriage turned off the main road and started up the long driveway that led to the Meechum house. This particular landaulet, with a liveried driver at the reins, was from Rosecrown, also in Lafourche Parish, and a neighboring plantation to Trailback. Riding in the carriage were Phillipe Doucette, his wife, Cassandra, and their daughter, Marie.

Phillipe looked at the two dark-haired, dark-eyed women, and wondered how he, by all definitions a rather ordinary-looking man, had managed to convince a woman as beautiful as Cassandra to marry him. Very little of Cassandra's beauty had faded and, today, at forty-four years old, she was as lovely as she had been on the day he first met her. She looked more like the older sister of the young woman beside her, than her mother.

Marie had inherited indomitable courage and strength of will from her father. But thank God, Phillipe thought, her looks came from her mother.

"You have been strangely quiet during the ride over here, Marie," Cassandra said.

"Have I, Mama?" Marie said the words *mama* and *papa* with the accent on the second syllable, in the manner of the French.

"Yes, you have. Is there anything wrong?"

"No, Mama, nothing is wrong."

Phillipe chuckled. "She is upset because she couldn't ride Prince to the party."

Cassandra gasped. "Marie, you didn't really want to ride your horse to the party, did you, dear? What lady would do such a thing?"

"A lady who has a horse like Prince. And a lady who can

ride as well as any man in the state," Phillipe boasted proudly.

"Why, we would be scandalized!"

Marie smiled, then reached across to put her hand on her mother's arm. "Papa is teasing you, Mama."

"Well, thank heaven for that. Still, you have been very quiet for the entire drive over."

"I suppose I have just been thinking about Lucinda's wedding."

"Yes, it is going to be lovely," Cassandra said.

"She has asked me to be one of her bridesmaids," Marie said.

"Has she? I wonder why she didn't ask you to be her maid of honor? Although I am certain she must have been influenced against it by her mother."

"Now, why would you say a thing like that, Cassandra?" Phillipe asked. "Mrs. Meechum has always been very nice to Marie."

"To Marie, yes. But, Phillipe, you must know that that woman has been aloof to me from the very moment you brought me to Rosecrown. For myself, it does not matter. But I would not want it to carry forward so that the same coolness would exist between Lucinda and Marie."

"Why, Mama, I have noticed no coolness. Mrs. Meechum has always inquired about you," Marie said. "And Lucinda and I are the best of friends."

"Of course you are, my dear," Phillipe said. He reached over to pat his wife's hand reassuringly. "Cassandra, I am sure any aloofness you may perceive is all in your imagination. After all, what reason would Diane Meechum have to dislike you?"

"None," Cassandra said. "That is, no *real* reason."

Phillipe gave his wife's hand an extra squeeze.

Up at the house, several tables and chairs had been set out at various places around the lawn; some down by the arbor, others under the pecan trees, and even a few beneath a trellis which, had it been springtime, would be dripping with purple wisteria. Johnny Meechum was holding court with several of the other young swains. Most of the single young women had gathered at the tables under the trellis. Marie took her plate over to join them.

"Wasn't Hunter Grant's trip to Texas the most exciting thing?" one of the girls asked. "They say he was right in the middle of a terrible battle!"

"I hear that Johnny is planning to go to Texas as well, only he doesn't want his mother to know."

"The only reason Johnny wants to go is because Hunter was there," another said. "I swear, if Hunter chopped his head off, Johnny would want to do so as well."

"Well, they are very good friends," another noted.

"They are more like brothers, than friends. Hunter's mother and father both died when he was only fourteen years old, and Mr. and Mrs. Meechum all but took him in."

"Yes. The wonder is, he didn't regard Lucinda as so much of a sister that he wouldn't marry her."

"There was no chance of that. Lucinda set her cap for him a long time ago. Poor Hunter never knew what was happening," one of the girls said, and they all laughed.

"They do look happy, don't they?" one of the others said, nodding toward the corner of the porch where Lucinda and Hunter were greeting well-wishers. Lucinda was wearing a lime-green dress, while Hunter had on a dark blue jacket and mustard-colored trousers, stuffed down into highly polished boots.

"Well, who wouldn't be happy, planning a wedding?" someone asked.

"Speaking of planning a wedding, Marie, when will you and Sam McCord be announcing your wedding plans?" another asked.

Marie was taken aback by the question. "*My* wedding plans?"

"Yes. Everyone knows that you and Sam are going to be married. We just don't know when."

The girls laughed.

"Oh, do tell us everything!"

"Let's not discuss my plans now," Marie said, sidestepping the question. "After all, this is Lucinda's day."

"Marie is right, this is Lucinda's day. Let's go over and

talk to her now. I want to hear more details about the wedding.''

So excited were the young women by the prospect of talking with Lucinda, that they failed to notice Marie didn't go with them. Instead, she wandered down the long, sloping lawn, away from the crowd, toward a small boat dock. She moved to the very edge of the dock and stared down into the water of the bayou, studying her reflection to see if she could see anything different about herself.

It all started when Sam McCord came over to the house yesterday afternoon and asked her to go horseback riding with him. He told her that he had something very important that he wanted to discuss with her.

"Shall we have a race?'' Marie challenged, leaning over to pat Prince on the neck as Sam swung into his own saddle.

"You're on!'' Sam shouted back, urging his horse forward immediately.

"No fair!'' Marie shouted, slapping her legs against the sides of her horse, even as she yelled, "Go, Prince, go!''

Prince burst forward like a cannonball, reaching top speed almost immediately. Marie bent low over his withers, laughing into the rush of wind with the pure thrill of the run, feeling as if she and Prince were one. They flashed down the road with Prince's hooves drumming a steady rhythm, kicking up little spurts of dust behind him. She urged her horse to an even greater speed and for a few dizzying seconds, had the fantasy that Prince was actually going to take off and fly!

She reached the grassy glen at the bayou nearly six lengths ahead of Sam, and had already dismounted and was praising Prince for the race he had run by the time Sam brought his own horse to a halt.

"If I could disguise you as a man, I could make a fortune betting on you in horse races,'' Sam said, laughing, as he dismounted.

"Oh? Do you want me to look like a man?'' Marie teased.

"Hardly,'' Sam said, putting his arms around her to kiss her.

Remembering that he had told her he had something important to discuss with her, Marie was convinced that he was going to ask her to marry her, and when Sam began kissing her, she, eagerly, kissed him back. As their passions increased, she made no effort to put a brake on them. Why should she? Would Sam not, soon, be her husband? And would it not then be his obligation to be responsible for the both of them?

Passions rose and blood heated, but Sam made no effort to slow things down. What followed was a series of delectable, but frightening, events, the memory of which was now hidden behind a sensory-laden fog of guilt. Now, her most vivid recollection of yesterday was coming to her senses as she was readjusting her clothing.

An innocent young girl had gone riding with Sam McCord yesterday afternoon. Less than one hour later, that innocence had been abandoned.

Overcome with guilt, Marie said not one word, nor did she look at Sam during their long, quiet ride back. When they reached the house they mumbled hasty good-byes, then Marie hurried inside. With a silent wave toward Phillipe Doucette, Sam rode off. Whatever it was he had come to talk about was never discussed.

Marie spent a sleepless night last night, praying that the Lord would forgive her for what she had done. Her transgression was still weighing heavily upon her conscience when she awoke this morning, and it had been that same guilt which caused her silence, so prolonged as to arouse her mother's notice during the drive over.

"You haven't taken ill, have you?" a man's voice asked.

Startled, Marie turned to see who had spoken to her and was surprised to see Hunter Grant standing at the other end of the little boat dock.

"Why, Mr. Grant! What are you doing here? Shouldn't you be with Lucinda, greeting the guests?"

Hunter's blue eyes twinkled in amusement, and he chuckled. "Correct me if I am wrong, Miss Doucette, but I thought you *were* one of the guests," he said.

"Well, yes, I suppose I am, but I didn't mean for you to look after me."

"Lucinda saw you walk down here alone and she was concerned that you may have eaten something that didn't agree with you. She asked me to make an inquiry."

"I'm fine," Marie said. Nervously, she touched her hair. "I just walked down here to look at the water, that's all. I'm ready to go back now."

Hunter looked at her as if he didn't quite believe her answer. He took a breath to ask another question, then reconsidered, and, instead, offered her his arm. "Good. Then, if you are ready to rejoin the others, I'll walk you back."

Marie put her hand through his arm. "Thank you," she said.

"By the way, where is Sam?" Hunter asked, as they started back. "I don't believe I have seen him today."

That is a very good question, Marie thought, though she didn't give voice to her thought. Where was Sam? She realized at that moment that his absence was one of the things that was causing her such distress.

"Oh, I'm sure he'll be along soon," Marie said, but the assurance sounded weak, even to her own ears.

MONDAY, OCTOBER 26, AT THE ABSINTHE HOUSE IN
NEW ORLEANS, LOUISIANA

Hunter Grant was in one of New Orleans's most popular establishments, drinking bourbon and water. An exceptionally beautiful girl, a quadroon with golden skin and doelike eyes came over to him. Putting her hands on his table, she leaned forward and smiled at him, managing to show a generous portion of her breasts as she did so.

"May I offer you another drink, monsieur?" the girl asked.

"No, I'm fine, thank you."

"Something else, then?" The girl raised up from the table and slid her hands down the sides of her hips slowly, provocatively. "I have a very lovely room upstairs, if you would care to come up for a visit."

Hunter took another swallow of his drink. "You are a beautiful temptress, Jolene," he said. He saluted her with his glass. "But I think, perhaps, I should stick to this."

"Such is the pity, Monsieur Grant," Jolene said. "I think we would be very good together."

"I have no doubt," Hunter agreed.

"Oh, here is your friend," Jolene said, nodding toward the redheaded young man who was just now coming down the stairs.

Johnny Meechum, looking considerably more flushed than he had when he went upstairs a few minutes earlier, pulled out a chair and sat at the table across from Hunter.

"That didn't take long," Hunter teased.

"No, I don't guess it didn't," Johnny replied. He smiled sheepishly, then brushed an unruly shock of hair back from his forehead. "Whew! I tell you the truth, Hunter, I do believe I am in love."

"Celeste is a very pretty girl, all right, but I don't know that—"

"Celeste?" Johnny interrupted. "No. I'm in love with Danielle," Johnny corrected. He saw Jolene walking by. "Say, darlin', could I have a drink over here?" he called to her.

"*Oui*, monsieur."

"That Jolene is a pretty little thing, isn't she?" Johnny asked. Then he turned his attention back to Hunter. "What makes you think I'm in love with Celeste?"

"Oh, I don't know. Maybe it is because she was the one you went upstairs with," Hunter replied.

"Oh, yes, now that you mention it, I guess I did go upstairs with Celeste, didn't I? But when we got upstairs I saw Danielle just coming out of her room so I . . ." Johnny giggled. "I switched girls and"—Johnny clapped his hands together—"it happened, just like that. Boom, I'm in love."

"You are in love?"

"I am in love," Johnny insisted. He reached for the drink Jolene brought him. "*Merci*, darlin'," he said, smiling at her. He turned his attention back to Hunter. "I'm serious, Hunter. If Danielle wasn't a quadroon, I'd marry her. Hell, I would anyway if I could, but the law says that one-fourth, even one-eighth, of a part of colored blood makes you colored. And a white can't marry a colored."

"That is the law," Hunter agreed. He smiled. "And right now I'd say that is probably a pretty good law, at least as far as you are concerned. Otherwise you'd let something other than your head do your thinking."

"I could take her to Texas," Johnny suggested. "I wouldn't even have to tell them about her touch of the brush. I could go to Texas and fight in their war, then get myself some land. We could get married there."

"Johnny, Trailback is one of the largest plantations in Louisiana, and you are your father's only son," Hunter said. "Are you saying you would be willing to turn your back on all that for this girl?"

"I guess not," Johnny admitted. "But Danielle is the kind of girl that can make you start thinking about things like that." Suddenly Johnny smiled broadly. "I'm not supposed to tell you this, but you're going to get half of Trailback as soon as you and Lucinda are married. Pop and I have already discussed it."

"Johnny, I can't do that," Hunter said. "I can't take your birthright from you."

"Ah, don't worry about it," Johnny said easily. "Listen, I've got an idea. Why don't you go upstairs and give Danielle a try? You'll see what I mean."

Hunter looked at his friend in surprise, then he burst out laughing. "What the hell do you mean, go upstairs and give her a try? Didn't you just tell me you were in love with her?"

"Yes."

"And now you want me to take her to bed?"

"Yes. Well, like you said, I can't marry the girl. Besides, what are friends for, if they can't share the good things of life?"

Hunter laughed again. "Thank you, but no thank you. If I did something like that, Lucinda would never again have anything to do with either one of us."

Johnny smiled conspiratorially and wagged his finger back and forth. "What Lucinda doesn't know won't hurt her. Besides, Lucinda is so in love with you that there is absolutely nothing you could do that would cause her to turn you out. What do you say, Hunter? You want to take advantage of the situation while you still can? Look, there she is over there, by that table. Have you ever seen anyone more beautiful?"

Hunter looked over at the young woman, and, sensing that she was the object of his scrutiny, Danielle flashed a brilliant smile, then thrust her hip out invitingly.

"You know what, Johnny? I think we ought to get out of here. Let's go find a card game somewhere."

"Uh-huh, your resolve is weakening, isn't it? You want to give Danielle a try, don't you?"

"No, my resolve is not weakening. I'm just ready to play cards, that's all."

"You've got an urge to stray, Hunter, my boy. I know that look."

"Come on, let's go," Hunter insisted.

"All right, if you insist." Johnny got up, then looked over toward Danielle, Jolene, and a few of the other women. Putting his hand across his stomach, he made a courtly bow. "Alas, ladies, I fear we must bid thee all farewell," he called.

"Good-bye, Monsieur Meechum, Monsieur Grant," the girls called back.

Johnny threw them all a kiss as they stepped out into the warm night air.

Three

Staying in the Vieux Carre, Hunter and Johnny walked for a short distance along the *banquette*, passing by little patio gardens and under iron grillwork balconies, until they came to a brightly lit establishment called the Golden Pigeon. The Golden Pigeon was many times larger than the Absinthe House, and much more elaborately decorated. It had crystal chandeliers which, along with the clusters of lanterns on the walls, provided a bright beacon that drew revelers to it like moths are drawn to a flame.

Inside, there were several tables covered in green felt, around which sat men playing cards. Hunter and Johnny joined one of the games. As Hunter sat down, he looked around the table, recognizing all the players except one. The player he didn't know was colorfully dressed in green and gold.

"Boys, this august gentleman is Don Juan Esteban Montoya," Emile Underhill said by way of introduction. Underhill was one of New Orleans's wealthier merchants.

"Are you from Texas?" Hunter asked.

"I am from Vera Cruz," Montoya said. "Not Tejas." He pronounced Texas in the Spanish fashion.

"That's a funny way of saying Texas," Johnny said. "I never heard it pronounced that way before."

"It is the way my people have pronounced it for three hundred years," Montoya said. "Why have you such an interest in Tejas?"

"Haven't you heard? There is a war going on over there."

"Hardly a war, senor. A few rebels are making a disturbance, that is all. Our soldiers will soon have things under control."

Johnny laughed. "Is that the way it looked to you, Hunter? Do you think the Mexican soldiers will soon have things under control?"

"The ones I saw at Gonzales ran like scared rabbits," Hunter said.

"Senor, the men you saw at Gonzales can scarcely be called soldiers. They are thieves, scoundrels, and brigands who have landed in the army to avoid prison. If the Norte-americanos chose to gage our army by those misfits they saw at Gonzales, then they will be making a serious mistake."

"What makes you think the rest of the army is any better?" Johnny asked.

"Because, senor, I am a major in the *zapadores,*" Montoya said proudly.

"What is the *zapadores?*"

"Engineers," Underhill explained. "Only in the Mexican army, the *zapadores* are sort of a cross between the engineers and the cavalry of our army. They are the most elite unit."

"Tell me, Mr. Montoya, if you belong to such an elite unit in the Mexican army, what brings you to New Orleans?" Hunter asked.

"I am here on family business. I have had a most successful visit to New Orleans, arranging for a market for the coffee beans my family grows," Montoya explained. "And, I am more properly addressed as 'Don' Montoya."

"Well, now, that's real friendly of you, Don, using your first name like that," Hunter said.

"*Don* is not my first name, senor. It is my title," Montoya explained.

"All right, Don. Whatever you say." By the twinkle in his eye, everyone else around the table realized that Hunter knew the difference and was just having a little fun at the Mexican's expense.

"Gentlemen, shall we play a little cards?" Underhill suggested, hoping to defuse the situation which, he believed, was beginning to get a little uncomfortable. He spread the cards out on the table in front of the other players, then flipped them over expertly. After that, he shuffled the cards and began to deal, his hands moving swiftly as a pile of cards appeared in front of each player.

Hunter won the first hand and Johnny the second. After that Hunter won steadily, to the increased agitation of Montoya, who quickly became the game's biggest loser. Thinking he held the winning cards, Montoya sought to recoup his winnings by betting particularly heavy on one hand, only to see Hunter win that one as well.

"Your run of luck seems . . . phenomenal," Montoya finally said.

"Not luck, *amigo,* skill," Johnny insisted.

"Senor Grant, I would like the opportunity to play against you, alone," Montoya said.

"That wouldn't be fair to the others," Hunter replied easily. "You aren't the only one losing here, and that would deny them the chance to recover their money."

Montoya looked at the table. Besides himself and Hunter, there were three other players.

"Suppose we take thirty percent from the pot, to be divided equally among these three?" Montoya suggested. "What would you gentlemen say to that?"

"That's all right by me," Johnny said. "I don't seem to be winning any other way."

"That's fine by me, too," Underhill agreed, and the third quickly assented, so that the decision was now up to Hunter.

"All right, Montoya, I'll play you."

"How about one hundred dollars on a hand of show-down?"

"That would mean two hundred dollars in one pot!" Underhill said loudly, mentally computing his share of the winner's pot.

The news that one hundred dollars was being wagered on one hand of showdown spread from table to table, and several of the other players in the establishment abandoned their own games to come over and watch this one.

"Choose the dealer," Hunter said.

Montoya looked up, then chose one of those who had just arrived.

Excited at being a part of it, the man chosen to deal sat at the table and picked up the cards.

"Senor Montoya, my name is Henry Code," the dealer said. "I am honored to deal for the two of you. Gentlemen, ante up."

Silver and gold coins were shoved to the center of the table, where they gleamed, softly, in the artificial light.

The cards were dealt and Hunter won the hand with a pair of fours.

"A pair of fours," Montoya said. "Not a very impressive hand."

"Maybe not, but it was good enough to beat yours," Hunter reminded him.

"Another one hundred dollars?" Montoya suggested, sliding the bet forward.

"All right," Hunter replied easily, pushing a stack of coins to the middle of the table.

Hunter won that hand with a pair of tens.

Montoya swore in Spanish.

"Mister, I don't know what you just said," Hunter said easily. "But I sure hope it wasn't anything a fellow might take offense to."

"We will play again," Montoya insisted.

"Seems to me like you ought to quit while you still got that fancy shirt you're wearin'," one of the onlookers suggested.

"Yes, and them pants," another added, and the crowd roared with laughter.

Montoya knew they were laughing at him, and that knowledge made him even angrier. He slid three hundred dollars toward the center of the table and stared at Hunter.

"We will draw one card," he said. "The high card wins."

Hunter matched the money without a word.

Montoya smiled coldly. "I did not think you would have the courage to play for three hundred dollars," he said.

"It doesn't take courage, Montoya, to play with your money," Hunter said.

Again the crowd roared with laughter, and Montoya's anger grew more intense. He made an impatient gesture toward the dealer and the dealer fanned the cards out.

"Draw the first card," Montoya said.

Hunter reached for a card, but before he touched it, Montoya reached down and grabbed his wrist, stopping him just short of the card.

"I have changed my mind, senor," he said. "I will play the card you were going to take."

"Be my guest," Hunter invited.

Montoya flipped over a king, then he grinned broadly. "Thank you for finding it for me," he said as he reached for the pot.

"Just a minute, Don Juan Montoya," Hunter said quietly. "I haven't had my turn." He picked a card, then turned it over slowly. It was an ace. The onlookers gasped in surprise.

Montoya stared at the card for a moment, then his eyes blinked rapidly, as if he couldn't believe what he was seeing. "Senor! I do not believe an honest man can win so consistently," he said.

Hunter's eyes grew cold and flat as he stared across the table at Montoya. All other sound in the room had ceased and everyone was looking at the two men who were sitting across the table from each other.

"You know what your problem is, Montoya? Mexicans can't play cards any better than they fight," Hunter said. "And even though you are a pissant in fancy clothes, you are still a Mexican."

"Pissant?" Montoya questioned. He looked around in confusion. "What is this, pissant?"

Underhill, who spoke Spanish, explained the term to him.

"*Que?*" Montoya shouted angrily. He stood up so quickly that he knocked over his chair. "Senor! I am a gentleman and an officer in the Mexican army. My family is of royal

Spanish lineage. How dare you refer to me as a pissant!''

"And how dare you accuse me of cheating?" Hunter responded. "Now, why don't you just take your losses like a man, and let's back away from this before it gets out of hand?"

"It is already too late, senor. I do not know how things are in New Orleans, but in Mexico, an insult to one's honor cannot be left unanswered."

Hunter's ice-blue eyes grew flat. "Are you calling me out?"

"If you mean, am I challenging you to a duel, the answer is *si*, senor. I am challenging you to a duel."

Hunter sighed. "Are you sure you want to do this?"

"You have left me no choice. My honor demands satisfaction."

"Very well, Senor Montoya, you shall have your satisfaction."

Montoya's smile showed no mirth. "You have just sealed your doom," he said. "I am the best swordsman in all of Mexico."

"That's very interesting, Senor Montoya," Hunter replied. "But, in case you have forgotten where you are, we aren't in Mexico. We are in New Orleans. And, in New Orleans, the challenged party has the choice of weapons. I choose pistols."

"Pistols?" Montoya replied in surprise. The look of confidence on his face was suddenly replaced by one of anxiety. "But, senor, swords are the weapon of choice for gentlemen."

"What does that have to do with us?" Hunter asked easily. "I do not pretend to be a gentleman, and by your poor sportsmanship, you have forfeited all claim to that distinction yourself. Pistols, Mr. Montoya." Now, Hunter smiled again. "Unless, of course, you wish to withdraw your challenge. Do so now, and it will end here."

Montoya blinked a couple of times, now much less sure of himself than before. "No, I . . . I will not withdraw the challenge."

"You'll need an arbitrator," Underhill said.

"What about Colonel Bernard Troupe?" another suggested. "He's directed more duels than just about anyone."

"*Colonel* Troupe?" Montoya said. "He is an officer, then?"

"Fought agin the British right here in New Orleans, back in 1815," Underhill said.

"Very well, he is acceptable to me," Montoya agreed.

"And a surgeon," someone else added.

"What about Dr. Hazelip?" Johnny suggested.

"I do not know this surgeon," Montoya said to Hunter. "But as I do not intend to make use of his services, I will defer to your judgment."

"Dr. Hazelip will do," Hunter said.

Colonel Troupe, who was in the establishment next door, was quickly summoned. He was a short, bald man already growing corpulent with success and middle age. There was an aura of command about him, and he assumed his position as arbitrator as soon as he arrived.

"Who are the disputing parties?" he asked.

Hunter and Montoya were pointed out to him.

"Senor Montoya, I must point out to you that I am personally acquainted with Mr. Grant. You may wish to find someone who knows you both, or who knows neither party."

"I do not think I can find anyone here who knows me," Montoya replied. "Nor, do I believe, can I find anyone who does not know Senor Grant. I am told you are an officer."

"I am a colonel in the militia," Troupe explained.

"I, too, am an officer," Montoya said. "I shall depend upon the integrity of one officer to another."

"Very good, sir, I accept the assignment. Now, my first duty is to see if this duel can be prevented. As you are the challenger, what would it take to satisfy you, Senor Montoya?"

"He has impugned my honor, and the honor of the Mexican army," Montoya said. "I demand an apology."

"I have already apologized once," Hunter said. "That should be enough."

"I also demand the return of money which I feel was taken dishonestly," Montoya added.

"That, I will not do, for to return the money would be an admission of guilt, and I am guilty of nothing."

"Then I am afraid I can be satisfied only on the field of honor."

"Very well, gentlemen, an honest effort having been made to prevent the duel, I now declare that a duel is the only answer. You will each need a second."

"I'd like to be your second, Hunter," Henry Code said quickly. "I feel as if I have a particular interest in this, since I was dealing the cards. And, if he accuses you of cheating, that's the same as accusing me of cheating."

"Have you any objections to Mr. Code acting as your second?" Colonel Troupe asked.

Hunter looked over at Johnny, who was just about to make the same offer. However, as it would be a terrible breach of courtesy to reject Henry Code's offer, especially under the circumstances proposed by Code, Hunter had no choice but to accept. Johnny, realizing this as well, shrugged his shoulders and smiled in acquiescence.

"Thank you, Mr. Code, I accept your kind offer," Hunter said.

"And who shall act as my second?" Montoya asked, looking around.

No one offered.

"Come, come, senors. Is there no one among you who will come to the aid of a foreigner who stands in need of assistance?"

Johnny looked around, and when he saw no one else making the offer, he spoke up.

"All right. If no one else will do it, I'll act as your second."

"You, Mr. Meechum?" Colonel Troupe asked. "But you are Mr. Grant's friend."

"That's right, I am his *best* friend," Johnny confirmed. "And about to be his brother-in-law. But it is worth being this Mexican peacock's second, just to see him get his comeuppance."

Montoya looked around. "But surely this will not do. Will no one else volunteer to act on my behalf?"

Johnny laughed. "What's the matter, Montoya? Are you afraid I will load your pistol with powder, and no ball?"

"The thought did occur to me," Montoya admitted.

"You need have no concern on that matter, Senor Montoya," Underhill said. "Colonel Troupe is an exacting arbitrator. He has, personally, killed duelists who took unfair advantage. He is your guarantee that the duel will be on the up-and-up."

"Very well then, Senor Meechum. I accept your offer."

"Mr. Meechum," Colonel Troupe warned. "I give you fair warning, sir. If you agree to be this man's second, I shall hold you to your honor in all accounts. Do you understand, and agree to that?"

"Don't you be worrying about me, Colonel Troupe. I'll play my role, and I'll follow all the rules," Johnny promised.

"Then so be it. You will act as Senor Montoya's second."

"Where and when shall this duel be fought?" Montoya asked.

"On Cypress Island in the Metairie Bayou, tomorrow morning at dawn," Colonel Troupe answered. He turned to Hunter. "Mr. Grant, I now offer you one last chance to satisfy Senor Montoya by apology, and by returning his money."

"No apology. No return of the money," Hunter said.

"Senor Montoya, I offer you one last chance to withdraw your challenge."

"The challenge stands."

"Very well, gentlemen, I shall see you both tomorrow at dawn," Colonel Troupe said.

TUESDAY, OCTOBER 27, 7:00 A.M., CYPRESS ISLAND, IN THE
METAIRIE BAYOU, LAFOURCHE PARISH

A heavy fog had moved in, masking Cypress Island in its shroud and making ethereal tracings of the Spanish moss which hung wraithlike in the limbs of the trees. The fog was so thick that Hunter, who was standing down at the waterline on the edge of the island, was unable to make out the opposite shore.

Behind Hunter, in the thick growth of trees which gave the island its name, a woodpecker drummed loudly, the staccato thumping echoing hollowly through the woods. The drumming was followed by the call of a whooping crane, then the chatter of a squirrel. A fish jumped, then reentered the water with a splash, sending concentric ripples to disturb the otherwise smooth, silver-gray surface of the bayou. Henry Code cleared his throat and Hunter turned to look at him.

"I sure hope this dampness doesn't foul the powder," Henry said. He was holding a small, felt-lined, wooden box. The box contained two dueling pistols, plus the powder horn and balls with the pistols that would be charged.

"We'll be using the same powder," Hunter replied. "If it is fouled for one of us, it'll be fouled for us both."

"I suppose that is true," Henry agreed. Henry moved down to the edge of the water to stand beside Hunter. "Do you see anything yet?"

"No, not yet, not through this fog."

"It's dawn, they should be here by now. I don't understand what's keeping them."

Hunter smiled. "What's the rush, Henry?" he asked. "To tell you the truth, I'm not in that big of a hurry to kill someone . . . or to get myself killed."

"No, I don't suppose you are," Henry agreed. Suddenly he held up his hand. "Wait! I think I hear something."

Both men strained to listen, then Hunter heard the telltale sound of oars, splashing quietly in the water.

"Yes, I hear it, too," Hunter said. "It sounds like a boat, coming our way."

They continued to stare into the fog toward the sound, until, finally, the boat materialized. The little craft moved steadily toward the shore until its three occupants could be easily recognized. They were Colonel Troupe, Dr. Hazelip, the surgeon, and Johnny Meechum. Montoya was not with them.

"Where is Montoya?" Hunter asked, as he stepped down to the water's edge and helped land the boat.

Johnny was the first one out of the boat, stepping lightly onto the shore. "We couldn't find him," Johnny said. "We went to the boardinghouse where he was staying but the cowardly son of a bitch had already checked out."

"You mean he ran?"

Johnny nodded. "Just like the Mexicans you saw at Gonzales," he said. "I guess they're all alike."

Hunter breathed a sigh of relief. "Well, then it is all over. We can all go home."

Hunter started toward his own boat, when he was stopped in his tracks by Colonel Troupe's voice.

"I'm afraid it is not over, gentlemen," Colonel Troupe said.

Hunter turned toward him. "What do you mean, it isn't over?" he asked.

Colonel Troupe pointed to Johnny. "Mr. Meechum, by agreeing to be Montoya's second, you must now take his place."

"That's not a very funny joke, Colonel Troupe," Hunter said.

"I am afraid it is not a joke, Mr. Grant," Colonel Troupe replied. "According to the code by which gentlemen live, Mr. Meechum, as Montoya's second, must now take his place in the duel."

"But that is ridiculous!" Johnny said. "I don't even know Montoya, except enough to know that I don't like him. I certainly don't intend to fight his battles for him."

"Nevertheless, you *did* volunteer to act as his second, and you did agree to be held to honor on all accounts," Colonel Troupe said.

"I only agreed to be his second because no one else would," Johnny answered. "And I didn't want the son of a bitch to be able to weasel his way out of the duel."

"But you are now honor-bound to take Montoya's place or you will forever be branded a coward and a man of dishonor."

"It doesn't matter whether Johnny agrees to take his place or not, because there will be no fight. I won't fight him," Hunter insisted.

"You must fight him, or you shall both be branded as cowards and dishonorable men," Troupe said dogmatically.

"Fine, then we shall bear the brand."

"No," Johnny said quietly.

"What?" Hunter asked.

"Think about it, Hunter. Could you live with the brand of cowardice, or dishonor?"

"Yes, if I had to."

"I can't. I'm willing to fight."

Hunter gasped. "Johnny, have you lost your senses? Do you know what you are saying?"

"I know exactly what I am saying," Johnny said. "Hunter, what is a man if he has not honor? If we are to be so adjudged, we will no longer be able to hold our heads up. We'll be scorned everywhere we go. And it will destroy the friendship we now have. I can not, and I will not, go through the rest of my life being called a coward."

"Johnny, this is crazy!" Hunter insisted. "This isn't your fight." Hunter looked at Colonel Troupe. "Suppose I offered, through Mr. Meechum, to return the money to Montoya, and to apologize for any intemperate words? Would that satisfy the terms of the duel?"

"As Montoya's second, I accept," Johnny said quickly, relieved that Hunter had found a way out. Johnny smiled. "And you don't have to return the money, I'll pay the bastard myself."

"I'm sorry, gentlemen, but that will not do," Colonel Troupe insisted. "Only the injured party can agree to the terms of satisfaction."

"Well, the injured party isn't here," Johnny said. "The cowardly bastard has run away. That's why I'm here, representing him."

"You can represent him in the duel, Mr. Meechum, but you cannot agree to any terms," Colonel Troupe said.

"But I don't want to fight Johnny! I have no quarrel with Johnny! Can't you understand that?" Hunter bellowed.

"You have no choice."

"I refuse."

"But you must, Mr. Grant. If you do not fight, dishonor will follow you both for the rest of your lives."

"I don't care."

"We are going to have to fight, Hunter," Johnny said.

"No."

"Fight me."

"No!"

Suddenly and unexpectedly, Johnny slapped Hunter hard in the face.

"Johnny, what the hell . . . ?"

"Fight me, damn you!"

"No!"

Johnny slapped Hunter again.

"Stop hitting me!" Hunter said sharply.

Johnny slapped him again. *"Fight me!"*

"Johnny, I . . ."

"Please, Hunter. Can't you see? We have no choice!" Now there were tears in Johnny's eyes.

Hunter sighed, then with a shrug of surrender, nodded toward Henry, who, having witnessed the scene in almost total shock, was still holding the little wooden case which contained the perfectly matched brace of dueling pistols.

"Are they loaded?" he asked.

"Hunter, you're not really going through with this?" Henry replied.

"God damn you, Henry, are they loaded?" Hunter shouted, his voice returning in echo.

"Yes, Hunter," Henry replied very quietly. "They are loaded."

"Very well." Hunter turned toward Johnny. Johnny, who just last night had sworn that he was in love with one of the girls of the Absinthe House, and had offered to share that same girl with him. Johnny, who was the brother of the woman Hunter was to marry. Johnny, who had been his best friend for many years. and who was the closest thing to a brother Hunter had. "Choose your weapon, Mr. Meechum," Hunter invited.

The two men continued to look at each other for a long, agonizing moment, then Johnny walked over to pick up one of the two pistols from the red felt. He hefted it, testing it for weight and balance, then he smiled wanly.

"I gave you these pistols for your twenty-first birthday, do you remember?" he said to Hunter. "Little did I know that we would someday use them against each other."

Hunter walked over to the box to take the remaining pistol.

"Gentlemen," Colonel Troupe said. "As you are now armed, kindly take your positions, standing back to back. I shall count off fifteen paces. At the fifteenth pace, you may turn and fire at will. I caution you now, I will shoot anyone who turns and fires before the fifteenth pace."

"Johnny, we don't have to do this," Hunter said, trying one last time to talk some sense into his friend.

"Take your place, Mr. Grant," Johnny answered.

Sighing, Hunter turned around and allowed Troupe to position Johnny behind him. The two men stood back to back, holding their pistols in their right hands with their elbows cocked so that the pistols were pointing up.

"Normally, at this stage, I would make a last-minute offer to mediate the dispute," Colonel Troupe said. "But, as one of the parties to the dispute isn't present, it cannot be mediated. Therefore, there is nothing left to do but proceed to the next step. Gentlemen, are you ready?"

"I am ready," Johnny said.

"Ready," Hunter replied.

"One!" Colonel Troupe called out.

Hunter heard the paces being counted off as he moved through the wet grass. Then, as he stepped off the paces, he formulated a plan. He would purposely miss his shot . . . and hope that Johnny did so as well.

At the fifteenth pace he turned and brought his weapon up to bear. Two pistols barked in the early morning fog. Johnny's bullet crashed into Hunter's right shoulder, just as Hunter pulled the trigger. Though he fully intended to miss, the impact of the bullet striking him in the shoulder caused him to pull his shot, and, through the billowing clouds of smoke, he was horrified to see a large, dark hole, suddenly appear in Johnny's chest.

"Johnny!" Hunter screamed in heart-wrenching agony. Throwing down his pistol, he ran toward his friend.

Johnny fell to his knees before Hunter could reach him. He looked up as Hunter got there.

"Oh, you are hit, too, aren't you? How badly are you hurt?" Johnny asked in a strained voice.

"Don't worry about me," Hunter replied. "What about you?"

"You ever know anyone to survive a bullet in the chest?" Johnny asked. He forced a laugh. "I can hear the angels' wings."

"Johnny, no, I'm sorry, I'm sorry!" Hunter cried. "I tried

to miss but the bullet in my shoulder pulled my aim off. Dr. Hazelip, come quickly!''

"Say, maybe you've discovered a new way to fight duels," Johnny said. "Try to miss and hope the other contestant hits you in the shoulder." Again, he tried to laugh, but this time the laughter turned into a spasm of coughing, and the coughing brought up blood.

"Do something, Doctor," Hunter demanded, as Hazelip bent to examine the wound.

"I am afraid the bullet has destroyed his lungs," Hazelip said. "There is nothing I can do. He is going to die."

"No! Take the bullet out! You're a surgeon, aren't you?"

"I'm a surgeon, Mr. Grant, not a wizard," Hazelip said.

"Hunter?" Johnny said. His voice was weaker now. "Hunter, don't blame yourself. I forced you into this."

"No, you didn't," Hunter said. "It was the code, the idiotic dueling code."

"Hunter? Hunter?" Johnny said, gasping. He drew three or four more labored breaths, then his breathing stopped.

Hazelip leaned forward and put his ear to Johnny's chest, getting blood on the side of his face as he did so. He listened for a heartbeat for a moment, then he straightened up and looked over at Colonel Troupe.

"This man is dead," he said.

"No! No!" Hunter shouted in a painful bellow. Seeing the dueling pistol still in Johnny's hand, he removed it, then ran back to retrieve the one he had dropped.

"Mr. Grant, what are you doing?" Colonel Troupe asked.

"I'm doing what I should have done this morning!" Hunter shouted back. He hurled both pistols far out over the bayou, then grabbed his shoulder in pain from the effort as the two expensive, perfectly matched and balanced weapons splashed into the water.

"The terms of this duel having been satisfied, I declare it over," Colonel Troupe said.

Hunter turned to look back at the pompous arbitrator.

"The terms have not been satisfied, and it is not over," he said coldly. "Not until Don Juan Esteban Montoya is held to account for this."

Four

NOVEMBER 2, 1835, THE VIEUX CARRE

Word of what happened on Cypress Island that foggy morning spread through New Orleans like wildfire. Merchants told the story to their customers . . . draymen and boatmen spoke of it at the docks . . . gamblers discussed it over their games of chance, and ladies of the evening exchanged the latest gossip while in bed with their clients. And, because Johnny Meechum and Hunter Grant had so frequently visited the Absinthe House, it was a subject of particular interest there.

"Imagine, shootin' your best friend like that."

"Well, what choice did he have? It was either go on with the duel, or live without honor."

"Yes, but I heard that Johnny Meechum turned the gun on himself, rather than shoot his best friend. If Grant really was a man of honor, he would have done the same thing."

"That's not true. I got it straight from someone who was there and he told me exactly what happened. He said Grant didn't want to fight, but young Meechum pushed him into it."

"Why would he have done that?"

"Because he didn't want to be branded a coward."

"They say that Grant is no longer received at Trailback. They say that the engagement with the Meechum girl is off, and they say that Angus Meechum has let it be known that he will shoot Grant if he ever sets foot on Trailback again."

"They say, they say, they say. Is that all you can say?"

"Well, that is what they say."

"Ssshh! Here comes Grant now!"

All conversation came to a halt when Hunter pushed through the front door to step into the Absinthe House. It was like that everywhere he went now, and if anyone could appreciate the humor, Hunter would have laughed out loud at the irony of it all. Here he and Johnny had been told that if they did not fight they would be totally ostracized by New Orleans society. So they fought, and what happened? Johnny was dead, and he was being ostracized.

Ignoring those who were ignoring him, Hunter stepped up to the bar, bought a bottle of bourbon, then took it over to a table where he sat, alone. Gradually, the conversation in the room resumed, though now it was in harsh whispers which could be heard but not understood. Several in the room glanced toward him, only to look away, quickly, when he caught their eye.

In the six days since the duel, Hunter had scarcely drawn a sober breath. He drank, trying to erase the terrible scene of Johnny dying in his arms. But it didn't matter. No matter how drunk he got, he could not forget.

"Mind if I join you?" someone asked, disturbing his reverie.

Looking up, Hunter recognized the intruder.

"Well, if it isn't Sam McCord," he said. With a wave of his hand, he took in the chair across the table from him. "Have a seat, Sam, and share my bottle with me."

"Thanks," Sam said, sitting down and reaching for the whiskey.

"On second thought, maybe you won't want to sit with me," Hunter suggested.

Sam turned the bottle up for several Adams apple-bobbing swallows. Then, with an audible expulsion of breath, he put the bottle down and wiped his mouth with the back of his hand.

"Why would I not want to sit with you?" he asked, replying to Hunter's question.

"Why, haven't you heard? I'm poison. If you hang around me, it'll rub off on you. People will begin talking about you, just the way they talk about me."

"I don't give a damn whether people talk about me or not. I won't be here. I'm going to Texas," Sam said.

"You are? But what about Miss Doucette?"

"What about her?" Sam replied.

"Aren't the two of you about to announce your engagement?" Hunter reached for the bottle.

"No," Sam answered, without elaboration.

Hunter didn't ask for clarification, figuring Sam would have told him, if he had wanted him to know. "Still," Hunter continued. "Why do you want to go to Texas? They are fighting a war there, in case you didn't know."

"Yes, I am aware of that," Sam said. "But I hear they are also giving away land, good land, to men who'll come and fight with them."

"You sound as if you have it all planned."

"I do. Why don't you come with me?"

Hunter shook his head no. "There's nothing in Texas for me."

"Is that a fact? Well, tell me this, Hunter Grant. Now that Johnny Meechum is dead, and the Meechum family has turned you out, what is there for you in Louisiana?"

Hunter shook his head. "Not much, I guess," he admitted.

Sam leaned forward, to press the advantage. "On the other hand, if you will go to Texas with me, you might find Montoya," he suggested.

Hunter's eyes grew cold, as if he were seriously considering the offer. Then logic returned. "And I might not find him there," he said. "Whereas, if his family is doing business here in New Orleans, Montoya will come back. And when he does come back . . . I'm going to kill the son of a bitch."

"You can't just kill him. You'll have to challenge him to a duel. And, according to the code, it will be a new duel."

"New duel, old duel, what difference does it make, as long as the son of a bitch is dead?"

"Well, for one thing, if you challenge him, he will get his choice of weapons. And you had better believe that he won't choose pistols. It'll be swords for sure. And if you fight him with swords, you might be the one that is dead."

"I don't care if the bastard chooses cannons," Hunter insisted. "I'll be ready for him."

Sam looked across the table at Hunter for a long moment, then he stuck his hand out. "Well, I wish you luck," he said.

"The same for you," Hunter said. Sam started to walk away but was stopped by Hunter's call to him.

"Sam!"

Sam looked back toward the table. "Yes?"

"When the bullets start flying, keep your head down."

Smiling, Sam touched the brim of his hat, then left the establishment.

TUESDAY, NOVEMBER 10, 1835, THE SABINE RIVER SETTLEMENT, COAHUILA Y TEXAS

The settlement was so temporary that it didn't even have a name. It hugged the Texas side of the Sabine River, the first settlement after leaving Louisiana on the trail of El Camino Real, or, the Road of Kings. The little town was no more than a clutter of canvas tents, a few huts thatched with reeds from the canebrake, and one or two wagons that had been abandoned by earlier travelers moving west.

The biggest tent belonged to a man named Luther Hagens. Hagens had gone to Texas to make his fortune, and was doing so, not off the land, but off the other people who were coming to the new land. He sold goods and liquor at inflated prices, took a rake-off from cards and other games of chance, functioned as a meeting house, post office, and, even as a provisional government, all for a price.

A few hundred yards away from the settlement, Sam McCord lay asleep in the canebrake. Here, the rushes grew to heights of ten feet or more, curving over at the top to form leafy caves and corridors that blotted out the sun. If one chose carefully, one could sleep throughout the day without being awakened by sunshine, or disturbed by passersby.

Sam was sleeping in such a spot when there was a gunshot not ten feet away from his head. Waking with a start, he sat up immediately.

"Did you get 'im, Bill?" a voice yelled.

"No." The answering voice was very close to Sam, but the thick cane prevented him from seeing the other two men. "Leastwise, I don't think I did. It's hard to tell."

"I told you, it don't make no sense to hunt rabbit in the canebrake. Even iffen you was to get one, more'n likely he'd hop off to die in the rushes and you'd lose him. Come on, let's go down to the riverbank and git us a big ol' catfish."

Sam picked up his hat and put it on, covering hair that was the same color as wheat straw. He heard a soft rustling sound and turned to see a rabbit looking out at him from behind a clump of cane.

"You gave those two men a pretty good run, didn't you?" he said quietly. "You also woke me up. I ought to shoot you myself and have you for breakfast."

As if he could understand the words, the rabbit turned and darted away.

Chuckling, Sam walked over to Hagens's tent. He had been told yesterday that there would be someone here today, recruiting soldiers for the new Texas army, and Sam didn't want to miss him.

Sam bought a breakfast of bacon, biscuits, and gravy, then found a stump to sit on. He had just finished eating when a man rode in, wearing what Sam assumed to be a military uniform of some sort. He had a blue, swallow-tailed jacket with gold epalets, and brown pants, with a red stripe down each pants leg. The man took a sheet of paper from his saddlebags, then nailed it to a tree. Three other men went over to look at it, and Sam joined them.

FREEMEN OF TEXAS

To arms! To arms!

We have prevailed on our fellow citizen, Wm. H. Wharton, Esq. to return and communicate to you the following express. and also to urge as many as may be possible to leave their homes to volunteer for the Army of Texas, armed and equipped for war even to the knife.

We are just now starting and thus must apologize for the brevity of this communication. We refer you to Mr. Wharton for a fuller explanation of our wishes, opinions, and intentions, and also for such political information as has come into our hands. If Texas acts promptly they will soon be redeemed from that worse than Egyptian bondage which now cramps her resources and retards her prosperity.

David Randon
Wm. J. Bryan
J. W. Fannin, Jr.

                                   F. T. Wells
                                   Geo. Sutherland
                                   B. T. Archer
                                   W. D. C. Hall
                                   W. H. Jack
                                   Wm. T. Austin

"You'd be this fella Wharton, would you?" someone asked.

"I am William Harris Wharton, at your service," Wharton replied.

"Glory be, you are impressive-looking in that uniform. Do you be a general?"

Wharton chuckled. "By profession, sir, I am a lawyer. By passion, I am a citizen of what is sure to become the Republic of Texas, and by appointment, a colonel in the Army of Texas."

"What does a fella have to do to get into that army?" one of the other men asked.

"It's simple," Wharton answered, taking off his hat and brushing back a curl that fell across his forehead. "All you have to do is arm yourself, then find someone who is raising a company and report to him. He will swear you in."

"What do you mean, someone who is raising a company?"

"Anyone who can raise a company of twenty men will be commissioned a captain," Wharton explained. "That is by order of Sam Houston."

"Where at can we find such a fellow?"

"I'm right here," Sam said quickly. "Captain Sam Mc-Cord at your service."

"Captain McCord, it is good to make your acquaintance, sir," Wharton said, sticking his hand out to shake Sam's hand. He did not challenge Sam's self-appointment. "As soon as you have enough men raised and equipped, please repair to the Texian camp outside San Antonio de Bexar, and there, present yourself to Colonel Ben Milam."

"San Antonio. Yes, sir," Sam said.

"Say, Colonel Wharton," one of the other men asked. "Iffen we was to join this here army, will we be given grants of land?"

"Yes," Wharton replied. "All the landholders in Texas have made a commitment to parcel out choice sections of land to those men who do their patriotic duty."

"How much land?"

"Eight hundred acres, plus a bonus of twenty-four dollars in gold."

"Whereat is this land?"

"There are choice sites all over Texas. Naturally, the first choice and a greater acreage will go to those who hold the higher rank, for they will be the ones who, by their industriousness, have raised the army for us." Wharton remounted. "Gentlemen, I leave you now, in the care of Captain Sam McCord. Good luck to you, and God save Texas!"

"Hurrah!" one of the men shouted and the others joined in.

"Captain McCord, won't you swear us in?" someone asked.

Sam stood at attention, then raised his right hand. "Raise your right hands," he ordered.

The three men raised their hands.

"Repeat after me. I, and state your name."

The men did so.

"Do solemnly swear to defend Texas against the Mexican bastards who are trying to take it away from the Americans, and to obey all the orders given us by Captain McCord and all other officers in the Army of Texas."

The men repeated the oath accordingly.

"Gentlemen, you are now members of McCord's company, the Army of Texas. Get your weapons and a horse and meet me here in one hour. We are going to San Antonio."

"Yahoo!" one of the men shouted as they hurried back to their "digs" to follow Sam's orders.

Luther Hagens had been watching the entire proceedings from his tent. With Wharton and the new recruits gone, he came over to speak with Sam, bringing a bottle with him. He offered Sam a drink, but Sam waved it aside.

"Thank you just the same, Mr. Hagens, but I need to watch my money more closely."

"There's no charge, Captain," Hagens said. "It's an honor to buy a drink for one of our patriots."

"In that case, thanks," Sam said, taking several generous swallows.

"I thought you had just arrived from Louisiana. I had no idea you had already raised twenty men for our army."

"Hagens, you know how to get to this place, San Antonio?"

"Sure do. All you have to do is follow the El Camino road."

"How long does it take to get there from here?"

"I'd say week, maybe ten days, with steady traveling."

"Yeah, well, I don't know how steady the traveling will be," Sam said. "I'm going to have to raise a few more men in order to make sure I have the twenty I need to stay a captain."

Sam took another pull from the bottle, then looked over toward the three men he had just sworn in. They were talking excitedly among themselves as they rolled all their gear up into a blanket.

"You mean you don't have twenty yet?" Hagens asked.

"No."

"Well, how many more do you need?"

Sam belched. "About seventeen more," he said.

Hagens laughed. "Sam McCord, anyone with as much brass as you've got, deserves to be a captain whether you raise the men or not."

LUNES, 16 NOVIEMBRE, 1835, ON BOARD THE SHIP GULF CHALLENGER, OFF THE COAST OF VERA CRUZ, MEXICO

Don Juan Esteban Montoya stood leaning into the ship's shrouding, looking toward the verdant shore as the vessel approached Vera Cruz. How beautiful Mexico was, and how it lifted his spirits to be returning.

It was now three weeks since he left New Orleans. It had not only been a successful business trip, it had been a pleasant adventure as well. That is, until the unfortunate incident of the card game.

On his last night in New Orleans, Juan had celebrated, with drink, the conclusion of a successful business trip. Although he did not drink so much as to be drunk, he knew now that he had undoubtedly drunk enough to affect his judgment. That is the only way he could explain why he let himself gamble so recklessly. And it was also, he believed, that same lack of judgment which caused him to challenge Hunter Grant to a duel.

Later that same night, Juan sobered up, and he began re-creating the events of the evening just concluded. He came to the realization that the fault had been entirely his. He had implied that Hunter Grant was being dishonest, even though he had no evidence to substantiate his accusation. Then, when Grant called him a "pissant," Juan let his temper take control of him.

As he lay in bed that night, Juan considered the possibilities that lay ahead of him.

If he fought the duel, one of two things would happen: Either Juan would be killed, which he certainly didn't want . . . or he would kill Hunter Grant. And, because Juan had reacted in temper, rather than reason, he didn't want that either.

Fortunately, there was a way out. He had already booked passage on board the *Gulf Challenger* and had been told to be aboard by three A.M. the next morning. If he reported to the ship as he was supposed to, he would be well at sea by the time the duel was scheduled to take place, thus there could be no duel, and no one would be hurt.

That was exactly what he decided to do.

"Pissant."

Juan said the English word aloud, then laughed at the sound of it. It would be a good word to remember.

As Juan stood on the deck, looking out at the coastline of his country, he wondered what happened out on Cypress Island that next morning, when he didn't show up. He was sure that they probably made several remarks about his lack of honor for failing to show . . . perhaps they even called him a coward.

The thought of being called a coward rankled him, but let them make their accusations. Juan did not lack self-esteem. He knew he was not a coward. He had been tested many times in battle and had never been found wanting. Let the Norteamericanos make their unkind remarks. They lived a thousand and more miles away, so their opinions meant nothing to him. It was more important that Juan have the satisfaction of knowing that no one was killed as a result of his unchecked anger.

Captain Lowry, the master of the *Gulf Challenger*, came over to speak to Juan.

"How does your homeland look to you, Don Juan?" he asked, indicating the rapidly approaching shoreline.

"I believe it is the most beautiful place in the world," Juan replied.

"Aye, 'tis a pretty spot, all right," Lowry agreed. "Lots of folks back home who have never seen anything of Mexico except for the desert country up north, have no idea how beautiful a country it really is."

"You'll come out to the *finca* as my guest, will you not, *Senor Capitano?*" Juan invited.

"Well, I thank you for the invite, Don Juan, but, regretfully, I must decline. I intend to set sail again as soon as we have taken on water and provisions."

"*Gracias, Capitano*, and to you, also, my thanks for a pleasant voyage."

Captain Lowry laughed. "Don't thank me, friend. It was God who gave us fair winds and calm seas."

Once ashore, Juan hired a carriage to take him out to the family farm which was located a few miles north of the city of Vera Cruz. By the time the carriage rolled to a stop in front of the large house, a servant, who had seen him coming, had already taken word to his family, and Juan's mother and father were waiting on the patio to greet him. Juan and his mother embraced as the elder Montoya paid the carriage driver and sent him on his way.

"I am so happy you are back home," his mother said. "Thanks be to God, your journey was a safe one." She crossed herself.

"Yes," Juan agreed, crossing himself as well. "Thanks be to God." He thought of the duel he had almost fought. Had he lost that duel, he would have been returned home in a coffin. Had he won, he would have returned a murderer in his own eyes. How foolish his gesture had been, and how glad he was that he had managed to come to his senses in time.

"And tell me of the trip, my son," his father, Jorge, asked. "Was it successful?"

"Very successful," Juan said. "The New Orleans merchants will take as much coffee as we can send them."

"Then we will send as much as they can take," Jorge replied, with a twinkle in his eye.

"Where is Ramon?" Juan asked, looking around for his younger brother. "Is he so busy with the senoritas that he can not come to welcome his own brother home?"

Juan's parents looked pointedly at each other.

"What is it? What is wrong?" Juan asked.

"Ramon has gone to the war," his mother answered.

"The war? What war?"

"With the Norteamericanos in Coahuila y Tejas," Jorge explained. "Have you heard nothing of this?"

"I heard that there was a very small fight near the town of Gonzales. The battle was over a cannon, I believe." Juan remembered the stories he had heard in New Orleans, and the shame he had felt at the description of Mexican soldiers running like scared rabbits. "But surely that has all been settled by now?"

"It was humiliating to have a ragged mob of gringos defeat our army," Jorge explained. "Santa Anna has sent General Cos, his own brother-in-law, to occupy San Antonio de Bexar, while the *presidente* has put himself at the head of an army which will march into Tejas to punish those who would make a rebellion against us."

"And Ramon?"

"Ramon is with Santa Anna. He has been commissioned a lieutenant," Jorge said.

"He is so young and so inexperienced," Juan's mother said.

"He is young, yes, but Ramon will make a fine officer," Juan said. "And I am very proud of him. But I am surprised that I have not also been summoned. I still hold a federal commission."

Jorge cleared his throat. "I did not want to tell you this on the first day of your return, but you have been summoned.

Orders have arrived for you as well.''

"Where are they?''

Jorge spoke authoritatively to one of the nearby servants, and, with a bow, the man ran into the house. He returned a moment later, carrying an envelope.

"*Gracias,* Pedro,'' Juan said, taking the orders. He looked at them for a moment, then smiled. "Good news! I have been promoted to lieutenant colonel and I am to be given my own regiment.''

"I know,'' Jorge replied. "I have persuaded Santa Anna to place Ramon in your command.''

"Juan, you will look after your younger brother, won't you?'' Juan's mother pleaded.

"Of course I will,'' Juan answered, putting his arms around his mother and pulling her to him.

"And you will stay for a while before you go?''

Juan looked at his orders. "*Si, Mamacita,* I do not have to report until after Christmas.''

Jorge smiled broadly. "Why wait for Christmas? We will have a fiesta now,'' he said. "Pedro, slaughter a goat. We will have *cabrito,* Juan's favorite.''

"*Si, Excellente,*'' Pedro replied, hurrying off to tend to the task.

Five

At one time, "Captain'' Sam McCord had as many as nine men in his "command.'' But one of them got kicked in the groin by a mule, two of them sobered up and had second thoughts about going off to fight in a war, and one took the ague so bad that he couldn't continue. Thus, when Sam reported to the Texians' encampment outside San Antonio, he had only five cold, tired, hungry, and dispirited men with him.

As they rode into camp on horses which were slab-sided from too little graze and even less oats, Sam saw several fires, each fire surrounded by men who were trying to keep warm. One of the men was wearing a military coat of red, a blue cockade cap, and a white belt, from which hung a saber. As he was considerably more impressive looking than any of the others in Sam's immediate view, Sam walked over to him.

"I beg your pardon, sir," Sam said. "Could you direct me to Colonel Milam?"

The man looked at Sam through narrow, distrusting eyes.

"And would you be tellin' me who 'tis that's doin' the inquirin'?"

"McCord. Captain Sam McCord."

The man snorted what may have been a laugh. "So 'tis a captain you'd be callin' yourself, is it?"

Sam cleared his throat.

"Well, I . . . I reckon not, if truth be known," he admitted. "I was told all you had to do to be a captain was to raise a company of twenty men. And as you can see"—Sam waved his arm toward the small group of men with him—"I've come up a mite short."

Suddenly, the man laughed. "Well, laddie, don't fret yourself over it. If you want to call yourself a captain, who the hell is goin' to stop you? It sure as hell won't be ole Ben Milam."

"Yes, well, that gets us right back to where we started, doesn't it?" Sam replied. "Where can I find this Ben Milam?"

The man picked up a twig, then leaned over and held the end of it in the flames until it ignited. Using the burning twig, he relit his pipe, then puffed several times before he spoke again.

"Well," he finally said. "I reckon that would be me."

"You're Ben Milam?"

"Aye, that I am, laddie, that I am. Now, what can I do for you?"

"I've come to join up," Sam said. "I, and my men."

"Is that a fact, now? You're a patriot of Texas, are you?"

"A patriot of Texas? Yes, sure, if that's what it takes."

"Do you hear this, boys?" Milam suddenly shouted to the rest of the dispirited camp. "While some of you chicken-hearts are talkin' about goin' home, we've got more brave lads who are comin' to join us. Now, what think you of that?''

"Let 'em come," someone said, walking by with his rolled blanket tied across his back. "Me an' these boys is goin' home where there's grub to eat, a fire to sit by, and a willin' woman to warm our beds."

Sam saw then that there were at least twenty or thirty who were getting ready to leave.

"Go on, then," Milam said. "Sure, an' be done with you, now. As far as I'm concerned, the whole bunch of you can go and be damned!''

Undaunted by Milam's tirade, the man calmly took a chew of tobacco, leaving some of it hanging in his beard. "I can't speak for these here other fellas, but come spring, iffen we're still fightin' ag'in the Mexicans, an' iffen I've got my crops in, I reckon I'll come back and join you."

"Don't you be troublin' yourselves none. As long as we got brave laddies like this," Milam said, indicating Sam, "we'll not be needin' the likes of you." Turning his attention away from the deserting men, Milam examined Sam.

"Tell me, Captain, from where do you hail?"

"Louisiana," Sam replied. "Near New Orleans."

"Louisiana, is it? Well, ole Jim Bowie is from Louisiana, and if you're half as good a man as he is, you're a good man. We've got good men from all over, who've come to join our fight: Tennessee, Missouri, Virginia, Alabama."

"You aren't from any place like that. From your speech, I'd make you a foreigner."

Milam laughed. "Aye, an' you've a good ear, laddie. I'm a Welshman. Now, how say you? Are you staying, or are you leaving?"

"I didn't come this far just to turn around," Sam said.

"Good lad."

"Tell me, Colonel Milam, would there be any food available anywhere? It's nearly time for sleepin' and these men haven't eaten today."

Milam looked at him. "Nor you, I suppose."

"No, sir."

Milam snorted, then nodded his head. "Whether you've got your twenty men or not, I'd say you've the makin's of a good officer, lookin' out for your men first. Come on along with me, I'll rustle you up some beans. Though, I can't say if there'll be any meat to go with it.''

"Beans would be fine," Sam said.

Filling his tin plate with beans, Sam found a log in front of one of the many blazing campfires, then sat down and began to eat. Milam came over to sit beside him. Again, Milam loaded his pipe.

"I don't know what it was that brought you to us," Milam said. Relighting his pipe, he took several puffs before completing his sentence. "But I appreciate the help."

"The land," Sam said, speaking with his mouth full.

"The land?" It was obvious that Milam didn't know what Sam was talking about. "What land?"

"We were told that everyone who joined the Army of Texas would be given eight hundred acres of prime farm land. Also, twenty-four dollars in gold."

"I see." Milam was quiet for a moment, then he spoke again. "Do you have your gold yet?"

"No, sir."

"And tell me. 'Twas it your thinkin' that I would be givin' it to you?"

"I gave it a passing thought."

Milam laughed. " 'Tis good that the thought was merely passing, for I've nothing like that for you."

"What about the land? Is that bogus, too?" Sam asked, looking up from his beans.

"If it is, will you be leaving?"

"There will be little to keep me here," Sam replied.

"Aye, little enough," Milam admitted. "Except honor," he added. "Does honor mean anything to you?"

Sam chewed his beans thoughtfully for a long moment, then he nodded.

"Honor means something," he said. "I'll not be speaking for the men I brought with me, but I'll stay."

"Good for you, lad, good for you," Milam said. "Now, about the land. I think you should know that if we lose this war, there won't be any land for anyone, not even the ones who have been here for years, because the Mexicans will kick us out." Suddenly Milam smiled broadly. "But if we win, lad. Ah, now, if we win, 'twill be a different story entirely. There will be all the land a body might want, just for the taking. An enterprising young man could settle himself down with a good woman, sire some sons to help out around the place, and in a few years be landed gentry the equal to any in the country. Have you a wife, lad?''

"No, no wife.''

"Ah, but you've a woman then? Is there someone back home you can send for after the war?''

Finishing his beans, Sam picked up a handful of sand and began cleaning his plate. In his mind's eye, he could see Marie Doucette as clearly as if she were standing right here before him: eyes as dark as agates, hair as black as a raven's wing, and a smile as beautiful as a golden morning. He could almost feel her trembling in his arms. Then the vision dimmed.

"No,'' he finally said. "No, there is no woman.''

"Milam! Ben Milam!'' someone began shouting, riding into camp. "Where at is Ben Milam?''

"Here, Prescott, I'm over here,'' Milam answered, rising from the log where he had been sitting talking to Sam.

Prescott guided his horse over to Milam, then swung down from the saddle.

"Colonel, iffen we're ever goin' to run them Mexicans outta San Antonio, there ain't goin' to be no better time to do it than right now,'' he said.

"What makes you say that, Prescott? Do you have something for me?''

Prescott smiled, then shouted back toward the darkness. "Jose. Come over here!''

A short, swarthy man, carrying a wide-brimmed sombrero, moved out of the shadows and stepped into the golden bubble of light that was cast by the campfire. He stood back, hesitantly.

"Don't be none a'scairt. Ain't no one here goin' to hurt you, long as you with me,'' Prescott promised.

Jose moved a little closer.

"Colonel Milam, this here is Jose Garcia,'' Prescott said. "He's my brother-in-law, so I trust him.''

"*Buenas noches,* Senor Garcia,'' Milam said, nodding.

"*Buenas noches,* Senor Colonel," Garcia replied.

"Go on, Jose, tell Ben Milam what you told me." Then to Milam, he added, "Jose has been with General Cos."

"Inside San Antonio?"

"Yes, sir. Go ahead, Jose, tell Colonel Milam."

"The soldiers with General Cos," Jose began. "They are not good soldiers. They are angry because there is no food. They are frightened because you are here with a big army. They do not like their officers, and many have said that if fighting begins, they will throw down their guns and surrender."

Milam looked at Prescott. "Can I trust this man to tell me the truth?"

"Colonel, I've known Jose for several years now. Like I said, he's my own wife's brother, the uncle of my children. I would trust my life to what he tells me."

"Yes, well, that may be what you are doing. Not only your life, but ours as well," Milam said. He stroked his chin for a moment, then he grinned broadly and stuck his hand out to shake Jose's hand.

"I am going to trust you, *amigo,*" he said. "You have brought us great news! That means that the Mexicans are even more dispirited than we are! One good attack and they will fold. Men!" he shouted loudly to the others in the camp. "Men, gather 'round!"

From all over the campsite, men began to appear. They stood in the orange glow of the campfires, their lanky, buckskin-clad bodies lighted in front, and dark in back.

"Men, this is Jose Garcia," Milam said, pointing to Prescott's brother-in-law.

"What's that Mexican bastard doing in our camp?" someone shouted.

"Hang the son of a bitch! Hang him for a spy!" another called loudly, and there were several enthusiastic endorsements of the proposition.

Jose's eyes flashed in fear, then he began glancing around like a trapped rabbit, looking for some means of escape.

"No, men, no!" Milam shouted loudly, holding his hands up to forestall any such plan. "Jose is on our side! He has brought news which is very helpful to us."

Milam's assurances calmed the crowd, and they stood by in interested silence to see what Milam had to say.

"Jose has been inside the Mexicans' camp," Milam reported. "According to him, their morale is at rock-bottom. I know Houston and some of the others have been advising us to wait, but I say we wait no longer. Already, we've seen some among us grow tired of waiting and leave. If we wait too much longer, we'll become as dispirited as the Mexicans. Lads, there is never going to be a better time to attack than right now."

"Attack?" someone said. "Attack what?"

Milam pointed toward San Antonio. "We are going to attack General Cos and his troops. I have reason to believe that the attack will be successful. And, boys, when we control San Antonio de Bexar, we will control the largest city in Texas. *Our* Texas!" he concluded with a loud shout.

"Yes, our Texas!" someone called back. "Let's run those bastards all the way to Mexico City!"

Milam took out his sword and drew a line in the sand.

"Who will go with old Ben Milam into San Antonio?" he challenged. "Who will follow old Ben Milam?"

Hundreds of voices roared in response, but Sam McCord was the first one to cross the line.

The night passed slowly, almost reluctantly from the earth. When the darkness lifted, slanting bars of morning sunlight revealed an army of Texians waiting just outside the city, determined to enter San Antonio.

Although it had been Milam who had rallied the men, Sam learned that it was Colonel Edward Burleson who was in over-all command. Burleson divided his army into two columns, one commanded by Ben Milam, the other by Francis Johnson. Sam, and the men who had come with him, were in Ben Milam's column.

"Now, listen to me, men," Milam said. "When you aim, aim low." As Milam was giving instructions to his men, he was walking back and forth and waving his sword for emphasis. "You don't do anyone any good by getting in so much of a hurry that you discharge your weapons into the trees."

"And be sure'n prime the pan!" someone shouted, and several laughed, because they had all heard stories of fights with the Indians when, in the heat of battle and pitch of excitement, men had poured in powder, wad, and shell, then snapped the trigger uselessly against a firing pan that was not primed, and thus would not discharge.

"Don't be afraid," Milam went on. "Just keep it in mind that the Mexicans will be as frightened as you are. Keep your own fear under control, and use the Mexicans' fear against them, and you'll come out of this little fracas just fine."

Sam looked around at the five men he had brought with him. He was sure that their faces were a reflection of his own; excitement, fear, and determination.

"All right, men, let's go," Milam said, starting forward. Johnson's column started toward San Antonio at the same time, and the attack was underway.

The Mexican sentries sounded the alarm as the Texians approached the outskirts of the city. Within moments after the alarm was given, firing broke out and the battle was joined.

The Mexicans, trained to fight in structured battlefield conditions, hurried to the center of the street where they formed into rigid battle lines. The first line of soldiers knelt to fire, while the second line dutifully awaited their turn. It was an awe-inspiring sight, but it was also a tactic which exposed every Mexican soldier to fire, whether they were in the front line or not.

The Texians, more used to fighting against Indians than in set-piece battles, fought as they had learned to fight. They scattered with the wind the moment they came into town, taking cover behind trees, houses, and walls. Sam dashed to the corner of a house where three others had also taken cover. Within a moment there were no Texians in view and, at first, the confused Mexicans thought they had turned back the attack.

The Mexicans quickly learned the truth, however, when a withering volley came from the Texians, who were firing from places of cover and concealment. The opening fusillade brought down a significant number of Mexican soldiers.

The accurate killing fire of the Texians quickly drove General Cos's troops to the middle of San Antonio. There, the

Texians took possession of two well-built houses which fronted Military Plaza. One was the De La Garza house, the other was the mansion of the Veramendis. Again, a situation was established whereby the Texians had the advantage of cover and concealment, while the Mexican soldiers were exposed in the open square of the plaza.

The air was rent with the sound of musketry and the boom of Mexican cannon fire. Thick, acrid smoke rolled across the town as the fight went on. Once, as Sam dashed across an open area, a Mexican cannonball came crashing in on the wall of what had been a beautiful hacienda. A second artillery blast did just as much damage to the house as the first, and it was quickly evident that the poorly trained Mexican cannoneers were going to be a greater threat to the houses and buildings of the town than they were to the Texian troops. The Texians, emboldened by their early successes, fought like demons, gradually pushing the Mexicans back through the town, from house to house, street to street, and plaza to plaza.

The fighting raged on for the rest of the day, ending shortly after the sun set. That night the homes, patios, and gardens of San Antonio's citizens were turned into fortified encampments as the Texians consolidated the gains they had made during the day's fighting. Low-lying clouds reflected back the flickering orange of both Texian and Mexican campfires, and flickering shadows gave false alarms to the sentries of both armies.

The Mexican family that owned the house where Sam McCord and Ben Milam were bivouacked, surprised Sam and the others by bringing out a steaming pot of beef and beans, and a platter of tortillas. They served the men without taking pay.

"I wonder why they did that?" Sam asked Milam.

"Because they live in Texas," Milam explained. "And they've got about as much to gain as we do by getting Santa Anna off our back. If truth be known, I expect nearly all the Texas Mexicans are on our side, though they can't always say so."

"It's as if they're turning against their own kind. I'm glad for their support, but it seems a little strange to me."

"Why so? Isn't that what your own countrymen did, back

during the Revolutionary War? Don't forget, they were all English subjects, yet they turned against the crown.''

"Yes, I guess so.''

Milam chuckled. ''Well then, take it from the point of view of a Welshman who views your Revolutionary War from the other side. There is no difference.''

From somewhere in the distance, a guitar started playing, then they heard a clear, melodic voice singing in Spanish.

"Seems funny, doesn't it?'' Milam suggested.

"What's that?''

"That we try to kill each other during the day, then sing to each other at night.''

"It is a pretty song,'' Sam said.

"Yes, it is.''

"What do the words mean?''

Milam listened for a moment, then he translated. ''It is a story about a man who loves one girl but is forced to marry another.''

"If he loves one girl, why is he marrying another?'' Sam asked.

"Because the girl he loves is a peasant and beneath him,'' Milam explained. He listened for a moment longer, then nodded his head. ''He goes on to tell her that his love for her is real, but that it must remain forever hidden in his heart.''

"I see,'' Sam said.

"It is a rather foolish song,'' Milam admitted, clearing his throat. ''But it does reflect the kind of thoughts men often have at times like these. I'll wager there are a few eyes over there . . . and over here as well, that aren't dry, about now.''

"Thanks for the translation,'' Sam said. He took his tin cup of coffee over to a nearby rock, then sat down to drink it and to listen to the music. Even though he couldn't understand the words, the poignancy of the song managed to get through to him. The more so, he realized, because it seemed to be speaking directly to him.

Sam recalled his conversation with the parish commissioner.

"Are you absolutely positive about your information?" Sam had asked.

"I have no doubt whatever," the commissioner had replied.

"But surely, that can't be true. Phillipe Doucette is a personal friend of President Andrew Jackson. He was personally decorated by him after the battle of New Orleans."

"That may be so," the commissioner said. *"But the census statistics do not lie."*

"McCord!"

Milam's call brought Sam out of his reverie. "Sam McCord! Where are you?"

"I'm over here, Colonel," Sam shouted back. He stood as Milam came over to see him.

"Sam, I want you to get this message back to Washington-on-the-Brazos."

Sam looked confused. "You want me to deliver a message, sir? When?"

"Right now. I want you to leave tonight."

"But, Colonel, the battle isn't over yet," Sam protested. "I'd rather stay and fight."

Milam smiled, then put his hand on Sam's arm. "I know you would, son," he said. "But what you have to realize is that we are engaged in a war, not just a battle. There will be other fights for you to participate in. In the meantime, the rest of Texas has to be told what's going on here. Can I depend on you?"

"You can depend on me," Sam promised.

"Good. I've written this message," Milam said. "Tell me what you think about it." Milam began to read aloud from the little scrap of paper: " 'We have, so far, had a fierce contest, the enemy offering a strong and obstinate resistance. It is difficult to determine what injury has been done him; many killed, certainly, but how many cannot be told. On our side, ten or twelve wounded, and two killed.' "

"That's very good, Colonel," Sam replied. "I'd say it paints a clear enough picture of what's going on around here."

"I'm glad you agree. Once you have delivered the message, come back and join us. After we kick the Mexicans out, we are going to occupy this town, so I'll be right here, waiting for you."

"I'll be back," Sam promised.

Six

"Captain McCord?"

Sam had been sleeping, and when he opened his eyes, he saw one of Sam Houston's lieutenants looking down at him.

"Yes, Lieutenant?" Sam said, sitting up and rubbing his eyes. "What is it?"

"General Houston sends you his compliments, sir, and says that he will see you now."

"It's about damned time," Sam grumbled. Getting up, he stretched and yawned, then moved around a little, to eliminate the soreness of sleeping on the ground. "Where is he?"

"He's over there in his headquarters tent," the lieutenant replied, pointing.

Sam started over in the direction indicated by the young lieutenant. He had actually delivered the message to Houston three days ago, in the naive belief that he would not only return to San Antonio immediately, but he would do so with at least a company of men with him.

That was not the case. General Houston was working on the *Proclamation of Sam Houston, Commander-in-Chief of the Army of Texas,* and he directed Sam to stay put until the proclamation was completed.

Sam stopped just short of the tent opening, then cleared his throat. Sam Houston, who was sitting at his field desk, looked up.

"Ah, Captain McCord, come in, come in," he invited.

Sam stepped into the tent, wondered for a brief moment if he should salute, then decided against it as neither he nor General Houston were traditional militarists.

"There is news from San Antonio," Houston reported.

"The fighting? How goes it?"

"The fighting has ended," Houston reported. "And it ended very well for our side. At the end, the Mexicans fortified themselves in the old Alamo mission, but they were unable to withstand the withering artillery fire of our troops. After five days of pitched battle, General Cos sent out a white flag and surrendered eleven hundred officers and men.''

"Surrendered? You mean they are our prisoners?''

"There are no prisoners," Houston said. "General Cos and his army were paroled on their oath that they will not, again, fight against us.''

"Do you believe Cos will keep his word?''

"If it were General Cos alone, I would believe him," Houston said. "But Santa Anna is far too vain a man to let this pass. The defeat of Cos will be too humiliating to him. Santa Anna will invade Texas, and I have no doubt but that Cos and his paroled army will be marching at his side.''

"Then I say, let them come! We'll whip them again!'' Sam said happily. "I knew Milam could do it! I just wish I had been there at the end, that's all.''

Houston pinched his nose, then cleared his throat. "Unfortunately, Captain, I'm afraid that not all the news from San Antonio is good.''

"What is it? What is the bad news?''

"Colonel Milam is dead," Houston reported. "He was killed by a bullet in the head on the third day.''

Sam shook his head. "I'm sorry to hear that, General. Milam was a good man and I figure Texas is going to need all the good men they can get.''

"I agree," Houston said. He reached over to the corner of his desk, where there stood a pile of just-printed circulars. "That is why I wrote this proclamation," he added.

"You've finished it?'' Sam asked.

"Yes. And I would like for you to take several copies back to San Antonio with you, so that they may be distributed among the men.''

Sam picked up one of the documents and glanced through it. He read the last couple of sentences aloud: '' 'Generous and brave hearts from a land of freedom have joined our standard before Bexar. They have, by their heroism and valor, called forth the admiration of their comrades in arms, and have reflected additional honor on the land of their birth. Let the brave rally to our standard.'

"Stirring words, General," he added.

"Thank you."

"I only wish you had finished it earlier, so I could have gotten back in time."

"In time for what?" Houston asked.

"Why, in time for the battle that I missed," Sam explained, as if unable to understand why Houston didn't understand.

Houston shook his head. "Captain McCord, you should forget about the battle at San Antonio. You must think only of the larger picture now. Believe me, your presence would have done nothing to prevent Colonel Milam from being killed . . . and, as evidenced by the fact that the battle was won without you, neither was your presence required to secure victory."

"I suppose not," Sam admitted. "Still, I would have liked to be there."

"So would we all, Captain McCord, so would we all. In the meantime, deliver these proclamations, then hold yourself in readiness as we raise our army. You will be called upon again, this I promise you."

CHRISTMAS DAY 1835, ROSECROWN PLANTATION

> Angels we have heard on high,
> Singing sweetly through the night,
> And the mountains in reply
> Echoing their brave delight.
> *Gloria in excelsis Deo*
> *Gloria in excelsis Deo*

The sweet sound of caroling came from both black and white throats as Rosecrown celebrated the Christmas of 1835. As was the tradition at Rosecrown, a huge table had been erected of boards and sawhorses, around which everyone, master and slave, would sit in communal meal to celebrate the birth of the Christ child. There was, however, one significant member of the Rosecrown family missing, and Phillipe, noticing his daughter's absence, spoke of it to his wife.

"Do you think she is ill?" Phillipe asked.

"No, I'm sure everything is fine," Cassandra answered. "She is probably just trying to decide what dress to wear." Cassandra held her hand up toward a large black woman who was nearby. "I'll send Millie up to her room to look in on her."

"Yes, please do. I do not want her to miss out on the celebration."

In her room upstairs, Marie was standing in the shadows caused by the closed curtains, looking at her nude image in the mirror. She put her hand on her flat stomach and pressed in, then released it, leaving a momentary impression of her palm, but nothing else. She leaned closer to the mirror and looked into her eyes, trying to stare into her own soul, to see if her sin was evident.

There was nothing there.

"Dear God, please," she said, breathing a small, quiet prayer. "Sam is gone. Don't abandon me now."

Her prayerful moment was interrupted by a knock on the door.

"Just a minute, Mama," Marie called.

"It ain't your mama, chile, it's me, Millie. Your mama done sent me to see is you all right?"

"Yes, I'm fine. I'm just getting dressed."

"Does you need some help?"

Marie started to say no, then, impulsively, she walked over to open the door.

"I'll just get your things and—" Millie started, then quickly closed the door behind her. "Lord, chile, you is naked!"

"I'm in the middle of changing clothes. Besides, you've seen me naked before, Millie."

"Yes'm, I knows I has, but you ought to be careful 'bout such things. That could'a been anyone outside your door. What if it had been one of the field hands?"

"Now what would one of the field hands be doing up here? Besides, you told me it was you."

"How'd you know I wasn't lyin'? I could'a been someone else, just sayin' I was me."

Marie laughed at Millie's convoluted logic. "I trust you," she said.

"Yes'm. Well, it's a good thing I wasn't lyin'. Now, let me help you get dressed so's you can get downstairs. This is Christmas Day. It's a day to be joyous."

"Is it? I wonder."

"What you mean by that? Miss Marie, is there somethin' wrong with you?"

"Look at me, Millie."

Millie looked at her for a moment, then averted her eyes. "You still naked," she said.

"I know I am, but I want you to look at me. Look very closely. Do you see anything wrong . . . anything different?"

"I don't see nothin' but a beautiful young lady what ain't makin' a whole lot of sense," Millie answered. "Now, be a good chile and get yourself dressed so's you can come down. All the people is askin' about you. This is a special day to them, too, you know. On Christmas Day, there ain't no one a slave, 'ceptin' to the Lord."

Millie often spoke of "the people" and "them" as if she weren't one of them, though she was. However, her position as head of the house was lofty enough that it did provide her with a sense of separation from the others.

Marie sighed. "All right, Millie. You go back downstairs and tell Mama that I'll be there shortly."

"Yes'm, I'll do that," Millie replied. Millie started outside, then, when she reached the door, she stopped and looked around. "Honey, you been mopin' aroun' here ever since Mr. McCord left for Texas. It wasn't right, what he done, leavin' without so much as a fare-thee-well, but what's done is done, and they ain't no need in you frettin' over it."

"But, Millie, you don't know—"

"Like I said, chile, what's done is done. That means the only thing you can do is accept the load the Lord done give you to carry."

"I'll try to remember that."

"And another thing," Millie said. "When you come downstairs you be smilin'. This the only day of the whole year that the people can be pure joyous. Don't you go spoilin' it for them with a sour look on your face."

"I won't," Marie said contritely.

Millie's stern disposition softened. "I don' like to speak harsh to you, chile," she said. "There ain't nobody in this whole world loves you more'n I do, 'ceptin' your mama and papa. I wants you to be happy. You know that, don' you?"

Marie nodded. "I know that. I've always known that."

Millie smiled. "Good. I'm goin' go down now and tell everyone that things is just fine."

In a one-room apartment upstairs at a ship chandler's on Canal Street, Hunter Grant lay on the bed with his hands laced behind his head, staring up at the ceiling. An empty glass was on a nearby table, alongside a whiskey bottle which, by lying on its side, gave mute evidence to being as empty as the glass.

Downstairs, on the street outside, Hunter heard someone wishing a "Merry Christmas," and, in the torpor of his hangover, he realized that today was Christmas. Hunter had passed the two months since the duel in an alcoholic fog.

Hunter looked around the room, at the peeling wallpaper, the unpainted woodwork, the bare floor, and the meager furnishings. It was quite a change from the house with the flower-filled courtyard he once owned and occupied on Bourbon Street. Then, Hunter had been a very successful cotton broker, and a part of the New Orleans aristocracy. His circumstances were now so reduced that he was barely able to sustain himself.

All this was a result of the duel. Hunter's feelings of guilt and remorse over having killed his best friend, his rejection by Lucinda and her family, and the ostracism of New Orleans "society" had driven him to intemperate use of alcohol and injudicious gambling habits. In order to support such behavior, he began to take greater and greater risks in his business. He reached the bottom when he sold several thousand bales of cotton that he did not have, to a group of Northern traders. It was a legitimate risk, for he was anticipating that a favorable move in the price of cotton within the next two weeks would work to his advantage. In fact, cotton moved in the opposite direction, and Hunter came up short. He was forced to liquidate all his holdings, just to make the contract good. That left him bankrupt, and his business, his house, even his horse, was taken over by debtors. He had barely enough money left to pay the meager rent on his room and keep himself supplied with cheap, but strong, whiskey.

Church bells began ringing outside, and, again, Hunter heard the sound of merrymakers wishing each other a Merry Christmas. He sat up in bed and had to grab his head in order to stop the spinning. He knew what was good for that. Another drink.

Hunter got up, then left his room and staggered down the stairs into the street.

"I hope you have a Merry Christmas, sir," someone said, doffing his hat as he walked by.

"It will be," Hunter replied. "If I can find a tavern open today."

VIERNES, 8 ENERO, 1836, SALTILLO, COAHUILA, MEXICO

The inside of the tent was lined with red, green, and white satin. A canvas floor covering was stretched over the level ground and an ornate Persian rug was spread upon the canvas.

In the middle of the tent stood a table that would have been at home in the finest dining room in Mexico City. It was set with silver, crystal, and china, all sparkling in rich array. A roast suckling pig, gleaming in a golden brown glaze, occupied the position of honor at the center of the table, surrounded by several plates of vegetables and fruits.

This was the field headquarters of Antonio López de Santa Anna, General of the Armies and President of Mexico. Lieutenant Colonel Don Juan Esteban Montoya, resplendently dressed in his *zapadores* uniform of blue trousers with a red stripe, a red, pigeon-tailed jacket with green lapels, epaulets, and a green collar, stood at attention as he reported to Santa Anna.

"Ah, Juan, you have waited a long time to report for duty," Santa Anna said. He was sitting at the table eating a piece of roast pork. A very beautiful, and very young girl was sitting beside him, with her hand lying, easily, in his lap. "I was beginning to grow worried that you would not come."

"My orders said that I need not report until after Christmas.

I am sorry if my delay was a cause for your concern, *Presidente*," Juan said contritely.

"*Si*. Well, you are here now, and that is all that matters. What do you think, Colonel Montoya? Is our army not impressive?" Santa Anna asked, holding his hand out in a sweeping and expressive gesture. "I have amassed the greatest army in the history of Mexico, and I am taking it to Tejas to crush that upstart group of Norteamericanos who have had the temerity to rebel against me."

"It is a grand army, *El Presidente*. More than enough, I would think, to end the rebellion."

"*Si*, but I intend to do more than merely end the rebellion. I plan to completely eradicate all foreigners from Tejas. And if that means killing everyone who opposes us, then that is exactly what we will do. Our government has, in fact, passed a law which states that, 'Any foreigner who takes up arms against the government of Mexico shall, when captured, be summarily shot.' And I intend to carry that law out to the last letter."

"It is a harsh law, General."

"These are harsh times, Colonel. Sit, eat with me."

"Thank you, General, but I have already eaten," Juan lied.

Juan had not yet eaten, but he could not bring himself to dine so sumptuously when he knew that the "magnificent" army Santa Anna was so proud of, was barely able to scrape up starvation rations to feed itself. That was because it was made up of conscripts, the draft filled by emptying jail cells and gathering the very dregs of society. There were many Indians in the army as well, untrained, ill-clothed, and unable to speak the language of the men who commanded them.

At this moment there were more than ten thousand such soldiers spread out in large, concentric circles around the headquarters. Because of its composition, it was an army without doctors, cooks, bakers, farriers, or supply specialists. The conscripts were sloppy, disorganized, and raucous.

In addition to the untrained and ill-equipped soldiers, the large encampment was crowded with wives, children, parents, girlfriends, prostitutes, officers' servants, horses, donkeys, cattle, sheep, goats, pigs, chickens, and pets. The officers made no effort to run these people off, for without their direct support, there would be nothing to eat. Whereas Napoleon's army traveled on its stomach, the army of Santa Anna, the "Napoleon of the West," traveled on what food the women could scavenge for their men. Enough women, feeding their own men, had the effect of feeding the entire army.

There was, however, a part of the army that held itself completely aloof from the conscripts. These were the two thousand or so professional soldiers, NCOs, and officers who were uniformed, disciplined, well-trained, and tough. They had made a life of the army, and they knew and trusted each other, forming a family that stuck together. Of this small corps, Santa Anna had a right to be proud, for it was as fine an army as any in the Western Hemisphere.

Major Manuel Quinterra, Juan's executive officer, was one of those elite men. He greeted Juan with a salute when Juan reported to the command post of his regiment.

"Welcome back, Colonel," Quinterra said. Then he laughed. "I suppose I shall have to get used to addressing you as colonel, rather than Juan." The two men had served as majors together in a previous campaign.

"Forget it, and I will teach you a lesson by putting you in the *calaboose*," Juan replied, though his laughter gave away the fact that he was teasing. After the salute, the two men embraced.

"And how was your trip to North America?"

"It was good," Juan answered without elaboration. "Is there anything to eat, Manuel? I am starved."

"Santa Anna did not invite you to dine with him?"

"He did, but I declined."

Quinterra laughed, then looked over at a captain, who took out a paper banknote and handed it to Quinterra.

"I knew you would not accept his invitation," Quinterra said. "And I bet Captain Monteclave as much. Come with me. I am certain the officers' mess has some beans and tortillas left."

Juan followed Quinterra to a place behind the tent where an iron kettle hung suspended over a wood fire. A little cloud of steam issued from the pot, perfuming the air with its spicy aroma. Juan ladled some of the beans onto a tortilla, then he rolled it all into a tube and began eating.

"Juan!" a happy voice shouted, just as Juan took his first bite.

"What did you call your commanding officer, Lieutenant?" Quinterra asked in mock sternness.

Ramon gulped, then came to attention and saluted. "My apologies, Colonel," he said, saluting.

Frowning, Juan returned his brother's salute, then, unable to hold the pretense of anger any longer, he broke into a big smile. Juan embraced his brother as he had Quinterra earlier.

"What is your company?" Juan asked.

"I am in Captain Mendoza's company," Ramon replied.

"Mendoza's company, eh?" Juan replied. "That is good. Mendoza is a fine officer and a good man."

"Yes, I suppose he is, if you say so," Ramon said with little enthusiasm.

Juan wiped a spill of beans off his chin, then sucked them off his fingers. He knitted his eyebrows as he looked at his younger brother.

"Why do you speak so? Do you think differently about Captain Mendoza?"

"I think he trains us too much," Ramon complained. "Every day we march, march, march. I am marching in my sleep."

Juan laughed. "Is that all it is? Well, I am glad he drills you with such regularity. When the campaign is hard it is good, sometimes, to be able to march in your sleep."

The other officers laughed at Ramon's expense, then Juan and his brother drifted over to a fallen log where the two caught each other up on the latest family news.

Later that night, Major Manuel Quinterra brought a bottle of tequila over to Juan's tent, and the two men talked of the impending military action.

"What I do not understand, is why the Norteamericanos in Tejas would be willing to make war against us when we have always treated them with such generosity," Juan said.

Quinterra licked some salt from the back of his hand, then took a large swallow of tequila.

"It is not just the Norteamericanos in Tejas, my friend," Quinterra said. "The decree that has denied Tejas any rights of self-rule is applied with as equal vigor against our own

people who live there. All who live in Tejas have been ordered to disarm themselves, Mexican and Norteamericano
alike. And, although our politicians would like us to believe
that this will be a war between Mexico and the Norteamericano invaders of our country, there are many Mexicans living
in Tejas who will join with them. They feel betrayed by the
renunciation of the Constitution of 1824.''

"Do you know for a fact that any Mexicans have joined
them?'' Juan asked.

"*Si.* During the battle in San Antonio de Bexar, the citizens
of the city, our own people, sided with the Texians,'' Quinterra said. "And when General Cos and his army was forced
to leave, these same Mexican citizens stood on the side of the
street and shouted insults.''

"Is that true? I have not heard such a thing,'' Juan said.
"How do you know this?''

Quinterra was quiet for a long moment before he answered.

"My wife's brother, Juan Seguin, was among them,''
Quinterra said in a flat monotone.

"Your brother-in-law has sided with the Norteamericanos?'' Juan asked.

"*Si.* Though, if you asked him, he would say that he has
sided with the Texians.''

Juan looked out across the extended campground. Around
hundreds of campfires, thousands of men, women, and children were bedding down for the night. From one part of the
campground he could hear guitar music and singing.

"It is not good to make war against your own people,''
Juan said.

"I agree, Colonel. But this war has been thrust upon us.
We have no choice.''

"*Si,*'' Juan replied. "We have no choice.''

Thank God, Juan thought, when war came he would be
fighting alongside his kinsmen and not, as Quinterra must do,
against them.

MONDAY, JANUARY 11, 1836, NEW ORLEANS

When Marie Doucette stepped down from her carriage in
front of the New Orleans police station, she attracted the at-

tention of several men, all of whom wondered what business could possibly bring such a beautiful young woman to the police station.

"Miss Doucette, you sure you don't want me to come in with you?" the carriage driver asked. "They's some powerful fearsome folks be hangin' out around a police station."

"Thank you, Julius, but I'll be all right," Marie replied. "After all, if one isn't safe when surrounded by the police, then when is one safe?"

"Yes'm, I guess you be right," Julius said. "I'll just wait right here for you." Julius tied the reins to a ring on the footboard, then leaned back in his seat. He tipped his hat forward across his eyes, folded his arms across his rather large chest, and closed his eyes.

Marie walked up the concrete steps to the front door of the building, then pushed it open and stepped inside. A tall man, with a high-crowned hat and a long blue coat was standing just inside the door, by the wall.

"Are you here for the court, miss?" he asked.

"No . . . yes . . . I don't know," Marie replied. "I wish to speak with Mr. Henry Code. I was led to believe that he would be here."

"Mr. Code? You might find him in the lawyers' room. It's the second door on the right."

"Thank you," Marie said.

As Marie walked down the hall she passed by a large, open, double-door. Glancing through it, she saw that court was in session. The judge was leaning back in his chair, his eyelids drooping heavily under bushy white eyebrows. At that particular moment the prosecutor was making a point, and he was emphasizing his statements by pounding his fist into his hand. The accused sat at his table, looking properly contrite.

Marie continued down the hall until she reached a door, where a sign read: LAWYERS' CONFERENCE ROOM. Beyond the door, the room had one large table surrounded by several chairs. One man was sitting at the table writing in a ledger. Marie stepped up to the table and cleared her throat. When the lawyer looked up he recognized her, and not expecting to see her in such a place, his eyes grew large in surprise.

"Miss Doucette," he said, standing so quickly that he

knocked over his chair. "What on earth is someone like you doing in a place like this?"

"I believe you are holding Mr. Hunter Grant in your jail," Marie said.

Henry chuckled. "It's not my jail, and I'm not holding him," he said. "It belongs to the city of New Orleans. And when one is drunk, disorderly, and commits assault, that's where one winds up."

"I am told you are his lawyer. Can you get him out of jail?"

Henry sighed. "Ah, now, there is the rub. I'm afraid there is very little left I can do for him," he said. "After all, this is his sixth court appearance for the same offense. I am afraid that the judge's patience has grown quite thin . . . as has mine, actually."

"But, surely, you can do something for him," Marie protested.

Suddenly Henry smiled. "Wait a minute, you are a close friend of Lucinda Meechum, aren't you? Praise the Lord! If you are bringing word that Lucinda has forgiven Hunter, you will be doing more for him than anything I could ever do."

Marie shook her head. "I'm sorry. I was not sent by Lucinda," she said.

Henry sighed. "That's too bad. I had hoped that, by now, she could have found forgiveness in her heart."

"You are more than Mr. Grant's lawyer. You are his friend as well, aren't you?"

"I *was* his friend, yes. But Hunter has repeatedly stated that he has need for neither friend nor counselor, though I have never known a man with greater need for both. But, tell me, Miss Doucette. If you are not here for Lucinda Meechum, then what *is* your interest in Hunter?"

"I would like to pay his fine and have him released to my custody," Marie said.

Henry shook his head. "I'm not certain the judge will even affix a fine this time. He may order Hunter to go directly to jail."

"Oh, but surely not!" Marie pleaded. "Hunter Grant is a gentleman, one of our city's leading citizens. The judge couldn't possibly consider putting him in jail with the likes of thieves and murderers.''

Henry clucked his tongue. "When Hunter Grant was brokering cotton he was, indeed, one of New Orleans's leading citizens. But his estate has so deteriorated that now he is not only without funds, if he were not in jail, he wouldn't even have a roof over his head.''

"Oh, what a tragic thing to happen to him," Marie said.

"I am curious, Miss Doucette. What use have you for Hunter Grant, that you would pay his fine and ask that he be released to you?''

"I will share that reason with Hunter Grant and no other," Marie replied.

Henry studied Marie for a long moment, then he nodded. "All right, I will see what I can do. But this is the last time I am going out on the limb for the likes of Hunter Grant." Henry walked over to stick his head through the door. "Constable?''

"Yes, sir, Mr. Code.''

"Kindly escort Miss Doucette to the courtroom. She has business there.''

"Yes, sir, right away. Come this way, miss," the constable directed.

The constable took Marie down the hall and into the courtroom, where he found a place for her near the very front. He touched his forehead in a half-salute, then left, while Marie sat down, feeling the stares of the others who had watched with interest as she entered.

A railing separated the gallery of the courtroom from the counsel tables and the judge's bench. Behind his bench the judge sat in somber robes.

"Would the defendant approach the bench?" the judge said.

The defendant, still the portrait of contriteness, appeared before the judge.

"Having pleaded guilty and shown the proper remorse for your offense, this court is moved to a lenient sentence. Thirty days in jail.''

"Defense thanks the court for its magnanimity," the lawyer for the defendant said as the prisoner was escorted away.

"Bailiff, call the next case, please."

"The court calls Hunter Grant," the bailiff said.

"What is the charge?" the judge asked.

"Your Honor, the defendant is charged with public drunkenness, disorderly conduct, starting a fight, inciting a riot, and extensive damage to private property," the prosecutor said, reading from a piece of paper.

The judge sighed. "Mr. Prosecutor, this couldn't be the same Hunter Grant who appeared before me two weeks ago, could it? And one week before that, and only three days before that?"

"It could be and it is, Your Honor. This is, in fact, the sixth time the defendant has appeared before this court," the prosecutor answered.

"Your Honor, may I point out that there are extenuating circumstances?" Henry Code called from his position at the other table.

"So, Mr. Code, you are still representing Mr. Grant, I see?" the judge said.

"Yes, sir, I am, though as Hunter Grant is now indigent, I am no longer in his employ, but am representing him as a result of an appointment by the court. And, as I said, there are extenuating circumstances to his behavior."

"Yes, yes, we all know Mr. Grant's story," the judge said. "If he was not prepared to live with the results of the duel, he should never have let himself be talked into one." The judge sighed. "But what is done is done. Bring the defendant before the bench."

A side door opened and Hunter Grant came into the room, preceded and trailed by burly bailiffs. When Marie saw him, she gasped in surprise. She knew that he had fallen on hard times but she was not prepared for just how rough and unkempt he would look. His clothes were dirty and torn, and his hair and beard were long and unkempt. There was nothing of the proud, confident, and, Marie thought, handsome young man she had known before.

"Look at you, Mr. Grant," the judge admonished. "Have you not even enough pride remaining to clean yourself up before appearing in my court? You have not even the appearance of a gentleman."

"What's that?" Hunter replied sharply. "I am not a gentleman, you say? Well, now, how can you say that, Judge? Did I not fulfill my . . . *honor* . . . and my . . . *gentlemanly* . . . obligation by putting a pistol ball in my best friend's heart?" The words *honor* and *gentlemanly* were uttered in a mocking slur.

"We are all aware, Mr. Grant, that you fulfilled your obligation to the code of honor as was proper for a gentleman of your station. What you have *not* done, sir, is behave as a gentleman of station *since* that time."

"Well, excuse me, Your Honor, if my behavior no longer finds favor with polite society. However, as I no longer consider myself to be a part of polite society, I really must tell you that I don't give a damn."

There was a tittering of laughter and snickers in the courtroom, brought to a halt by the rapping of the judge's gavel.

"Mr. Grant, as it is obvious that you—"

"Excuse me, Your Honor. May I approach the bench?" Henry asked.

"If you feel you have something to add," the judge replied. The judge removed a handkerchief and blew his nose loudly as Henry Code stepped up to talk to him. There was a long moment of quiet conversation during which the judge listened, then looked pointedly toward Marie. After another moment, the judge nodded and put his handkerchief away.

"Mr. Grant, your lawyer has pleaded you guilty," the judge said. "Do you concur?"

"Who am I to question my lawyer, Your Honor?" Hunter said sarcastically. "After all, doesn't he have my best interests at heart?"

"He does, sir. He does indeed," the judge replied. "Approach the bench for sentencing."

With a guard on either side of him, Hunter walked up to stand before the judge.

"Have you anything to say, Mr. Grant, before I pass sentence?"

"No, Your Honor."

"Very well. It is the decision of this court that you be fined one hundred dollars. If you cannot pay the one hundred dollars, you will be required to serve six months in jail. Have you sufficient money for the fine?''

"I have no money at all, Your Honor," Hunter answered.

"Your Honor, there comes now before this court, one Miss Marie Doucette," Henry said.

"And what is the purpose of Miss Doucette's appearance before this court?" the judge asked.

"Your Honor, Miss Doucette appears for the purpose of paying Mr. Grant's fine," Henry said.

"What?" Hunter barked loudly, turning around quickly to see Marie who, at that moment, was just getting up from her seat. "Like hell she will! Your Honor, I cannot accept that. I will *not* accept it!"

" 'Tis neither yours to accept nor decline, Mr. Grant," the judge said. "That money is due the court, and the court will make the decision."

"Well, decide against it!" Hunter said. "I'll serve the time. I'll not have a woman paying my fine!"

"And I'll not have a self-confessed man at the docket telling me what to do, sir!" the judge replied, emphasizing his point with another bang of the gavel. "Miss Doucette, the court grants you permission to make the fine for this defendant. You may pay the clerk."

"And, if Your Honor please, the second part of the arrangement?" Henry said.

"What arrangement?" Hunter asked. "What second part?"

"Oh, yes," the judge said, as if just thinking of it. "Mr. Grant, you are herewith discharged to the custody of Miss Doucette for a period of indentured servitude to her of no less than six months," the judge concluded his sentencing with a bang of his gavel. "Court is adjourned."

"What? Indentured servitude?" Hunter shouted at the top of his voice as the judge and the gallery began leaving the court. Hunter turned to his lawyer. "Henry, what the hell is going on here?"

"I'm sorry, Hunter, this was the best I could do for you," Henry answered with a shrug of his shoulders. He began picking up papers from the table and stuffing them into his case.

"What do you mean, this is the best you can do for me?" Hunter looked over toward Marie, who, having paid the fine to a clerk, was now standing just on the other side of the railing, waiting for him. "Well, your best isn't good enough. I'll not go with her," he said. "She just wasted her money paying my fine. I'll serve my six months in jail."

"I'm afraid it wouldn't be six months, now, Hunter. It would be five years."

"Five years? What do you mean five years? The judge said six months!"

"That was before he declared you to be Miss Doucette's indentured servant. Should you fail to go with her now, your status would be the same as that of a runaway slave. And the penalty for running away from one's master in this state is five years in prison."

"Damn your hide, Henry! I thought you were my friend! How could you do this to me?"

"Don't blame me!" Henry replied sharply. "The fault lies with yourself, Hunter Grant. You, alone, are responsible for your sorry state of affairs. And if Miss Doucette has enough compassion in her heart to pay your fine and keep you from jail, then the very least you can do is show her some gratitude. Or, if you can't muster up any gratitude, then show her some common courtesy. You have not yet sunk below that point, have you, Hunter?"

"I . . . I'm sorry," Hunter said quietly.

"Don't apologize to me. Apologize to Miss Doucette," Henry suggested. Henry picked up the last of the papers and closed his case. He started to walk away, then he stopped and looked back at Hunter.

"Hunter, I know the despair you went through when you killed your best friend. I know the bitterness of being turned against by the very society whose code of honor you sought to fulfill. And I can understand the heartache of being rejected by your fiancée and her family, a family so close to you that it was as if it were your own. Hell, I even feel partially responsible for it. I know that if I had not volunteered so quickly to be your second, Johnny would have served in that capacity and he would be alive today. But, what is done is done, and I have done all I can do to make it up to you. So I'm telling you now, from here on out, keep yourself on the straight and narrow. I won't be representing you anymore. If you get into trouble again I shall ask the court to appoint a new lawyer for you. As of now, we're quits, you and I. I don't know what Miss Doucette has in mind for you, but my final piece of advice is for you to do anything she asks you to do. This may well be your last chance at recovering your self-respect." Spinning on his heel, Henry walked quickly away.

"Henry, I . . ." Hunter called after him, but when Henry didn't turn around, Hunter didn't complete his statement. Instead, he just stood there, watching his erstwhile friend walk away.

"Mr. Grant?" a woman's soft voice said from behind him.

Hunter turned and glared at Marie, his features set in such a disagreeable expression that the young woman gasped, then took a step backward, with fear and indecision registering in her eyes.

Feeling bad at frightening her, Hunter softened his expression.

"I apologize for my appearance, madam," he said with a slight bow that managed to recall, at that moment, some of his old courtliness. "I must look a sight."

Marie smiled hesitantly. "I admit, you don't look much like you did the last time I saw you," she said. At the quizzical expression on Hunter's face she hastened to add: "It was at the cotillion at Trailback, when your engagement to Lucinda was announced."

Hunter nodded. "Ah, yes," he said. "The cotillion. Well, I am afraid, Miss Doucette, that the . . . *gentleman* . . . you saw on that occasion no longer exists."

"Come with me, Mr. Grant. Perhaps a haircut, shave, bath, and some new clothes will bring that gentleman back."

"It may make me appear more presentable," Hunter said. "But it will not bring back one who is dead."

Seven

ROSECROWN PLANTATION

Phillipe Doucette stood in the living room of the manor house, looking out toward the stable. He was watching Hunter Grant carrying water into the barn to be used to take his bath. Behind Phillipe, Marie and her mother, Cassandra, were seated on the large settee.

Millie came into the room then, carrying a bundle of clothes.

"Miss Marie, I done look through all your papa's things to find clothes he don't wear no more that would be fittin' for a gentleman like Mr. Grant to wear and I come up with these."

"What's that?" Phillipe asked, turning around. "You're giving him my clothes?"

"Papa, did you see how he was dressed? The meanest field hand on our plantation has better clothes. It would be positively un-Christian not to give him something to wear."

"Marie is right, dear. We can't very well have him running around here in absolute rags," Cassandra said.

"Yes, well, that begs the question, doesn't it? Why is he here in the first place?"

"Just think, Papa, if he had married Lucinda, he would be our neighbor now," Marie answered.

"Yes, but he didn't marry Lucinda, did he?"

"And do you think it is safe to have him here, dear?" Cassandra asked. "After all, he did murder the Meechum boy."

"Mama, he did not *murder* Johnny Meechum," Marie said. "He killed him in a duel."

"Well, there is very little difference between a duel and murder, in my opinion. Besides, to fight a duel against his own best friend . . . a boy he grew up with. It just seems awful to me, that's all."

"He had no choice, Cassandra, he had to fight the duel,"

Phillipe said. "The real criminal here is that fool, Colonel Troupe, for forcing the issue. Because of Troupe, a perfectly innocent man is dead and the life of another has been ruined."

"Then you are on Mr. Grant's side?" Marie asked quickly.

"I do not condemn him for doing what he was forced to do," Phillipe said. "But neither do I condone his behavior of late. That he has not been able to live with the consequences of his action denotes a weakness of character."

"You won't make me turn him out, will you, Papa? He has no other place to go."

Phillipe sighed and stroked his chin, then went back to looking toward the barn.

"I won't make you turn him out," he said.

Millie, who had been standing by listening quietly to the entire exchange, held up the bundle of clothes.

"Do it be all right for me to take these to the gentleman?" she asked.

"Yes, give him the clothes with my compliments," Phillipe said.

"*Merci,* Papa." Marie hurried to him to embrace him in appreciation.

"But, dear, what if Mr. McCord should come back and find Mr. Grant here? That would not look good, would it?" Cassandra asked.

"By going off to fight in a war that is of no concern to him, Mr. McCord has shown himself to be a man without honor. Should he return, he would not be welcome here."

"But, Papa, what if he returned to marry me?" Marie asked anxiously.

"After what he has done, I could not let him see you."

"Papa, no, you don't mean that."

"Oh, but I do mean that," Phillipe insisted. "He has shown, by his indifference to your feelings, that he is not the man you should marry."

"But I *must* marry him!"

"*Why* must you marry him?"

"Because . . . because everyone expects it. If I don't marry him, I will be ruined. I will never be able to hold my head up again."

"Nonsense, my dear," Phillipe said. "The expectations of

others should have nothing to do with how you live your life. I say that Sam McCord isn't the man for you, and there will be no more discussion of it.''

"But, Papa," Marie started.

Phillipe held up his hand to quiet her dissent. "Daughter, I said that is the end of it."

"Yes, Papa," Marie said, her eyes filling with tears.

"Now look what you have done," Cassandra said. "You have made her cry."

"There, now, don't cry," Phillipe said, walking over to put his arms around his daughter. "There are plenty of other men who are anxious to pay court to you. And why shouldn't there be? You are the most beautiful girl in the parish, and in the state as well." Phillipe smiled. "And don't forget, with no brothers or sisters, there is also Rosecrown in the bargain. I've no doubt that you'll be married soon enough, my dear, and to someone much more suitable than the absent Mr. McCord."

When Marie went out to talk to Hunter Grant later that afternoon, she found him, now cleaned up and wearing acceptable clothes, sitting on the roof of the barn with a hammer and chisel in his hand.

"Mr. Grant! What are you doing up there?" she asked.

Hunter picked up a pile of shake shingles to show her. "I'm repairing the roof of your barn," he answered. "Have you forgotten that I am your slave?"

"But I don't intend for it to be like that," Marie said. "Come back down, please."

Shrugging his shoulders, Hunter moved down the slope of the roof toward the ladder. With his hair trimmed, his beard shaved, and wearing clean clothes, he looked more like the Hunter Grant Marie had known before.

Hunter climbed down the ladder, then walked toward her, brushing his hands together.

"You have something else you want me to do?"

"Yes," Marie said. "I want you to pack your belongings."

Hunter snorted what could have been a laugh. "I have no belongings," he said. "You may recall that you told Julius to burn the clothes I was wearing."

"I'll give you some money," Marie said. "I want you to go into town and buy whatever clothes might be necessary for you to take a trip . . . a long trip."

"Where am I going?" Hunter asked.

"To Texas," Marie replied. "And you aren't going alone. I'm going with you."

Hunter stroked his chin for a moment as he studied the beautiful young woman in front of him.

"You want to go after Sam McCord, don't you?"

"Why do you ask that?"

"It's true, isn't it? I know that he went off to Texas. Why are you going after him?"

"Because," Marie said quickly. "He has sent for me."

"Kind of odd for a fellow to send for his fiancée instead of coming for her, don't you think?" Hunter asked. "What does your father think about you trailing out there after him?"

Marie thought of the conversation she had with her father that very morning. "Papa doesn't know that he has sent for me," Marie said. "And please, you mustn't tell him that we are going."

"Oh, you don't have to worry about that, because we aren't going."

"But I *must* go to him, don't you understand?" Marie pleaded. "Besides, you belong to me. If I wish, I can force you to take me to him."

Hunter smiled and shook his head. "You can force me to take you to the Sabine River, but you can't force me to cross it."

"What do you mean?"

"Think about it, Miss Doucette. Once we cross the Sabine River into Texas, the judge's order would no longer be valid and I wouldn't be your indentured servant anymore. I could walk away from you and there wouldn't be a thing you could do about it."

"Oh!" Marie gasped, putting her hand to her mouth. "Oh, I never thought of that!"

"Is that the reason you paid my fine and had the judge release me to you? So I could take you to Texas?"

"Yes," Marie replied in a weak voice.

"Then I am afraid you have wasted your money. By the

way, why haven't you told your father?''

"Because he would try to stop me.''

"Of course he would, as would any thoughtful parent.'' Seeing that she was truly upset, Hunter softened the tone of his voice. "Miss Doucette, it is for your own good that I am turning you down. You must understand that Texas isn't settled like Louisiana. I speak from experience, because I have been there. It is a vast, wild country, still mostly unsettled except for savage Indians. And if that weren't enough, there is now a war going on between the Texians and the Mexicans. Such a trip would be very dangerous.''

"For an ordinary woman, perhaps. But, as you may know, Mr. Grant, I am an excellent rider, and I have a wonderful horse. I am sure that Prince could get me out of any difficulty I might get in.''

"I know all about Prince,'' Hunter said. "And I know what a good rider you are. But it takes more than horsemanship to survive in that land.''

"That is all the more reason why you should take me. I know I would be safe with you.''

"I couldn't guarantee your safety,'' Hunter warned. "I can't even guarantee my own. Trust me, you'll be much better off here.'' Hunter pointed to the roof of the barn. "On the other hand, you do deserve the best I can give you. So, as long as I am here, I'll fix your roof, repair your fences, curry Prince, or do any kind of labor that you or your father may have for me. But if Sam McCord wants you to come to Texas, he is going to have to come for you himself.''

"If you will not take me to Texas, then I shall go by myself.''

"I would hope you don't mean that,'' Hunter said.

"Oh, but I *do* mean it,'' Marie said resolutely. She took a rolled-up piece of paper from the sleeve of her dress and handed it to Hunter. "Here. This is for you.''

"What is it?'' Hunter asked.

"It is your release. You are free to go.''

"My release?''

"Your servitude is no longer required, nor desired,'' Marie said. "Actually, I was going to give it to you the moment we started for Texas anyway. So you see, crossing the line would have made no difference, you would have been free long before that." Marie sighed. "But, since you aren't going to take me, I may as well give it to you now."

Hunter unrolled the paper and looked at it. It was, as Marie indicated, a document that released him from any further obligation to her.

"Thank you," Hunter said. "I'll pay you back the money you spent paying my fine."

"How?"

"How? I don't know. I just will, that's all."

"Mr. Grant, I was prepared to forgive your debt, plus pay you five hundred dollars."

"That is very generous," Hunter agreed. "But if I let you do that, you would be subsidizing your own tragic fate. By the way, just where, in Texas, *is* Sam McCord?"

"I . . . I don't know."

"You don't know? Well, what did the letter say? Where did he ask you to meet him?"

"It just said Texas."

"Texas? Miss Doucette, do you have any idea how big Texas is? McCord could be anywhere out there."

"I'll find him. With or without you, I'll find him," Marie said.

"Excuse my bluntness, Miss Doucette, but anyone who would run off and leave a beautiful woman like you behind, then send for you . . . not come for you, mind you, but just send for you, telling you only that he is somewhere in 'Texas,' without being more specific, is not worthy of you."

Somewhere in the recesses of his mind, in a memory dimmed by several weeks of immoderate drinking, Hunter could recall Sam McCord visiting with him briefly, just before he left. It had been a strange conversation, in which McCord seemed not at all concerned about leaving Marie behind.

"I'm sure he had other things on his mind when he sent the letter," Marie said.

"Perhaps," Hunter answered. "But have you considered the possibility that he was purposely being vague because he doesn't really want you to come? He may very well have taken himself a senorita by now. And, if you want my opinion, you're much the better off for it."

"Thank you, sir, but I do not care for your opinion," Marie said in a choked voice. "Now, if you will excuse me?"

"You're going to thank me for this in the morning, when you've had time to think it through," Hunter said. "Believe me, Miss Doucette, Texas is not a place for someone like you."

"Good day, Mr. Grant," Marie called back over her shoulder. "You may keep the clothes you are wearing, but, please leave Rosecrown."

"I will, as soon as I repair the roof."

"Someone else will repair the roof," Marie said. "I want you off this place, now!"

Hunter looked at the shake shingles he had put together for the job, then he glanced up toward the roof where the patch job was needed. A part of him wanted to go ahead and do the job anyway, no matter what Marie said, but, as she was so insistent, he merely shrugged his shoulders, then turned and walked slowly away.

TUESDAY, JANUARY 12, 1836, THE ABSINTHE HOUSE, NEW ORLEANS

The room was quite large. In the middle of the room, on a raised platform, was a huge bed, covered with a deep blue silk spread. The walls of the room were wainscoted with white painted wood on the bottom, and red flocked wallpaper above.

This was not the first time Hunter had been upstairs at the Absinthe House. He had done so several times since being turned out by Lucinda. But this was one of the few times he had been up here sober, and he found himself looking around the room with some interest.

The door opened and a young woman moved through the door in an effortless glide. This was Danielle, the same quadroon with whom Johnny had been so stricken on that last night before the duel. Johnny was right about Danielle being beautiful. With her high cheekbones, golden skin, liquid brown eyes, long, thick, black hair, and shining red lips, she was pretty enough to take one's breath away.

"I am so pleased to have you finally visit me, Monsieur Grant," Danielle said.

"What do you mean, finally? I've been here before, haven't I? I seem to recall it."

Danielle nodded. "*Oui,* you have been here before, monsieur, but, always, you have been so drunk that I feel you did not fully appreciate your visits."

"I must have appreciated them, or I wouldn't keep coming back," Hunter quipped.

"Perhaps that is true," Danielle conceded. "At least, that is always one's hope, isn't it? Whatever your reason for coming, my purpose is to give pleasure, and I cannot help but think it would be more pleasurable for you, if you knew that I was enjoying it as well."

"And do you think you will, this time?" Hunter asked.

Danielle smiled. "*Oui,* monsieur. I very much think that I shall."

Danielle walked over to the bed and pulled down the covers. Then she turned her back to Hunter and began undressing.

Hunter watched, fully appreciating the experience this time, as Danielle exposed first her shoulders, then her back, and finally her legs until she was completely nude. Not until she was totally nude did Danielle raise the corner of the sheet and slip into the bed. She did so without letting Hunter see any more of her than the long, golden curve of her back. Once in bed, she folded the sheet back to invite him into bed with her. He started to get in, but she stopped him.

"But, monsieur, are you going to wear your clothes to bed?" she asked, with a musical tinkling laugh.

"No," Hunter said, feeling quite foolish. "No, I guess I should take them off, shouldn't I?"

Quickly, Hunter undressed, then got into bed and slid under the sheets beside her. Danielle put her hand on him, and he felt himself awakening, quickly, to her touch.

Danielle was actually younger than Hunter, but with a mother who was half-white, and a father who was all-white, she had been bred, almost from birth, to provide sexual pleasure. Schooled by her courtesan mother, Danielle was the handmaiden of Eros. She was so skilled at determining the pleasures and wants of the particular man that she was with, that she could almost make him believe that she was just for him. She was a skilled and enthusiastic lover, and using all the tricks she had learned, she gave as well as took, often becoming the aggressor.

Hunter lost himself in the pleasure, letting Danielle lead the way. She knew from experience just how long a man could ride the building wave of his desire before reaching the crest, and as they made love, Danielle orchestrated everything, a movement here, a position there, until, finally, Hunter reached the exquisite point of his release, and, locking her arms and legs around his naked back, Danielle held him to her, keeping him inside her, as they shared that one, final moment of explosive ecstasy.

A short time later they lay side by side in the shadows of the room, without touching and without speaking. Gradually the noises of conversation and laughter began drifting up from the big common room below, invading their silence, and the mood was broken.

"Monsieur Grant?" Danielle said when she knew that the moment was past.

"Yes."

Danielle raised up on one elbow and looked down at him. The action had the effect of flattening one of her breasts, while pulling the other into the shape of a pear, pushing the little button-hard nipple into a beam of light from the bedside lantern. Though it was a totally unconscious move, it was a very provocative pose.

"Once, when you were here, you gave me a small box. Do you remember that?"

"A box?" Hunter was looking at her nipple, and he was having difficulty concentrating on what she was saying to him. He shook his head. "No, I'm sorry, I don't remember. What was in the box?"

"I do not know, monsieur, I have never opened it," Danielle replied. She brushed a fall of hair back from her eyes and the action returned a mound of flesh to the flattened breast.

"You haven't opened it? Why not?"

"The box was not meant for me, monsieur. Your instructions were for me to keep the box for as long as you were intoxicated. But if ever I was to see you sober, I was to give it back to you. You are sober now, monsieur. Would you like the box?''

"Wait a minute," Hunter said. He sat up in bed and ran the tip of his finger across his moustache. "You know, Danielle, now that I think about it, I think I *do* remember giving you a box. I don't remember what is in it, but it seems to me like it was something important. Do you have it here, in your room?''

"*Oui*, monsieur," Danielle replied. She got out of bed and padded, naked, over to a large chifforobe. As she stood there, rummaging through the drawers, Hunter was treated to a vision of her total nudity. It was almost enough to make him forget about the box. Finally she located a small wooden case, then held it up for him. "Here it is," she said.

Opening the box, Hunter immediately recognized the papers inside. They were warehouse receipts, and they were all made out in his name.

"Damn! I had forgotten that I had these things!" he said as he began sifting through the receipts. "When I couldn't fulfill the contract, I had to come up with over a thousand additional bales of cotton. The only way I could do that was to liquidate all my assets and put out buy orders. After I satisfied the contract, I killed the buy order, but not until I had already purchased several more bales of cotton than I actually needed. I was left without money, though I did have several bales left over, which I promptly converted to warehouse receipts. I must have given them to you for safekeeping.''

"*Oui*. You did," Danielle replied.

Hunter spread the receipts out on the bed and examined them. "According to this, I have warehouse receipts crediting me with . . ." he paused for a long moment, then whistled softly, "I have three hundred and twelve bales! Lord, I had no idea I had that much cotton. I wonder what it's selling for today? Danielle, get me today's *Picayune!*''

Slipping quickly into a dress, Danielle left the room, then returned a few moments later with the newspaper. Hunter went immediately to the commodities column and checked the price of cotton. "It's selling at eight cents a pound," Hunter said. "That's forty dollars a bale for three hundred and twelve bales. That's . . . twelve thousand four hundred and eighty dollars! Danielle, can you believe it?" he said almost reverently. "I've got money! More than that, I'm a wealthy man!"

Gleefully, Danielle clapped her hands. "I am joyous for you, Monsieur Grant!" she said.

WEDNESDAY, JANUARY 13, 1836, TRAILBACK PLANTATION

Hunter rode out to Trailback Plantation for one more attempt at reconciliation with Lucinda and her parents. He had been sober for the entire week, and, by selling his cotton, had reestablished himself as a man of means. It was his hope that, by pulling himself together and once more establishing his place in society, Lucinda and her parents would give him another chance.

Hunter was met at the front gate by one of the slaves.

"Afternoon, Mr. Grant. We ain't seen you 'roun' these parts too much lately."

"That's true, Troy, but then I haven't exactly been welcome around these parts," Hunter replied. He hooked one leg across the pommel and looked up the long road toward the house. "Is the family in?"

"Yes, sir, they all be there. They was out takin' their lunch on the veranda no more'n a few minutes ago, so I know they still be there. It's sure good to see you again."

"Thank you, Troy. I can only hope the family shares your enthusiasm," Hunter said. "But I'm afraid they don't."

"No, sir, I don't thinks you goin' to find much of a welcome from them," Troy agreed.

Hunter rode up the drive. As he approached the front of the house, he saw Angus Meechum standing on the veranda just above the steps, his hands on his hips. Hunter got down from his horse.

"You shouldn't have bothered to dismount, Mr. Grant," Angus said coldly. "You won't be staying long."

"Mr. Meechum, as you may have heard, I have sobered

up, and I am no longer destitute in funds, though I shall remain so in spirit until this is cleared up between us. I beg of you, let me speak with Lucinda. Just for a few minutes.''

"If you were as sober as a judge and rich as a king, it would make no difference. My hate for you is as strong now as it was on the day this happened. It was all I could do not to meet you with a pistol as you rode up this morning.''

"Please, Mr. Meechum. Can't you understand that I have suffered from this as much as any of you? Johnny and I were the best of friends! You must know that!''

"It is a funny kind of a friendship that would cause one of you to kill the other.''

"It could have just as easily gone the other way,'' Hunter said. "He could have killed me.''

"I wish, with all my soul, that he *had* killed you, so that it would be you lying in the grave, and my own son standing here before me.''

"No, Mr. Meechum, you don't really mean that. For if he were standing here now, Johnny would be going through the same hell I am going through. I know you wouldn't want that.''

"What I want, Mr. Grant, is for my son to be alive. Can you give that to me?''

"No, sir, you know that I cannot.''

"Then you have no business here.''

"Let me see Lucinda, just for a moment,'' Hunter pleaded. "Let me hear, from her own lips, that she has not forgiven me.'' ·

At that moment the front door to the house opened and Lucinda came outside. With her golden hair shining brightly in the afternoon sun, and her green eyes sparkling as if from some inner light, Hunter thought that he had never seen her looking so beautiful. That she was so beautiful, and at this moment so unapproachable, made the situation all the more painful.

"I have not forgiven you, Mr. Grant,'' Lucinda said. "Is that what you wanted to hear?'' Her voice was as cold as stone.

Hunter cleared his throat. "All right, Lucinda,'' he said. "I am ready to accept the fact that there will never again be anything between us. But I cannot live the rest of my life knowing that you hate me so.''

"I am afraid you have no choice, Mr. Grant," Lucinda said. "For, surely, I will hate you as much on the day I die, as I hate you now."

As Hunter looked at Lucinda, he wondered how those lips that had once kissed him and filled his ears with such sweet endearments could now utter words of such hate-filled bitterness. He thought of the taste of her, and of the feel of her body against his, and he knew that he would never again feel an emptiness or a loss as severe as what he was feeling at this very moment.

"I'm sorry," Hunter said weakly.

"Yes, well, you have had your say, Mr. Grant," Angus Meechum said. "I think you had better be going now."

Because Angus Meechum had been nearly a father to Hunter, the loss of his respect and affection was nearly as painful to Hunter as was the loss of Lucinda's love.

"Yes, sir, I'll be going," Hunter said with a resigned sigh. Troy, who had come up from the gate to hold the reins, now handed them to Hunter, and Hunter remounted. "Thank you for your time," Hunter said, touching his forehead in a half-salute.

"Mr. Grant?" Angus said.

"Yes, sir?"

"I would advise you not to come onto Trailback again. I intend to give all my slaves and my hired hands orders to shoot you on sight, should they see you on my land."

Nodding, Hunter clucked at his horse, then pulled its head around and rode away. He had made one last effort to effect a reconciliation. That effort failed, and he wouldn't be trying anymore. Meechum's threat to have him shot on sight if he set foot on Trailback meant nothing to him, since he had no intention of ever coming back, or ever attempting to see Lucinda again. And, with that decision made, the process of mending his broken heart was begun.

Eight

Hunter Grant knew that the first thing he needed to do in order to restore his self-respect was to settle all debts and obligations he had incurred during his protracted period of intemperate behavior. That included paying back Marie Doucette, who had bailed him out of jail, then released him from his bond of servitude.

It was to repay . . . and to thank her, that he rode out to Rosecrown. Phillipe Doucette met him at the foot of the steps, leading up to his long, columned front porch.

"Where is my daughter?" he demanded anxiously.

"I beg your pardon?" Hunter replied, surprised by the question. He dismounted and tied his horse to the hitching. "You mean she isn't here?"

"She is not here, as you well know, since she went with you. So where is she? Where did you leave her?"

"Mr. Doucette, you'll have to forgive me, but I don't have the foggiest idea what you are talking about. I owe your daughter one hundred dollars and I came out here today to repay her."

"Did you not take her to Texas?"

"My God! You don't mean to tell me that she went alone?"

"Then you did know about it?" Phillipe accused.

Hunter shook his head. "No, I didn't. That is, we talked about it, because she wanted me to take her. I refused, because I thought the trip would be too dangerous for her."

"Then it is even worse than I thought," Phillipe said. "I thought you had taken her, and even though I was angry with you, I was comforted by the fact that she had you to protect her."

"Why didn't you stop her?"

"I did not have the opportunity to stop her. Her mother and I did not even know she was contemplating such an ad-

venture until we discovered this." Phillipe pulled a piece of
paper from his pocket, then showed it to Hunter.

> Dearest Mama and Papa,
>   Forgive me for sneaking off in the middle of the
> night like this, but if you had known I was going, you
> would have tried to stop me. And I cannot be stopped,
> I must not be stopped. I am heartsick over Sam
> McCord's continued absence, and I am going to Texas
> to find him.

"Oh, the little fool," Hunter said, putting his hand to his
head. "How long has she been gone?"

"She's been gone for a week now. She left during the night
of the same day she brought you here," Phillipe answered.
"Her mother is in bed, now, sick with worry. And I am beside
myself. I cannot think why, for the life of me, she would do
such a thing."

"And you thought I took her?"

"I was certain of it."

"Mr. Doucette, Marie told me she received a letter from
McCord, asking her to come to him. Do you know where the
letter was mailed from?"

"A letter asking her to come to him? I know of no such
letter," Phillipe said. "Anyway, how could a gentleman write
such a letter?"

"That is the same question I asked," Hunter replied. "I
told her that McCord wasn't much of a man to send for her.
If he wanted her, he should come get her, and I refused to
have anything to do with it."

"What did she do when you refused?"

"She did nothing. She released me from my bond."

Phillipe pinched the bridge of his nose. "More difficult to
understand than why he sent such a letter, is why Marie would
respond to it? To think that she would cause us such grief
and worry, just to find him. I mean, consider yourself. Would
you have gone to Texas, and then sent for Lucinda?" Phillipe
caught himself, almost as quickly as he said it. "Please, forgive me," he said. "It was insensitive of me to speak of the
Meechum girl under the present circumstances."

"It doesn't matter," Hunter said. "That part of my life is behind me. But you are right. If I had a woman like Marie, I certainly wouldn't send for her and take the chance of having her travel alone. And I would not have thought Sam McCord to be such a person."

"Nor would I, but we were obviously mistaken in our judgment of him," Phillipe said.

Hunter took out several gold pieces. "I have come here to repay my debt to her. And, since she isn't here, I would appreciate it if you would take the money I owe her."

Phillipe started to take the money, then he pulled his hand back. "No, you keep the money," he said.

"I would rather not keep it. I cannot regain the respect of others until I am, once again, able to respect myself. And that, I cannot do, as long as I am indebted to your daughter."

"That may be, but you don't owe the money to me, Mr. Grant. You owe it to Marie. Give it to her."

"Can you not hold it until she returns?"

"If you really feel a responsibility to her, you would go to her now, and give her the money."

"Go to her?"

"Mr. Grant, please, I am begging you," Phillipe said. "For me, and for her mother, I want you to find our Marie and bring her back to us."

"I wouldn't even know where to look," Hunter complained.

"Look in Texas."

"Do you have any idea how big Texas is?"

"She is a young woman, traveling alone, searching for a man. That kind of person is bound to leave some sort of trail," Phillipe said. "You can find her. I know you can."

Hunter stroked his jaw for a long moment. "Suppose I do find her, Mr. Doucette? If she left of her own accord, she may not want to be found. What's more, she may not want to come back."

"If she genuinely has no wish to return, then don't force her to do so. Her mother and I will take some measure of comfort just in knowing that she has come to no harm. I know that you have fallen on difficult times. I will pay you handsomely if you will do this."

"Thank you for your generous offer, Mr. Doucette, but my situation is not as difficult as it once was."

"Then if money will not persuade you, call this an act of penitence," Phillipe suggested.

"An act of penitence?"

"You killed your best friend in a duel, did you not? And even though it was a situation beyond your control, I know that you have suffered. Perhaps an act of Christian kindness . . . such as finding our daughter and returning her safely to us, will bring peace to your soul."

Hunter chortled. "You know, I must be going out of my mind," he said. "Because, in a crazy way, what you are saying makes sense to me. All right, Mr. Doucette. I will look for her."

Phillipe grabbed Hunter's hand and shook it hard, smiling through tears of gratitude.

"Thank you, my boy, thank you," he said. "And God go with you in your quest."

FRIDAY, JANUARY 15, 1836, THE SABINE RIVER SETTLEMENT

Since arriving at the settlement two days earlier, Marie Doucette had worn pants and a jacket and had kept her hair bundled up under an old slouch hat. For her own security she decided it would be best to dress and pass herself off as a man. It also made it much easier to ride.

So far she had managed to get away with it, but this morning she felt a strong need to take a bath, and she knew that it would be difficult to maintain the ruse. For in order to do so, she would have to leave the main camp and find a secluded place in the river.

Having done so, Marie was now standing knee-deep in the water, bathing. Should anyone from the camp happen onto the site, they would have gasped in surprise over the fact that the young man they knew as Mike was actually a young woman, as beautiful as a water sprite. She was slim, with smooth, unblemished skin and small, exquisitely formed breasts, topped by tightly drawn nipples. The eyes of her beholder would, no doubt, gaze in awe at the inverted triangle of dark hair at the junction of her legs, glistening now with droplets of water that sparkled like tiny diamonds.

After Marie finished her bath she pulled on clean trousers and a loose-fitting shirt, then, once again, carefully coiled her hair around her head so it could be concealed beneath her hat. Then she slipped a leather vest over her shirt and, to the casual observer, she looked, once again, like a young man.

Ever since arriving here, Marie had avoided people as much as possible. She spoke only when necessary, and then in a low voice. So far, no one had guessed her secret.

Marie had sneaked out of the house in the middle of the night, explaining in the note that she left for her mother and father that she was *"heartsick over Sam McCord's continued absence,"* and was *"going to Texas to find him."*

Marie was determined to find him, on her own if need be, though she still hoped to enlist someone to her cause. She had come to the settlement hoping to join a wagon train, thinking that it would be a safer and more certain way of getting to Texas to find Sam, than to go alone. She was disappointed when she learned that the wagon train would have to wait for more members. Then, yesterday afternoon, five more wagons arrived. The travelers called a meeting for this morning, and it was Marie's hope that, with eleven wagons, the wagon master might now feel that it was safe enough to go on.

After she finished her bath, Marie hurried over to the meeting. Still dressed as a man, Marie leaned against a nearby willow tree, watching and listening as the various members of the train discussed the pros and cons of leaving the settlement. Some felt that they now had enough, but others were more cautious, as Marie soon learned.

"I say we go on," one of the men said. "I want to get settled into my place in time to put in this year's crops."

"Settled into your place? How do you know you even have a place?" another asked.

"Because I have it bought and paid for, that's how I know," the man replied. "And I've got the deed in my strongbox."

"If the Mexicans win this war, that deed ain't goin' to be worth the paper it's printed on," the second man scoffed.

"I'd like to see a bunch of Mexicans run me off my land," the man with the deed challenged belligerently.

"Look, worryin' about the Mexicans runnin' us off our land is just the half of it," another said. "They's a better than an even chance we won't even get through if we go now. They say that Santa Anna's bringin' the whole Mexican army up to Texas, and iffen that's true, why, he could wipe out the lot of us easy as steppin' on a bug."

"What do you think, Mr. Parker? Would it be safe to go?" someone asked John Parker, the wagon master.

"From Santa Anna's army, yes, you are safe," Parker answered. "His soldiers may stop us, they may even turn us around and send us back, but I don't believe they would use more force than is necessary, and I don't think they would rob us."

"See there, I tole you we didn' have nothin' to worry about!" the first man said triumphantly.

"But," Parker added quickly, holding up his hand to get everyone's attention. "There are others, men who aren't as gentlemanly as Santa Anna and his army."

"What others are you talking about?"

"Renegades," Parker said. "Deserters who have formed roving outlaw bands who are totally without honor."

"I ain't likely to be put to fear by no bunch of Mexican deserters," one of the men scoffed.

"They aren't all just Mexicans," Parker said. "There are some Americans as well. Mexico doesn't have a lock on desperadoes."

"It still don't make me no never mind. We can handle near anythin' that comes up, iffen we all stick together. I say, let's go."

"That's big talk comin' from you, Coley. You got no one but yourself to look out for," one of the others said to the bold speaker. "They's some of us here got families, ol' folks, and little children to think of besides ourselves. That's why I ain't goin'."

"Then I ain' goin' neither," another man put in.

"Well, if they don' go, then I sure ain' gonna go," a third man said. "That would cut our strength down to nine wagons. I don't think that's enough to get us through Texas safely."

"If you don't go, that cuts it down to eight, and I'm not goin' to try it with only eight wagons," another man said.

"Well, then, there you have it," Parker said, closing the meeting. "We ain' none of us goin' till some more wagons show up."

"When will that be?" someone asked.

"Who knows?"

"I heard tell of a party formin' up a train under a fella by the name of Reynolds," someone said. "It's supposed to have ten wagons with it."

"All right," Parker said. "Most likely that new train will be here within the month. At that time we'll have enough wagons to go anywhere we want. Until then, my advice to ever' one of you is just to sit tight right here in camp. Make sure your wagons is in good repair and that you have fully recruited your animals. Get lots of rest. You're goin' to need it."

Marie was very disappointed when she realized that the wagon train wasn't going on. She wished desperately to continue her journey. She had to find Sam McCord. She just had to! Whether she went with the wagon train, or traveled alone, she was determined to go on.

The bold man, the one with the land deed who was so anxious to go on, walked over to a water barrel and scooped out a drink. Marie watched him silently. Perhaps she could hire him to take her to Texas. He seemed as bent upon going as she was.

"I heard someone call you Coley," Marie said.

"That's right. Dan Coley," Coley said, looking at her over the rim of the water dipper. "What can I do for you, mister?"

"I guess you're disappointed that the wagon train isn't going on," Marie said.

"This isn't a wagon train. This is a group of old women," Coley said, underscoring his scornful statement with a healthy-sized spit.

"I'm thinking about going on alone," Marie said. "Of course, if you and I were to go together . . ."

Coley laughed out loud. "Is that supposed to make me feel safe? Having a little peach-fuzzed youth like you along? Sonny, you're goin' to have to find yourself another way. I ain't got no sugar-tit for you to suck on. Now, get away from here and leave me alone."

That night, as Marie lay on her bedroll and stared up at the stars through tear-dimmed eyes, she thought of the humiliation she had suffered this afternoon. She couldn't go back to Coley, not after the way he had treated her. But she was determined to resume her search. She had no choice. She had to find Sam McCord.

Then Marie got an idea. If no one would take Mike with them because he was a "peach-fuzzed youth," maybe they would take a young woman. Tomorrow, Marie would try again to find a sponsor. Only this time she would make no effort to hide her sex.

"Good morning, Mr. Hagens," Marie said, walking up to Hagens's tent just after sunup the next morning. "The coffee smells awfully good. I'll have a cup, if you don't mind."

Hagens grabbed the pipe out of his mouth and his eyes opened wide at the vision of a beautiful young woman walking up to his establishment as cool as a breeze.

"Glory be!" he said. "Where in blazes did you come from?"

"Louisiana," Marie answered. "I told you the first day I was here that I was from Louisiana."

"You told me the first day? Look here, miss, I ain't never even seen you before. If I had, I wouldn't likely forget."

"I'm afraid I wasn't completely honest with you," Marie said. "I let neither my true identity, nor my true gender, be known. You know me as Mike."

Hagens leaned forward to examine Marie more closely.

"Glory be!" he exclaimed. "It *is* you."

"That's right. Mr. Hagens, I have got to go on to Texas. I can't wait for any more wagons to show. I'm willing to hire someone to take me. Do you have any idea where I might find such a person?"

"Tell me, miss, what's so all-fired important out there that you're willing to risk life and limb?" Hagens asked.

"I am looking for someone. A man by the name of Sam McCord. Would you happen to know anything about him?"

"Sam McCord? Yes, seems to me like I do recollect someone by that name comin' through here a couple months ago.''

Marie's face lit up with excitement. ''Oh, sir, do you know where he might be?''

''From what I hear, he fought with Burleson at Bexar. He may be there yet.''

''Bexar?''

''It's also called San Antonio.''

''Where is San Antonio? Is it far?''

''I'll say it is. San Antonio is halfway across Texas,'' Hagens explained.

''At least that narrows my search down some,'' Marie said. ''When I started, I knew only that he was in Texas. Now that I know where to go in Texas, all I have to do is hire someone to take me.''

Hagens shook his head. ''Well then, you got yourself a problem, miss, 'cause there ain't no one around here who would do a fool thing like that.''

''I'll find someone who will,'' Marie insisted.

When, by the end of the day, she had found no one, Marie sat morosely by her fire, cooking a couple of pieces of bacon for her supper.

''You are Senorita Doucette?'' a voice called softly from the dark beyond the circle of firelight.

Shielding her eyes against the glare of the campfire, Marie looked toward the sound.

''Who is there? Step up closer to the fire, please, so that I can see you,'' she said.

A short, swarthy man, holding his sombrero respectfully in front of him, stepped out of the shadows. He stood quietly for her inspection.

''Who are you?'' Marie asked.

''My name is Carlos Alvarez,'' the Mexican replied.

''What can I do for you, Mr. Alvarez?''

''I am told that you wish someone to take you to San Antonio de Bexar,'' Alvarez said.

''Yes, I do. Do you know someone who will take me?''

''*Si*, senorita. I, Carlos Alvarez, will take you.''

Alvarez was such an unlikely looking person to undertake such a task that Marie almost laughed. On the other hand,

Alvarez was Mexican, and, under the present circumstances, being Mexican might well be an advantage. And her offer of one hundred dollars in gold had not produced any other takers.

"Do you know where San Antonio is, Mr. Alvarez?"

"*Si,* I know where it is. I have been there many times before."

That made Marie feel better. If Alvarez had been there several times before, how difficult could it be to reach?

"You know my offer?"

"I have been told that it is for two hundred dollars in gold," Alvarez said.

"You were told wrong. It is for one hundred dollars."

"San Antonio is a long way from here."

"One hundred dollars is a lot of money."

Alvarez stood for a moment longer, turning his hat in his hand as he tried to decide. Finally he nodded.

"Very well, senorita. I will take you for one hundred dollars in gold. Do you have a wagon?"

"I have a horse."

"Sell the horse. Buy a mule and a wagon."

"Sell my horse? But no, Mr. Alvarez! Prince is a wonderful horse! I could never sell him."

"If he is a wonderful horse, you could get two mules and a wagon," Alvarez suggested. "Trust me. If you want to go to San Antonio, it is much better to do it in a wagon."

Marie thought of Prince, and how hard it would be to part with him. But she thought, too, of Sam McCord, and she knew that she had to find him, and would do whatever it took to accomplish that feat. Even if it meant selling Prince. She sighed. "All right, if I have to, I will," Marie said. "Once I get a wagon, how soon can we leave?"

"If you get a wagon and a team of mules today, we will leave in the morning," Alvarez promised. "That is, if you do not mind leaving on *Domingo.*"

"*Domingo?*"

"Sunday. The Lord's Day."

"No, I don't mind," Marie said.

"Then we go *mañana.*"

*   *   *

Bright and early in the morning of the next day, Marie's wagon was waiting in front of Hagens's tent. Marie saw immediately why Alvarez had insisted on her getting a wagon. Alvarez had no horse of his own. The wagon and team of mules would serve both of them.

Marie sat on the seat of the wagon while Alvarez filled the water barrel from the river. The wagon master, John Parker, came up to stand beside the wagon. He stroked his long black beard as he looked up at her.

"Miss Doucette, are you serious about going through with this foolish adventure?" Parker asked.

"I am," Marie answered. She brushed an imaginary piece of lint from her skirt, for the wagon would also allow her to dress in keeping with her gender. In fact, one might have thought she was going for a leisurely ride down Canal Street in New Orleans, rather than beginning a thousand-mile foray into war-torn Texas.

"I wish you would wait and go with the rest of us. It would be a lot safer."

"I hardly see how my presence would make the trip any safer for the rest of you," Marie said.

Parker cleared his throat. "I meant, it would be safer for you, Miss Doucette."

"Do not worry about me, Mr. Parker. I shall get along just fine," Marie said.

"I'm not so sure about that. I'm afraid the time may well come when you will wish that you had never made that offer to Alvarez."

"Why do you say that?" Marie asked quickly. "Have I something to fear from my guide?"

Parker chuckled.

"No, you've nothing to fear from Alvarez. He is a decent enough man, and he will serve you as faithfully as he can. It is just that he will be limited in what he can do, just as any of us would. But he allowed the idea of a little gold to cause him to overlook those limitations."

Alvarez returned to the wagon then, groaning under the load of the full water cask. He set it in its place on the wagon bed, secured it with a length of rope, then wiped the sweat from his brow. He nodded at Parker.

"Senor Parker," Alvarez said.

"Why are you taking her, Alvarez?"

"She is a woman who needs help," Alvarez replied. "I will help her."

"Yes, for a little gold. Come on, Alvarez, you know damn well Texas is crawling with scum, Mexican and American, who'd give anything to have such a woman. Do you really intend to expose her to such danger?" Parker asked.

Alvarez climbed up onto the driver's seat. "I can avoid the soldiers," he said. "I know a secret way."

"Miss Doucette, I beg of you, one last time. Don't do this thing," Parker said.

"Thank you for your concern, Mr. Parker," Marie said. "But I am sure I will be just fine with Senor Alvarez."

"Are you ready, senorita?" Alvarez asked as he picked up the reins.

"I am ready."

Alvarez released the wagon brake, then slapped the reins against the back of the mules, and the team leaned into their harness. The wagon started to roll. They turned onto a road that had been cut through the canebrake and a few minutes later the encampment disappeared from view.

Marie settled into her seat for the long ride.

Nine

TUESDAY, JANUARY 19, 1836, SAN ANTONIO DE BEXAR

The town of San Antonio de Bexar consisted of two plazas and several streets. One plaza, called "Military Plaza," was dominated by two sturdily built homes, one was the De La Garza house, the second, the mansion of the Veramendis. The other plaza was dominated by a large church and courtyard to tend to the town's spiritual life. Its more secular needs were met by half-a-dozen cantinas, all of which did a booming business with the Texian soldiers who had occupied San Antonio ever since the defeat of General Cos.

San Antonio de Bexar was bordered on its west end by San

Pedro Creek. The north, south, and eastern environs of the town were guarded by a horseshoe bend in the San Antonio River. A small footbridge at the east end of town crossed the river, then a dirt road ran approximately four hundred yards across gently rolling ground to reach the Alamo mission.

In the largest of the cantinas, Sam McCord sat, having a drink with Green Jameson. Jameson was the military engineer in charge of converting the Alamo into a fort.

"I don't think anyone back in San Felipe, or Washington-on-the-Brazos, fully appreciates the problems we are facing here," Jameson was explaining. "The Alamo simply was not designed to be a fort. It was designed to be a church, and it didn't even do a very good job of that, as witness the fact that it has now been abandoned for many years."

"I don't know, Green, it might be all right," Sam said. "I mean the wall around the grounds is pretty thick and pretty high. If you want my thinking, you're doing a pretty good job of turning it into a fort."

"If you do too good of a job, you'll be wasting your time. General Houston wants you to blow it up," another voice said, and the two men looked up to see who it was. Sam recognized him at once.

"You're Jim Bowie, aren't you?" Sam said, smiling as he stood and extended his hand.

"That's what they call me," Bowie replied, shaking Sam's hand. Bowie's eyes narrowed as he studied Sam. "I know you, don't I?"

"Yes, sir, I'm Sam McCord, from Louisiana."

"McCord? Yes, yes, I remember you, now. I met you when I was Phillipe Doucette's guest at Rosecrown."

"Yes."

"How is the family Doucette doing?"

"They are doing fine, sir."

"And their daughter, Marie, is she your wife, now?"

"We are not married."

Bowie raised his eyebrows. "Oh? Well, I don't know what you did to mess things up, boy, but if you let her get away, it is going to be your loss."

"Yes, sir, I suppose so," Sam said without elaboration.

"Excuse me, Colonel Bowie," Jameson said. "But what

do you mean, when you say Sam Houston wants us to blow the Alamo up?''

"Hell, son, I didn't stutter," Bowie said. "Blow the place up means blow the place up. Put gunpowder along the walls and knock them down. Haul off what cannon you can and spike the rest. Leastwise, that's what he sent me here to tell you to do."

"You came from General Houston?"

"I did," Bowie said. Suddenly the front door burst open and someone shouted into the room.

"Colonel Bowie, can I dismiss the volunteers, sir?"

"You may, indeed, Mr. Cahill," Bowie called back. "And you may tell the boys that the first round is on me."

"Yes, sir! Thank you, sir!" When the information was relayed back outside, there was a loud roar of approval, followed by a massive surge of bodies through the front door, heading for the bar to get their free drinks.

"You brought an army with you?"

"Thirty men, all volunteers," Bowie said. Bowie suddenly broke into a spasm of coughing. It was a deep, racking cough which continued for several seconds. When the spell passed, Bowie's face was bathed in sweat, despite the coolness of the temperature.

"Are you all right, sir?" Jameson asked.

Bowie held up his hand. "I've been touched with some sort of recurring fever," he said. "The doctors can't figure out what it is, but each attack is worse than the one before."

"Maybe you should be in bed," Sam suggested.

Bowie shook his head. "What good would that do? I feel just as bad in bed as I do out. And if I were in bed, I wouldn't be here now, would I?"

"That's true," Jameson said. "And we can certainly use every man we can get."

Bowie filled his glass, then took a drink of whiskey before he spoke again.

"How many do you have here now?" he asked.

"Just under one hundred."

"So you can see what a welcome sight you are, Colonel Bowie," Sam said. "Your volunteers will increase our strength by a third."

Bowie shook his head no. "Sorry, gentlemen, but as I told you, I am here, under orders from Sam Houston himself, to help you destroy the Alamo, then pull out."

"Why would he want us to do that?" Jameson asked. "We won this position after a bloody battle."

"And the loss of some good men," Sam added.

"That is true. And General Houston wants me to tell you that you have the admiration of all Texas for that. But he thinks Texas will be better defended if the men here become more fluid. He wants us to strike and fall back, strike and fall back, until Santa Anna's supply lines are extended, and we have worn him down. In that way, General Houston contends, we will be able to amass our army and strike a fatal blow when Santa Anna is most vulnerable."

"Is that the general's suggestion? Or is it his order?" Colonel Neill asked. Sam and Jameson, seeing the arrival of their commanding officer, stood in greeting. "Hello, Colonel Bowie. I'm glad you're here," Neill continued, sticking out his hand in greeting.

"Well, now, Colonel Neill, I'm not really a military man, as you well know," Bowie replied. "But I have always heard that a commander's 'suggestion' is an order."

"That is true, when the commander is fully cognizant of the situation," Neill said. "I'm not sure that Houston is."

"Then you tell me. What is the situation here?" Bowie asked.

Pulling up a chair, Neill and the others sat back down to the table. By now the room was filled with Bowie's men, and their loud talk and frequent laughter caused the four men to have to raise their own voices to continue their conversation.

"I will be very frank with you, Colonel Bowie. Our situation is one of the utmost desperation," Neill said. He took a piece of paper from his pocket. "I would like to read to you part of a letter I sent five days ago, by courier." Clearing his throat, Neill began to read: " 'My men have been in the field for the last four months, they are almost naked, and this day they were to have received pay for the first month of their enlistment. The pay has not come, and almost every one of them speaks of going home.' " Neill skipped over a few lines, mumbling to himself, then he continued. " 'We are in a torpid, defenseless situation, we have not horses enough to send out a patrol or spy.' '' He folded up the letter then and stuck it back in his pocket.

"If that is the case here, then you, undoubtedly, agree with General Houston," Bowie said. "We should abandon the Alamo."

Neill shook his head. "On the contrary, sir, I do not agree."

Bowie looked surprised. "But you just said that you were in a defenseless position."

"Be that as it may, we will defend the defenseless," Neill said.

"You're not making any sense, Colonel Neill."

"I am making absolute sense," Neill replied. "It is absolutely imperative that we remain here, for the Alamo is the only obstacle standing between Santa Anna and an unimpeded drive, clear across Texas. Besides, even if I wanted to abandon my position, I don't have the mules or oxen required to haul away the cannon. And I can't just leave them here for the Mexicans."

Bowie looked at Sam and Jameson. "You two boys feel the same way?" he asked.

"I don't know about anyone else, but I'm staying," Sam said.

"I certainly can't go," Jameson said. He took another drink of whiskey, then wiped the back of his hand across his mouth and smiled broadly. "Besides, I've got work to do. I have to turn this mission into a fort if we are going to 'defend the defenseless,' '' he added, quoting Colonel Neill.

"And you really think you can make a stand here?"

"Colonel, if we could be properly supplied, we would do our duty and fight better than fresh men," Jameson said. "For we have all been tried, and we have confidence in ourselves."

"Tell Houston that, when you return," Colonel Neill suggested.

Bowie stroked his chin, then sighed. "You're going to have to get somebody else to do it," he said.

"Why is that?"

"Because my men and I will be staying here with you."

Neill smiled, then stuck his hand across the table. "Thank

you, Colonel. Thank you very much.''

"But that brings up a problem. If your condition is as bad as you say it is, my men and I will be putting an even greater strain on your meager resources.''

"It is a price we will willingly pay for your support,'' Neill said.

"Perhaps the price doesn't have to be so dear,'' Bowie suggested. "With your permission, Colonel Neill, I will renew some old acquaintances with a few of my Mexican friends here in San Antonio. I think I can round up enough additional food and supplies to not only make up for what my men will use but to take care of the garrison as well.''

"My permission, Colonel? You have more than my permission. You have my most enthusiastic support and my undying gratitude!''

"I'll get started on that first thing tomorrow,'' Bowie said. "Now, if you don't mind telling me, I'd like to hear just what you have done in the way of fortifying the mission.''

"That has been the job of Green Jameson here, and Lieutenant Almeron Dickerson,'' Neill said.

"Dickerson? I heard a little about him. He's an artillery officer, isn't he?''

"Yes, sir,'' Jameson said. "And he has been most helpful in planning the construction, since much of it has to do with the placement of the guns.''

"Well, seems to me like figuring out where to put the guns would be about your only problem. I mean there's already a wall around the place, isn't there? And it's high and thick, from what I recall.''

"That's true. But there are no embrasures in the wall through which we can fire our guns without being exposed. And there are no parapets to allow the men to fight from the top of the wall. And last, but not least, the wall doesn't even go all the way around the grounds,'' Jameson concluded.

"How much does it lack?'' Bowie asked.

"There is a seventy-five-foot gap on the southeast side, which I am sealing off with a palisade of logs, earth, and stone. But the gap in the wall isn't our main problem.''

"What would that be?''

"The sheer size of the thing."

"The size? Why, it seems plenty big enough to me," Bowie replied.

"Big enough? That's just it. It's too big, much too big for our purposes. We have a perimeter wall that is a quarter-of-a-mile in length, and we have considerably less than two hundred men to defend it. Now, if we had a thousand men . . ." Jameson's eyes blazed in excitement. "Well now, give us a thousand men, and time to complete my modifications, we could defend it against the entire Mexican army."

"Which may be what is coming after us," Bowie said, turning up the bottle to take a drink. "My informants tell me that Santa Anna is in the process of putting together the largest army ever raised in Mexico."

"I have no doubt but that your sources are correct," Neill said.

"Show me the fortifications," Bowie said. "And if there is anything you need me to do to help, let me know."

Jameson took a piece of paper from his pocket and spread it out on the table. On it was a to-scale drawing of the Alamo.

"We started here, with the seventy-five-foot gap between the church and this building that we call the Low Barracks," Jameson said, pointing to the place on the drawing. "We closed that gap with a high palisade of upright timbers, backed by an earthen embankment from which riflemen can fire. In addition, we have shored up any weak spots in the existing wall with sloped banks of earth and timbers, and we have built parapets of earth and timber inside the walls, which will enable riflemen to fire in all directions."

Jameson continued. "Here, just outside the south gate, I am constructing a lunette—"

"A what?" Bowie interrupted, looking up at the intense young engineer.

"A lunette. It is a circular gun position," Jameson explained. "Technically, it is on the outside of the main wall, but it is well enough fortified by itself to afford the gunners some protection, so it is almost as if it were a part of the wall itself. I am putting a couple of six-pounders there."

"And over here?" Bowie asked, pointing to the west wall.

"We're using the building that runs along the west wall as

officers' quarters, and I have built a parapet that will allow us to bring an eight-pounder onto the roof of the quarters. Also, here in the southwest corner I am putting the eighteen-pounder. That is our biggest gun and I want it facing in the direction from which the Mexicans will come."

"Good idea," Bowie agreed.

"And, of course, I've done the same with the north and east walls. Until, finally, we come to the church. Though the roof and bell tower have fallen in, I believe this to be the most secure part of the entire fort, containing as it does the double walls of the fort and the building. At the rear of the church, we have built a long, sloping platform which will allow us to elevate three twelve-pounders." Jameson pointed to the cattle pen and horse corral just outside the eastern wall. "I'm afraid these areas can't be defended. When the fighting starts, we'll have to abandon them."

"And what is this?" Bowie asked, pointing to a place inside the plaza, near the well.

"Let us hope that we do not have to use this, Colonel Bowie, for by the time we get to it, it will be over for us. However, I figure we may as well make them pay dearly for their victory, so we are putting a couple of eight-pounders there," Jameson explained. "The blacksmith has been busy cutting up horseshoes and chain."

"Horseshoes and chain?"

"That's how these guns will be loaded," Sam explained. "If the Mexicans do break through the walls, they are going to have quite a welcome in store for them."

"That part doesn't have to happen if Fannin will reinforce us," Colonel Neill said.

"Is he going to come to our aid?" Bowie asked.

Neill shook his head. "I don't know. He's had some crazy idea about attacking Matamoros, but that doesn't seem to be going anywhere. He knows we are here, and he has had ample opportunity to reinforce us, but as yet we have heard nothing from him."

"I know Fannin," Bowie said. "And if I were you, I wouldn't count on him."

Neill stood up. "Colonel Bowie, since assuming command here, I have learned one bitter lesson. And that is, don't count on anyone but yourself. Again, I welcome you to San Antonio, but if you would excuse us, Captain Jameson and I have work to do back in the fort.''

Jameson stood and, again, extended his hand to Bowie. "I, too, am glad to have you with us, Colonel.''

Bowie laughed. "Gentlemen, perhaps I had better wait to see how things turn out before I say I'm glad to be with you,'' he said.

Sam stood as well, but Bowie raised his hand.

"Colonel, do you mind if I keep Captain McCord here for a while? He's from my part of Louisiana and I'd enjoy the opportunity for a little talk.''

"You may stay, Captain,'' Neill said.

"Thank you, sir,'' Sam answered. He sat back down.

Bowie called a serving girl over, and speaking in fluent Spanish, ordered something.

"Have you had your supper?'' Bowie asked.

"No, sir, I thought I'd go back to the barracks to eat.''

"What? Salt pork and bread?'' Bowie waved his hand in dismissal. "Forget about that. Stay here, eat with me, my treat. I have just ordered for both of us.''

"Thank you.''

"Colonel Bowie, I never had the opportunity to tell you how sorry I was to hear about what happened to your family.''

Bowie got a faraway look in his eyes. "It's been almost three years now,'' he said. "A cholera epidemic was sweeping through Texas, so I sent Ursula and our two babies to her parents' home in Monclova to be safe, while I stayed here, in San Antonio, to look after things. But God sometimes plays tricks, even on the most obedient of all His creatures, and while I, sinner that I am, was spared, my wife, my two children, and my in-laws were struck down.''

"It was a terrible tragedy. All who heard of it back in Louisiana mourned with you.''

Bowie tossed down a full glass of whiskey. "I've learned one thing from it,'' he said.

"What's that?''

"They haven't yet made enough whiskey to drown real sorrow.'' He cleared his throat as if by so doing he could

clear his mind of the terrible thought. "So, tell me, Sam. I'm
always curious about folks who come to Texas. What brought
you here?"

Sam shrugged. "A sense of adventure, I suppose."

"I came looking for adventure, too, originally," Bowie
said. "But I didn't have anything back in Louisiana except a
reputation for making trouble. You, on the other hand, had a
lot to stay for. Rosecrown, for example, is much larger than
any piece of land you are likely to get here . . . and it is already developed into a fine plantation."

"You speak of Rosecrown as if it belonged to me."

"I know who it belongs to," Bowie said. "But I also know
that, as Phillipe has no son, it is his intention to leave the
plantation to the one who marries his daughter. And it was
my understanding that you would be that person."

"That is an assumption that some people made," Sam replied. "But no formal commitment was ever made."

"No formal commitment?" Bowie stared at Sam. "Why
do you say that as if you are defending yourself in a court of
law?" he asked. "Is the thought of marrying such a beautiful
and wealthy young woman so odious to you?"

"No, of course not," Sam replied quickly.

"Then why do you act as if it is?"

"Pardon me, Colonel Bowie, I don't wish to be rude,"
Sam said. "But I really don't think this is any of your business."

"No, I don't suppose it is," he agreed. "But you can't
blame a man for being curious when he hears a story like
this. I mean, here you were, practically engaged to one of the
most beautiful young ladies in all of Louisiana, with her father's plantation at your feet, and you turn your back on all
of it. You must admit that it can make one wonder."

"Colonel Bowie, when you were married to . . . your wife
. . . was there ever any difficulty because she was . . . ?"

"She was what?"

"Uh, she was different."

"How do you mean, she was different?"

"Well, sir, she was Mexican, was she not?"

"She was."

"And you are American. Besides which, you are fair, and

she was dark. You came from different backgrounds, different cultures. That never bothered you?''

"Is that what's troubling you?'' Bowie asked. ''Are you having difficulty because Marie is Creole?''

Sam paused for a moment before he answered. ''Something like that, yes.''

"My God, man, how bigoted can a person be?'' A serving girl brought the food. *"Gracias, muy bonita conchita,"* Bowie said to her. The girl, blushing at the compliment, smiled and withdrew. ''You think that girl is pretty?'' Bowie asked.

Sam looked at her. ''Yes,'' he said.

"She is Mexican.''

"I know.''

"There is no room for prejudice out here,'' Bowie went on.

"I know,'' Sam said again. He sighed. ''But sometimes there is a situation that is beyond one's control.''

Bowie tore off a piece of tortilla and used it to rake some spicy beans onto his fork. ''Tell me something, McCord. Did you run out on that girl?'' he asked.

Sam was silent.

"You did, didn't you?''

Sam nodded.

"Without even so much as a good-bye?''

"I'm afraid so.''

"Does she know where you are?''

"I'm sure that, by now, someone has told her that I am in Texas.''

"Well, if you want my opinion, she's probably better off without you,'' Bowie said, the disapproval obvious in his voice.

"I am certain you are right,'' Sam said contritely.

That night, Sam McCord sat up on the roof of the officers' quarters on the west wall, looking back toward San Antonio. Here and there within the little town, he could see bright bubbles of light, the brightest coming from the same cantina where he had taken his supper with Bowie and where, now, a dance was being held. Sam could hear the music; the strum-

ming guitars, the rhythmic maracas, and the high clarion wail
of a cornet. He could also hear the raucous conversation and
frequent laughter of the men who, tonight, were taking time
away from the hard work of fortifying the Alamo in order to
relax with the young women of the town.

So far, Sam had not made the acquaintance of any of the
young women, although there had been many opportunities
to do so. Many of the other soldiers here, especially those
who were single, had been quick to form relationships with
the Mexican women of the town. Of course, not all the
women here were Mexican. Almeron Dickerson's wife, Susanna, was with her husband, along with their baby daughter,
Angelina. Susanna was a very pretty woman, blond and blue-
eyed.

Both Almeron and Susanna were from Tennessee, but even
coming from the same culture and background was no guarantee against controversy as Sam learned. One night when he
was a dinner guest in the Dickersons' home, they told him
the story of their wedding.

It happened back in Tennessee. Almeron was about to
marry a young woman who had been picked out for him by
his parents. He was already in church, standing back in the
sanctuary, peeking through a crack in the door at the pews
which were packed with his, and his bride-to-be's family,
friends, and neighbors. He was waiting for his intended to
walk down the aisle.

Just as the processional began, Susanna, who was to be one
of the bridesmaids, came into the room. What neither the
bride-to-be nor Almeron's parents knew, was that Susanna
and Almeron had been carrying on a secret romance for the
previous several months. That romance would have to end
the moment Almeron was married.

"Almeron, you can go out there and marry Ann," Susanna
told him, "and that will be the end of it for us. Or . . ." she
let the word hang.

"Or what?" Almeron had asked.

"Or we can both go out the back door, right now, where
I have two horses saddled and waiting for us. We can leave
Tennessee and go someplace where we can make a new life
for ourselves . . . together."

Almeron told Sam that it took him less than ten seconds to make up his mind.

"But what about your family?" Sam had asked. "What about your friends and neighbors? Didn't you care what they might say?"

"You know what, Sam? I didn't give one little damn about what they had to say then, and I don't give one little damn about what they might have to say now," Almeron said. "Sue and I loved each other, and I figured that was all that was important. Neither of us have ever had a moment of regret."

As Sam sat out on the roof of the officers' quarters, recalling that conversation, something in the sky caught his attention, and he looked up in time to see a falling star.

Was it an omen? If so, of what? Of his mistake-ridden past, or of his uncertain future?

His thoughts turned then to Marie Doucette, and he recalled that afternoon, three months ago, when he had gone over to see her. He had asked her to go riding with him, because he had just learned something that, if it was true, could only mean the immediate end of their relationship. He needed to confront her with the information, to ask her right out, if it was true.

But she had never been more beautiful to him than she was that day. She was so beautiful, so trusting, and so vulnerable that he couldn't bring himself to confront her. On the contrary, he felt an overpowering need to comfort her, to tell her that everything would be all right . . . even though he knew that it wouldn't be, that it couldn't be, no matter how much he might want it.

He took her into his arms and began kissing her on the cheek and temples. Their kisses and caresses deepened, and Sam waited for Marie to call a stop to them, as she always did, before things went too far. But Marie didn't resist and, almost before he realized it, they were making love on the grass in the meadow by the bayou.

After that, Sam could not make himself say what he had come to say. Over the next few days he conducted his own investigation to see if what he had learned about her was true. When he determined that it was, he came to the only acceptable conclusion. He would have to leave Louisiana. Marie would, undoubtedly, be hurt and confused by his mysterious disappearance, but it would, at least, spare her shame and humiliation.

Ten

TUESDAY, JANUARY 19, 1836, ALONG THE TRAIL OF EL CAMINO REAL, IN COAHUILA Y TEXAS

They had been three days on the trail. Three days of vast, unsettled land. As Marie looked out over the countryside they were passing through, she could clearly see the attraction such a place might have for so many people. Here was wonderful land, stretching for as far as the eye could see, and as they had not seen another living soul since they left the Sabine River settlement, there was obviously no problem of overcrowding.

Each night, at camp, Alvarez would lay a blanket out next to the fire for Marie, then move several feet away to spread his own blankets.

Marie was standing up to the rigors of travel fairly well, though this morning the smell of breakfast made her nauseous, and she had to walk away from the campsite for a few moments of privacy. When she came back, Alvarez was looking worriedly at her.

"All you all right, senorita?"

"Yes, I'm fine," Marie said. She pointed to the skillet and smiled wanly. "I've never been much of a breakfast person anyway," she said. "And for some reason the smell of it this morning . . ." She let the sentence hang.

"*Si*, I *comprendo*," Alvarez said. He held up a coffee cup. "Coffee?"

"Yes, thank you. I think I could drink some coffee," Marie said.

Alvarez poured a cup, then handed it to Marie. The tin cup was hot, and Marie set it down quickly.

"Thank you. Uh, *gracias*," Marie said, smiling at him.

As the two had their breakfast, Marie studied Alvarez over her coffee. Thus far on the journey she had found him to be a quiet, pleasant man, not at all frightening, though he was Mexican, and Mexicans were who everyone seemed to be afraid of right now. Thus far they had not spoken about the war that was dividing the Americans from the Mexicans.

"Senor Alvarez, why are they fighting in Texas?" Marie asked.

"Ah, senorita," Alvarez replied. "Why do men go to war anywhere? Because they do not follow God's law, and because there is much greed among them."

"Is greed what is causing this war?"

"*Si.*"

"Greed on the part of the Mexicans, or on the part of the Texians?"

"There are no Texians, senorita," Alvarez said. "There are only Norteamericanos who have come to Tejas."

"Then you are saying that this war is the fault of the Americans?"

"No," Alvarez answered. "Many of the Norteamericanos have come to Texas legally. They have bought land and they wish only to settle down and be good citizens of Mexico."

"What is wrong with that?" Marie asked.

"There is nothing wrong with that. It is a noble ambition. But *Presidente* Santa Anna does not wish to let the Americans do this."

"Why not?"

"Maybe it is because some Mexicans fear that the Americans will become too many and too strong. Or maybe it is because many feel that the Spanish land grants should stay only with Spanish-speaking people. I think there is much hate between the two sides."

"Do you hate the Americans?" Marie asked.

"I hate no one, senorita, except those who give me reason to hate them."

WEDNESDAY, JANUARY 20, THE SABINE RIVER SETTLEMENT

"Hunter! Hunter Grant, is that you?"

Startled at being recognized in this place, Hunter stopped

his horse, then looked toward the person who had hailed him. He saw a tall, thin man coming toward him, smiling broadly.

"Jules Clay!" Hunter said, recognizing one of the men he had done business with in Gonzales. Hunter swung down from his horse and went toward Jules with his hand extended. The two men shook hands warmly.

"Well," Jules said. "I see you are in Texas. Come to join us in our fight?"

"Not exactly," Hunter said.

"Not exactly? What does that mean, not exactly? You are here, aren't you?"

"Yes, but I'm looking for someone."

Jules got a puzzled expression on his face. "Looking for someone? Look here, Hunter, you haven't become a lawman, have you? Because if there's somebody here fighting for Texas, we aren't going to look too kindly on you taking him back to Louisiana, no matter what he may have done."

Hunter chuckled. "It's nothing like that, Jules, I'm certainly not a lawman," he said. "And I'm looking for a woman."

Jules smiled broadly. "Oh, a woman. Well, in that case, I wish you all the luck in the world. Is she a Texas gal?"

Hunter shook his head. "She's from Louisiana. Her name is Marie Doucette."

"Wait a minute. You say her name is Marie Doucette?"

"Yes. Have you seen her? Is she here?" Hunter asked.

"I haven't seen her, but I heard about her. I'm pretty sure that's the girl Hagens was telling me about."

"Hagens?"

"He runs the trading post here. And just about everything else in the settlement," Jules said. "Come with me, I'll introduce you."

"The woman I'm thinkin' about left three . . . maybe four days ago," Hagens said, cutting off a piece of chewing tobacco. "Come here dressed like a man, ridin' a big black horse." He stuck the plug in his mouth. "I tell you true, she could handle that horse, too."

"That would be Marie Doucette," Hunter said. "She was

as good a rider as any man in Lafourche Parish and owned the best horse.''

''*Did* own him,'' Hagens said. ''He belongs to me now.'' Hagens pointed to a pen beside his store and Hunter saw Marie's horse.

''How did you get him?'' Hunter asked. ''Half the men in Lafourche Parish have tried to buy that horse without success.''

''She traded the horse for a wagon and a team of mules,'' Hagens explained.

Hunter looked at Hagens in surprise. ''She traded Prince for a wagon and a team of mules?''

''She was one determined lady.''

''Yes, I'm beginning to realize just how determined. How much do you want for the horse?'' Hunter asked.

''He's a good horse.''

''I know he's a good horse. And I know that you have the right to make a little profit. So how much do you want for him?''

Hagens smiled, then got a couple of tin cups and held them under the whiskey barrel. ''Come on over here and let's jaw for a while. We'll work something out,'' he said.

An hour later, Jules and another man came over to the stable where Hunter was not only seeing to his own horse, but was taking possession of Prince.

''What did you find out about the girl?'' Jules asked.

''She left here with a Mexican by the name of Alvarez,'' Hunter said. ''They're heading for San Antonio, looking for Sam McCord.''

''McCord is there, all right,'' the man with Jules said.

Hunter looked up from the horses to see a rather smallish man, with a nose that was a bit too large for his face. ''Who are you?'' Hunter asked.

''Austin.'' The man broke into a series of spasmatic coughs, and for a moment he clutched a handkerchief to his mouth. Finally, regaining control, he spoke again. ''Stephen Austin, at your service, sir.''

Although Hunter had never met Stephen Austin, he had

heard of the man who, with his father, had opened Texas to American immigration.

"Mr. Austin, it is a pleasure to meet you," Hunter said, shaking Austin's hand.

"The pleasure is all mine, Mr. Grant. I have heard of the business you have negotiated with our Texas cotton planters and I assure you, sir, such business dealings are, and will be, the key to the survival of Texas in whatever status it eventually finds itself."

"Mr. Austin, you said that Sam McCord was at San Antonio?"

"Yes. There was a battle there some weeks ago in which General Cos and the Mexicans were driven out of the town of San Antonio de Bexar. Now Colonel James Neill and a handful of ill-armed, ill-clothed, and unpaid Texans are trying to convert the Alamo into a fort." Austin began coughing again.

"The Alamo?"

"It is an old Spanish mission, located just to the east of the town," Austin explained, once he had the coughing under control. "It is a church, with an enclosed courtyard, and an engineer, Green Jameson, is in charge of building the fortifications, but I feel, as does Sam Houston, that it is a hopeless task. Neill and his men would better serve Texas if they would abandon the Alamo and join with the army Houston is putting together."

"Have you sent word to that effect?" Hunter asked, patting Prince on the neck.

"We have, sir, and it has gone unheeded. I thought perhaps you could persuade them to leave."

Hunter looked up in surprise. "Me? What makes you think they would listen to me?"

"You know Sam McCord, don't you?" Austin asked.

"Yes."

"Then try to persuade him. Although he has only recently arrived in Texas, Sam McCord has already earned the respect of Texians. If he could be convinced that withdrawing from the Alamo is the most prudent course of action, then it would greatly help our cause."

"I know McCord, true enough," Hunter said. "But he is

his own man. If he's made up his mind about staying, I don't think there is much I could do to change it. Have you attempted to convey this information by any other means?"

"Yes. General Houston sent Jim Bowie to talk to Colonel Neill. But I don't think that will do us any good."

"Why not? Jim Bowie is quite well-known, isn't he? Surely he will be listened to."

"Jim Bowie is a drunk," Austin said, matter-of-factly. "What's more he is an adventurer. He is just as likely to be persuaded by Neill, as he is to persuade Neill."

"Your characterization of him as a drunk is a little harsh, isn't it, Stephen?" Jules said. "After all, it isn't as if he has no justification for his drinking."

"Justification or not, a drunk is a drunk," Austin said. "Do you not agree with me, Mr. Grant?"

Hunter cleared his throat. "I don't like to judge anyone until I have walked in their shoes," he answered. Left unsaid was the fact that, until quite recently, he was walking in those same shoes.

"Yes, well, perhaps you are right. I shouldn't be too harsh on Mr. Bowie. After all, he is helping us, and General Houston seems to have a great deal of confidence in him. But, back to you, Mr. Grant. We are prepared to help you find Miss Doucette, in return for your carrying our message to Sam McCord."

"And just how do you propose to help me?" Hunter asked.

"By appointing you a captain in the provisional Army of Texas," Austin said. "And providing you with twenty men."

"Twenty men? I don't need twenty men."

"You'd better take them, Hunter," Jules urged. "You never know what might happen. With a young woman and a Mexican alone out there . . ." Jules let the sentence hang.

Hunter ran his hand through his hair. "All right, I'll take the twenty men with me, but only until I find her. And, just so that you know, the moment I find her, I'm taking her back to her family."

"Perhaps not," Jules suggested. "According to Hagens, the lady seemed pretty determined to find McCord. Someone that determined might not be ready to go back to Louisiana, just because you want her to. What do you plan to do if she insists on going on?''

"I guess I'll just have to cross that bridge when I come to it," Hunter answered.

"Hold up your right hand," Austin said.

"Why?"

"Because I'm about to swear you in. When you cross the bridge you were talking about, you'll cross it as a captain in the Army of Texas," Austin replied.

LUNES, 25 ENERO, 1836, SALTILLO

A few days before moving his army north, Santa Anna decided to have them pass in review. Massed bands played stirring martial music while scores of red, white, and green flags snapped in the breeze.

First came the cavalry, dressed in blue trousers and gleaming brass breastplates, then the *zapadores,* holding their beribboned lances high, followed by the dragoons, resplendent in green and red, then finally by the infantry, dressed in white trousers and blue jackets with red and green trim, and wearing tall hats. Broad white bandoleers crossed every infantryman's chest, while red blanket rolls resting atop the packs each infantryman carried added to the color and spectacle.

As Santa Anna took the salutes from horseback, he moved back and forth with the restless energy that was his hallmark.

What Santa Anna did not know, and what his officers hid from him, was the fact that the cavalry, *zapadores*, dragoon, and infantry troops Santa Anna reviewed were the same men, over and over again, for as they marched by, they hurried around to get into position at the end of the line, thus making the army look fuller, and better prepared than it actually was. That was because, among the conscripts, not one soldier in ten had a uniform. Most wore the loose-fitting white trousers and shirt that were the native dress of the peasantry. Nearly all were barefooted, while those who did have shoes were wearing open-weave sandals.

When Juan passed in review, he raised his sword handle to his chin, then looked right, in salute, toward Santa Anna.

The gleam in Santa Anna's eyes told Juan that *El Presidente* was either unaware of the ragtag condition of most of his army, or he was totally unconcerned.

MONDAY, JANUARY 25, 1836, ALONG THE TRAIL
OF EL CAMINO REAL

On the tenth day of their journey Marie and her driver came to a farmhouse. Although Alvarez had been a pleasant enough companion thus far, he was not much of a talker, and, craving some conversation, Marie smiled in anticipation as they approached the house.

As it turned out, her company was just as eagerly sought, for the husband and wife and two small children, one boy and one girl, turned out to greet them enthusiastically as they approached the house.

"The name's Amon Thompson, and you two are a welcome sight," the man called. "Come inside and rest. Drink some water and stay to supper."

"Thank you, Mr. Thompson," Marie replied, stepping down from the wagon gingerly, then stretching her aching muscles.

"Senor Thompson, may I tend to the mules?" Alvarez asked.

"Of course," the man agreed. "Come with me, and I will help you."

Marie went inside the house at the woman's insistence. She sank down onto the settee and gratefully accepted a glass of cool water.

"It comes from our well," Mrs. Thompson said. "It's the best tasting water in the world."

Marie drank it appreciatively. It did taste much better than the slightly rank water from the barrel she and Alvarez were carrying.

Marie looked around the rustic house. It was unpainted, and the boards were loosely fitted together, as if the house had been built by one man, working alone. But it was exceptionally clean, and there was a charm, almost a beauty to the place. She could see that Mrs. Thompson was very proud of it.

"You have a nice home," Marie said.

The woman smiled broadly. "When Amon asked me to come out here with him, I told him that I wouldn't leave Missouri unless he could promise me a house just like the one we were living in there. He agreed and, well, here we are."

"You are farming here now?"

"Yep. More'n twenty-five hundred acres," the woman said proudly. "Back in Missouri some of the wealthiest landowners in the county are farmin' a lot less."

"My! What are you growing on a farm this large?"

"Children, for one thing," Mrs. Thompson replied with a laugh. She pointed to the two youngsters who were looking on in undisguised fascination. Marie smiled at them and the little girl, embarrassed at having her scrutiny returned, looked away.

"My, what a lovely locket you are wearing," Marie said to the little girl.

"Her grandmother gave it to her," Mrs. Thompson said. "Laura, show it to the nice lady."

The little girl walked over to Marie and held the little heart-shaped gold locket up for Marie's inspection.

"It contains a miniature of my mother," Mrs. Thompson said. "She said she didn't want us to forget her, as if we would." Mrs. Thompson was pensive for a moment. "It's a hard thing, leaving your family like we did."

"Yes," Marie said, thinking of her own situation. "It is."

"What about you and your husband? You have no children?" Mrs. Thompson asked.

"My husband?"

Mrs. Thompson nodded toward the barn.

"Oh, you mean Senor Alvarez?" Marie smiled. "He isn't my husband. He is my guide. He is taking me to San Antonio."

"San Antonio? I hear that's a long ways off. Why in heaven's name do you want to go there?"

"Because the man who is going to be my husband is there. A man named Sam McCord. Perhaps he stopped here?"

Mrs. Thompson shook her head. "No. The name don't mean nothin' to me, I'm afraid."

They heard voices then, as Alvarez and Mr. Thompson came back from the barn.

"Here come the men," Mrs. Thompson said. "They'll be wantin' their supper. You, too, I reckon. Ridin' all day like you done has to build a powerful appetite."

"Yes, it does," Marie agreed.

The supper that Mrs. Thompson prepared that evening was as bounteous as a Christmas feast. She had both fried and baked chicken, half-a-dozen different vegetables, freshly baked bread, a pie, and a cake. Marie was pleased to note that Alvarez was also welcomed at the table. Because he was Mexican, she knew that some would turn him away.

"Senor Alvarez has been most gracious during our journey together," Marie said as she helped Mrs. Thompson clear the table after their meal. "But he is Mexican, and I feared that there would be some difficulty because of the war between his people and ours. I am glad that you made him feel welcome."

"Well, my dear, we are all God's children," Mrs. Thompson said. "I don't want my children fighting amongst themselves and I can't see as how the Lord would like His children fighting amongst themselves either. I don't know anything about this war. It hasn't reached us yet and I hope it never does. The fact is, I don't understand wars at all . . . especially wars against people I like. And I like nearly all the Mexicans I've ever met."

When the two women came back into the dining room, Alvarez pointed to a guitar that was standing in the corner.

"Does someone play the guitar?" he asked.

Mr. Thompson chuckled. "A fella came through here 'bout a year ago, carryin' that guitar on his saddle. He asked if he could leave it with us, said he was afraid it'd get broke if he carried it with him. I told him I'd look out for it, and it's been a'sittin' there in the corner ever since."

Alvarez walked over to the instrument and picked it up, gently, lovingly.

"This is a very fine guitar," he said. "I can understand why the man did not wish to take it with him."

Alvarez strummed it a couple of times.

"It is not in tune," he explained, as he began twisting the tuning keys.

"Do you play that thing?" Amon asked.

"Yes," Alvarez answered.

"Play somethin' for us."

"I don't know, it isn't my guitar."

"Senor Alvarez, please play for us," Marie said. "It's the least we can do to repay the Thompsons for their hospitality."

"Very well, if you will forgive my clumsy effort," Alvarez replied. He played several chords, then stopped. Marie started to ask him what was wrong. Then she saw that he was bowing his head, almost as if in prayer. Was he praying? If so, for what? That he would play well?

After a few more seconds of silence, Alvarez began to play once more. The music spilled out, a steady, unwavering beat with two or three poignant minor chords at the end of phrases, but with an overall, single-string melody weaving in and out among the chords like a thread of gold, woven through the finest cloth.

The music spoke of joy and sorrow, pain and pleasure. It moved into Marie's soul, and she found herself being carried along with the melody, now rising, now falling. Perhaps it was the moment, the quiet, the softly lit room, but Marie had never been so deeply moved by music. She sat spellbound for several seconds after the last exquisite chord had faded away. Then, when Alvarez put the instrument down, Marie began to applaud enthusiastically.

"Bravo, Senor Alvarez. Bravo!" she said. "That was wonderful!"

"Yes," Mrs. Thompson agreed. "It truly was."

Later that evening, Mr. Thompson and Alvarez sat on the front porch drinking Thompson's home-brewed liquor. Marie helped Mrs. Thompson ready the children for bed. They went most reluctantly, because they were still excited over their visitors. Marie had to promise them that she wouldn't leave without telling them good-bye.

*   *   *

Explaining to Mrs. Thompson that she wanted only coffee for breakfast, Marie stood out on the front porch drinking the coffee and watching the sun rise while the others had their breakfast. She looked toward the western hills where the purple shadows of night still clung in the draws and notches. She thought of Sam McCord and wondered what he was doing, and what he was thinking about. Did he know that she was coming after him? And if he did know, what would his reaction be?

"Are you sure you don't want anything to eat?" Mrs. Thompson asked, coming out onto the porch behind her.

"No, thank you, I'm not really much of a breakfast person," Marie insisted.

"Maybe you'll feel more like eating around lunchtime. I packed a nice big lunch for you to take with you."

"Mrs. Thompson, you shouldn't have done that. You have your own family to feed."

"Nonsense, child. Near' everything we eat comes from right here on our own place. We've got plenty enough to spare."

"Thank you, Mrs. Thompson. You have been very kind, in more ways than you know."

"I hope you find Sam McCord, honey. And I hope he is good to you."

Before Marie could answer, Alvarez came outside. The wagon was ready for them, the mules standing quietly in their harness. Alvarez helped Marie into the seat, then he walked around and climbed up himself. With the Thompsons waving good-bye, they drove off.

"How much longer, Senor Alvarez?" Marie asked.

"About two weeks, maybe."

"Let's travel as quickly as we can."

"I will do the best the mules can do, senorita," Alvarez said.

In just over two weeks, she would come face-to-face with Sam McCord. How would he react to seeing her? What would he think about her coming to Texas after him? Would he be angry, or pleased?

Eleven

The rocking motion of the wagon had lulled Marie into a light sleep. She thought, later on, that if she had not been dozing, if she had been more alert, she would have seen the riders coming up behind them. Perhaps she could have warned Alvarez. Still, he would have been able to do very little. At least he had died quickly, without ever knowing what had happened.

The shot that killed Alvarez awakened Marie from her slumber and she screamed. She watched in horror as Alvarez tumbled from the seat, the back of his head red with blood. The mules bolted, and the reins fell out of Marie's reach so that she had to ride helplessly on the seat of the wagon, holding on for dear life.

Riders swooped down on the wagon and quickly moved along both sides. The lead rider grabbed the mules and pulled back on them until the wagon came to a stop. Another dozen riders joined the first one, and they all looked down at Marie. They wore uniforms, of sorts, incomplete and augmented with sombreros and scarves.

They were Mexican.

The riders were talking among themselves in Spanish. Marie couldn't understand what they were saying, but the tone of their voices and the expressions on their faces made it plain that they were discussing things she did not want to hear.

"What are you doing?" she asked. "What do you want?"

"Ah, senorita, a lady as pretty as you should never ask a man what he wants," one of the riders said. As he spoke, Marie saw another rider approach. This one was more elaborately uniformed than the rest, with epaulets of gold braid. Marie guessed that he was the leader.

"Who are you?" Marie asked.

"I am Captain Ricardo Lopez, at your service," he said.

He removed his hat and bowed gallantly.

Marie realized that in other circumstances she might have considered him handsome. At the moment, however, his fine-featured face was lost on her.

"Captain Lopez? If you call yourself an officer, I can only hope that you are a gentleman as well."

"*Si*, I am a gentleman. And, as a gentleman, I should apologize for the rude suggestions made by my men, though, if you do not speak Spanish, you didn't understand them."

"I speak no Spanish."

"That is good, senorita. Their suggestions were quite bold. But of course, you must forgive them. They are convict soldiers, you see."

"What are convict soldiers?" Marie asked in a frightened tone. She did not like the sound of the term.

"Just what it implies. They are convicts, the scum of the earth," Lopez said easily. "They are here, not out of patriotism, but because the army is an alternative to prison. They have all been convicted of crimes . . . robbery, murder . . . rape." He paused before saying the last word, to give it added emphasis, though it needed no emphasis to frighten Marie.

Marie gasped.

"But do not worry, my pretty one. If you will put yourself in my hands, I will personally guarantee your safety."

"Thank you, Captain Lopez," Marie said. She turned and looked behind her. Alvarez's body was lying in the road, unmoving.

"Alvarez is dead, I'm afraid," Lopez said.

Marie gasped in surprise when she heard Lopez call her driver by his name. "You *know* him?"

"*Si*. We are cousins, and we played together as children."

"You killed your own cousin?"

"No, not I," Lopez said. "It was one of my men."

"But you are their commanding officer. You are responsible for what they do."

"In an ordinary army, under ordinary circumstances, senorita, that would be quite true. But my men are not ordinary soldiers, and these are extraordinary circumstances. The rules of conventional warfare and gentlemanly behavior have been suspended, not only by my side, but by yours as well."

"I have no side in this war. You can have all of Texas, for all I care."

Lopez laughed. "It is too bad, senorita, that you cannot extend your generous offer of Texas in the name of your American criminals, Sam Houston, Stephen Austin, and Jim Bowie."

"Jim Bowie?"

"Ah, you know Jim Bowie?"

"Yes, I know him. He and my father are very good friends."

"Jim Bowie is the worst of the rebels, for he married the daughter of one of our noblemen and was accepted by our people. Then his family was killed by the sickness."

"Yes, we heard that," Marie said. "It was a terrible tragedy."

"It was a blessing," Lopez said unexpectedly.

"How can you say that such a terrible thing could be a blessing?"

"Because they did not live long enough to see him betray his adopted country." Lopez said something in Spanish, then one of the soldiers dismounted and climbed into the driver's seat beside her.

"I have ordered him to drive you to our headquarters," Lopez explained.

"What will happen to me there?" Marie asked.

"That all depends on you."

"How?"

"If you cooperate with me, I promise that you will be released unharmed. If you do not cooperate with me, then perhaps I shall let my soldiers have their way with you."

Cold fear swept through Marie, but she said nothing.

"I take your silence to mean that you will cooperate with me." Lopez's dark eyes flashed brilliantly, as if from some inner light, and he smiled, his white teeth gleaming against his dark face. "Ah, wonderful, wonderful," he said, when she didn't protest.

Lopez signaled, and his men began to move. They rode fast, and the driver of the wagon lashed out against the mules, trying to force them to keep pace with the others. Soon the team was covered with foam, and Marie begged the driver to be easy with the poor animals, but the soldier understood no English and disregarded her desperate gestures.

Finally they came to a stream, and Marie caught sight of a cabin and a cluster of tents on the far side. The wagon plunged through the shallow river behind the horsemen, throwing water and sand over Marie's face and clothing. The men reined in their mounts when they reached the opposite bank.

Lopez swung down from his horse and walked over to the wagon. He offered his hand to help Marie down. Stiff and aching from the hard ride, she accepted his help. She needed to walk around and stretch her muscles a bit.

"What is this place?" she asked.

"It is called the Taylor Cabin, because the cabin once belonged to a family of Norteamericanos named Taylor," Lopez said. "The Taylors no longer have any use for it, so I have taken it over. It serves as my headquarters."

"Where are the people who used to live here?"

"Dead, senorita," Lopez said easily. Marie looked at him sharply. "But we didn't kill them," he added. "They were killed by desperadoes who are without honor and without a flag. Such men fight only for profit."

"And you are *with* honor?" Marie asked sarcastically. "Is it honorable to kill a poor helpless driver and capture a woman who were doing you no harm?"

"Senorita, I, at least, fight under my country's flag," Lopez said. "Are you hungry? We will eat and talk."

Lopez led her behind the house to the backyard where a Mexican woman was cooking over a wood fire. The pungent aromas of the food assailed Marie's senses, making her realize how hungry she was.

"Do you wish to rest, senorita? There is a hammock under the two shade trees beside the hacienda," Lopez offered.

Marie was too frightened to rest, but she hoped that if she accepted his offer, she would at least be out of sight of the other soldiers. She thanked Lopez as she walked toward the hammock.

"Who is the woman who cooks for you?" she asked.

"Her name is Rosita," Lopez answered. "The men captured her in San Felipe."

"They *captured* her? But she is Mexican."

"She is also a woman, and she serves their needs."

"Serves their needs?"

"When the men need a woman, they take Rosita," Lopez said simply.

"You mean all of them?" Marie asked, incredulous.

Lopez chuckled. "Rosita is an ugly cow, too old to attract men. She pretends that she is held captive against her wishes, but when we leave she does not try to run away. I think she enjoys her position. You should be thankful for her. As long as my men have her to serve them, I can offer you my personal protection. If you will excuse me now, I will prepare for dinner."

"You may do as you wish, Captain," Marie said. "I am not a guest to whom you must excuse yourself. I am your prisoner."

"I only sought to make your time here more comfortable. Forgive me." Lopez touched the brim of his hat in a salute, smiled, then left.

Marie sat down in the hammock. She could hear the conversation and the laughter of the men. Though she understood none of what they were saying, she found their laughter unnerving, and she knew they were talking and joking about her. She was glad she couldn't understand them.

When, after awhile, Lopez returned, Marie nearly didn't recognize him. He had bathed and shaved, and he was wearing a splendid uniform of green, red, and gold. On his head, he wore a wide-brimmed hat, resplendent with feathers and other ornamentations. In a ballroom in New Orleans, the handsome Captain Lopez would have cut such a dashing figure that all the women would have taken their dance cards to him to sign. Here, on the banks of a muddy stream in the wilds of Texas, he looked so incongruous that Marie felt an irrational urge to laugh, but she prudently controlled it.

"Allow me to introduce myself more properly, senorita," Captain Lopez said. He removed his hat, then made a sweeping, formal bow.

"I am Don Carlos Sebastian Lopez, formerly a colonel on the personal staff of General Santa Anna."

"You were on the personal staff of the president of Mex-

ico?'' Marie asked, surprised that he had once held such a
high position.

"*Si*, senorita. With my cousin, Major Alvarez."

"I knew that Alvarez was a gentleman," Marie said. "But
he didn't tell me he had served on the general's personal staff.
But what happened? Why were the two of you sent here?"

"It is a story often heard, I am sure," Lopez replied. "Too
much liquor, a pretty girl, and a moment of indiscretion."

"Major Alvarez put a young woman in a compromising
position? That does not seem like him."

Lopez chuckled. "You did not know him long, but you
knew him well. Better even, than his superiors, because you
are correct. Alvarez was innocent, but he took the blame for
my actions."

"Why would he do that?"

"Because I persuaded him to. I knew the punishment
would be less harsh for him."

Marie listened in shocked silence.

"You see, senorita, for Alvarez, the punishment was easy.
He was merely cashiered from the army and banished from
Mexico City. Had I taken complete responsibility, Santa Anna
would have surely had me shot, due to my many previous
indiscretions. But, because Alvarez assumed the blame, I was
simply demoted for allowing one of my officers to transgress
so. With my reduced rank, I was then sent up here to take
command of the dregs you now see around you." Lopez
looked toward the men, one of whom was talking with Rosita.
"Ah," Lopez sighed. "I don't know which of us suffered the
greater punishment. To have been reduced from the glory and
honor of such a position to this . . . or to have been cashiered."

Marie's voice was cold and accusing when she spoke. "Alvarez gave up everything for you, and you had him killed."

"No, senorita, I did not have him killed." Lopez held up
one finger as if explaining something to a child. "One of my
men killed him without my knowledge. I didn't even know
who the victim was until I saw the body."

"But you showed no remorse, no grief," Marie said.

"I am a soldier," Lopez replied. "In time of war, I have
no time for remorse."

''Couldn't you at least punish the man who killed your cousin?''

''But who killed him? And what punishment would you have me mete out?'' Lopez smiled. ''But, enough of this unpleasant talk. Come, there's no elegant dining room in the cabin, but it will be better than taking your meal out here. We shall dine together.''

The table in the small house was set with a clean white cloth and with crockery that Marie assumed had belonged to the late owners. Her heart sank at the thought of eating off dishes that must have been the pride and joy of a woman who now lay in a shallow grave somewhere nearby. But Marie knew she would need nourishment, so she closed her mind to all other thoughts.

Lopez poured a clear liquid into a glass. ''Drink this. It will make you feel good.''

Marie, whose experience with liquor was limited to an occasional glass of wine, looked at the drink uneasily.

''What is it?'' she asked.

''It is called tequila. It is native to my country.''

Marie put the drink down. ''I'd rather not,'' she said.

''Senorita,'' Lopez said, his eyes flashing angrily. ''You have no choice. You may drink quietly and willingly with me, or I will turn you over to my men and you will drink with them, whether you want to or not.''

Marie, frightened that he would turn her over to his men, picked up the glass and forced the drink down. It burned her throat, and she found the taste unpleasant.

Lopez filled the glass a second time.

''Drink!'' he ordered again.

Marie looked at him pleadingly, but she saw no compassion in the gaze he returned. She drank the second glass.

The third glass went down more easily, but she felt a spinning lightness in her head.

Time seemed distorted after that. She vaguely remembered eating the meal. Then the food was gone and Rosita cleared the table. Candles were lit, and Marie realized that it had grown dark outside.

Lopez stood up, clicked his heels in front of her, bowed elegantly, then raised her hand to his lips.

"Senorita, I thank you for your delightful companionship this evening. I now bid you good night."

Surprised, and relieved that the evening had come to no more than dinner and a few drinks, Marie dipped her head politely.

"Thank you for your courteous behavior, Captain," she said.

Lopez took in the cabin with a sweep of his hand. "The cabin is yours for the night," he said. Picking up his hat, he left.

Marie continued to sit at the table for a moment or two after Lopez left. Her head was still spinning, and when she tried to stand, she lost her balance and, with a gasp, fell back into the chair.

Rosita came into the room then.

"Rosita. Are you sleeping in here as well?" Marie asked.

Rosita held out her hand. "Your clothes, senorita," she said.

"I beg your pardon?" Marie asked in surprise.

"Give me your clothes," Rosita said.

"Give you my clothes? I most certainly will not. Why on earth would I want to do a thing like that?"

"It is the orders of the captain," Rosita said.

"But why? He has been such a gentleman! Why does he want me to take off my clothes?"

"He is afraid you will try to run away. If you have no clothes, you will not run."

Marie pointed to the door. "Well, you just go back out there and tell him that I will not run, but I have no intention of taking off my clothes."

Rosita opened the door and two of the convict soldiers stood just on the other side, leering at her.

"If you do not take off your clothes for me, senorita, these men will take them off for you."

Defeated, Marie nodded her acquiescence. Rosita smiled and closed the door, shutting the soldiers out of the room.

Marie took off her dress and handed it to Rosita, hoping that would satisfy her, but it didn't. The woman stood silently, holding her hand out for more, until, reluctantly, Marie had stripped herself totally naked.

Rosita looked at Marie coldly, dispassionately, then she took the clothes and closed the door. Marie was alone, helpless, naked, and a prisoner in the wilds of Texas. Despite all that, she was not frightened. Perhaps her fear, like all her other emotions, had been dulled by the drink. Or, perhaps she had grown accustomed to danger during the past several days. Whatever the reason, she was able to remain calm, and she was proud of that.

Marie climbed into the bed and covered herself with a patchwork quilt. For an instant, she thought of the hours of work the late owner of this house must have put in on the quilt, but she could not retain the thought. Her head was still spinning from the liquor and the horrible events of the day.

Marie was surprised at how good it felt to lie down. It had been a terrifying and exhausting day, and she fell asleep within moments of closing her eyes.

Lunes, 1 Febrero, 1836, Saltillo

Santa Anna and his immediate entourage, consisting of three wagons filled with all the things that could make his encampment luxurious, departed Saltillo early in the morning, heading north, toward the Rio Grande. He gave instructions to his generals to move the army out in parade formation, thus providing the local citizens with visible evidence of the power of the Mexican Expeditionary Force. By extension, he would also be impressing them with his own power.

The officers' corps and the professional army led off, so that the parade began as a beautifully uniformed and well-disciplined army on the move. Once they were gone, however, the march rapidly deteriorated into the jerking, staggering movement of conscripts and camp followers. As a result, those who watched the army leave were left with the impression, not of the grand army Santa Anna wanted to show them, but of a poorly equipped, disorganized, slovenly band of outcasts.

At noon, Juan Montoya stopped to give his horse a rest on a small promontory. From this vantage point he could observe the line-of-march of the army. He looked out over the expeditionary force as it stretched out for many miles, from the impressive elements of the professional corps at the head of the column, all the way back to the stragglers bringing up the rear. Lifting his canteen from his saddle pommel, Juan took a drink of water and was just reinserting the cork when Major Quinterra arrived.

"Our regiment is well-positioned in the line-of-march, Colonel. We have no stragglers," Quinterra reported. "Even the two conscript companies assigned to us are keeping up."

"Good," Juan said. Juan looked up at the sky. "Manuel, I believe we may be in for a winter storm this night," he said.

"Surely not, Colonel," Quinterra challenged. "It is a very warm day."

"*Si*, it is very warm now. But we are going north across the highlands, and I have been in this country before. It can become very cold, very quickly." He pointed to the west. "And I think there may be snow in those clouds."

"If there is, Colonel, we may be in for it," Quinterra replied. "Many of our men are from the lowlands near the coast. They are not dressed for cold weather and I doubt that any of them have ever even seen snow."

"Their lack of preparation is what worries me. Have our sergeants circulate through the men," Juan ordered. "Collect all extra blankets and coats, then redistribute them, seeing to it that as many men are protected as can be accommodated."

"Those from whom we take the coats and blankets will not be pleased," Quinterra said.

"Tell them it is for the good of the regiment," Juan said.

"*Si*, Colonel."

Following Juan's orders, Major Quinterra set the sergeants to work, redistributing the extra coats and blankets. As Quinterra had suggested, some of the old hands griped about it, however they had no choice but to comply. As a result of Juan's foresightedness, by midafternoon, everyone in the regiment was provided with some sort of protection against the weather.

As the day drew on, the wisdom of Juan's orders was quickly seen. In the late afternoon the temperature started dropping. What had been a balmy, sixty-degree, sunny day, was, within a period of half-an-hour, twenty degrees colder, and the soldiers began hugging themselves against the sharp wind. Juan could feel ice crystals in the cold air and he knew that a snowstorm was imminent.

By early evening, the temperature had dropped to below freezing, and snow began to fall. At first the snowfall was a few icy crystals only, but soon the flakes grew bigger and the snowfall became heavier, until, by dark, Santa Anna's army was marching through a blizzard.

As Quinterra had suggested, the soldiers from the tropical lowlands had never before encountered such weather, and they suffered terribly. Very quickly, the ground was covered with as much as fourteen inches of snow, and as men and animals began to collapse in frozen fatigue, they were quickly covered over, becoming white mounds along the route of march. Not only soldiers, but the women and children who were following the army, suffered from the cold and the snow. The conscripts in the other regiments, whose own commanders had not prepared them as Juan had his men, began to die. They died in twos and threes, then in dozens, then by scores, and finally by the hundreds.

Juan, who was properly dressed, nevertheless suffered from the cold. He wrapped a scarf around his face to ward off the stinging, icy spray as he pressed forward.

"Colonel! Look at that!" one of his captains reported, pointing to a little mound of snow. There, half-a-dozen poorly clothed men were digging through the snow, stripping the bodies of what little clothes they had, so they could put them on themselves. "They are leaving the dead naked. You men! Get away!" the captain shouted.

"No, Captain, leave them be!" Juan responded quickly.

"But, Colonel, do you not see? They are showing no respect for the dead!"

"Captain, don't you understand? We have no obligation to our dead," Juan explained. "Our obligation is to keep alive as many as we can."

The captain, who was himself well-protected against the brutal cold, looked on for a moment at the ill-clad and desperate, freezing men. Then he nodded.

"*Si*, Colonel," the captain said. "You are right. The poor

devils must do whatever they can to survive. I will make no effort to stop them.''

Shortly before ten o'clock that evening, the army was ordered to halt for the night. Immediately after stopping, all generals and regimental commanders were summoned to Santa Anna's headquarters.

"General Santa Anna will, no doubt, want an accounting of how many men we have lost in the march,'' Juan explained to Quinterra as he prepared to go forward. "How badly has our regiment suffered?''

"In our regiment, no one has died, Colonel,'' Quinterra replied. "Your idea of dividing up the coats and blankets was very smart. If the other commanders had done the same thing it would have saved many lives.''

"But there was not enough for all, even if everyone would have shared,'' Juan said. "See that a proper camp is made and that the fires are kept going all night,'' he added. "I go now to Santa Anna's headquarters.''

Wood fires roared in the two stoves which were set at opposite ends of Santa Anna's large command tent. The fires were hot enough to cause the chimneys to glow red halfway up to the canvas roof. The stoves were throwing off so much heat that, despite the blizzard conditions outside, Juan was too hot in his coat and scarf. As Juan looked around at the other commanders who had gathered for their briefing with Santa Anna, he saw that they, too, were uncomfortably warm inside the tent.

"Where is the general?'' Juan asked.

"He is 'busy,' '' one of the other generals answered, then he made a motion with his hands, to indicate that Santa Anna was engaged in his opium habit.

The generals and colonels of Santa Anna's staff spent several minutes in quiet conversation, discussing the brutal winter storm that had hit them. Calculating the numbers of casualties supplied by the others, Juan realized that, by morning, the cold could well claim as many as two thousand victims. One in five would be lost before the first shot was fired.

After keeping his staff standing around for an uncomfortably long time, Santa Anna finally approached them, coming from the corner of the tent where he had been surrounded by giggling young women. Dressed in trousers and shirtsleeves only, he was wiping his face with a silk handkerchief.

"The ignorant peons have made it much too hot in here," he complained. "It seems to me a simple thing to keep the temperature regulated. Why they cannot do this, I do not understand." He put the handkerchief away. "So, senors, how went the first day's march?"

"It went well, *Presidente*," one of the generals answered quickly. "The trailing elements are moving into their encampment now."

Juan was shocked by the answer. Had they not just been talking of the hundreds upon hundreds of men who had died, and were dying, of cold and exposure? He looked at the other colonels and saw that they were staring at the ground. They knew that the general had decided that Santa Anna would hear nothing but positive reports, and none of their number would be the one to tell him otherwise. Like the others, Juan said nothing.

"Are they being fed? And are they clothed and protected against the weather?" Santa Anna asked.

"*Si, Presidente,*" the general said again.

Santa Anna smiled broadly and rubbed his hands together.

"Wonderful, wonderful," he said. "And now these people who call themselves 'Texians' will see the foolishness of arousing the anger of the Napoleon of the West. The parade we held at our departure this morning was *magnifico*, was it not? How splendid our army looked!"

"*Si, Presidente,*" the general who was the spokesman for the staff replied. "It was most impressive."

"Senors, we will sweep through Tejas like a *tempestad de fuego*, leaving death and destruction in our wake," Santa Anna said. "It will be one thousand years before anyone dares to challenge Mexico again."

"*Si, Presidente.* One thousand years," the general mumbled.

Santa Anna stretched and yawned, then looked toward the corner of his tent where one of the prettiest of the young women in his entourage, her full breasts spilling over the scoop neck of her blouse, was already making the bed. She glanced over at him and smiled invitingly. As Santa Anna looked at her, his tongue darted out to lick his lips. His dark eyes looked carnal, and a small red gleam seemed to flash from somewhere deep down inside.

"Senors," Santa Anna said. "The march today was tiring . . . for all of us. I suggest that we all go to bed early so that we may get as much rest as we can. We have many more such days ahead of us. Good night."

To a man, the generals and colonels of Santa Anna's staff came to attention and saluted. The chief of staff spoke for all of them: *"Buenos noches, Benemerito en Grando Heroico."*

When Juan awakened the next morning, a pristine blanket of snow covered everything in sight. No longer visible was the trail of an army on the move. There were no footprints and no signs of an encampment. Even the fires they had built the night before were covered now in a mantle of white. It was as if no one had been here.

The darkness lifted, only to be replaced by a heavy morning fog. Not until then did the rest of the army begin to awaken. The women followers were first, moving slowly and painfully through the cold mist, breaking the ice on the surface of the water barrels in order to get water to make coffee, while the men went through the same ice-breaking ritual in order to shave and attend to their morning ablutions.

"Good morning, Senor Colonel," Juan's striker said, greeting him as he stepped out of his own tent. The sergeant handed Juan a cup of coffee, steaming hot. Juan was as appreciative of the warming effect the tin cup had on his hands, as he was of the coffee's bracing sustenance.

Suddenly the morning was interrupted by a series of shots, and when Juan looked around to ascertain the cause, he saw his brother running toward him.

"Juan!" Ramon shouted, forgetting in his excitement to address his older brother by his rank. "Juan, we are being attacked!"

"What? Attacked? By Texians?" Juan asked.

"No. We are being attacked by Comanches! They are going after the conscripts!"

"Quinterra!" Juan shouted. "Get a platoon of *zapadores*

mounted, quickly! Sergeant, saddle my horse!''

''*Si, Colonel!*'' Quinterra and Juan's striker answered, as one.

As the two men hastened to carry out Juan's orders, Juan ran back into his tent to get his sword and pistol belt. He was still strapping it on when his sergeant brought his horse to him. Normally, Juan would not participate in a platoon-sized action, nor would he be expected to. But the thought of Comanches having the audacity to attack his own regiment right under his very nose so angered him that he swung into the saddle and waited as the others mounted.

Major Quinterra, who was himself mounted and ready to go, had been selective in assembling a platoon so that all who answered his call were professional soldiers, experienced in battle, well-armed, well-mounted, and eager to serve their colonel. It was, perhaps, the single most effective fighting unit in the entire army.

Juan drew his sword, then stood in his stirrups as he looked out over the hastily assembled platoon. He noticed immediately that in addition to himself and Major Quinterra, there were two or three company-grade officers, so eager for battle that they were willing to fight in the ranks.

''Forward, men!'' Juan shouted, waving his sword.

As if sharing the same bloodstream and musculature, men and horses surged forward as one. Startled soldiers and camp followers looked on in awe as Juan's *zapadores* galloped through the encampment at full speed. Sparkling crystals of snow flew up in glistening sheets of white, the miniblizzard created by the horses' hooves. The eyes of the steeds gleamed yellow, almost as if illuminated by some inner light. Clouds of steam issued from their flared nostrils, and with the sound of the hoofbeats silenced by the snow, and the platoon shrouded in the early-morning fog, the galloping riders gave the appearance of a ghost army, sent from hell by Diablo himself.

Some of the more superstitious crossed themselves and mouthed a quick, fearful prayer as the platoon swept by.

On the extreme western flank of Juan's regiment, where the lightly armed, ill-clothed, and untrained conscripts had made their own poor accommodations for the night, a mounted raiding party of Comanches was, at that very moment, swooping down upon the helpless camp. Taking advantage of the weakness of their adversaries, the Indians were indiscriminately looting and killing men, women, and children.

"There they are!" Juan shouted, bringing his sword forward, pointing out an Indian who had just brought down a fleeing woman with one swing of his war club.

Juan rode down the Indian who had just clubbed the woman. He thrust his saber through the Comanche's heart, plunging it in, then withdrawing the bloody blade even as the Indian tumbled, dead, from his saddle. A ripple of explosions sounded as the attacking soldiers fired, at nearly point-blank range, into the surprised Indians.

Seeing that the tide of battle had turned against them, those Indians who survived the first volley jerked their horses hard about in an attempt to flee. Many of them were forced to drop their ill-gotten loot.

"Continue the chase!" Juan shouted. "After them! Hound the heathen bastards all the way to hell!"

With a battle cry in their throats, the *zapadores* pressed their advantage over the Indians, some of whom had dismounted to tend to their looting, and were now forced to flee on foot. Juan saw one Indian get the back of his head blown off by a point-blank blast from a double-shotted pistol. As the *zapadores* pressed the pursuit, they galloped on through the camp and out into the snow-covered high desert beyond.

His immediate blood-lust fulfilled, Juan turned command of the platoon over to Major Quinterra, then dismounted to gage the damage the Indians' raid had done. Ramon, who had brought word of the attack, was just now returning from Juan's headquarters. He stood with his brother as they looked around the encampment of the conscripts. The bodies made dark forms on the white snow, highlighted with great swaths of red blood. The men, women, and children who had survived the savage attack, were now weeping quietly over their dead.

"Our army has been on the march but one day," Ramon said to his brother. "And, already, we have lost nearly a fourth of our number."

''*Si*, Ramon,'' Juan agreed. ''But those who survive until we reach Tejas will be the stronger for it.''

''Always, when I thought of war, I thought of flags waving and bugles playing,'' Ramon said. He took in the pitiful scene with a sweep of his hand. ''I never imagined it would be like this.''

''War is never as one imagines it,'' Juan said. Juan swung back into his saddle, then looked down at his brother. ''Return to your company, Lieutenant,'' he said. ''We will be getting underway soon.''

''*Si*, Colonel,'' Ramon replied, saluting his brother.

Twelve

Tuesday, February 2, 1836, the Taylor Cabin

It had been four days since Lopez and his men swept down upon Marie and her guide, killing Alvarez and making her their prisoner. For four days she had been kept naked and locked in the little cabin. The only good thing about that four days was that Lopez and his men were gone, leaving only Rosita to watch over Marie.

Marie tried to make friends with Rosita, but no matter how hard she tried, she couldn't break through to her. Then she learned why Rosita was so unfriendly. The Mexican woman was jealous of her.

''You are so beautiful,'' Rosita said. ''When the men return, I fear they will look only at you and they will forget about Rosita.''

''Then help me escape,'' Marie pleaded. ''Bring me my clothes. That way I will be gone when the men return.''

''I cannot,'' Rosita said. ''If I help you escape, I will be beaten.''

That was two days ago, and since then, Marie had seen Rosita only when Rosita brought her meals. Then tonight, Marie was awakened by laughter and loud voices. With a feeling of dread, Marie realized that Lopez and his men had returned.

She sat up in bed and looked around the room. The moon was shining through the window so brightly that she could see, even into the shadows of the corners. Outside the cabin she could hear guitar music, singing, and laughter.

Marie crept out of bed and across the floor of the little cabin where she discovered that, for the first time since being brought here, the door wasn't locked!

Quickly and quietly, Marie wrapped herself in the quilt, using as a belt a short strip of cloth that she had modified for just such a purpose. Thus, with her modesty, if not her dignity, preserved, she opened the door and stepped out into the moonlight. She pressed herself against the outside wall of the cabin and began to edge slowly along it. A short distance from the cabin there was a remuda where all the horses were tied. Marie knew that if she could make it that far without being seen, she could mount one of the horses and get away. With a head start, she knew that she could outride any man.

She was startled by a shout that came from somewhere very close by, then by the crash of a bottle, followed by drunken laughter. Thinking she had been discovered, Marie's heart nearly stopped. It took but a moment, however, to realize that the soldiers were so intoxicated that they were oblivious of her. Cautiously, she continued to creep through the darkness until she reached the corner of the house where she paused, planning the path she would take across the open area to the remuda. She took a deep breath, ready to run.

"No, senorita," a quiet voice said. "Don't try it. My soldiers would only catch you, then their anger would be such that I could not stop them from having their way with you."

Marie gasped. "Captain Lopez!"

Captain Lopez stepped out of the shadows into the moonlight.

"*Si*, it is I. Did you miss me these past few days, senorita?" Lopez asked.

"Captain, you have no right to keep me here," Marie said. "I demand that you return my clothes to me at once, sir, or . . ."

"Or what, senorita?"

"Or . . . or you are no gentleman!"

Lopez laughed out loud. "Senorita, I have already admitted

that I am no gentleman. Now, go back inside, *por favor*."

Angry and disappointed, Marie returned to the little cabin that had been her prison. She sat on the edge of the bed in frustration.

A few moments later the door opened and Lopez stepped inside. He was carrying a small, burning brand, and with it, he lit a candle that stood on a table near the door. As the candle flamed, a golden bubble of light helped the bright moon push back the darkness. The candle flickered, casting wavering shadows on the wall.

"What do you want?" Marie asked. "What are you doing in here?"

Lopez smiled and his brilliant white teeth flashed against his face. He raised the little flaming twig to his lips and blew it out, then laying it aside, he began unbuttoning his green, red, and gold military tunic.

"What? What are you doing?" Marie asked again in a soft, frightened voice.

"Ah, *caramba*, senorita, you have been much on my mind. I think you are the handmaiden of Diablo. You have crowded out all other thought. From the time we found you, I have known that I must have you."

"No," Marie said, cowering from him. "Please, Captain Lopez, don't do this."

Lopez put his hand on her neck. At first Marie cringed, thinking he might choke her, but his touch was amazingly gentle, as if he were feeling for her pulse.

"Once, as a young boy, I picked up a bird that had broken its wing," Lopez explained. "I could feel the heart of the bird beating very fast, just as yours is now, and I knew that it was frightened of me." Lopez closed his fingers around her neck, more securely, but still, gently. "I think that you, my pretty one, are that bird. You are very frightened, but I do not wish to hurt you, as I did not wish to hurt that bird."

Lopez moved his hand down from Marie's neck to her shoulder, then across her breast. Fear held Marie immobile.

"I think perhaps you will like this, no?" Lopez said.

"No," Marie said, her throat so constricted with fear that she could barely utter the word.

"Let me see you, senorita," Lopez said. He untied her

makeshift belt, then, with a quick jerk of his hand, pulled the quilt away from her. Realizing that she was now naked before him, Marie put one arm across her breast and the other between her legs in an attempt to shield herself from his intense gaze.

"*Dios,* you are a very beautiful woman, senorita," Lopez said, almost reverently. "You have set me on fire."

"Please, Captain, I beg of you, leave me alone."

"I want only to bring you pleasure, my pretty little bird," Lopez said. He pushed Marie back on the bed until she was lying down. Still holding her arms across her in strategic positions, Marie looked up at him through eyes that were wide in fear. She tried, one more time, to reason with him.

"Captain, surely you will not force yourself upon a woman who has placed herself under your protection. No gentleman would do such a thing."

Lopez smiled broadly as he unfastened his belt and let his trousers drop. He stepped out of them, and, within another moment, was as naked as she. "Have you forgotten, senorita, that I am no gentleman?"

Suddenly Marie heard shooting outside. The shots were rapid and earsplitting, and the music and laughter of the soldiers changed suddenly to cries of fear and pain.

"*Dios!* Pablo! *Quien es?*" Lopez shouted, turning away from Marie. He started toward the door, then realizing that he was naked, came back to grab the quilt and wrap it around himself before he went outside.

Outside the cabin, Marie heard loud voices, speaking English.

"Look out for the girl!" one voice shouted. "Watch where you are shooting, men! Don't hit her!"

Marie was shocked and thrilled to realize that she knew that voice! It was Hunter Grant! She closed her eyes and bit her lip, not daring to believe that he had come for her.

There was more shooting and more shouts, then the sound of horses galloping away from the compound.

"Captain Grant! They're getting away!" someone shouted.

"Go after them!" Hunter called. "Chase the bastards back to Mexico! I'm going to look for the girl!"

Footsteps approached the cabin. Marie sat quietly, scarcely

daring to breathe as she looked at the door.

"Miss Doucette, are you in there?" she heard Hunter call.

Marie tried to answer, but she was so traumatized by recent events that her throat was constricted and she couldn't make any words come out.

"Are you all right?" Hunter called again. This time there was more anxiety in his voice.

Though she tried a second time, Marie still couldn't answer.

Suddenly the door exploded into the room, flying off its hinges in splinters. Holding a pistol in one hand and a knife in the other, Hunter stood just on the other side of the threshold, looking in, warily. Then he saw her.

"Marie! Thank God, you are all right!" He put his weapons away. "When I didn't get an answer I. . . ." Hunter stopped in midsentence, as if just now noticing that Marie was naked. He stood there and stared at her in unabashed intensity.

"Captain Lopez took my clothes," Marie explained. Her voice was quiet and weak.

"I'll kill the son of a bitch," Hunter said menacingly. "When I catch him, I'll murder him. Any man who would force himself upon a woman doesn't deserve to live."

"But he didn't force himself on me."

Hunter continued staring at her, then he looked down at Lopez's clothes, which were lying in a crumpled heap on the floor. The bedding was disarranged, and Marie's naked body was flushed.

"I see," Hunter said coldly. "How disappointed you must be at my untimely arrival."

"Your untimely arrival? What are you talking about?" Marie asked. She couldn't understand the sudden change in the tone of Hunter's voice. At first it had been solicitous, now it was almost belligerent.

"It doesn't take a genius to figure things out, Miss Doucette. Lopez was wrapped in a quilt as he rode off, and I can see that these clothes are his. You are naked and you say he didn't force himself on you. One can only conclude that you were a willing participant."

"What?" Marie gasped. Her eyes filled with tears. She was

going to tell him that Lopez didn't force himself upon her because he was interrupted before he could accomplish the foul deed. How could Hunter have so completely misunderstood?

"Are you going to try and convince me that nothing happened?" Hunter asked.

"No," Marie said flatly.

"I didn't think so."

"It is neither my obligation, nor my intention, to convince you of anything," she added.

"Where are your clothes?" Hunter asked.

"I don't know where they are. I haven't seen them for four days. Ask Rosita," Marie said. "If she is still here."

Hunter went outside for a few moments, then he returned carrying a dress.

"This is all I could find," Hunter said. "The Mexican woman says they took the rest of your things."

Marie took the dress, then stared pointedly at him for a few seconds. "Mr. Grant, I know that I no longer have any secrets from you but would it be too much to ask you for a little privacy so that I might get dressed?"

"I'm sorry," Hunter said. "Of course I will give you some privacy. I'll be waiting for you just outside."

Marie began dressing, putting on clothes for the first time in four days. It didn't matter that this was the same dress she was wearing when she was captured. It didn't matter that it was dirty. It was clothes and for that she was very happy.

A few moments later Hunter knocked on the door. "Miss Doucette, are you dressed? May I come in, please?" he called.

Without answering him, Marie walked over and opened the door, then turned and walked away from him. Hunter stood, waiting for an invitation to come in.

"May I?" Hunter asked, indicating with a wave of his hand that he wanted to come in.

"Have I really any choice, Mr. Grant? From what you think of me now, I assume you will do as you wish."

"Please?" Hunter said, again making a motion with his hand.

"Come in," Marie said.

Hunter cleared his throat. "Miss Doucette, I want to offer my most sincere apology," he said. "I was wrong."

"I beg your pardon?"

"I spoke to the Mexican woman, Rosita," Hunter said. "She told me what happened. I am sorry for my misconception and my boorishness. I don't expect you to forgive me. My behavior was inexcusable."

"Yes, it was."

Silently, Hunter looked at the floor in contrition.

"However, that being said, I will now tell you that I am very glad you arrived when you did. Although I am curious as well. What are you doing in Texas?"

"I have come for you," Hunter replied. "Your father sent me to bring you back."

"No, Hunter, please, you mustn't try and take me back," Marie said, using his first name in an attempt to persuade him. "I have to find Sam McCord. I know where he is now. He is in a place called San Antonio de Bexar."

"Yes, I know he is there."

"You know he is there? You've seen him?"

"No, but I have spoken with those who have," Hunter replied. "Miss Doucette—"

Marie smiled. "Surely, after all this, you now know me well enough to call me by my given name," Marie interrupted.

"Marie, do you know why Sam is in San Antonio?"

"Not exactly."

"I am told that there will soon be a big battle there," Hunter said. "And Sam is there with a group of men who, as I understand it, are trying to convert an old church into a fort. San Antonio is going to become a very dangerous place, very soon. It is not a place any rational person will want to be. This is as far as I'm going to let you go."

"This is as far as *you* are going to let me go? What gives you the right to say such a thing?"

"It is an obligation, more than a right," Hunter answered. "I feel a duty to your mother and father to take you back."

"What about me, Hunter? Do you feel no obligation toward me?"

"I do indeed," Hunter said. "Which is all the more reason

I don't intend to let you put yourself in such danger."

"Hunter, you can force me to go back with you if you choose to. There is nothing I can do to stop you," Marie said. "But if you do so, then you had better make me your prisoner and keep me bound, hand and foot. Because I tell you now, I intend to find Sam McCord, and I will get away from you at the first opportunity."

Hunter ran his hand through his hair as he studied the determined young woman.

"Does it mean that much to you?"

"It means everything to me."

"Marie, I know that love is supposed to make someone blind to another's faults," Hunter said. "But consider what you are doing. Sam McCord ran out on you and you are chasing him. Have you no pride at all?"

"Pride?" Marie replied. She shook her head and, unbidden, tears came to her eyes. "Oh, Hunter, how little you understand. It is too late for pride. Now, there is only time for shame."

Hunter looked confused. "What do you mean by that?"

"I *have* to find him, and he *has* to marry me. Don't you understand? Must I explain it to you as one would explain it to a child? I am pregnant, Hunter. I am going to have Sam McCord's baby."

"Oh," Hunter said. Once, as a boy, a fall from a tree had knocked the breath out of him. For just a moment, he felt that way now, so unexpected was this news. He stared at Marie for a long moment. "Oh," he said again softly. He brushed his hand through his hair. "I . . . I didn't know."

"No, of course not. No one knows," Marie said. "Not my parents, not Sam McCord. No one."

"Are you sure that—"

"That it's Sam McCord's baby? Of course I am sure." Marie sobbed. "Oh, how wanton you must think I am," she said.

"No, Marie," Hunter said quickly. "I wasn't going to ask that question. I was just going to ask if you are certain you are pregnant."

"Oh," Marie replied self-consciously. "Oh, yes, yes, I am absolutely certain."

Hunter sighed. "All right. I can see, now, why it means so much to you. I guess we'll go on."

"We?" Marie asked.

"Yes, we. There is no way I'm going to let you go by yourself. Especially not in your . . . uh . . . condition. We'll leave, first thing in the morning."

"Oh, thank you, Hunter! Thank you!"

Spontaneously, Marie threw her arms around Hunter's neck, then leaned into him. He was acutely cognizant of her body against his . . . not only because he had seen it in all its naked glory a few minutes earlier, but also because he was now aware that there was a baby growing inside.

Bars of bright sunlight spilled in through the window and the smashed door of the cabin. A bird called impatiently outside, and in the distance could be heard the hammering of a woodpecker. The morning sounds aroused Marie and she found herself slowly abandoning sleep.

Marie was still fully dressed, having lain on the bed the night before to get what rest she could. She stretched, then got out of bed and walked across the small room. The door lay in splinters where Hunter had kicked it in the night before. She looked outside, blinking a few times at the brightness of the morning sun.

"Good morning," Hunter said. He was squatting beside a campfire. A brace of forked twigs bracketed the fire, and a green willow branch bridged the two. A pot of coffee was suspended over open flames and Marie could smell the aroma of the coffee as it brewed.

"Good morning," Marie replied hesitantly.

"Are you ill?"

"Ill?"

"I have heard that women who are going to have a baby are sometimes ill in the mornings."

"Yes," Marie said. "That is true, and I have been ill, but the illness seems to have passed, these last few days."

"Then perhaps you are not . . ."

Marie shook her head. "No," she said. "I am pregnant."

"Are you certain you will be able to go on? I mean, shouldn't you be more careful now, in your condition?"

"My condition? I'm pregnant, Hunter, I'm not dying," Marie said. She looked around at the white-gray residue of last night's campfires. There was not a spark left alive in any fire except the one Hunter was using. "Where are the others?" she asked.

"What others?"

"Your soldiers. The men who were with you."

"They're gone."

"Gone where? Aren't they going to San Antonio with us?"

"No. They were merely volunteers to help me find you. Now that you are safe, they are free to go their own way."

"Then it will just be the two of us?"

"Yes."

"Oh."

Hunter poured two cups of coffee, then brought one over to Marie. "I don't know why that should concern you. You were alone with Alvarez, were you not?"

"Yes, but he was Mexican."

"So?" Hunter blew across the lip of the cup to cool his coffee.

"Well, there was really no chance that we . . . uh . . . that he and I . . ." Marie let the sentence die.

Hunter smiled. "Don't worry, Miss Doucette. I will do nothing to compromise your honor."

Although Hunter made the comment matter-of-factly, the words seemed to mock the fact that she was pregnant, and unwed so that, in the eyes of many, including her own, she no longer had any honor to be compromised.

"How are we going to go?" Marie asked. "Captain Lopez took my team and wagon."

"It's just as well. We'll travel faster by horse," Hunter said. "And I brought one for you. It's over in the remuda."

Marie looked toward the remuda, then let out a little gasp of pleasure.

"Prince!" she said. "Oh, Hunter, you brought Prince!" She hurried over to the horse and Prince, recognizing her, nuzzled her hand. "Oh, Prince, I'm so glad to see you."

"How glad can you be?" Hunter asked sarcastically. "You sold him."

"I had to sell him," Marie defended hotly. "I needed the team and wagon."

"Tell that to your horse," Hunter said. "I'm not the one you have to explain yourself to."

"You're right," Marie said. "I don't have to explain anything to you."

Hunter walked over to his saddlebags and dug something out. Turning toward Marie, he tossed it to her. "You'd better wear this," he said.

"Pants and a shirt," Marie said. "Men's clothes."

"It'll make you sit the horse easier," Hunter explained. "Besides, if anyone is watching us, I'd just as soon they think it's two men on the trail, instead of a man and a woman. It might be safer that way."

"All right," Marie agreed. She finished her coffee, then went inside the cabin. When she came back out a few minutes later, she was wearing the pants and shirt Hunter had given her. Hunter had already saddled his own horse and was just finishing with hers.

"Let's go," he said, swinging up into his own saddle and starting off at a canter without looking back. Marie quickly mounted Prince and caught up with him.

"Hunter, are you all right now?" she asked.

"What do you mean?"

"I mean about what happened with you and Johnny and Lucinda."

Hunter was quiet for a long moment, before he answered. "What's happened has happened," he said. "If I have learned anything, it's that nothing is going to change it."

"Still, I know that it hurt you terribly. And I think the Meechum family, and especially Lucinda, were unfair."

"How can I expect them to forgive me, if I can't even forgive myself?"

"But you have forgiven yourself," Marie said. "I mean look at how you have pulled yourself together. You were . . ."

"A drunk?"

"I wasn't going to be so blunt about it."

"Why not? It's true, isn't it?"

"Whether it was true or not, it is no longer so. And I think

Lucinda is a fool for letting you get away.''

Hunter chuckled.

''Why do you laugh?''

''I was just thinking. Lucinda and Sam should get together. Since they are both fools, they would be perfect for each other.''

Despite herself, Marie laughed as well.

Supper was a rabbit that Hunter killed, then cooked over a fire. Just before they went to bed, Hunter threw a few more pieces of dry wood into the blaze so that they would have a fire to push away the night chill.

Marie lay on her blanket, watching burning red sparks climb a column of heated air up into the sky. There, the tiny red dots joined the stars spread out in the vast cathedral vault above. She called over to Hunter.

''Are you still awake?''

''Yes.''

''Isn't it lovely out here? No bedroom could ever have a nicer ceiling. The stars are absolutely beautiful.''

''Yes,'' Hunter said. ''They are.''

They were quiet for a moment longer.

''Marie?''

''Yes.''

''About last night.''

''What about last night?''

''When I came upon you . . . naked . . .''

''You've already apologized, Hunter. You don't have to apologize again. Just don't think about it.''

''No, you don't understand. I'm not talking about what I thought, or what I said.''

Marie raised up on one elbow and looked over toward him. She could barely make out his shadow, lying wrapped in his blanket, on the other side of the fire.

''Then what are you talking about?''

''About what I saw,'' Hunter replied. ''I can't get it out of my mind. I close my eyes and there it is. There you are. I have never seen anyone . . . or anything as beautiful.''

''No, Hunter, you mustn't say things like that.''

''I know. Especially the way things are. So I won't mention

it again,'' Hunter's disembodied voice replied. ''But I just want you to know that I don't intend to forget it.''

LUNES, 8 FEBRERO, 1836, THE RIO GRANDE RIVER

Colonel Juan Montoya sat his horse atop a small rise on the Texas side of the Rio Grande. With his spyglass, he searched the nearby hills and wood lines for any sign of the enemy, but saw no one.

Behind him, he heard a low, rumbling sound, like a prolonged roll of timpani. The drumming began to swell, growing louder and louder until it was like thunder. The sound made Juan's stomach quiver and it filled the trees with its pounding until finally, bursting over the crest of the embankment, Juan could see its source.

Major Quinterra was riding at the head of Juan's regiment, bent low over his horse's neck. The horse was in full gallop and its mane and tail were streaming out behind, its nostrils flared wide, and the powerful muscles in its shoulders and haunches throbbing.

Following Quinterra was a flag bearer, and above him, Juan could see the red, white, and green ensign snapping in the wind. Then came the entire body of men, all urging their animals to the fastest possible pace.

These were the *zapadores,* cavalry, and dragoons of Juan's regiment. The infantry and conscripts had been detached from the regiment and given over to other elements within Santa Anna's army. What remained of Juan's regiment was a much smaller, but very swift, and very professional fighting force. The regiment was then attached to the brigade of General Jose Urrea. Urrea's brigade separated from Santa Anna's army and proceeded to Matamoros, where, according to Santa Anna's spies, Colonel Fannin would be attacking.

When General Urrea reached Matamoros without sighting Fannin, he sent Juan's regiment across the river into Texas. ''If Fannin is there, crush him,'' Urrea ordered. ''If he is not there, wait for him.''

As a result of those orders, Juan's regiment became the first of Santa Anna's army to reach Texas, and Juan was the

first of his regiment, having turned temporary command over
to Quinterra half an hour earlier so he could ride on ahead.

The column of men hit the water and sand. Silver bubbles
flew up in a sheet of spray, sustained by the churning action
of the horse's hooves until it fell back like rain. Seeing his
commander, Quinterra turned the column toward the little
rise, halting them just short of Juan. Dismounting, and holding the reins of his horse in his left hand, Quinterra saluted
with his right.

"Colonel Montoya, I have the honor, *Senor Commandante*,
of reporting that your regiment has crossed the river in force
and awaits your orders!"

"Thank you, Major Quinterra," Juan said, returning the
salute. "Have the men make camp there," he added, pointing
to an area just inside the wood line. "There is ample wood
and water, and we will be able to observe all approaches."

"*Si*, Colonel," Quinterra replied. He turned and shouted
the orders back to the subordinate commanders.

"Did you see any sign of the rebels?" Juan asked, as he
and Quinterra dismounted.

"No, Colonel," Quinterra replied. "Did you?"

"No," Juan said. "Though it does not seem possible that
we have come this far without opposition. I believe the Norteamericanos have missed their best opportunity to stop us."
He stroked his chin. "But as you see, we are here. And here,
we shall stay, until we get further orders."

At supper that evening, Juan shared a bottle of wine with
several of his officers, including his brother, as they discussed
the latest intelligence brought to them by courier from General Urrea.

"Colonel Fannin did not leave Goliad," the courier reported. "Our sources say that he is still there, with some
ninety men."

"Only ninety?" Juan asked.

"*Si.*"

"Then he was wise not to attempt to stop us. Still, with
ninety men, he could have engaged in a program of striking
and falling back."

"Striking and falling back?" Ramon asked. "What would

be the use of that, my brother? Surely he could not hope to defeat us with only ninety men?''

"He would not attempt to defeat us,'' Juan explained. "Such a strategy would have no purpose other than to inflict casualties upon us, while exposing himself to the minimum of risk. Using that tactic, I believe he would be singularly successful. I think he was foolish not to take advantage of the situation.''

"Perhaps Colonel Fannin lacks the bravado for such activity,'' Quinterra suggested.

"The Norteamericanos may have many shortcomings, my brother, but a lack of bravado is not one of them.''

"Then why did he not come out? Why did he not attack us? As you pointed out, Colonel, he has much more to gain than he does to lose, by such activity.''

"Perhaps they are amassing their army for one grand battle, in a place to be chosen by them,'' Juan replied.

"I do not think Colonel Fannin, nor any Norteamericano fighting with the rebels, has the military skills necessary to pull off such a plan,'' Quinterra said.

"Don't underestimate the Texians,'' Juan said. When Quinterra made a face, indicating that he did not like the term "Texian,'' Juan was quick to explain why he used it.

"They call themselves Texians, and so shall we. After all, it is not every Norteamericano we are fighting. It is only those who have come to Tejas to abuse our hospitality. And then, only those who have joined the Tejas army, to take up arms against us.''

Quinterra scoffed. "Our spies have brought us reports of this Tejas 'army.' '' He twisted his mouth as he said the word *army*, in order to show his disdain for it. "Never has a more ragtag collection of men been assembled,'' he continued. "They wear buckskin breeches as if they are uniforms; some new, soft and yellow, while others are hard and black and shiny with grease and dirt. There is not more than one military tunic among any twenty men, and their mounts vary from horses to ponies to mules.''

"But do not forget that it was a ragtag army just like the one you are describing that was successful at Gonzales and that defeated General Cos at Bexar,'' Juan said.

"General Cos," Quinterra replied, punctuating the word with an expectoration. "Juan, you and I both know that Cos is an old woman who has his commission only because he is the brother-in-law of the *Presidente*."

"That may be true, Manuel. But he was in command of an army of professionals. And I blame our fellow professional officers, as much as I do Cos, for their failure. They made the primary mistake in warfare. They underestimated their enemy. Just as Santa Anna is doing now."

"But Santa Anna has raised an army of fifteen thousand men," Quinterra said. "An army of that size proves that he is not underestimating the enemy."

"Fifteen thousand men, *si*. But of that fifteen thousand, there are thirteen thousand men for show, and only two thousand men for fighting," Juan said. "Did you know that our gallant *commandante* has already ordered a special medal to be struck and issued to all the soldiers for our victory over the Texians?"

"I have heard rumors of such a thing," Quinterra replied.

"It is not a rumor, my friend. It is for real. I, myself, have seen the design. It is an eagle with a snake in its beak, and a sword in its talons."

"What a noble design!" Quinterra said.

"A noble design, I agree," Juan replied. "But I think we should not too quickly adorn our tunics with the medal, lest we anger the Gods of War."

Juan heard a commotion and he stood up from the little collapsible cot where he had been sitting and walked to the tent flap to look outside.

"What is it, Sergeant? What is going on out there?" Juan called.

"I do not know, Colonel," a voice answered from the dark. "But I will find out for you."

Juan waited for a moment, then the sergeant called to him. "Colonel Montoya?"

"*Si?*"

"Our men have taken a prisoner," the sergeant said.

Juan stepped out into the night. "Have the prisoner brought to me."

"*Si*, Colonel," the sergeant answered.

A moment later, a young officer in charge of the guard detail saluted. "Colonel, we found this man spying on our encampment."

"I beg of you, senor, have mercy on me! I was not spying!"

"You are not Anglo?"

"No, senor! My name is Salvador Nuñez. I am Spanish, like yourself, senor. Like all my countrymen!"

"Colonel, our pickets caught him in a tree, observing our camp," the officer reported.

"But I was not spying!" Nunez insisted.

"If you were not spying, what were you doing?"

"I am on the way to Matamoros to visit my mother and my sister. I saw many soldiers and I was frightened," Nunez said.

"If you have done nothing wrong, you have no need to be frightened," Quinterra suggested.

"*Si*, senor, that is true if you are speaking of the fine soldiers of the army of Mexico. But what of the soldiers of Tejas? I think they are not as principled as you, and were a lone Mexican to fall into their hands, they would, no doubt, kill him quickly."

"Have you seen an army of Norteamericanos?" Juan asked.

"I have seen them in San Antonio," Nunez said. "They have been there since General Cos ran away."

The young officer flinched at Nunez's use of the term "ran away," but Juan and Quinterra barely managed to suppress a smile.

"How many Tejas soldiers are in Bexar?" Juan asked.

"This, I do not know, senor. Many, I think."

Juan studied the frightened man for a moment, stroking his chin as he did so. There was a long, uncomfortable beat of silence, during which Nunez was barely able to suppress a whimper. Finally, Juan spoke.

"Take off your clothes," he ordered.

"*Que?*" Nunez asked in surprise.

"Take off your clothes," Juan said again. "Lieutenant, find Private Nunez a uniform. He will be in our army."

"*Si*, Colonel," the young lieutenant said.

"But, senor, I do not wish to be in the army," Nunez

protested. "My mother and my sister are waiting for me. I have family."

"All of our soldiers have mothers and sisters who wait for them. And, like you, many do not wish to be in the army. Still, they do their patriotic duty without protest, as you shall."

"But, senor?" Nunez protested again. "Have I no choice?"

"He is colonel to you, Private Nunez," the lieutenant said authoritatively. "And you do have a choice. You can serve the Mexican people, or you can be shot as a spy. Which shall it be?"

Nunez smiled wanly. "But of course, I shall be proud to serve the Mexican people," he said.

"Manuel, bring his clothes into my tent," Juan said, turning and walking back to his tent before the surprised Quinterra could ask him what he wanted with a peon's clothes.

When Quinterra stepped into Juan's tent a few minutes later, he was carrying Nunez's clothes on the end of a stick. Juan was sitting on his bed, pulling off his boots. He had already removed his uniform and was now wearing only his long underwear.

"Colonel Montoya, what are you going to do?" Quinterra asked.

Juan smiled. "I am going into Bexar to have a look around," he said.

"Have you gone mad? Such dangerous expeditions are not for colonels!"

"Ah, Manuel, but I do not go as a colonel." Juan pointed to the clothes Quinterra had just brought into the tent. "I go as Pedro Bustamante." He was using the name of one of his father's servants.

"I beg of you, Juan, do not take this risk," Quinterra said. "Send someone else. Let me go."

"Thank you for your concern, my friend," Juan said, as he stepped into Nunez's trousers. He wrinkled his nose against the odor. "But in order to fully understand the situation in San Antonio, I should go and see for myself. I leave you in command, until my return."

Thirteen

Each morning on the trail started exactly like the morning before. Hunter and Marie would be on the trail for an hour before the sun peeked up over the edge of the distant horizon, sending bars of light out to push away the darkness. There was a sameness to the days, as well. Hunter was a hard rider, but he saw to it that their horses were watered frequently and rested often. And, when the sun reached its apex, Hunter and Marie would dismount and walk beside their horses. It was always after dark when they quit the trail and wiped down the horses. Afterward, Marie would sleep the sleep of the exhausted.

After dark on the sixth day of traveling, Marie was rubbing down her horse when Hunter told her he had a surprise.

"We're going to have beans for supper," he said. "I thought a slight change in fare would be good for us."

"Impossible," Marie replied. "You have to soak beans for a long time before you cook them. Otherwise they are no good."

"I did soak them. I've been soaking them since last night." Smiling, Hunter held up a pouch. "I put them in this skin last night and covered them with water. We can have them cooked in less than an hour. I found some peppers, too."

"Oh, Hunter, that sounds wonderful," Marie said. "Not that I haven't been grateful for the game you've provided, mind you. It's just that I was beginning to wonder if I would ever eat anything besides wild meat again."

Hunter laughed. "I was beginning to feel that way myself. I've been saving these beans ever since we started, but I think it's about time we ate them."

"I'll gather some firewood," Marie offered.

"Go ahead. I'll rub down the horses."

As Marie gathered the wood, she let her mind wander a

little. Suppose there had never been a Lucinda Meechum to break Hunter's heart? And suppose there had never been a Sam McCord? Suppose she and Hunter were making this trip under different circumstances? If things had been different, she and Hunter might well be married and moving to Texas to find land and start a family of their own, like the Thompsons. Suppose the baby was Hunter's baby?

Such fantasies were wonderful to contemplate, but Marie had to return to reality. The baby she was carrying wasn't Hunter's, it was Sam McCord's. And Hunter was taking her to San Antonio so she and Sam McCord could be married . . . if Sam McCord would marry her. She knew that the possibility existed that he would not marry her, and if that were the case, she didn't know exactly what she would do. She knew she couldn't force him to marry her, nor, she believed, would she want to.

She put those thoughts out of her mind, and returned to thinking about the journey she and Hunter Grant were making together. The last several days had been hard, yes, but if she was honest with herself, she would have to admit that there were many things about it that she liked. She loved wrapping up in her blanket by an open wood fire. And she loved looking up at the brilliant points of light, far overhead. The stars were so distant and cold-looking. She wondered what made them glow.

Sometimes a star fell to earth. Her father's friend, Jim Bowie, claimed to have made his famous knife, the knife they named after him, from the metal he found in a fallen star.

Marie had once seen a fallen star, and it looked just like a piece of rock to her. It didn't glow at all. Why did stars glow when they were fixed in the sky? And what held them up there?

When Marie finally returned to the campsite she had a large armload of wood and she dropped it inside the little circle of rocks Hunter had fashioned. He used his flint and tinder, and in a few minutes he had a fire going. He suspended a pot above the flames and began to cook the beans.

In the distance a coyote howled, and when Hunter saw Marie shiver, he moved over to sit beside her.

"It's just a coyote," he said.

"I know it is. But they sound so mournful."

"That's just the way we think they sound. The truth is, that's a happy yell."

"A happy yell?"

"Absolutely. That coyote has his mate with him, and he's telling the world about it. Like this."

Hunter cupped his hand to one side of his mouth and let out a yelping howl, much like the coyote's, complete with the long, mournful wail at the end.

Marie laughed out loud. "You are crazy," she said.

"Maybe so. But that's the way I'd tell people about it if . . ."

"If what?"

"If you belonged to me, instead of Sam," Hunter said.

"Hunter, no, it's not good for—" Marie started, but before she could finish her statement, Hunter kissed her.

The kiss was thrilling in its intensity, and though she wanted to fight against it, the blood in her veins heated quickly, and a little whimper, not of protest, but of pleasure, escaped from deep in her throat.

"Oh, Hunter, how can you do this to me?" she asked. "You know my situation . . . the way things are."

"Tell me you don't want me to kiss you," Hunter said.

"Please," Marie said. But did she mean please stop, or please go on? She couldn't answer that herself.

Hunter ran his hands lightly over her body. He stopped at her breasts and he could feel the heat coming through the shirt she wore, setting fire to the palms of his hands. He began to unfasten her shirt, hesitating for one agonizing moment between each button, as if expecting her to challenge him.

Marie gave no challenge. She knew she should protest, but she could not. She was on fire, and she was afraid that if she spoke at all it would be to whimper a demand that he go on, further and faster.

Without her challenge, Hunter continued to unbutton the shirt until it hung open, causing her naked flesh to glisten orange in the glow of the campfire. He slipped her shirt off from her shoulders, and then down her arms until Marie was naked from the waist up. He bent down to kiss her breasts, even as his hands moved down to her hips and thighs. He unfastened her trousers, and a moment later she raised herself up so that he could remove them.

Marie was mesmerized. She was aware that she was nude, and a small voice, deep inside, pleaded with her to stop now, before it was too late. But another stronger, and more insistent voice urged her to go on, and she was shocked at her own actions when she found her hands on the buttons of his clothes.

Within another moment, Hunter was as naked as she.

Marie thought of the coyotes, and, for one strange, wild moment, she felt as if she were one of them. She and Hunter were naked and wild, like the animals, and the thought of it was more liberating than anything she had ever experienced in her life.

Hunter settled down over Marie. He could feel her skin, smooth and soft beneath his muscled body. He looked down at her and fixed the image in his mind as a flood of sensations swept over him with dizzying speed.

Marie pulled him down to her, pushing up against him as he thrust into her. For the second time in her life, she was having sex. For the first time in her life, she was making love, though, until this moment, she hadn't truly realized the difference.

Hunter moved against her, matching his deep, plunging thrusts with her bucking motions so that they were, for that moment, joined not only physically, but spiritually as well. They were on a quest for fulfillment, not as a man and a woman, but as lovers together on a pilgrimage. They would reach their ultimate goal, when they reached it, together.

Marie felt as if she had been lifted up to the level of the stars that burned so brilliantly above them. Her body was wound as tightly as the mainspring of a clock. Then pleasure burst over her, a tiny tingling that began deep inside, pinwheeling out faster and faster until her entire body was caught up in a whirlpool of excitation.

Hunter was swept up in the maelstrom with her, catching up quickly, then rushing ahead in a burst of ecstasy. Beneath him, he felt Marie's body convulsing in pleasurable shudders as involuntary cries escaped from her throat and he let himself go in one explosive orgasm which pulled and whipped at him until he was completely spent.

Afterward, they lay together for a long moment, floating with the pleasant sensations that stayed with them like the warmth that remains after a fire has died out. Finally, Hunter rolled away from her and lay beside her, inert now, where he had been so powerful but moments before. His breathing came hard for several moments before it stilled.

Hunter started to get up, but Marie put her hand on his naked shoulder.

"No," she said. "I'll take care of the meal. You just lie here."

Marie walked over to the campfire. She stirred the pot of simmering beans with a wooden spoon, then lifted it away from the fire and set it on a rock to cool. She took tin plates and spoons from Hunter's saddlebags, spooned out a generous portion of beans and peppers for each of them, and walked back over to sit beside Hunter. She was still naked, and the sensuality of it sent shudders of pleasure through her again.

Hunter, seeing her shiver, thought that she was cold. "Don't you want to get dressed?" he asked, sitting up to take the plate she offered him.

"No," Marie said, smiling back at him. "I don't want to get dressed now, or ever again."

Hunter chuckled. "That's fine by me," he replied. "But it might cause a few folks to talk, first town we ride into."

"Let them talk," Marie teased.

They ate a leisurely meal, and Marie could not remember when she had tasted anything more delicious. She didn't know if it was the change of fare, or if the food had been seasoned by the experience they had just shared.

"The fire is dying," Hunter said, after they finished eating. He started to get up.

"Don't worry about the fire," Marie said. "We'll keep each other warm tonight."

They spread their blankets next to each other, then, pulling the other blanket over them, pressed their naked bodies together. They kissed again, and when Hunter's need returned, Marie was ready for him. They made love slowly and deliberately and, afterward, fell asleep in each other's arms.

The next morning Marie awakened before Hunter. They were lying nude together, and for a moment, in the cold light of day, she felt a twinge of embarrassment. The feeling passed quickly, however, as she recalled the rapture they had shared the night before.

There was a clear stream near their camp, and Marie decided to enjoy a cool bath. She walked down to the water's edge and waded in, smiling. At least now, one inconvenience had been taken care of. There had been other occasions during their travel together when she had wanted a bath, but propriety had prevented it. Now she felt no need for modesty before Hunter Grant, and she would take a bath wherever she had the opportunity.

When Marie returned to the camp, she found Hunter already dressed and both horses saddled.

She felt an unwelcome twinge of embarrassment. Strangely, the fact that he was dressed while she was not, made her feel all the more naked. Hunter paid particular attention to the saddle fastenings, pointedly avoiding looking at her. That made her even more aware of her nudity, and now she felt herself blushing.

"I overslept," Hunter said. "You should have awakened me."

"I'm sorry," Marie said. "I wanted to take a bath."

"Yes, well, get dressed now. We have to go."

Marie was puzzled by Hunter's strange behavior. "Hunter, is anything wrong?" She walked over to touch him.

"No," Hunter said, walking away from her. "It's just that . . ."

"What?"

"I lost control of myself last night. I'm sorry. I had no right to force myself on you like that."

"But you didn't—"

"For God's sake, Marie!" Hunter said sharply. "You are pregnant with another man's child! Did you forget that?"

Marie's eyes filled with tears, and she turned away from him.

"Yes," she finally answered. "I guess, for a moment, I did forget."

"It's not something we can afford to forget again," he said.

"Now, get dressed. We have to find him in time to give your baby a name."

MIERCOLES, 10 FEBRERO, 1836, SAN ANTONIO DE BEXAR

Dressed in the clothes of a peon, Juan rode slowly into town, doing nothing that would get him noticed. A burst of laughter spilled out of a nearby cantina, and when Juan looked toward it, he saw three men coming out. They were wearing buckskin clothes, and they were carrying a single jug of whiskey which they passed back and forth, drinking from it in the peculiar way of holding it on their shoulders and turning their heads to the mouth of the jug.

"Hey," one of them said, passing the jug to another and wiping his mouth with the back of his hand. "Let's ask this here Mex fella."

Startled, Juan realized they were talking about him. Not wanting to engage in any conversation, he turned his horse and started to ride away.

"Amigo!" the man shouted. "Amigo, hold up there!"

Juan stopped his horse and waited, as the three men came toward him.

"Me an' my friends here, is havin' us a little argument."

"Warn't no argument, 'twas a discussion."

"All right, a discussion, then. And we figure, you bein' Mex an' all, you could answer it."

"What makes you think this here Mex could answer it, Bill? Look at the poor sumbitch. I bet he ain't never had no woman in his life."

"You don't need no money to get a woman, if the woman be willin'," Bill replied. He giggled. "Hell, if you needed money, we'd all three still be virgins."

"That's the truth," the third man said.

"All right now, Mex, here's the question," Bill said. "Which one is better in bed? A Mexican gal, or a colored gal?"

"No speak English, senors," Juan said.

"Well, shit, this feller ain't no help a'tall," one of the three said. "Let's go find someone else."

Juan rode away, but as he did, he heard one of the Americans.

"You boys notice anythin' peculiar about that there Mexican fella?"

"No."

"Me neither."

"Well, I did. I was just noticin' his horse. For a poor man, he's sure ridin' hisself a good horse."

Juan stiffened. He had ridden his own horse, because he wanted a mount he could depend upon if he had to get away quickly. He should have realized that someone who really knew horses would recognize the incongruity of a peon on such a horse. He decided he would be better off by leaving the horse somewhere while he looked through the town on foot.

Dismounting, Juan walked up and down all the streets of San Antonio. He saw several Norteamericanos, all of whom were laughing and joking as if they didn't have a care in the world. Their behavior surprised Juan. He didn't know if they were unaware of the approaching Mexican army, or if they were so confident that they were completely unconcerned.

The music of a guitar and trumpet summoned him to the largest of the cantinas. He went to the back and sat at a table near the wall, ordering a tequila and a spoonful of salt.

"And make certain the glass is clean," Juan ordered, though as soon as he issued the order, he wished he could call it back.

"*Si*, senor," the waiter said quickly. The look in the waiter's eyes indicated some confusion, for although Juan looked like a peon, he sounded like a nobleman.

"I know I am but a poor peon," Juan added. "But don't we have as much right to clean glasses as the rich?"

The waiter smiled, then looked around the room as if sharing a secret. "Sometimes, if the nobleman is *muy el grando*, I will polish his glass, and then I will spit in his drink," he said.

Juan laughed. "That is a fine joke to play," he agreed, relieved that the waiter's suspicions were apparently allayed.

A moment later, the waiter returned and put the tequila and a small dish of salt in front of Juan. "As you can see, senor, the glass is clean,'' the waiter said. ''And I did not spit in it,'' he added.

''*Gracias.*''

''Hunter Grant,'' a voice said.

Juan froze. Hunter Grant was the name of the man with whom he had almost fought a duel. Putting his hand up to cover his face, he looked around to see if Grant was in the room.

''Yes, Hunter Grant, that's his name.''

The conversation was coming from the table next to his, and neither of them was Grant. Obviously they were just talking about him. Slowly nursing his drink, Juan listened to their conversation.

''You know, Sam, I met Hunter Grant when he came to Gonzales to negotiate a cotton deal. He seemed like a fine, upstanding gentleman then, but I have heard that he has turned into a drunk. Could that be true?''

''I'm sorry to say that it is true.''

''But why?''

''It's a sad thing, Al,'' Sam said. ''It all started with the duel.''

''The duel? What duel?''

''Didn't you hear? Hunter was challenged to a duel by some uppity Mexican son-of-a-bitch who was in New Orleans on business. But the Mexican couldn't find anyone to act as his second, so Johnny Meechum said he would.''

''Who is Johnny Meechum?''

''Johnny Meechum was Hunter's best friend.''

''If that is so, why would Meechum act as second for the Mexican?''

''Folks say it was because Meechum didn't want to see the Mexican weasel out of the duel. Which is funny, 'cause that's just what happened.''

''So there wasn't no duel?''

''Yeah, there was a duel,'' Sam said. ''And that's the bad part. You see, what happened is, the arbitrator made Meechum fight the duel in the Mexican's place, and Hunter Grant killed him.''

At that precise moment, Juan had just taken a drink, but he was so shocked by what he heard, that the tequila went down the wrong way. He gasped and dropped his glass as he went into a spasm of coughing.

"Hey, amigo!" someone shouted. "Iffen you cain't handle your liquor, you oughtn't to be in here with the big boys!"

Everyone laughed.

"*Pardone,*" Juan said. Getting up from the table, he exited quickly, the laughter of the Texians rolling out behind him.

Juan walked over to the hitching rail and stood there for a long moment.

What had he done? By running out on the duel like that, he had caused an innocent man to be killed! And the life of another to be ruined, for according to what he heard, Hunter Grant had become a derelict, all because of his actions. No, not his actions, he decided. His inaction. His cowardice.

Juan's face burned with shame, and he was overcome with remorse for what he had caused. Crossing himself, he said a quick prayer, begging God for forgiveness, for he knew he could never forgive himself.

The sound of gunfire startled Juan, and he looked around quickly.

"Dead center!" someone shouted.

"Hell, it was easy to do. I just pretended it was one of Santy Annie's soldier boys," another answered.

Juan drifted, along with several others, down to the end of the street, where some buckskin-clad men were shooting at a row of bottles, lined up on a two-wheeled cart. What made the exhibition amazing was the distance the men were from their target. The bottles were at least two hundred yards away.

"All right, it's my turn," one of the shooters said. He was a tall man, with long, wavy hair. Like the others, he was wearing buckskin shirt and trousers, but he was also wearing a fur cap, with a fox tail hanging from the rear of the cap. He licked his thumb, then rubbed it against the side of his gunsight.

"Does that spit make you shoot better, Davy?" one of the Americans in the crowd asked, and the others laughed.

"You don't expect me to give you boys all my secrets now, do you?" Davy replied. He pointed to the bottles on the cart. "You see the third one from the left? I'm going to take off the neck, but leave the rest of the bottle."

"Hell, they can't nobody do that."

The man called Davy grinned. "Just watch me," he said. He raised his rifle to his shoulder.

The rifle flashed and boomed, and a large puff of smoke poured from the end of the barrel as it kicked back against Davy's shoulder.

Juan was looking at the bottle Davy had pointed out, and he saw the neck explode in a shower of tiny, sparkling pieces of glass. The fat part of the bottle remained untouched. It was the most impressive display of shooting he had ever seen, and when the others applauded, Juan applauded as well.

"Hey, Davy, when ole Santy Annie comes, how many of his soldier boys do you reckon you'll kill?" someone asked.

"Oh, about as many as I've got lead and powder for, I reckon," Davy answered easily.

Juan hung around while some of the others gave demonstrations of their shooting prowess. Although none of the others were able to call their shot so precisely as to break the neck off, there were very few bottles which were spared, and all this from a distance of two hundred yards. This, Juan knew, would give the Texas defenders a remarkable killing range.

"Cease fire! Cease fire!" someone shouted, riding up quickly, then leaping down from his horse.

"Colonel Travis, what is it? What's wrong?" the one called Davy asked.

"Colonel Crockett—"

Davy held up his hand. "No, now, I thought we had this straight. I don't want to be a colonel. I'm just a private. Maybe a 'high' private, but a private, just like all the rest of my Tennesseeans. Why don't you just call me Davy? All the boys do. Now, what's wrong?"

Travis was a tall, sinewy, rawboned man with reddish hair and a ruddy face. He ran his hand through his hair and sighed.

"I'll tell you what's wrong," Travis said. He pointed to the distant targets. "You and your Tennesseeans are out here shooting away precious ammunition as if we had all of it in the world. Are you too stupid to realize that we are short of supplies?"

Crockett's eyes narrowed, and he stroked his chin as he

studied the intense young officer. "Well, now I reckon I did know that," he said. He held out his hand toward the group of Mexicans who had gathered to watch the shooting demonstration. By coincidence, his finger happened to be pointing directly at Juan. "And I reckon if there are any spies in this bunch of Mexicans here, you just told them, too."

"But, what were you thinking, to waste ammunition so?"

"I thought maybe a little shooting demonstration might do a couple of things. First, seeing how well my Tennesseeans shoot might make the Mexicans hesitate just a mite, before trying to storm the Alamo. And the other thing is, by doing a little public target shooting, I thought we might be able to hide from them just how critical our lead and powder supply is."

"Oh, so this was your idea of military strategy, is that it?" Travis asked.

Crockett studied Travis for a moment, before he answered. "You might say that," he finally said.

"Might I suggest, Crockett, that you leave such things up to those of us with experience?"

"You'd be talkin' 'bout that cannonball you fellas shot off at Anahuac, would you?" Davy asked. He was referring to an incident the previous June, when Travis rallied a force of twenty-five men and a cannon and led them to Anahuac. There, they fired a single cannonball and the Mexican officer and his forty-four soldiers surrendered and promised to leave Texas.

Travis cleared his throat. "Among other things," he replied.

"Well, I reckon you got me there," Davy admitted. "Seein' as how I've never fought in any real war, 'ceptin' against the British and three or four different Indian tribes."

The Tennesseeans laughed.

"Colonel Crockett, how do you put up with such ill-mannered and boorish behavior?"

Davy put his hand on Travis's shoulder. "Take it easy, son," he said. "I'll be the first to admit that my Tennesseeans aren't much on military discipline and all that. But when it comes down to the fightin', why I reckon you'll be glad to have 'em around."

"Colonel Crockett—"

"I told you, just call me Davy."

"*Colonel* Crockett," Travis said again. "Without some discipline, our situation is hopeless."

Davy laughed. "Hell, Travis, it *is* hopeless, I thought you already knew that. That's why Houston wants us to pull out."

"I have no jurisdiction over you or your men," Travis said. "If you want to pull them out, I can't stop you."

"I don't plan on pullin' them out, or keepin' 'em in. Being as all my Tennesseans are volunteers, I figure that's a decision each one of 'em is goin' to have to make for himself."

"And you?" Travis asked.

"Oh, I reckon I'll stay, Travis, seein' as I got no place else to go. The problem is, when I got defeated in my last run for the U.S. Congress, I got just real upset with the folks back in Tennessee."

"Tell 'im what you told 'em, Davy!" one of his men shouted.

"I told 'em I was goin' to Texas, and they could all go to hell."

"And if Davy stays, we all stay," one of his men shouted.

"That is, long as you don't make us start drillin' with them soldier boys you got in there," another shouted. " 'Cause I'm a'tellin' you now, we ain't a'goin' to do that."

"No, an' we ain't a'goin' to run aroun' salutin' ever'body and sayin' sir, neither," another added.

"Watch your manners, boys," Davy said gently. "This here is a colonel, and we're going to show him some respect."

"Whatever you say, Davy," the most boisterous of his men said contritely.

"Colonel Travis, my men and I stand ready to serve at the discretion of the garrison," Davy said.

Travis was somewhat taken back by the sudden change in Davy Crockett's attitude and manner of speaking, and he blinked, then cleared his throat.

"Thank you, Colonel Crockett," he said. "I trust that you will be generous with your advice."

"You'll get advice, all right. I've never been one for holding that commodity back, whenever I thought it might be needed.''

"I, uh, shall be looking forward to it," Travis said. "And, please carry on with your target practice."

"Target practice? Hell, Colonel, you mean target shootin', don't you? We don't need no practice," one of the Tennesseeans shouted and the others whooped and yelled in support.

"I guess not," Travis admitted. "When the time comes, your marksmanship will be our most valuable weapon."

At that precise moment, a long rifle roared and, two hundred yards away, another bottle burst into a shower of glass.

"That was a Mex," the man who fired the rifle said. "And I hit him right betwixt the eyeballs."

Fourteen

Juan was shaken as he rode out of San Antonio de Bexar that same evening, on the way back to his encampment. He had heard of the prowess some Norteamericanos had with the long rifle, but he had never actually witnessed it before today. The weapons his men were carrying wouldn't shoot more than seventy yards, and at that distance, only the most skilled marksman could hit his target. On the other hand these men, the ones calling themselves Tennesseeans, were hitting very small targets at an incredible two hundred yards!

Given the small number of defenders, Juan had no doubt but that the Alamo would fall. On the other hand, given the fortification, range, and marksmanship of their weapons, victory was going to come at a terrible cost in Mexican lives.

THURSDAY, FEBRUARY 11, 1836, ALONG THE TRAIL
OF EL CAMINO REAL

The store stood in the shade of a spread of oak trees. A crudely lettered sign identified it as LEDBETTERS. The building had obviously undergone several renovations since it was first built. Starting out as a store, a bar had been added, then a barbershop, and finally two rooms out back to serve as a hotel. The result was a rambling, unpainted wooden building that stretched and leaned and bulged and sagged until it looked as if the slightest puff of wind might blow it down.

A man was sweeping the porch when Hunter and Marie stopped out front. He was large, with a bushy beard, and wearing an apron that may have been white at one time. When the two riders approached he wiped his hands on it, and greeted them with a smile. A nondescript yellow dog was sleeping on the front porch, so secure in his surroundings that he did nothing more than briefly open his eyes when Hunter and Marie arrived.

"Hello, gents, hello. Ledbetter's the name. Get down and come inside. I got near 'bout anythin' in there a couple of fellers like you might want."

The two riders dismounted, then stepped up onto the porch. Marie leaned down to pat the dog's head just before they followed Ledbetter inside. The interior of the store was patterns of shadow and light. Some of the light came through the door, but most of it was in the form of gleaming dust motes illuminated by bars of sunbeams stabbing through cracks between the boards.

In the back of the store, a woman was on her hands and knees, using a pail of water and a stiff brush to scrub the floor. She looked up and brushed a strand of pale brown hair back from her forehead. Her eyes were gray and one of them tended to cross. When she stood to walk toward them it revealed the fact that she had tied up her skirt to keep from getting it wet. That exposed her legs all the way above her knees almost to the bottom line of her bloomers.

"Either one of you boys lookin' for a good time?" she asked.

"I beg your pardon?" Marie asked.

"Oh, you're a young one, ain't you?" the woman said. She reached out to chuck Marie under the chin. "That's all right, honey, I got a particular way with the young ones."

"What are you doing?" Marie gasped, drawing away from her.

Hunter laughed. "Take off your hat," he said to Marie.

Marie took off her hat, then shook her head, allowing cascades of dark curly hair to fall down to her shoulders.

"Glory be, it's a woman!" the woman said, startled by the revelation.

Ledbetter laughed out loud. "I guess they got you there, Linda Sue," he cackled. "Yes, ma'am, they got you good."

"Well, how was I supposed to know?" Linda Sue complained. "She's dressed like a man."

"It makes traveling easier," Marie said.

"Don't worry none about it, miss, you don't need to explain anything to her," Ledbetter said. "Go on back to work, Linda Sue," he added, dismissing the cleaning woman, and would-be prostitute, with a wave of his hand.

"I was just tryin' to be friendly, is all," Linda Sue muttered as she walked back to her pail.

"Now, folks, what can I do for you?" Ledbetter asked, turning his attention back to the travelers.

"We'd like some coffee," Hunter said. "Some beans, a side of salted pork. And, would you have any horehound candy?"

"Got a whole barrel of it, shipped in from St. Louis just last month," Ledbetter said.

"We'll take a sack of that," Hunter said.

"Nice of you to buy candy for your missus," Ledbetter said.

"I'm not—" Marie started, but Hunter interrupted her.

"What she's saying is, I'm the one with the sweet tooth," Hunter said.

"But you do share it with her?"

"Absolutely," Hunter said, warning Marie with a glance not to tell them that they weren't married.

"Good for you. Say, that was a real shame 'bout that family, wasn't it?"

"What family?"

"Thompsons, I think they was. His name was uh, let me see . . ."

"Amon?" Marie asked fearfully.

Ledbetter snapped his fingers. "Yes, Amon, that's what it was. Had two kids, a boy and a girl."

"What about them?" Marie asked.

"You mean you haven't heard? They was found killt, all four of 'em."

"Oh, no!" Marie gasped. Tears sprang to her eyes.

"Did you know them folks?"

"Hunter, that's the family I was telling you about," Marie said. "The ones that were so nice to me."

"Who did it?" Hunter asked.

"Don't nobody know for sure, but they're figurin' it was a bunch of Mexicans . . . soldiers maybe, or conscripts who had deserted and turned outlaw."

Marie was crying softly.

"Look, I'm real sorry about blurting it out in front of your missus, like I done."

"She'll be all right," Hunter said. He put his arms around her and she came to him without hesitation. "What's the news on the war?"

"The latest I've heard is, they's a bunch of Texians holed up in a place called the Alamo at Bexar. But if they's any fightin' gone on there, I ain't heard nothin' about it yet. Also, the convention is still meetin', still tryin' to decide whether or not to declare independence. How do you feel about that?"

"I'm from Louisiana," Hunter said. "I don't have any feeling about it, one way or the other."

"Hell, mister, I'm from Missouri. But I'm a Texian now. So will you and your missus be, oncet you get to where you're goin'. The way I look at it is, do we want to raise our kids as Mexicans or Texians? I say Texians."

"If you put it that way, I agree," Hunter said.

Ledbetter smiled. "Thought I might talk you around to my way of thinkin'. Wish I could make it to the convention. I'd have 'em all talkin' independence."

"No need for you to go. From the talk I've heard, I figure that's the way it's going to be," Hunter said.

"Can't be none too soon from my reckonin'," Ledbetter said. "You folks wait here, I'll start gettin' your stuff together."

Hunter continued to hold Marie, who had been crying ever since hearing about the Thompsons. "Are you all right?" he asked.

"They were such wonderful people," Marie said. "And

they had such dreams of the future.''

"I'm sorry," Hunter said. "I wish there was something I could do.''

"You are doing something," Marie said. "You're taking me to Sam.''

For a moment, Hunter had felt very comfortable with Marie in his arms. When she mentioned Sam's name, however, he realized that he had no right to feel that way, for she was another man's woman.

"That's right," Hunter said, quietly. "I'm taking you to Sam.''

JUEVES, 11 FEBRERO, 1836, SANTA ANNA'S ENCAMPMENT

"It is good to have you back, Colonel," Major Quinterra said.

"It is good to be back," Juan replied. Having just returned, Juan was stripping out of the peon's clothing and redonning his uniform.

"I have orders to inform you as soon as you return, that General Santa Anna wishes to see you right away.''

"That is good," Juan said, "because I want to see him. Manuel, did you know that the Texian defenders of the Alamo have rifles and marksmen who can break small bottles from distances of two hundred yards?''

"I have heard tales of these long rifles," Quinterra said. "But I believe such tales to be exaggerations.''

"No, they are not," Juan said. "The feat of breaking small bottles from a distance of two hundred yards?'' Juan pointed to his eyes. "This, I have seen with my own eyes. Orderly!'' he called.

A private stuck his head in through the tent flap.

"Si, commandante?"

"Burn these," Juan said, kicking the clothes over to the orderly.

"Si, commandante."

Juan finished buttoning his tunic and, once again, he looked like a commanding officer.

"Well, it is time to make my report to the general.''

"I am told you went, yourself, to San Antonio de Bexar," Santa Anna said.

"*Si*, General."

"And what did you find there? Were the Texians quaking in their boots?"

"No, General."

"No? Are they that brave, or that foolish?"

"Perhaps a bit of both, General," Juan replied. "Also, they do not believe that we can attack them before spring, because there is not enough forage for our horses between here and there."

"They are correct," Santa Anna said. "The forage is too sparse for our animals." Santa Anna smiled. "But we will go anyway. Surprise is the strongest ally in any battle, Colonel."

"I agree, General. But what about our horses?"

"Many will die of starvation," Santa Anna said, matter-of-factly. "But what matters the death of a dumb animal, if it secures victory? Now, tell me, Juan. How many Texians are there?"

"My guess is between one hundred and fifty and two hundred," Juan said. "And, I believe they are waiting on reinforcements from Colonel Fannin. If he reinforces them, they may have as many as six hundred inside the fort."

Santa Anna scoffed. "Six hundred, against our magnificent army. We will have five thousand men on the field. That should be enough to dislodge them."

"General, if I might make a suggestion?"

"*Si.*"

"Must we attack the Alamo?"

"*Si*, of course we must attack. What would you have us do? Surrender to them?"

"No, General. I would have us pass San Antonio by, and leave them there. I believe we should strike the Texian up-starts at their capital. That would be like attacking a plant at its roots. Do that, and the fruit will wither on the vine."

"The time for showing leniency is past, Colonel. The Norteamericanos are going to learn that the price of revolution is very high. And that price shall be extracted in lives."

"*Si,* but it is a price we shall pay as well. Especially if we attack the Alamo. General, are you familiar with the long rifle?"

"The long rifle? What is this long rifle?"

"It is a weapon with a very long barrel. The long barrel makes the ball travel very far, very accurately."

"Why are you speaking of such a weapon?"

"Because, Excellency, all the defenders of the Alamo are equipped with this weapon. And I, myself, saw a demonstration of its effectiveness. The Texians are expert with that weapon, and they shall have the advantage of a fixed, fortified position. In addition, they have had ample time to reposition the artillery pieces General Cos abandoned. They have made a formidable fortress of the old mission."

"I was informed by my brother-in-law that the Alamo cannot be made into a fort."

"I would not have thought it possible either, General. But the Texians have done so."

"And is it your belief, Colonel, that the fort is so strong that we cannot capture it?" Santa Anna asked.

"No, General. If we attack, we will prevail."

"Then why do you question the attack?"

"Because if we attack, we will suffer a terrible loss of men."

"What do you consider a terrible loss?"

"Perhaps as many as one thousand," Juan said.

Santa Anna laughed derisively. "You were not the one who should have gone to Bexar," he said. "You are too easily impressed."

One of Santa Anna's aides came over at that point. "General?" he interrupted.

"Yes, what is it?"

"There is an officer outside the tent who wishes an audience with you."

"An audience about what?"

"I don't know, Excellency," the messenger replied.

"Send him away," Santa Anna said with an impatient wave of his hand.

"He says he is a relative of yours, Excellency."

"What? Another relative?" Santa Anna looked at Juan and

sighed. "The bane of the powerful, Juan, is their relatives." He turned to his aide. "Very well, Lieutenant, show him in."

As he waited, Santa Anna held his wine goblet out to be filled, and the dark red wine had just been poured when the visitor came in. Santa Anna looked over at the visiting officer, then he smiled.

"Don Ricardo Lopez," Santa Anna said. "We meet again. Of course, you know Colonel Montoya?"

"*Si*, Excellency," Lopez said, bowing his head slightly toward Juan. "Juan, it is good to see you again."

"It is good to see you, Ricardo," Juan replied.

Santa Anna looked at Lopez's uniform. "I see you have managed to keep your commission."

"*Si*, though I have been demoted to captain, Your Excellency."

"A captain?" Santa Anna said. He shook his head and clucked sadly. "Surely you would have been a general by now, had it not been for your indiscretions. Where is the other fool who was caught up in all that? What was his name? Alvarez? The one you persuaded to take the responsibility for your indiscretion?"

"As I took the responsibility for yours, Excellency?"

Santa Anna laughed. "Ah, yes, I do recall that, now. It was I who dallied with the wife of the minister of the treasury, wasn't it? And you did accept the blame, I believe."

"In return for your sparing my father from execution," Lopez said.

"And I did so. You will be pleased to hear that your father is living happily in his own home, none the worse for his attempted rebellion."

"It wasn't a rebellion, General. He merely stood for election."

"Against my wishes," Santa Anna replied. "I consider that treason. Well, enough of that. Where is Alvarez?"

"Alvarez is dead."

"Dead? What a shame," Santa Anna said in a voice that expressed no feeling at all. "So, tell me, Ricardo, why have you come here?"

"I have come to bring news of the Norteamericanos at San Antonio de Bexar," Ricardo said.

"You have been there?" Santa Anna replied.

"No, General."

Santa Anna pointed to Juan. "This man has just returned from there. He advises me that we will lose as many as one thousand men if we attack. Do you agree with him?"

"Perhaps there will not be a battle," Lopez suggested.

"No battle? Of course there will be a battle. Why would you suggest otherwise?"

"Because Sam Houston has ordered Colonel Neill to abandon his position."

"Interesting," Santa Anna said. He looked at Juan. "Houston wants his men to abandon the Alamo and Colonel Montoya wants us to go right by, without doing battle. It would appear that there are men of weak hearts on both sides of the question."

"Whatever you may think of me, General, the officers and men of the Alamo are not weakhearted."

"Oh? And who are these officers?"

"There is Colonel Neill, of course. He is the *commandante*. And there is Colonel James Bowie. Of course you know him."

"Yes, I have heard of him."

"And Davy Crockett. He is one of the men who put on a demonstration of his marksmanship, and he was the best."

"Yes, I have heard of Crockett, too," Santa Anna said.

"And we must not forget Colonel William Travis."

"Travis? I have not heard of Travis. Did you learn anything about him while you were in Bexar?"

"*Si*, General," Juan replied. "In the cantina, I heard the men talking about him. He is a man with a checkered past. It is said that while he was in Alabama, his wife took a lover, and, in rage, Colonel Travis killed the lover and came to Texas."

"Then we know that he is a man of courage," Santa Anna said.

"*Si*. He is also one who believes that his destiny is great fame, or an early death."

"Good, because I intend to provide Colonel Travis with his destiny . . . that of an early death. We are not bypassing the Alamo," Santa Anna said. "And when news of my great victory over the defenders of the Alamo travels around Texas ... when the other so-called citizen soldiers hear what fate awaits those who dare to challenge my power and authority, the rebellion will end. Now, Colonel, you have been absent from your command far too long. I think you should return to your men."

"*Si,* General," Juan said, saluting.

Lopez watched Juan leave, then he turned to his cousin. "He is a good and conscientious officer," Lopez said.

"Though perhaps a bit overcautious," Santa Anna said. Suddenly Santa Anna smiled and rubbed his hands together. "Ricardo, have I ever thanked you for the service you performed for me?"

"*Si,* Excellency. You spared my father."

"I know that, but I was thinking of something a bit more tangible. I have an idea. For tonight, and tonight only, I shall give you a choice of any young lady in my entourage, after I have chosen for myself."

"*Gracias,*" Lopez said.

Santa Anna turned to one of the guards who stood nearby at such controlled attention that he looked like a statue.

"You," Santa Anna said to the soldier. "Have the women brought in."

The soldier left to do Santa Anna's bidding, and a moment later half-a-dozen giggling young women were ushered into the tent.

"I think I shall grant you the privilege of sharing the bed of your *presidente* tonight," Santa Anna said to one of the girls. She smiled proudly and stepped away from the rest of the girls to stand beside the general.

"And now, ladies," Santa Anna said, pointing to Lopez. "This is Don Ricardo Lopez. In repayment for a valuable service he once performed for me, I have given him the right to choose from among you, the woman he wishes for the night. If he chooses you, I command you to please him, or I shall have you returned to Mexico City tomorrow to serve in a brothel."

"Choose me, senor," one of the women said. "I will be happy to please you."

The girl who spoke was slender, and she moved with an easy grace. She had long, blue-black hair, and Lopez was suddenly reminded of the young woman he had kidnapped, the one he would have known except for the untimely arrival of the Texians. Her name was Marie, and the memory of her had haunted Lopez since the moment he left her.

This young woman was not quite as tall, and her eyes were not quite the same shade, but, with subtle lighting and some imagination she could become Marie in his mind.

"*Si*," Lopez said, pointing to her. "You will do nicely."

The girl lay beneath Lopez, raising her hips to meet his thrusts. Lopez looked down toward where their bodies joined and let his eyes travel up her nude body, across the flat stomach, rippled now with muscles. He looked at her breasts, and the tightly drawn nipples.

The girl's eyes were closed, and she was biting her lips in ecstasy. She jerked her head from side to side and her long, blue-black hair spread out around her head like a mane. Suddenly she opened her eyes and looked up at Lopez. That spoiled the illusion.

"No," Lopez said. "Close your eyes! Close them!"

The girl did as he ordered but asked, "Why must my eyes be closed?"

Her question further destroyed the illusion, for she spoke flawless Spanish, whereas Marie Doucette spoke English.

"Don't talk," Lopez ordered.

Lopez stared down at the girl who was thrashing beneath him. Her body had the same shape, and her hair was the same. When he squinted, he could almost put the right face there, but when she opened her eyes, that spoiled it for him.

The girl began moving with an urgency that told him she was approaching a climax, and Lopez closed his eyes and saw the picture he needed. The vision hit his body with a flood of eroticism, and he felt himself erupting into her.

The body belonged to one of the girls of Santa Anna's personal entourage. But in his mind, Lopez saw Marie Doucette. And it was good. Oh, it was so good!

Thursday, February 11, 1836, on the trail of El
Camino Real

They crossed the Brazos in midafternoon. The river lay
before them, bright and shining, flowing majestically. At this
point it was shallow enough to promise an easy crossing.

A small log building stood on the other side of the river.
Even from where she stood, Marie could see the crudely lettered sign that identified the cabin as the Brazos Crossing
Saloon. She could also see half-a-dozen horses tied up out
front. She started into the river, but Hunter called to her.

"Wait," he said.

"What is it?"

"Look at the saddles of those horses. See the silver *con-
chas?* Those are Mexican saddles."

"That doesn't necessarily mean anything, does it?"

"No," Hunter admitted. "There are lots of Mexicans who
don't want anything to do with the war, and there are even
more Mexican saddles. Still, it seems a little odd to see so
many of them together in the same place."

"Do you think there's something wrong?"

"I don't know. But, given what happened to the Thompson
family, we must be careful. I think you should stay here and
let me go in first. If everything is all right, I'll come out and
get you."

"No," Marie answered. "What if something goes
wrong?"

"If that happens, I'll have a better chance of defending
myself if I don't have you to worry about."

"But I—" Marie started.

"Don't argue, Marie," Hunter said preemptively. "Just
stay out here. Stay on this side of the river until you see me
wave. If anything goes wrong the river will slow them down
enough to give you a good start." He smiled reassuringly.
"And with Prince, and the way you ride, that's all you'll
need."

"All right," Marie agreed. "But please, be careful."

"I will be," Hunter promised.

Marie patted Prince's neck while Hunter forded the shallow river. She watched him dismount and walk into the saloon. She held her breath for a long moment, then let out a sigh of relief when he reappeared and waved her over.

Marie squeezed her heels against Prince's side, and the stallion cantered into the water, sending sheets of silver spray flying to either side. She tethered her horse in front of the saloon and went inside. The inside of the building was so dark that it was difficult to see at first, so she stood there for just a moment, to let her eyes adjust to the dim light. Finally she saw Hunter sitting at a table near the back of the room, and she went over to sit with him. Almost immediately, the saloon owner put glasses of whiskey in front of them.

"I can't drink whiskey," Marie protested.

"Just pretend to drink it," Hunter suggested. "I'll switch glasses with you in a moment."

"All right," Marie said. She held the glass up to her lips. Even though she didn't open her mouth, she could feel the fire of the pungent liquid on her lips.

Someone walked up to the bar and showed the saloon keeper something. They discussed it quietly for a moment, then the saloon keeper, in an agitated voice, said loudly: "I'm not in the jewelry business, Dockins. If you want another bottle you're going to have to pay for it just like everyone else. Dollars or pesos, it don't matter to me, but it's got to be one or the other."

"But this here locket belonged to my mother," the man called Dockins replied. "Seems to me like you'd give me somethin' for it for sentiment."

"Not interested," the saloon keeper said.

Dockins turned away from the bar and looked out over the saloon. He held out a small gold chain from which dangled a heart-shaped locket.

"How 'bout any of you fellas in here?" he addressed the saloon patrons. "Anyone here want to buy a locket that belonged to my mother?"

Beneath the table, Marie put her hand on Hunter's leg and squeezed it tightly.

"What is it?" Hunter asked under his breath.

"That locket," she said.

"You mean you want me to buy it?"

"No!" Marie hissed. "Hunter, I think I saw that same locket on the little Thompson girl!"

"Well, let's just have a closer look," Hunter suggested. "Mister," he called to Dockins. "You want to bring that locket over here?"

"Sure thing, pard," Dockins replied. "I'll sell it to you for five dollars." He handed the locket to Hunter, who showed it to Marie.

"That's it," she said. "That's the same locket I saw on the little Thompson girl."

The smile left Dockins's face. "They know we kilt the Thompsons, boys!" he shouted. "Kill 'em both!"

Dockins reached for his gun, but Hunter's pistol roared before Dockins could draw. A hole appeared in Dockins's chest as the ball from Hunter's gun smashed into him. His shirt flooded red, and he coughed as he fell.

Two men who were standing at the far end of the bar turned toward Marie and Hunter and fired their pistols. One of the balls came so close to Marie that she could feel it whizz past. The other one missed by a somewhat wider mark, and, like the first, crashed into the wall behind her.

The pistols had to be muzzle-loaded, and neither Hunter nor the two ruffians at the bar had time to reload for a second shot.

"You take the little one," one of the men shouted, pulling his knife as he started toward them. "I'll gut the big son of a bitch!"

Marie looked at them in horror as they started toward her. Both were holding wicked-looking knives, and she knew that, in a second, she and Hunter would be ripped to pieces.

"Marie, the pistol!" Hunter shouted, pointing to the weapon which had been dropped, unfired, by Dockins.

Marie seized the pistol and handed it to Hunter. He aimed at the nearest attacker and shot him as he lunged for Marie. A hole appeared in the man's forehead and he tumbled over backward. A second shot rang out at almost the same moment, and the face of the second man, who had raised his knife against Hunter, suddenly assumed an expression of surprise. Then, slowly, he tumbled forward, dropping his knife with a clatter. A gaping wound yawned in his back.

Marie looked toward the bar and saw the saloon keeper holding the smoking rifle that had saved Hunter's life.

"Thanks," Hunter called over to him.

"No thanks needed," the saloon keeper answered. "The way I see it, all us Texians got to stick together till this here war is over. And we cain't hardly do that till bad apples like these fellas has all been weeded out."

Fifteen

FRIDAY, FEBRUARY 12, 1836, THE ALAMO

There was a ladder just outside the door of Sam McCord's room that led to the roof of the officers' quarters. Climbing the ladder, Sam walked across the roof, then leaned against the wall and looked over toward San Antonio. Although the sun was not yet visible, the horizon behind him was streaked with bands of pink and pearl gray, while the horizon before him was still dark. He could see squares of golden light, cast through the windows of the houses where early risers were already beginning to sit down to breakfast. The entire town was covered by a wisp of woodsmoke from the dozens of fireplaces which burned to push away the predawn chill.

Sam pulled his own coat more tightly around him and thought of the conversation he had had with Colonel Neill on the day before. Colonel Neill was leaving the garrison due to illness in his family, and he had asked Sam to help him pack. During the packing, Colonel Neill surprised Sam, by asking if he would like to go to Washington-on-the-Brazos as a special representative of the men of the Alamo.

"You won't have any official position," Neill explained. "The army has already elected two representatives at large to vote in the convention."

"Then what would be the purpose of my going?" Sam asked.

"You could carry a message for us," Colonel Neill explained. "I don't think anyone in Texas really understands what is going on here. We are in the perfect position to stop Santa Anna right in his tracks, but we are going to have to have some support.''

"Colonel, surely there are men who are more articulate than I,'' Sam replied. "At the very least, you should get someone who is a Texian. I am only a few months removed from Louisiana.''

"But you have fought for Texas, Sam. And that makes you more of a Texian than someone who has not, even though they may have lived here for many years,'' Neill replied. "And there is another thing.''

"What is that, sir?''

Neill interrupted the conversation for a moment, then walked over to the door of his quarters. He stuck his head outside and looked both ways before returning.

"I didn't really want to bring this up,'' Neill continued. "But you are an intelligent man. I'm sure you have figured it out for yourself. You must know that if you stay here, you are going to die.''

"Maybe not.''

"Sam, don't harbor any false hopes,'' Neill said. "We are outnumbered forty to one. Oh, I am certain that we will make the Mexicans pay dearly for their victory, but victory they will have, and it will be total. It is my belief that not one defender will be spared.''

Sam nodded, then sighed. "That is my belief as well,'' he admitted.

"Then my God, man, if you know that, why are you hesitating to take the opportunity I have offered you? By leaving now, on a legitimate military mission, you will be able to save yourself . . . with honor. The choice is yours.''

"Yes, sir,'' Sam said. "The choice is mine.''

When he finished his packing, Colonel Neill fastened the buckles to the straps that held his bag closed. "Has my horse been saddled?''

"Yes, sir, it's right outside,'' Sam answered.

"Then I'll be going. I've left orders with Colonel Travis that authorize your transfer to Washington-on-the-Brazos. I am leaving him in command of the garrison. But you'll have to make up your mind quickly, Sam, for the orders are only good for twenty-four hours. After that, it will be Travis's decision as to whether you leave or stay."

"I understand, sir," Sam said, as he walked out to Neill's horse with him.

"Oh, and there is one other thing you may wish to consider," Neill said.

"What is that, sir?"

"Bowie told me that you left someone back in Louisiana. A young woman that you were expected to marry."

"That was none of Bowie's business," Sam said. "And with all due respect, sir, it is none of yours either."

Neill held up his hand. "I realize that, Sam," he said easily. "I only bring it up to say that, if you have any lingering doubts as to whether or not you did the right thing, this may give you an opportunity to set things right." Neill mounted his horse.

"Garrison, attention!" Colonel Travis called, when he saw Neill mounted. The soldiers who had been drawn up into formation, came smartly to attention.

"Present arms!" Travis shouted. Travis rendered the hand salute while, behind him, two rows of soldiers brought their rifles up to the present arms position.

Neill returned the salute, then slapped his heels against the side of his horse. "Good luck to you, men!" he shouted as his horse started, at a trot, toward the gate. "I shall return as quickly as I can to share your fate!"

That had all taken place yesterday afternoon, and last night Colonel Travis reminded Sam of the standing orders and asked if he intended to leave today. Sam promised the new young commander that he would make his decision before breakfast.

The smell of brewing coffee and baking biscuits told him that, like the town before him, the garrison was preparing breakfast for the new day. Sam would have to make his decision soon.

"Johnny! Johnny, get some firewood, would you?" Sam heard one of the young enlisted men shout.

"All right."

Turning away from the wall, Sam walked back across the

roof to look down inside of the Alamo. As there was no central mess hall, the men were responsible for cooking their own meals and they generally did this by forming small mess-groups of from three to five men.

Sam looked down at the garrison soldiers as they went about their morning duties, some tending fires, others cooking meals, still others feeding the livestock. Sam knew that every soldier here had served several weeks without so much as one dollar being paid to them. What made them stay? They knew as well as anyone that the chances were very good that they would all be killed. And yet, without money, with practically no provisions, and with the sure and certain knowledge that they were going to die, they stayed.

"Private Lindley," Sam called down to the soldier named Johnny.

"Yes, sir?" Lindley replied, looking up toward the roof.

"Where are you from?"

"Sangamon County, Illinois, sir," Lindley replied.

"Pretty country back there?"

"Yes, sir. It's beautiful."

"Why are you here?"

"I beg your pardon, sir?"

"Why are you here, in the Alamo?"

"Why, I'm here to stop Santa Anna," Lindley answered. The expression on his face showed that he was puzzled as to why Sam would even ask such a question.

"Yes, that is why we are all here," Sam said. "But what I want to know is why are you, John Lindley from Sangamon County, Illinois, here?"

"Cap'n, I don't know as I could rightly put an answer to that question," Lindley replied. "But when you get right down to it, I reckon it's because I figure that anyone who was to run now would be a coward. And I don't want to be no coward."

Sam smiled. "Good enough answer, Lindley. Carry on."

"Yes, sir," Lindley replied, continuing his quest for the firewood.

Sam climbed down the ladder and went into his room to get paper, ink, and a quill. He had made his decision, but before he told Travis, he wanted to share it . . . and his reasons for making it . . . with his mother and father, back in Louisiana.

Dear Mother and Father,

As this is the first time I have written you since my untimely departure from Louisiana, this letter must come as a shock to you. I am certain that there are many back home who have branded me a fool for leaving, especially as my engagement to Marie Doucette was all but announced. Perhaps even you are wondering why I left as I did.

Let me say quickly, that it was through no fault of Miss Doucette's. She is a wonderful girl and has never given me the slightest cause to doubt her devotion or fidelity. There was a compelling reason for my absenting myself but I have taken an oath not to divulge that reason. In the meantime, if there is to be scandalous talk, let such talk be about me, and not about Miss Doucette, who is wholly innocent in this unhappy state of affairs.

If you have not heard from other sources by now, I will inform you that I am a member of the Army of Texas, my rank being that of captain. I am with Colonel Travis's garrison at San Antonio de Bexar, which is a town in the western part of Texas. Here, we have fortified an old mission, called the Alamo, and here we shall make our stand.

You may wonder why I, from Louisiana, would throw my lot in with the Texians. But you may well ask that of all the others who are here as well, for nearly all are from some place other than Texas. However, we have a determination to see Texas free and independent from Mexico. Besides, we all now consider ourselves "Texians."

There is a powerful force of Mexicans arrayed against us. Some say there are as many as four thousand or more camped at the Rio Grande. They are said to be preparing ferryboats to cross the river and march against us, but we know not when they may come. I do know that we are badly prepared to receive them.

I am afraid that a great number of our volunteers will leave tomorrow as the end of their second month is up and there have been no clothes, provisions, or pay furnished them. It seems to me poor thanks for the patriotic men who have stood by their country in its hour of trial. They are owed $7 each, for four months.

We are now one hundred and fifty strong. Jim Bowie is here. I know you remember him, Father, but as I recall, you did not much care for him. However, he is a hero in Texas and has the rank of colonel. He is ill now, with some sort of coughing and fever, but he has been appointed to the command of the volunteer forces, while Colonel William Travis is in command of the regular army troops who are in garrison here.

Until now, Colonel Neill was our commander, but he left for home, yesterday, due to an illness in his family. There was much regret at his departure by all of the men, though he promised to be with us in twenty days at the most.

Before he left, Colonel Neill offered me the opportunity to go to Washington-on-the-Brazos where a convention is being held to decide the fate of Texas. I would have no vote in the process, but would merely carry the request that our little garrison be reinforced, a request that has, so far, gone unsatisfied. I had until noon today to give my answer and, only this morning, did I decide that I will not go, but will instead, stay here with my friends and comrades in arms to meet Santa Anna.

And now, Father and Mother, I must tell you that if I stay here, I will, most assuredly, be killed. Do not weep for me, for this is my decision, willingly made. Please understand, it is not that I welcome death, but I, and all others who wait with me to share this fate, do strongly believe that an honorable death is to be preferred over a dishonorable life.

Your loving son,
Sam McCord

Finishing his letter, Sam blew on the ink to dry it, then he began folding the paper to prepare it for the day's courier. There was a knock on his door.

"Yes, Courier, I have a letter for you," he called over his shoulder.

"It's not the courier, Captain McCord. It is I, Colonel Travis."

Quickly, Sam stood. "Come in, Colonel, come in," he called.

Travis stepped into Sam's room, then looked around. Like most of the other unmarried officers of the garrison, Sam had a cot, a chair, and a desk.

"I know I gave you until noon," Travis said. "But if you have made your decision, I would like to know it now."

Sam held up the letter. "I have made my decision," he said.

Travis nodded. "Then God go with you. Plead our cause well," he said.

Sam shook his head. "I am staying, Colonel," he said. "I am sending this letter out, today, by courier, informing my parents of my decision."

For just a moment, Travis's eyes grew so deep as to be windows to his soul. He blinked once or twice, and Sam could almost believe that they were covered with a sheen of tears.

"Colonel?" Sam asked.

Travis cleared his throat. "May the Lord bless you, Captain, for your courageous decision," he said.

" 'Tis no more courageous than any other who is staying here," Sam reminded him.

"Oh, but it is, Captain," Travis insisted. "I am afraid that it is only the fear of being branded a coward that keeps many here. You, on the other hand, could leave without having that stigma, for you were given an honorable way out. Despite that opportunity, you have chosen to stay. That is a courageous decision."

"Well, perhaps it will all work out," Sam said. "Reinforcements may yet arrive."

"Yes, that is my hope as well," Travis said. "In fact I hope, by a series of letters, to inform the rest of Texas about our plight. In that light, I wonder if you would tell me what you think of this letter?''

Sam took the letter Travis handed him. It was written in a bold, very legible, hand.

> To His Excellency, General Sam'l Houston:
>
> You have no doubt already received information, by express from La Bahia, that tremendous preparations are in the making on the Rio Grande and elsewhere in the interior for the invasion of Texas. Santa Anna by the last accounts was at Saltillo, with a force of two thousand five hundred men and guns. Sesma was at the Rio Grande with about two thousand men, and he has issued his proclamation denouncing vengeance against the people of Texas, threatening to exterminate every white man within its limits.
>
> As this is the frontier post nearest the Rio Grande we will, no doubt, be the first to be attacked. We are illy prepared for their reception as we have not more than one hundred and fifty men here and they are in a very disorganized state. Yet we are determined to sustain the garrison for as long as there is a man left; because we consider death preferable to disgrace, which would be the result of giving up a post which has been so dearly won, and thus opening up the door for the invaders to enter the sacred territory of the colonies.
>
> We hope our countrymen will open their eyes to the present danger, and wake up from their false security. I hope that all party dissensions will subside, that our fellow citizens will unite in the common cause and fly to the defense of the frontier.
>
> I fear that it is useless to waste arguments upon them. It will take the thunder of the enemy's cannon, the pollution of their wives and daughters, the cries of their famished children and the smoke of their burning dwellings to arouse them. I regret that the government has so long neglected a draft of the militia, which is the only measure that will ever again bring the citizens of Texas to the frontiers.

Money, clothing, and provisions are greatly needed at this post for the use of the soldiers.

I hope Your Excellency will send us a portion of the money which has been received from the U.S. as it cannot be better applied, indeed we cannot get along any longer without money, and with it we can do everything.

For God's sake, and the sake of our country, send us reinforcements. I hope you will send to this post at least two companies of regular troops.

In consequence of the sickness of his family, Lt. Col. Neill has left this post to visit home for a short time and has requested me to take the command of the post. In consequence of which, I feel myself delicately and awkwardly situated. I therefore hope that Your Excellency will give me some definite orders, and that immediately.

The troops here, to a man, recognize you as their legitimate governor, and they expect your fatherly care and protection.

In conclusion let me assure Your Excellency, that with two hundred more men I believe this place can be maintained, and I hope they will be sent us as soon as possible. Yet should we receive no reinforcements, I am determined to defend it to the last, and should Bexar fall, your friend will be buried beneath its ruins.

> Sincerely,
> William B. Travis
> Commanding
> San Antonio de Bexar

Sam looked up at the intense young commander after he finished the letter.

"Colonel Travis, I think it is a very moving letter," he said. "If it doesn't get us some action soon, then nothing will."

"Thank you for your kind words," Travis said.

Sam cleared his throat.

"What is it?"

"Jim Bowie," Sam said.

"I haven't seen him today," Travis said. "I don't know if he is in bed with his fever . . . or in town with his drink."

"I know what you mean, sir, but Bowie *is* commander of the volunteers, and, as there are more volunteers than regulars, I am wondering if there will be a problem?"

Travis ran his hand through his hair. "If Colonel Bowie could stay sober long enough to discuss it, perhaps we can work something out," he replied. "But, now that you bring him up, are you aware of what he did this morning?"

Sam shook his head. "No, sir," he replied.

"He marched into town with a troop of armed men, each one of them as drunk as he, to confront Colonel Seguin. There, he demanded the release of Antonio Fuentes. Fuentes, mind you!" Travis said angrily. "I, myself, sat on the tribunal which found Antonio Fuentes guilty of theft, disorderly conduct, and attempted mutiny."

"What was Bowie's reason for releasing the prisoner?" Sam asked.

"He didn't release just one prisoner. He released at least half-a-dozen prisoners," Travis insisted. "It is his intention to use them as labor crews."

Given their current situation, Sam thought it might be a good idea to use the prisoners on labor crews, but he said nothing about it, for he had no wish to further upset his commander.

"Bowie has been elected as commandant of the volunteers, thus his rank and authority are equal to my own," Travis said. "But, barring specific orders to the contrary, I am commandant of the post, and thus, consider my position is supreme."

"Yes, sir. You'll get no argument from me," Sam said.

The next morning, Travis came to Sam with another letter.

"I have been thinking about what you said about Jim Bowie," Travis said.

"With regard to what, sir?" Sam replied.

"With regard to the delicacies of our relative positions," Travis said. "Therefore, I have written another letter, and I would value your opinion of it. Would you care to read it?"

"Yes, sir, I would be glad to," Sam said, taking the letter from Travis.

His Excellency, General Sam'l Houston:

I wrote you an official letter last night as commandant of this post in the absence of Col. Neill, and if you had taken the trouble to answer my letter from Burnam's I should not now have been under the necessity of troubling you.

My situation is truly awkward and delicate. Col. Neill left me in the command, but wishing to give satisfaction to the volunteers and not wishing to assume any command over them I issued an order for the election of an officer to command them with the exception of one company of volunteers that had previously engaged to serve under me.

Bowie was elected by two small companies, and since his election he has been roaring drunk all the time; has assumed all command, and is proceeding in a most disorderly and irregular manner, interfering with private property, releasing prisoners sentenced by court-martial and by the civil court and turning everything topsy-turvy. If I did not feel my honor and that of my country compromised I would leave here instantly for some other point with the troops under my immediate command, as I am unwilling to be responsible for the drunken irregularities of any man.

I hope you will immediately order some regular troops to this place, as it is more important to occupy this post than I imagined when I last saw you. It is the key of Texas from the interior. Without a footing here the enemy can do nothing against us in the colonies now that our coast is being guarded by armed vessels. I do not solicit the command of this post but Col. Neill has applied to the commander in chief to be relieved and is anxious for me to take the command. I will do it, if it be your order, for a time until an artillery officer can be sent here. The citizens here have every confidence in me, as they can communicate with me, and they have shown every disposition to aid me with all they have. We need money. Can you not send us some? I read your letter to the troops and they received it with acclamation. Our spies have just returned from the Rio Grande. The enemy is there one thousand strong and is making every preparation to invade us. By the 15th of March I think Texas will be invaded and every preparation should be made to receive them.

In conclusion, allow me to beg that you will give me definite orders immediately.

> William B. Travis
> Commanding
> San Antonio de Bexar

"Like the other one, sir, this is a very good letter," Sam said, handing it back to Travis.

"I wonder," Travis said.

"You wonder what?"

"Am I writing these letters for Sam Houston? Or am I writing them for posterity?"

"Either way, Will, it is good that we have someone who can tell the rest of the world what is going on here."

"Do you have any children, Sam?"

"No."

"I don't either," Travis replied. He held up the letter. "This may be the only bridge to the future you and I will ever have."

"Colonel Travis, may I see you for a moment, sir?" Lieutenant Dickerson called.

"Yes, Almeron, of course," Travis said. Before he left he smiled at Sam, then put his hand on Sam's shoulder. "On the other hand, Sam, if Fannin arrives with his troops, we could have a glorious victory. In that case, we may well meet as old men at some event in the distant future and recall these times with the fondness old men have for such memories," he said.

"I'm sure we will, Colonel," Sam replied. He watched the young commander walk off with Lieutenant Dickerson, busily engaged in conversation about the placement of some cannon. He saw one of Bowie's men passing by.

"Clark?"

"Yes, sir?"

"Where is Bowie?"

"Last time I seen 'im, he was goin' into town to the cantina," Clark said.

"Thanks."

Sam saddled a horse, then rode into town. There was no clearer evidence of the difference in the command philosophies of Bowie and Travis than what Sam was seeing here. Back inside the Alamo, the regular soldiers were working hard to shore up the defenses. Those who weren't working were drilling, or standing guard. Here, many of the volunteers were dallying with the women of the town, while half-a-dozen others were in front of the cantina, some of them passed-out drunk.

Sam tied off his horse, then pushed through the clacking beaded entryway. Bowie was sitting at his normal table in the back of the room. Sam was glad to see that he was eating, which meant that he probably was not yet drunk.

"Sam, my friend." From underneath the table, Bowie's foot found a chair and pushed it out for Sam. "Have a seat. Join me."

"Thank you," Sam said.

"Want something to eat?"

"I've eaten, thank you."

"Well then, stick around until after I've finished, and we'll have a drink together. Hell, we'll have several drinks together."

"Colonel Bowie, before you . . . uh . . . do that . . ."

"Before I get drunk, you mean? Hell, say it, man. I don't deny it," Bowie said.

"No, sir. I was going to say before you have another bout with your fever."

"All right. What is it about?" Bowie was eating chicken and he took a bite from a drumstick.

"It's about Travis."

"Travis is a popinjay. A self-inflated bantam rooster," Bowie said derisively.

"He is the commanding officer of the post."

"Of the regulars," Bowie said quickly. "I'm commanding the volunteers."

"I know. That's the problem."

"What's the problem?" Bowie asked sharply.

"Colonel Bowie, think about it. There are two groups of men here, and, as you pointed out, two commanders. But there is only one post, and we have only one mission. We are here to stop Santa Anna."

Bowie laughed. "Stop him? We may slow him down some, but we won't stop him. He'll cut through us like a hot knife in butter."

"Then, in that case, don't you think some sort of arrangement could be worked out between you and Travis? Something that would satisfy you both and, at the same time, give the men some stability."

Bowie lay the cleaned drumstick bone down, then picked up a napkin and wiped his hands and face. "You're serious about this, aren't you?"

"I'm very serious," Sam said. "If I'm going to stay here and get killed . . . and I believe that is a very good possibility . . . then I at least want the opportunity to do as much damage to the Mexicans as I can. And the more the two of you fight, the less damage we are going to inflict upon the enemy."

Bowie sighed. "Yes, well, I have to hand it to the runty little son of a bitch. He does keep those men of his working. Hell, I can't even keep my men sober."

Sam wanted to say that he might have better luck keeping his men sober if he, himself, would stay sober. But he said nothing.

"Yes, sir, and when the time comes and we have a wall to stand behind, and a parapet to shoot from, I expect there are going to be several of us glad that he kept his men busy."

"All right, I'll go see him," Bowie said.

"When?" Sam asked.

Bowie laughed. "Right away," he promised. "Before I get drunk."

Sam smiled easily. "Thanks," he said.

Proof that Sam's talk with Bowie bore fruit came the next day, when, once again, Travis brought a letter for him to read.

His Excellency, General Sam'l Houston:

By an understanding of today, Col. J. Bowie has the command of all the volunteers of the garrison, and Colonel W. B. Travis of the regulars and volunteer cavalry.

All general orders and correspondence will henceforth be signed by both until Col. Neill's return.

William B. Travis
James Bowie
Commanding
San Antonio de Bexar

"It's the best I can do under a most difficult situation," Travis said, when Sam finished reading the letter.

"It will work, Colonel Travis. You can make it work," Sam said.

"I can make it work, because I must make it work," Travis agreed. "And I thank you for using your good offices with Bowie to bring about the compromise."

"The compromise was yours, Colonel. Yours and Jim Bowie's. All I did was to get him to come talk to you," Sam said. "Both of you are responsible men. I was certain that if you got together, you would put your differences aside long enough to work something out for the good of us all."

"Yes, well, I think what Colonel Bowie finally came to realize is that I have no particular ambition to command this place. In fact, I have repeatedly asked that General Houston send an artillery officer in my place, for this is, rightly, an artillery bastion. However, we are often placed upon a road that is not of our own choosing and when that occurs, we can do nothing but make the best of it. And that is what I shall do as long as I am here."

"And I've no doubt, Colonel, but that your best will, in turn, elicit the best from all who serve under you," Sam insisted.

Travis reached out and put his hand on Sam's shoulder. "That is my belief as well," he said. For a moment, he got a faraway look in his eyes. "That Texas is to lose such magnificent men in the time when she will need them most, is my biggest regret."

"Yes, sir," Sam replied. Travis's words were too close to a truth that, by tacit agreement, most of the defenders avoided, therefore no further response was necessary.

Travis cleared his throat. "Yes, well, let's get on about our business, shall we? Have you given any more thought to the patrols I asked you to lead?"

"Yes, sir," Sam said. "If you'll step over here and have a look at the map, I'll show you."

The two men moved over to the small table beside Sam's bed. A map was spread out on the table. Sam pointed to the map.

"We know from our previous scouts that Santa Anna's army is camped upon the Rio Grande, but we don't know who or what is around us on our other three sides. Over the next several days, I plan to reconnoiter this entire area. If Fannin is going to join us, the route between here and Goliad must be clear."

"I agree," Travis said. "You may proceed according to your plan, Captain."

Sixteen

FRIDAY, FEBRUARY 12, 1836, ON THE TRAIL OF EL CAMINO REAL

Marie held their horses while Hunter stood at the top of a hill, peering through a spyglass at the valley before them. After several long moments, he came back down from the crest, collapsing the glass and putting it back into his saddlebags.

"They look like Mexican soldiers," he said. "Not the main army, but more than we want to contend with."

"Can we get through?" Marie asked anxiously.

"I wouldn't want to take the risk of trying to get through them," Hunter said. "I think we would be better off to go around."

"Whatever you say, Hunter," Marie agreed without question.

For a day and a half, Hunter and Marie rode hard, always keeping a line of hills or trees or rocks between them and the Mexican soldiers who were in the area. Then, late in the afternoon of the third day, they reached the town of San Antonio de Bexar. They were immediately besieged with questions by people from the town, as well as from the fort.

"Is there fighting anywhere else?"

"Do the others know we intend to make a stand here?"

"Have you seen any Mexican soldiers?"

"Do you know where Santa Anna is?"

Hunter answered all of the questions. He knew he wasn't telling them anything they didn't already know, but was merely satisfying their eagerness to talk to someone from outside.

"We didn't see Santa Anna's main army, but from the number of smaller units we observed, I've no doubt that he is on his way," Hunter said.

"Let 'im come," someone said. "We're ready for him."

"What brings you folks here, anyway?"

"We're looking for—" Hunter started, but before he could finish, Marie interrupted.

"Hunter, wait," she called.

Hunter looked back toward her.

"What's wrong?" he asked.

"I . . . I want to think about this," Marie said. "In the meantime, let us see if there are any rooms available, A place where we can stay."

"You might try the Dickersons," someone answered before Hunter could even ask the question.

"Dickerson? Would that be Almeron Dickerson?" Hunter asked.

"One and the same. Do you know him?"

"Yes, he's a good man. I met him in Gonzales. Where is his house?"

"They are renting the Musquiz house, on the southwest corner of Potrero Street and the Main Plaza."

Hunter shook his head.

"Here, let me show you," the informant said. He motioned for Hunter to join him in the plaza, then he pointed. "Do you see that house down there that juts out onto the corner? The one with the green flower box?''

"Yes."

"That's it. I'm sure you and your missus could stay with them."

"This isn't my wife," Hunter replied. "But maybe she can stay there, and I'll find someplace else."

"It shouldn't be hard for you to find a place. Especially if you join the volunteers. They'll have plenty of room for you out at the old mission."

"Thank you," Hunter replied. Touching his hat to bid the helpful citizen good-bye, Hunter and Marie began riding in the direction of the Dickerson house.

"Marie, I don't understand," Hunter said, when they were out of earshot of the others. "I was about to ask that man where Sam was, and you stopped me."

"I know."

"Why?"

"I . . . I'm scared, Hunter."

"Of what?"

"Of what Sam might do when he learns that I am here. Or rather, of what he might not do."

"But you came all this way just to find him."

"I know I did." Marie sighed. "I'm afraid I have made a big mistake."

Hunter reached over and put his hand on hers. "It's too late to think about that now, isn't it?" he asked. "You're here, Sam McCord is here, and there is a baby on the way. Seems to me like that baby is the only important thing now. I don't think either one of you have any choice."

"I suppose you are right. Still . . ."

"Marie, would you like me to find Sam for you?"

"Oh, would you, please?"

"And do you want me to talk to him as well?"

"Talk to him?"

"Tell him why you are here."

"Oh, no, I . . . I couldn't ask you to do that," Marie said. "That's something I am going to have to do myself."

"We'll see what happens," Hunter said. When they reached the Dickerson house Hunter swung down from his horse, then walked across the little dirt patio to knock on the door. An attractive, young blond woman came to meet them.

"Hello, Mrs. Dickerson."

The woman studied Hunter for a moment, then broke into a broad smile. "Why, land a-Goshen, I know you," she said. "You are Hunter Grant. A few months ago, you came to Gonzales to buy cotton."

"Yes, I did. You have a good memory, Mrs. Dickerson."

"Well, come in, come in, the both of you." She looked up at Marie. "And you must be the Lucinda I heard so much about. I'm Susanna Dickerson."

"I'm pleased to meet you, Mrs. Dickerson."

"Please, call me Susanna," the woman replied. "If we are going to be friends, we should use first names, don't you think?"

"Yes, I think that would be a good idea. And you can call me Marie."

"Marie?" Susanna looked surprised, then she cut a quick glance toward Hunter.

"I'm sorry, Mrs. Dickerson, but you assumed who she was before I could tell you. This isn't Lucinda Meechum."

"Oh, my," Susanna said. "Now that I think about it, I do recall hearing something about the engagement between you and Miss Meechum being broken off." Susanna looked at Marie. "That was so rude of me. Please forgive me."

"There is nothing to forgive," Marie replied. "It was a perfectly honest mistake. I am Marie Doucette."

"Doucette?" Now Susanna's surprise grew even more pronounced. "Would you be Sam McCord's Marie Doucette?"

"Yes!" Marie answered happily. "Yes! Then Sam *is* here?"

"He's here. He has quarters inside the Alamo," Susanna replied.

"Since you know of me, he must have spoken about me."

"Oh, indeed he has," Susanna replied. "I think he is going to be very surprised, and very happy, to see you."

"Yes, I am sure he will be one," Marie said. "The question is, will he be the other?"

"Whatever do you mean, dear?"

"Nothing," Marie replied. "It's just that he's not expecting me, is all."

"Then the surprise will be all the sweeter," Susanna insisted.

"Mrs. Dickerson, I was told that you might have an extra room Miss Doucette could rent," Hunter said.

"I have an extra room, that is true," Susanna answered. "But it isn't for rent."

"I see. Then do you have any suggestions as to where Miss Doucette might stay?"

"Wash out your ears, Hunter Grant," Susanna replied. "I said it wasn't for rent . . . I didn't say she couldn't live here. Marie is welcome to stay with Almeron and me for as long as she likes. I'll not be charging her for it."

"That is very kind of you," Marie said.

"You must be exhausted, poor thing. Why don't you take a rest? I'll have supper on before long."

"And wait until you try her fried peach pies," Hunter said. "My mouth starts watering again, just thinking about it."

Susanna smiled at the flattery. "That's right," she said. "I do seem to recall sending a few of the pies back with you."

"Well," Hunter said. "I suppose I should go out to the mission and see if I can find accommodations for myself. But, I leave you in good hands."

"Hunter, if you see Mr. McCord . . ." Marie started, then she stopped.

"Yes?"

"Perhaps you could tell him about, uh . . ."

"Don't worry about it, Marie. I'll take care of everything," Hunter promised.

"Thank you," Marie said gratefully. "I guess I'm not quite as brave as I thought I was."

Hunter looked at Marie and, for a long moment, their eyes held each other, silently. Susanna listened to the exchange and saw the way they looked at one another. Then she withdrew with the excuse that she would have to "see to supper."

"Mr. Grant seems to be a very nice man," Susanna said a moment later, when Marie came into the kitchen with an offer of help. "I recall that I liked him when I met him in Gonzales."

"Yes," Marie said. "He is a very good man."

"But then of course, so is your Sam," Susanna was quick

to add. "Almeron says Captain McCord is one of the hardest working officers in the entire garrison, and all the men like him."

"I'm glad. Shall I set the table?"

"Yes, if you'd like. You can use those bowls over there," Susanna said, looking up from the pot of stew that she was stirring. "Sam McCord is your man, isn't he?"

"I beg your pardon?"

"I don't want to make another mistake as I did when you and Mr. Grant arrived and I called you Lucinda."

"Oh. Yes, Mr. McCord is my man."

"You can see how I might be confused," Susanna said. "I mean, what with your arriving with Mr. Grant and all. And, I must say, for someone who is about to see her man for the first time in what has to be a few months, you seem unusually pensive."

"Yes, I suppose so," Marie said.

"If you don't want to talk about it now, I won't bother you with any more of my questions."

"Thank you. It's not that I want to be rude or anything . . . it's just that I'm not sure I have the answers."

"I understand, dear," Susanna said. "Believe me, life can be pretty confusing sometimes."

When Marie finished setting the table she put the back of her hand against her forehead, brushing away a fall of blue-black hair. "Susanna, if you don't mind, I think I will take you up on your offer to rest a little."

"Of course I don't mind. You just go back into that room and lie down. I'll call you in plenty of time for supper."

"You are very kind," Marie said.

Marie went into the back of the house and lay on the bed. Her eyes fell upon a crucifix on the wall opposite, and she crossed herself and said a little prayer: "Dear God, what am I going to do? I am carrying Sam McCord's baby, but I know now, that I am in love with Hunter Grant."

INSIDE THE ALAMO

"Lieutenant Dickerson speaks very highly of you, Mr. Grant, so I would be most pleased to have you join us,"

Colonel Travis said. "If you can stay sober, that is. Quite frankly, I have been given the intelligence that you are a drunk, and I have enough drunks to contend with now, thank you."

"I *was* a drunk," Hunter admitted freely. "But I am no longer."

"Raise your right hand, and I'll swear you in."

"I have already taken an oath of allegiance to Texas, when Stephen Austin appointed me a captain of volunteers."

"A captain?" Travis replied.

"Yes."

"Just what we need, another captain, with no troops to command."

"Colonel Travis, it is not necessary that I retain the rank of captain. It was only a temporary appointment," Hunter said. "In fact, just long enough to bring you instructions from Austin."

"And what are those instructions, Mr. Grant? That I abandon the Alamo?"

Hunter blinked in surprise. "You already know?"

"I know that Houston, and Austin, and all of the rest of our leaders who have no idea what is going on here want it abandoned." Travis made a fist with his right hand, and pounded it into the palm of his left to emphasize his point. "But here we stay, and here we stand!" he said. "This is the gate to all of Texas. If we could stop, or cripple Santa Anna here, we would have our victory."

"I see," Hunter said.

Sighing, Travis turned away and started to pick up some papers. "Under the circumstances, therefore, you are free to go . . . Captain."

Hunter shook his head. "No," he said. "I've come this far, I've delivered the message, what you do with the message is up to you. But if you are going to stay, I reckon I'll stay with you."

Travis smiled. "Good for you, Captain," he said. "But as a captain? I'm afraid we have no position for a captain."

"Then I'll stay as a private."

"Excuse me, Colonel," Almeron pointed out. "But it

might be good to have another officer who isn't a part of Bowie's volunteers.''

"Yes," Travis said, stroking his chin. "Yes, Almeron, you may be right at that. All right, I will make you an officer. I'll appoint you to the most junior officer position, that of cornet. Are you willing to serve in that capacity?"

"Yes, of course."

"Then, welcome to Bexar, Mr. Grant. Almeron, find quarters for him."

"Yes, sir," Lieutenant Dickerson replied. "Come with me, Mr. Grant, if you please."

Hunter followed Almeron across the open area to a low-lying building along the west wall.

"You'll be billeted here, in the room right next to Captain McCord," Almeron said, pointing.

"By the way, where is Captain McCord? I have something I would like to talk to him about."

"You want to tell him about bringing Miss Doucette to Bexar?" Almeron replied.

Hunter looked over at the lieutenant in surprise. "How did you know that? I haven't said anything to anyone about it."

Almeron chuckled. "You have her staying with Susanna, do you not? We are a very close-knit community here, and news travels fast."

"Then McCord probably already knows," Hunter said.

Almeron shook his head. "Not necessarily. Captain Mc-Cord took out a patrol early this morning and he isn't expected back until after dark."

"Then I shall wait for him. I want him to hear it from me first."

Hunter was standing just inside the front gate that evening when the six men of McCord's patrol returned. He remained in the shadows as Sam McCord rendered his report to Travis.

"Did you spot Santa Anna?"

"No, sir. We saw several scattered units of the Mexican army, but, as yet, no sight of Santa Anna and his main force," Sam reported.

"How about Fannin or any reinforcements that might be coming to our relief?" Travis asked.

"I'm afraid not. We saw none of our own people."

"They are probably still gathering the men together. They'll come," Travis insisted. "You'll see. They'll come. In the meantime, my compliments, Captain, on rendering a good report. Dismiss your men, then get yourself some supper."

"Thank you, sir," Sam said, saluting Travis. One of the other men, who had been on the patrol with Sam, took his horse from him, then started leading Sam's animal, as well as his own, toward the corral.

"Thank you, Mills," Sam said.

"No problem, Cap'n," the young soldier called back over his shoulder.

"Hello, Sam," Hunter said, stepping out of the shadows at that moment.

Sam looked surprised, then he smiled. "Why, Hunter Grant!" he said. He came over to shake Hunter's hand. "So, you've come to Texas after all."

"Yes."

"I am happy to see you, my friend. But I must tell you that you picked one hell of a time to join us. There are less than two hundred of us here, and Santa Anna is invading Texas with, depending on who you are listening to, from two to six thousand men. I'm afraid it is going to get very interesting around here."

"That's all right, I've always been someone who is ready to see the varmint."

"Have you had your supper?"

"Yes, thank you, but I'll have a cup of coffee with you while you eat."

"It's good that you are drinking coffee. The last time I saw you, I seem to recall that your drink of choice was somewhat stronger."

"It was, but I have managed to put that behind me," Hunter said.

"And what about the Meechums? Has all that been resolved?" Sam asked, as he filled his plate with beans, bacon, and bread.

"I have resolved it by putting it behind me," Hunter replied.

"Sometimes that's all we can do," Sam agreed. "I know that's what I have done."

"No, I don't think you have."

Surprised by the strange reply, Sam looked up. "What do you mean?"

"Sam, where can we go to talk?" Hunter asked.

"I thought we were talking."

"No, I mean really talk."

Sam nodded toward the ladder that stood against the wall just outside the door to his room. "Let's climb up on top of the officers' quarters," he suggested. "I find myself spending more and more time up there now, anyway. It affords a good view of the town, and we won't be disturbed."

The two men climbed to the roof, then walked over to the wall. Sam set his plate on the wall and used it as a table. From overhead, thousands of stars winked down at them, while golden bubbles of light shined in the town before them. The high-pitched sound of bagpipe music floated across the darkness which separated them from the town, and Sam chuckled.

"That'll be John McGregor and his pipes," he said. "Sometimes he gets on that thing and then Davy Crockett starts sawing away on his fiddle. They call themselves playing music, but I've always felt they were just trying to see who could make the most noise."

"It doesn't sound bad from over here," Hunter said.

"Now that you mention it, I guess it doesn't, at that. Maybe that's because we are far enough away. At any rate, the men seem to enjoy it. So, tell me, Hunter, what is it you wanted to talk about?" He used a crust of bread to rake through the bean juice on his plate.

"Sam, Marie is here."

Sam looked up. "What? How in God's name did she get here?"

"I brought her."

Sam sighed. "Hunter, would you mind telling me why you would want to do a damn fool thing like that?"

"She left me no choice. She was determined to come, and it was either I come with her and look out for her, or let her face the dangers alone."

"Well, you can just take her back to Louisiana with you, because I have no intention of seeing her."

"Sam, if you feel that way about her then why the hell didn't you have the decency to tell her that before you left Louisiana? You toyed with her, then you left without one word as to why you were leaving."

"It wasn't anybody's business why I left."

"It was her business."

"All right, let us say that I might grant that it was her business. Even if that is true, what business has it become of yours?"

"It is my business because I . . ." Hunter started, then he stopped.

"Because you what?"

Hunter paused for a long moment. "Because I love her," he finally said quietly.

"I see," Sam said. He took a bite of bread, then stared out toward the town. Hunter watched a vessel near his temple work as he chewed thoughtfully.

"You know, I've never said that aloud before," Hunter said. "In fact, I don't think I even realized it before now."

"Hunter, I have to tell you, this whole thing is getting more confusing to me. If you love her, as you say you do, then why are you so insistent upon bringing her to me? My God, man, why didn't you just run off with her, somewhere, and leave me out of it?"

"Believe me, I wish I didn't have to bring her to you. I wish I could go to her, and tell her how I feel."

"Then do it!"

"I beg your pardon?"

"Do it," Sam said again. "Don't let me stand in your way."

"I can't," Hunter said. "You are the one she has come to marry."

"I'm sorry to hear that. Because if that is why she is here, she has wasted her time."

"Damn you, you *will* marry her," Hunter snapped. "You have no choice, don't you understand?"

"No, I don't understand."

"*Sam, Marie is going to have your baby!*"

Sam stopped eating. Without a word, he put his fork down onto the plate, then walked several feet away. He stood at the wall for a long moment, resting his forearms on the parapet, with his hands clasped together, just on the other side. Hunter gave him a few moments alone, then he went over to him.

"I'm sorry you had to learn about it this way," Hunter said. "But you really gave me no choice."

"How far along is she?"

"You tell me," Hunter replied. "Since it is your baby, you ought to be able to figure it out."

"That would have to be October," Sam said. "That would make her going into the fourth month."

"Now that you know, Sam, what are you going to do about it?"

"I'm not going to do anything about it."

"What do you mean you aren't going to do anything? Don't you understand what I am saying to you? You are the reason she is here! You, and the baby she is carrying."

"Hunter, I *can't* marry her."

"Sweet Jesus, I never thought of that. You are married to someone else, aren't you?"

"No."

Hunter looked confused. "Well then, I don't understand, Sam. If you aren't married to anyone else, why can't you marry her?"

"The law will not allow us to get married."

"What do you mean, the law won't allow it?" Hunter asked. His confusion deepened.

Sam turned toward Hunter, and in the bright light of the moon, Hunter could study his face closely. He didn't think he had ever seen anyone reflecting a deeper sense of pain.

"I didn't want to have to tell you this, Hunter. I didn't want to have to tell anyone. But Marie Doucette is an octoroon. She is one-eighth colored, and that makes her, by the laws of the state of Louisiana, a Negress. I cannot marry her ... and neither can any other white man."

Hunter gasped.

"Sam, surely that can't be true," he said. "She is Phillipe Doucette's daughter. Phillipe Doucette is from one of the finest, wealthiest, and most respected families in the entire state.''

''That is true,'' Sam replied. ''But it is not from Phillipe's side of the family that Marie gets her taint. It is from Phillipe's wife.''

''Cassandra Doucette?''

''Yes, although, given the circumstances, I am quite certain that Cassandra is a wife in practice only. I am certain that she is not the beneficiary of any marriage license or ceremony.''

''But that can't be true, Sam. I have seen Cassandra Doucette many times,'' Hunter insisted. ''She is as white as you or I. And there isn't a more gracious woman in the entire parish.''

''I don't dispute you. But haven't you ever wondered why, at parish functions, we never met any of her people?''

''No, I don't think I ever thought about it, one way or the other.''

''Well, I did. If I was going to marry into that family, I wanted to know where she came from, so I conducted a little investigation.'' Sam sighed. ''God, if I had it to do all over again, I would not be so curious.''

''What did you find out in your investigation?'' Hunter asked. Despite himself, he was caught up in the same curiosity now, and cursing himself because of it.

''Her name is Cassandra Cote, and she was the most prized quadroon in *The House of the Chrysanthemum.*''

''*The House of the Chrysanthemum.* I have heard of that,'' Hunter said.

''It was once the most exclusive of all the sporting houses in New Orleans. They say it cost fifty dollars just to step through the doors. But that was over twenty years ago. It is no longer in business.''

''What happened to it?''

''Phillipe Doucette bought it, then closed it,'' Sam said. He sighed. ''I suppose he thought that if all the evidence of Cassandra's former life was erased, no one would ever discover the secret of her past.''

''But you discovered it.''

''Yes, God help me, I discovered it,'' Sam said. ''Though

I would give anything if I had not.''

"Perhaps you have just been listening to rumors and innuendos," Hunter suggested.

"No, it is true," Sam insisted. "The information I received was quite detailed.''

"Does Marie know?''

Sam shook his head. "I am sure that she does not know. And that is the problem.'' Sam looked into Hunter's face again, as if begging for understanding. "Hunter, surely you can see how it was! If I had posted the banns for marriage . . . and if someone had come forth with the information about Marie's mother, then I would not only have been prohibited from marrying Marie, then Cassandra would have been exposed, Phillipe scandalized, and Marie publicly humiliated. I could not let her suffer through all that.''

"I see what you mean," Hunter said.

"But that was before I knew she was pregnant. I'm afraid this complicates things.''

"What is so complicated? She is carrying your baby, you marry her. It is as simple as that.''

"But we just went through all of that. I can't marry her, don't you understand? I just told you, it is against the law!''

"Miscegenational marriage is against the law in Louisiana. But we are under Mexican law here. And while I don't know all there is to know about Mexican law, from the observations I have made since arriving in Texas, what with Mexicans marrying Americans and so forth, I'm sure that such restrictions don't apply.''

"Even if they don't, marriage is a big step. It's not something a person should do without giving it a great deal of thought.''

"It seems to me like the time for thinking is over," Hunter said. "And as for the big step, what step can be bigger than fathering a baby?''

Sam sighed. "You are right," he said. "Of course you are right, and I feel like a scoundrel for even suggesting that I might not do the right thing by her. Where is she now?''

"She is staying with the Dickersons.''

"That is a good place for her. The Dickersons are good people. I'll go out there and talk to her in the morning. If she accepts my proposal, I'll marry her.''

"Good," Hunter replied.

But if the idea of Sam marrying Marie was good, Hunter wondered, why was it making him feel so bad?

Seventeen

Not since word of Santa Anna's coming had San Antonio been so alive with activity as it was that evening. The citizens of the town, American and Mexican alike, were invited to the wedding. The Mexicans wore their most colorful costumes, and they laughed and sang and danced to the music of guitars and maracas. Their children played games, then blindfolded one another and swung long sticks at the gaily decorated piñatas that hung from the rafters. Whenever one of the children broke open a piñata, the others whooped with joy and scurried to discover what prizes had spilled from the smashed vessel.

The entire plaza was festooned with greenery, and it seemed impossible that a great battle could be just hours away.

In a room in the Dickersons' house, Marie stood in front of a mirror as Susanna helped her dress for her wedding. The sounds of the celebration floated in through the window, and a child's squeal of delight told them that another piñata had been broken.

Marie hurried over to look out the window.

"Look, Susanna, Americans and Mexicans are celebrating together. Is it possible that soon they will be fighting one another?"

Susanna nodded grimly. "I can't explain what makes men so foolish," she said. "I gave up trying a long time ago."

"They are all celebrating my wedding, and yet they don't even know me."

"It doesn't matter," Susanna said. "A wedding reminds them all of happier times."

The church on the plaza was lighted with over two hundred candles, and the soft light bathed the faces of the guests in glowing gold. Although Jim Bowie had been fighting a particularly troublesome bout of the fever which continued to plague him, he recovered in time to escort Marie down the aisle, for she had asked him to be her surrogate father. Sam was waiting at the altar for her.

Mexican law required that all marriages be Catholic marriages. As Marie was already Catholic, she was perfectly at ease with the requirement. And even though the priest who performed the ceremony was Spanish, the wedding service was performed in Latin, so even that was familiar to her. The priest made the sign of the cross, and in Marie's mind, the trappings of war fell away. This was a real marriage, sanctified by God, and it didn't matter that it took place in a Mexican church in a little town that was practically under siege. The ritual was no different than it would have been had it taken place in the grandest cathedral in New Orleans.

Once, during the ceremony, Marie looked over at Hunter and their eyes locked for a long time. At that precise moment Hunter got a vivid memory of how Marie had looked, beneath him, the last time they made love, and when he saw her look away in quick embarrassment he believed that, somehow, she had just experienced the same thought.

"I now pronounce you husband and wife," the priest said, and Sam took her in his arms and kissed her. She was now married.

"Okay, boys! Let's celebrate!" Bowie shouted the moment the ceremony was over. "Davy, how about you and McGregor cranking out some of that caterwaulering you call music?"

"Caterwaulering is it?" Davy answered, goodnaturedly. "Why, I'll have you know that when I was in the United States Congress, I had dignitaries from all over the world comin' to hear me play."

"Yeah, they were tryin' to figure out what it was!" one of the other Tennesseeans shouted, and everyone laughed.

The dancing started almost as soon as the music, and from the banter and laughter, anyone who didn't already know the situation would be hard-pressed to realize that this was a beleaguered garrison.

* * *

Hunter left the party, then walked back across the bridge toward the Alamo, which loomed big and dark against the night sky. He nodded at the guard on duty at the lunette just outside the south gate, then went inside the fort. He stopped at the well and drew up a bucket of water, then dipped in the scoop for a drink. The well, everyone was quick to point out, was one of the Alamo's most important assets, for it meant that, even if they were placed under siege, they would not be cut off from water.

As the party continued in town, Hunter was glad to be away from it. It was as if, by so doing, he could put behind him the fact that Marie had wed another. Hunter crossed the large, open plaza to the north wall, then climbed up onto the parapet. There he saw a soldier standing guard and tapping his foot to the music which was floating across the open area between the fort and the town.

"You're the new cornet, Mr. Grant, aren't you?" the soldier asked.

"Yes," Hunter replied. "I'm sorry, you'll have to forgive me, but I haven't yet learned everyone's name."

"My name is Highsmith, sir. Benjamin Franklin Highsmith, at your service," the young man answered.

"Benjamin Franklin, is it? You have quite a name to live up to."

"Yes, sir, I reckon so."

"Where are you from, Highsmith?"

"Well, sir, I was borned in St. Charles, Missouri. Only it wasn't yet a state when I was borned. But I come to Texas with my folks back in 'twenty-three when I was just a tyke, so I don't hardly remember much about Missouri."

"How old are you now?"

"I'm eighteen, sir."

"Eighteen?"

"Last September."

"Aren't you rather young to be in here?"

"Ain't too young a'tall," Highsmith said. "If you take a look around the place, you'll see others just as young."

"I suppose so," Hunter admitted.

A loud burst of laughter reached them.

"Sounds like the folks in town is really havin' a lot of fun," Highsmith said.

"You want to go over there?"

"I can't, sir. I'm posted to guard duty for another two hours."

"I'll stand your guard duty for you."

Highsmith looked around. "I don't know, sir. I don't know if I can."

"Of course you can. Don't worry, I'll tell your commander I relieved you."

Highsmith smiled broadly, then handed his long rifle over to Hunter.

"Thank you, sir!" he said. "Oh, and if you see anything, you aren't supposed to shoot, you're just supposed to get word to the sergeant of the guard."

"I'll do that," Hunter promised. He took the rifle, then stepped up to the wall and looked out toward the north. He turned back once, but Private Benjamin Highsmith was already hurrying toward the gate in order to join in the festivities.

Hunter had taken the young man's duty . . . he wished, by some magic, that he could trade places with him. Then he would see the marriage as a respite in the work and the tension of the garrison, an occasion for having a good time.

Instead, he saw the marriage only as a symbol of his breaking heart.

Later that evening, while the celebration continued in town, Marie and her husband returned to the fort, and to the room that they would now share. The door opened and Sam stood there in the silver light of the moon. With the door open Marie could hear the music and the clear, high voice of a singer. Sam shut the door and the music grew quieter.

"Good evening, Mrs. McCord," Sam said.

"Good evening, Mr. McCord," Marie replied.

Sam put his arms around her, and though Marie didn't push him away, she did grow tense.

"What is it?" Sam asked, confused by her action.

"Nothing is wrong."

Sam started to unbutton Marie's dress. She made no attempt to stop him, but neither did she help him. After a few buttons, Sam stopped.

"Marie, this is our wedding night."

"Yes, I know. I'm sorry," Marie said. "I guess I'm just overwhelmed by everything. Please, have some patience with me."

"All right," Sam said. "It's understandable, I suppose. I mean you have to be exhausted by the long trip here. Then, to come into a situation like this. It's a wonder you have any wits about you at all."

Marie smiled, and put her hand on his. "I'm glad you understand."

"And you are in love with another," Sam added, almost as an afterthought.

Marie gasped. "What?" she asked.

"Tell me if I'm wrong," Sam said. "You have fallen in love with Hunter Grant."

"Oh, Sam, I am so sorry," Marie said. "I didn't intend to fall in love with Hunter. I came here looking for you. It just happened."

Sam held up his hand to stop her from any further explanation. "No, you don't have to apologize to me," he said. "I am the one at fault, here. I am the one who ran away."

"I want you to know, however, that I take my marriage vows very seriously," Marie said. "I will not be unfaithful to you, Sam McCord. And I will raise our child in a way that will make you proud."

"I know I am late in telling you this, Marie. And it is my own foolishness which has caused all of this. But I love you."

"I love you, too, Sam, I truly do," Marie replied. "Whatever has happened between Hunter and me has not caused my love for you to be diminished. It is just that, now, everything is so confusing. Please, just give me a little time."

Sam put his arms around her and held her close for a long moment, then he kissed her on the forehead. "I will be as patient as you want me to be." He smiled. "The reward will be well worth the wait."

DOMINGO, 21 FEBRERO, 1836, THE RIO MEDINA

Colonel Don Juan Esteban Montoya was gathered with several other officers in Santa Anna's tent, on the banks of the Rio Medina. The invading force was now only twenty-five miles from San Antonio, and Juan had to give Santa Anna his due, for despite the lack of forage and the vast, harsh, unforgiving land between the Rio Grande and here, Santa Anna had made good his boast of moving his army across the unforgiving wasteland.

It had been a brutal transit, for one could track the army by the hundreds upon hundreds of dead animals left in its wake. And it wasn't only animals who suffered, for the casualties continued to run high among the soldiers as well.

"Senors, I have just received news that a wedding is taking place tonight, inside the Alamo."

"A wedding, General?" Juan replied, puzzled as to why this would be news of importance.

"*Si.* One of the rebels, Captain Sam McCord, is marrying a young woman named Marie Doucette."

"Marie Doucette?" Lopez interrupted.

"Why do you ask, Lopez? Do you know this Marie Doucette?" Santa Anna asked.

"*Si.* Marie Doucette was traveling with the traitor Alvarez when we caught up with him and killed him."

"I hope you did not dishonor yourself with her," Santa Anna said.

"She was treated with dignity, General. And, as I had no military use for her, I set her free," Lopez said.

"Is she a beautiful woman?" Santa Anna asked.

"*Si, Excellente.* Her beauty is beyond description."

Santa Anna smiled. "Good!" he said, enthusiastically. "It is good that she is a beautiful woman, for, the more beautiful the bride, the more gala the celebration. And, tonight, we want the celebration to be *el grando*, for while the rebels are dancing and celebrating, we will attack."

"Attack? General, we are still twenty-five miles away,"

Juan reminded him. "It is not possible to move the army that quickly."

"You are correct, Colonel. We cannot move the entire army. And that is the beauty of our plan, don't you see? We are twenty-five miles, and too far for any of their scouts to have seen us, so they will not be expecting you."

"Me, *Senor Presidente?*"

"*Si.* I want you to lead your *zapadores* in a surprise attack tonight. Tonight they celebrate, but tomorrow, we will dance on their graves. "Colonel Montoya, you and your *zapadores* will give us that victory."

"*Gracias, Excellente.*"

"After you crush the pathetic little group in the Alamo, there will be nothing to stand between us and their so-called capital. We will have all the rebels subdued before they can even raise an army to defend themselves. So, Colonel Montoya, as you can see, the entire Texas campaign may well hinge upon how well your *zapadores* perform tonight."

"We will not let you down, *Excellente,*" Juan promised.

"We are to lead the attack?" Ramon asked, his eyes shining in excitement.

"*Si,* tonight."

Ramon's face split in a wide smile. "Juan! Do you know what this means?" Ramon asked, so excited by the prospect that he failed to call his brother by his rank.

"*Si.* It means, tonight, we will be doing battle."

"Oh, but it means so much more than that!" Ramon insisted. "Years from now, school children will read of the great civil war in which we kept Texas from being stolen from us. And they will read that the most decisive battle was the battle of the Alamo, won by Colonel Don Juan Esteban Montoya! We will go down in history!"

"We, brother? How will you go down in history, when I plan to leave you behind?" Juan asked.

Ramon was crestfallen. "Leave me behind?"

"*Si.* We will be traveling very fast, so the tents and packs will be left behind. I need someone I can trust to look after them."

Ramon's eyes grew wide in shock. "Juan! You would not

leave me here, on the eve of this important battle, merely to do the task of a storekeeper, would you?'' he asked.

Juan and Quinterra could no longer keep a straight face, and Juan laughed out loud.

"No, my brother," he finally said. "I will not make you stay here. When we make our attack tonight, you will be with me. But you must promise me to be careful, for if you were killed while under my command, I would be unable to return home and face our parents."

"Accolades go to the bold, Juan, not to the careful," Ramon replied resolutely. "But don't worry about me. I have had a dream. And in the dream, I was visited by San Miguel. And this, he told me." Ramon held up his finger. "I will be killed by a rebel bullet."

Juan laughed. "If the patron saint of battle told you this, then it must be true."

"Return to your platoon, Lieutenant," Quinterra said. "And ready them for action. We will carry rifles and lances."

"*Si*, Major," Ramon answered happily, saluting both Quinterra and Juan before he hurried off.

"Manuel . . ." Juan started.

"Do not worry, *amigo*," Manuel said, interrupting Juan before the question could even be asked. "I will look after your brother."

"*Muy gracias.*"

The rain started in the early afternoon. It moved across the Rio Medina and fell on the *zapadores* as they prepared for their attack. It slashed into the trees, and rolled out of the hills, filling gullies and flooding plains. The rain grew even heavier as the afternoon wore on and the ground where the great army was encamped turned into a great quagmire, so that the men and horses slipped and slid as they moved around, pulling their feet from the sea of mud with increasing difficulty.

Juan stood just inside the open door of his tent looking out at the storm, listening to the music it made. The rain was perfectly orchestrated, from the rhythmic percussion and harmonic bass notes of the large, booming drops, to the delicate trills and melodious tinkling of water that ran down the sides of the tent. It cascaded across the rocks and stones to form puddles, streams, and rivulets, all of which ran together to feed the swelling river.

Juan saw Quinterra coming through the rain toward him, nearly obscured by the gray wash of the heavy downpour. The poncho he was wearing was doing little to keep out the rain and his uniform and moustache were dripping wet.

"Colonel, we have a problem," Quinterra shouted. He had to shout to be heard above the roar of the falling water.

"You know the code of the *zapadores*, Manuel," Juan replied. "There are no problems. There are only solutions that have not yet been applied," Juan was only half-teasing when he said it.

"*Si*, Colonel," Major Quinterra said. "But one of the solutions we have not yet applied is how we are going to get across the river."

"The river? Is this not the place to ford the river?"

"At noon today, Colonel, we could have forded the river quite easily. But with this accursed rain, the water is now six feet deep, and rising. In addition, the current has become very strong."

Juan's younger brother, Ramon, seeing Quinterra approaching Juan, had come over to listen to the conversation.

"So what are you suggesting?" Juan asked Quinterra.

Quinterra shook his head. "I think it will be impossible to cross," he said. "We will have to wait until the water recedes."

"No!" Ramon said quickly. "We cannot call off the attack! Juan, you know that General Santa Anna will insist that we go!"

"Ramon may have a point, Manuel," Juan said. "Any man who would kill as many horses and men as our esteemed leader did in bringing us here, is not likely to accept the fact that we were stopped by a little water."

"A *little* water, Colonel?" Quinterra said. "Have you looked closely at that river? Juan, if we try and move our *zapadores* across now, we will lose at least three-fourths of them, maybe more!"

"But if we call off the attack then we will not get another chance. After tomorrow, the entire army will be there and our *zapadores* will be robbed of the victory. We must go to-night!'' Ramon said.

"Perhaps I should take a closer look at the river," Juan suggested.

"*Si,*" Quinterra agreed. "I think that would be a good idea."

Juan stepped back inside the tent just long enough to put on his own poncho, then he and Quinterra walked down to the river's edge. Before he even got there, however, he could see that Quinterra was right. What had been a shallow, slug-gishly moving stream this morning, was now three times wider than it had been. No longer sluggish, it was now a mighty, rolling river, sweeping logs and limbs downstream as it chewed away at the banks on either side.

"Look there," Quinterra suggested, pointing to a tree, around which the river surged. "At one o'clock today, that tree stood on dry land. Now, half of it is underwater."

"I think you are right, Manuel," Juan said. "We have no choice. It is impossible to cross the river as it is."

Manuel chuckled. "You tell your brother," he said. "I do not want him to think . . .''

Suddenly a horse and rider galloped by them. Juan and Quinterra's surprise grew to shock when they saw that the rider was Ramon Montoya.

"Ramon!" Juan called.

"Tell the others to follow my example!" Ramon shouted back over his shoulder. "When they see that I am safely on the other side, they will know that the river can be crossed!"

"Ramon, stop! Come back here! That is an order!" Juan yelled.

"Stop that man!" Quinterra ordered in a loud voice, and two men who were close to the edge of the river made an attempt to get to him, but Ramon was riding too fast and he brushed right past them, then plunged into the river.

"Ramon!"

Almost immediately the horse lost its footing. When its feet lost purchase, the horse tried to swim, but the current was much too swift and the terrified horse was moving down-stream much faster than it was making any forward progress.

"Get ropes, quickly!" Juan shouted, running down to the

edge of the river. "Ramon! Ramon, hang on!"

Now, even Ramon was aware of his worsening predicament, and he leaned forward, trying to urge the horse across the stream. Unseen, by both Ramon and the horse, was a huge log which was sweeping down the river. Quinterra saw it.

"Ramon! Ramon, watch out for the log!" Quinterra shouted.

At Quinterra's warning, Juan looked upstream and saw the big log bearing down on his brother. He cupped his hands around his mouth and shouted.

"Ramon, the log! Look out for the log!"

The roar of the rain and the rushing river was so loud that Ramon couldn't hear the warnings, and he was so busy trying to stay on the horse that he didn't bother to look upstream. The log hit horse and rider with full force. Both animal and man went under, and for a long moment Juan could see nothing but churning water where his brother had been.

"There is the horse!" someone shouted, and, looking in the direction indicated, Juan saw the animal resurface. The horse was absolutely motionless, other than the motion provided by the swiftly flowing river.

"It's dead!" Quinterra said. "The horse is dead!"

"Where is Ramon? Where is my brother?" Juan shouted anxiously. "Everyone! Look for my brother!"

By now the commotion had brought several of the *zapadores* down to the water's edge, for the men all loved and respected their commander and shared his fear over the fate of the young lieutenant.

"*Commandante!*" a sergeant called, pointing. "*Commandante!* There!"

Juan saw then what the sergeant saw. Ramon's body was floating, facedown, in the river.

Eighteen

DAWN, TUESDAY, FEBRUARY 23, 1836

There was a great flurry of activity just outside the Captain and Mrs. McCord's quarters, and when Marie opened her eyes she discovered that she was alone in the room. She dressed quickly, then went to the door to have a look.

Many who had been staying in San Antonio de Bexar were now streaming into the fort. Carts full of belongings squeaked across the plaza, and tall, solemn men were walking beside somber-looking women. Marie saw Sam coming toward her, smiling.

"Good morning," he said.

"Sam, what is it? What's going on?"

"The Mexicans in town are saying that Santa Anna has arrived," Sam said.

Marie gasped. "He's here?"

"Not yet. But Colonel Travis has ordered everyone inside the gates."

"Oh, Sam, what about Susanna and little Angelina? They are still in town!"

"They won't be much longer," Sam replied. "Almeron just rode into town to pick them up."

Hunter Grant was in town. Jim Bowie's sickness was getting progressively worse, so Hunter volunteered to help him escort his two sisters-in-law and their children into the fort. The Veramendi house, where the two women lived, was just across the plaza from the Dickerson house, and Hunter was standing out front when he saw Lieutenant Dickerson arrive on horseback. Susanna, carrying a cloth bundle in one hand, and their fifteen-month-old baby in the other, came out of the house to meet him.

"Give me the baby!" Dickerson shouted. "Jump on behind me and ask me no questions."

Susanna handed the baby and the bundle up to Dickerson,

then he held out the stirrup for her and reached his hand down to help her mount.

"Are you coming into the fort, Mr. Grant?" Susanna called over to him.

"Yes, ma'am," Hunter answered. "I'll be in shortly."

"Don't delay! They say the Mexicans are just over that rise," Susanna said.

An old Mexican woman came out into the plaza and watched all the scurrying activity of the refugees.

"Oh, you poor people," Hunter called. "You will all be killed!"

Two civilians came riding by. "Are you Mr. Grant?" one of them asked.

Hunter nodded.

"I'm Dr. John Sutherland. This is John W. Smith," Sutherland said. "Colonel Travis's compliments, sir, and he asks if you will ride out with us to see what we can see?"

Hunter looked back toward the Veramendi house. Bowie was just coming out with a babe under each arm.

"I'll be along as soon as I help Bowie with these people," Hunter said.

"Go ahead, now, Hunter," Bowie said. "I can get them all right." Bowie staggered under the weight of the children, and Hunter had to grab them quickly. Sweating profusely, even though the temperature was brisk, Bowie leaned against the front of the house and mopped his forehead with a handkerchief.

"Look at you. You are so weak you can barely stand."

"I'll be all right," Bowie insisted. "Go on, go with them. I've been telling Travis for days what we were facing, but I don't think the cocky little son of a bitch has believed me. Let's see how he takes the news from you."

"You go, Senor Grant," one of Bowie's sisters-in-law said. "We will look after Senor Jim, as he looks after us."

"All right," Hunter agreed. "I'll go. I'll check in on you when I get back."

Hunter mounted his horse, then rode out with Sutherland and Smith. They rode at a fast trot, and, five minutes later, reached the top of a hill, about a mile and a half away. Smith was the first one to the crest of the hill.

"Great God almighty," Smith said, when he reached the top of the hill.

Hunter urged his horse up the hill, then he dismounted with the others. He could see now why Smith had made the comment he made.

There, about a mile beyond the hill, was an awesome sight. A seemingly unending line of Mexican cavalrymen, stretched out in battle formation. The Mexican soldiers were beautifully uniformed, with half-a-dozen officers riding up and down in front of the formation, with drawn swords.

"Look at that," Hunter said. "They can't have a soldier left in Mexico."

"Hell, how could they have *anyone* left?" Smith replied. "There aren't that many people in all the towns and cities west of the Mississippi River combined."

"We'd better get back and warn the others," Sutherland suggested.

The three men remounted, then turned their horses for the gallop back. They were just getting started when Dr. Sutherland's horse, which was unshod, slipped and fell, landing on Sutherland's legs.

"Ahhh! Damn!" Sutherland shouted.

Hunter and Smith pulled up.

"Doc, are you all right?" Hunter called back to him.

"I'm all right," Sutherland said, though Hunter saw him wincing in pain as he managed to get back onto his horse.

Once down the hill, the three men urged their horses to the greatest possible speed, and they covered this distance back in about three minutes. A lookout, posted in the belfry of the church, started ringing the bell, though, by now, nearly the entire town was evacuated.

Just before noon, the last of the refugees filed into the Alamo, and Travis ordered the gates closed, and the bars lowered.

There were, Hunter knew, no more than one hundred and fifty fighting men in the Alamo, quartered in two barracks and several smaller structures along the east and west walls. There were also about twenty-five noncombatants crowded into the roofless church, a refuge now where, a short time before, it had been the setting for a marriage.

Hunter went with Sutherland and Smith to report on what they saw.

"How many soldiers are there?" Travis asked.

"Hell, Colonel, there was so many you couldn't count them," Smith said. "There are hundreds . . . no, thousands of them."

"Colonel Bowie, Mr. Crockett, would you please assemble all of your men in the plaza in front of the church in one hour?"

"We'll be there, Will," Davy said.

Travis looked over at Bowie. "Colonel?"

Bowie didn't answer.

"Colonel Bowie, I know we have had our differences," Travis said. "But I, for one, am ready to put those differences aside."

"I agree," Bowie said. "I'll have my men there."

"Is this going to be a closed meeting, Colonel? Or can the civilians come, too? Seems to me like we all got a stake in this."

"Everyone is welcome," Travis replied.

Across the plaza from where Travis was meeting with Bowie and Crockett, Sam stuck his head into his room to speak to his new wife.

"Sam, why are all these people coming in from the town? What is it? What is going on?"

"It's here, Marie, what we've been waiting for. Only it's come a bit sooner than any of us expected. Santa Anna has moved his army into position." He took her hand. "Come with me, I'll show you."

"Where are we going?" Marie said.

"Onto the roof," Sam replied. "You can see everything from up there."

Marie climbed the ladder onto the roof of the officers' barracks, then, following Sam's directions as to where to look, she saw what appeared to be tiny toy soldiers. She examined them through a long spyglass, and she caught the flash of sunlight on the shiny breastplates of the Mexican cavalrymen.

"So many of them," Marie said, lowering her glass.

"There are a lot more of them than there are of us. That's for sure," Sam said.

"When do you think they will attack?" Marie asked.

"Soon, I would think," was all Sam could say. "Soon."

A little later, Marie joined the other civilians to gather around the military formation that was drawn up in front of the church. She stood alongside Susanna, who was watching over Angelina. The little girl was sitting in the dirt, happily playing with a stick.

"Ladies and gentlemen of the garrison," Travis began. "Officers and men. These three brave men have brought us news." He nodded toward Sutherland, Smith, and Hunter. Dr. Sutherland was now on crutches, his leg having been broken by his fall. "Although, by now, our predicament is clear to anyone who might climb the wall for a look."

Travis began pacing up and down in front of the assembly. "I regret to tell you that our situation is very critical. I have sent repeated messages to Colonel Fannin at Goliad, inviting him in the strongest terms, to come to our aid, but he has refused our pleas for help. The only other town close enough to send reinforcements is Gonzales, which is about sixty miles east. I have written a message and will be sending it to them."

Travis held up the message, cleared his throat, and began to read: " 'The enemy in large force is in sight. We want men and provisions. Send them to us. We have one hundred and fifty men and are determined to defend the Alamo to the last. Give us assistance. P.S., send an express to San Felipe with news, night and day.' " He called Hunter forward, and handed the note to him. "Mr. Grant, guard this note with your very life," he said. "Now, get going."

Hunter took the note, then turned to leave. He looked out over the assembly of men and women who were standing anxiously before him. In the back row, he saw Marie, and he knew at that moment that he couldn't leave her. She was no longer his responsibility. Indeed, he no longer had any right to even consider her. Despite that, he knew that he couldn't leave, knowing that she was still here, awaiting her fate with the garrison.

Hunter stopped for a moment, then turned and started back toward Travis.

"Is something wrong, Mr. Grant?" Travis asked.

"Get someone else to go, Colonel," Hunter said. "I'm not going."

"You will go, sir!" Travis said sharply. "I have given you an order!"

"With all due respect, Colonel, I refuse your order," Hunter said.

"What are you going to do with him, Colonel? Shoot him?" someone called, and the others laughed.

"If the boy wants to stay, leave him be," Davy Crockett said. "I'm sure you can get one of the civilians to deliver the note." Davy nodded toward Smith and Sutherland. "Why not ask these men?"

Travis sighed. "Would you gentlemen deliver the note for us?"

Smith reached for it. "I'll take the message, Colonel," he said. "And I'll bring back help, I promise."

"Dr. Sutherland, I would appreciate it if you would go with him," Travis said. He nodded toward Sutherland's leg. "I don't know how much use you'll be to us here, seeing as you can't get around that well. On the other hand, two of you might have a better chance of getting through."

"Whatever you say, Colonel," Sutherland said.

At a signal from Captain Jameson, one of his men brought two horses for Smith and Sutherland, and the two men mounted.

"Gentlemen, as our Mexican friends say: *Via con Dios,*" Travis said.

"Open the gates!" Dickerson called to the front gate and the two soldiers who were guarding the gate got it open just as the two riders galloped through them. Then, the gates were closed once again.

Davy Crockett spoke up then, his clear voice sounding unafraid and resolute. "Colonel, assign me to some place and I and my Tennessee boys will defend it all right."

"Mr. Crockett, you have been a member of the United States Congress, sir, yet you came here as a private. I would prefer to appoint you to a command."

"No, sir," Davy said. "I have come to aid you all that I can in your noble cause, and all the honor I desire is that of defending the liberties of our common country."

Davy Crockett's words brought applause from the crowd, and Colonel Travis walked over and put his hand on the frontiersman's shoulder. "All right. Then to you shall go the honor of defending the place that is most vulnerable. I want you and your Tennesseeans at the palisade between the church and the low barracks."

"If that's where you want us, that's where we'll be," Davy answered.

Travis turned to Green Jameson. "Captain Jameson, how do we stand on shells for our heavy cannon?"

"We've got plenty of grapeshot," Jameson answered. "We made it ourselves. Almeron, here, cut up all the horseshoes we could find. I tell you, that's going to make some terrible kind of grapeshot. It'll cut the Mexicans down like a wheat scythe."

"Good," Travis said. "See that there is plenty of it near the guns. All right, men, we have a long day's work ahead. I suggest we get to it."

"Colonel?" Sam spoke up.

"Yes, Sam?"

"It seems to me that Santa Anna could squeeze us out in a siege if he had a mind to. That is, unless we do something about it."

"You have something in mind?"

"I thought I might take a handful of men outside the fort to search for food. Maybe we could round up some grain and livestock."

"That's a good idea, Sam," Travis agreed. "As it is, we don't have enough food in here to feed this many people throughout a long siege."

"All right, take some volunteers and go out and find what you can," Travis suggested. "Jameson, Dickerson, cover them with your cannon."

"I'll go, Sam," Hunter volunteered.

It took less than five minutes for a dozen men to be mounted, and ready for action. Sitting his saddle in front of them, Sam gave instructions.

"We're going out the gate, then we are going to follow the irrigation ditch around the east wall, then the north wall, and on down the hill toward the fields, just north of the town. There's cattle in those fields, and wheat and corn in the barn. Mr. Grant, you will take half the men. Find a wagon and fill it with grain. The rest of the men and I will round up the cattle."

Hunter nodded his assent, then the group rode over to the gate. At a signal from Sam, the gate was opened, and the men moved outside.

It took them fifteen minutes to work their way all around the fort because they were moving slowly and bending low over their horses to diminish the profile. Then, leaving the irrigation ditch, but still riding in defilade, they rounded a hill to come upon a large field, where fifty or more cattle were peacefully grazing.

"There are the cattle," Sam whispered. "Hunter, there's the barn." He pointed.

"Let's go," Hunter called to his men, and his group turned away from the others and sloped down the long hill toward the barn.

"Christ! The place is full of Mexicans!" one of the riders shouted, as they reached the edge of the barn and saw that, indeed, an entire company of men was encamped there.

The Mexican company had posted a guard and the guard, suddenly seeing Texians upon them, raised his rifle and fired.

Hunter's horse reared, then fell, and Hunter had to roll to one side to avoid being crushed. He leaped to his feet and tried to catch the horse, but it darted away, leaving Hunter afoot, his pistol in his hand.

Some of the Mexicans were already mounted, and one of them now galloped toward Hunter, smiling broadly at the prospect of an easy kill. Hunter fired and the Mexican soldier pitched out of his saddle.

There was no cover and Hunter was out in the open, unmounted, not a good place to be. Another mounted Mexican loomed on his right. From behind him, Hunter heard a shot. The bullet hit the Mexican's horse and it stumbled, throwing the rider over his head.

Sam, seeing that Hunter's group had run into trouble, galloped up to him, holding his hand down to help Hunter mount behind him. Hunter leaped onto the horse and the two men galloped to the cover of a nearby group of rocks. Hunter slid down then and ran to one of the rocks as a bullet whistled by his ear. He squeezed down behind the rocks and began reloading.

Sam came down with him, then raised up and aimed his shotgun. It roared like a miniature cannon, and the smoke billowed out before them. With so much shooting now, the field was covered with a cloud of acrid smoke. By now, half-a-dozen Mexicans lay dead, but not one Texian had received so much as a scratch.

The few remaining Mexicans, suddenly realizing that they were now outnumbered and outgunned, turned and ran.

"Run, boys, run!" Sam shouted, firing his other barrels into the air. The Texians whooped and shouted in excitement over their victory. Sam pointed toward the barn.

"There's a wagon, if you find grain," he said.

"I'm sure it's in the crib," Hunter said.

It was, and it took less than an hour for the wagon to be loaded, a couple of the horses to be hitched to it, and the little party to start back toward the Alamo. The gates were opened to let a wagonload of corn and wheat, plus some thirty head of cattle, inside.

"Hurrah!" someone inside the Alamo shouted, at seeing the unexpected bounty delivered into their hands. "Hurrah for Texas, boys, hurrah!"

Others joined in the cheer, then hurried over to congratulate the men who had run the risk to bring them food.

"Well, we've food and water to last out any siege," Travis said. "If they want us, they'll have to come get us."

"It's beginning to look like that's exactly what they've got on their mind," Bowie said. He had another spasm of coughing, then, when it was over, said, "Travis, I think maybe you'd better climb up on the wall and take a look."

At Bowie's suggestion, not only Travis, but Sam, Hunter, Almeron Dickerson, and half-a-dozen others, including even Susanna and Marie, climbed the ladder to the parapet which looked over to the west wall toward the town.

"What is it?" Travis asked. "What did you bring us up here for?"

"You see that flag they got flyin' from the church belfry?" Bowie pointed out.

"I see it."

"Look real close, Travis, and you'll see that it's not the Mexican flag," Bowie said. "It's a solid red banner."

"What does that mean?"

"It's a signal," Bowie explained. "A red banner means no quarter for the enemy. What they are telling us, Travis, is that they intend to take no prisoners."

"Oh, God in heaven!" Susanna gasped.

Travis looked over toward Susanna and Marie. "What are they doing up here?" he asked.

"When you get right down to it, I guess they've got as much right to be up here as anyone. We're all in this together now, unless you do something about it."

"Do something about it?" Travis replied angrily. "Man, what do you propose that I do?"

"You might send them a message."

Travis paused for a moment, then he looked down toward Dickerson and Jameson, who were standing by the big, eighteen-pound cannon. "Lieutenant Dickerson! Is the gun loaded?"

"Yes, sir!"

"Throw them an eighteen-pound iron ball!"

"Yes, sir!" Almeron said, and a moment later the fort trembled under the firing of the cannon. Those on the parapet watched the black ball hurtle through the sky, then crash into a wagon, sending pieces of wood scattering.

"That's their answer," Travis said resolutely.

"You aren't much of a negotiator, are you, Travis?"

"Shot and shell are the only terms of negotiation Santa Anna understands," Travis said.

"I'll say this for you, Travis," Bowie said. "You have certainly done all in your power to make that the case." Bowie's face grew very white then, and he had to lean against the wall to keep from falling.

"Colonel Bowie, you are ill, sir. I suggest that you repair to your quarters," Travis said.

"So you can have the command all to yourself?" Bowie replied in a voice that was now much weaker than it had been just a few days ago. Once again, he had to mop the sweat off his brow.

At that moment, from the town, they heard the sound of a bugle playing.

"What is that?" Travis asked. "What is that song?"

"It is the *Deguello*," Bowie said in a weak voice. "Fire and Death. Like the flag, it means, no quarter."

"All right, gentlemen, I think we all know where we stand now," Travis said. "Officers, to your posts. Ladies, please clear the parapet."

"Captain Jameson, will you help me to my quarters, please?" Bowie asked.

"Yes, of course," Jameson said.

Hunter watched Jameson help Bowie down the ladder. Then he looked over toward Marie and Sam, as Sam helped her down. Seeing them together like that was more than he could take, so he walked back to the wall and stared out across the open ground toward San Antonio.

He was a fool for bringing her here. He should have talked her into marrying him. They could have gone somewhere else and begun living their lives as husband and wife. Who would know that the baby wasn't his?

As he stared out toward the Mexican soldiers who were maneuvering into position in the outskirts of the town, he saw someone that so arrested his attention that all previous thought went away.

"Lieutenant Dickerson?" he called. Dickerson was just finishing with the reloading of the cannon.

"Yes?"

"Do you have a spyglass down there?"

"Sure do," Dickerson said, walking down the platform to hand it to Hunter. "See something?"

"I'm not certain," Hunter said. He opened up the telescope, then looked out toward the town. "I'll be damned," he said. "It's him."

"Beg your pardon?"

Hunter snapped the spyglass shut and returned it to Dickerson.

"Colonel Don Juan Esteban Montoya," he said.

"He is the one who caused the duel?" Dickerson had heard the story.

"Yes."

Dickerson smiled. "Well, my friend, it looks as if you are going to get your chance at him, after all."

"If I can pick him out of all the rest," Hunter replied. As both Hunter and Dickerson turned their backs to the wall at that precise moment, neither of them saw Green Jameson exit through the gate, then ride toward the town beneath a white flag.

One of Juan's officers escorted Jameson to him. "What do you want?" Juan asked.

"I want to speak with Santa Anna," the Texian replied.

"What for?"

"I have a message for him from Jim Bowie."

Juan studied the messenger for a moment, then nodded to Quinterra. "Have you searched him for a hidden weapon?" he asked.

"No, Colonel."

"Do so."

Quinterra spoke to two of the guards, and they began a thorough search. Then, satisfied that he was not carrying a hidden weapon, they stepped back.

"No weapons."

"Come," Juan said to the man. Ordinarily, he would let one of his junior officers escort such a messenger to Santa Anna, but he did it himself because he wanted to hear what was going on.

Santa Anna was sitting in a chair with his boots off. There were two women on the ground beneath him, each of them washing one of his feet. Juan took the messenger to him.

Santa Anna looked up, and the messenger saluted.

"Your Excellency, I am Captain Green Jameson, of the Army of Texas."

"There is no Army of Texas," Santa Anna snorted, not bothering to return the salute. "There are only a ragged band of rebels and outlaws."

"Very well, sir. Then I come bearing a message from that ragged band of rebels and outlaws."

One of the women took Santa Anna's foot out of the basin of water and began drying it with her hair.

"And for what purpose have you come, Senor Jameson?"

"Colonel James Bowie, cocommander with Colonel William Travis of the Alamo garrison, respectfully asks if you will agree to the same terms we imposed upon General Cos when we captured the Alamo?"

"And what terms were those?" Santa Anna asked. Now the other woman was drying his other foot, also with her hair.

"It would be a surrender, Your Excellency, in which the Texian defenders would be disarmed and allowed to return to their homes."

Santa Anna snorted what might have been a laugh. "Do you think I am a fool, Jameson? Why should I let men go so that they can fight me at a later time?"

"We would sign paroles, as did General Cos's men," Jameson promised.

Again, Santa Anna chortled. "Don't you realize that nearly everyone who was with General Cos is with me now? Including General Cos himself?"

Jameson shook his head. "No," he said.

"So, Senor Jameson, if we did not keep our word to you, how can we expect you to keep your word to us?"

"We're Texians," Jameson said resolutely.

"I see. And that makes you more honorable?"

Jameson's silence said it all.

Santa Anna pointed to his boots, indicating that he wanted them pulled on.

"Go back to your commander and tell him this," Santa Anna said. "I will accept only unconditional surrender. Nothing less. If you fight me, I will capture the fort and put every man to the sword."

Juan could see Jameson's temple throbbing in anger.

"I will take your message, General," Jameson said.

Juan walked out with Jameson. "Captain," he said. "You and your men should have abandoned the post before we got here. Now it is too late."

Jameson swung into the saddle of his horse, then looked down at Juan.

"You fellas come get us," he said. "And do your damnedest. But I think you should know that, for every one of us you kill, we will kill eight to ten of you."

Juan smiled. "In your anger and bravado, I think you may be exaggerating," he said.

"Think so?" Jameson replied, as he turned his horse. "I should tell you, I built the fort. I know what it is going to take to capture it. Oh, you will eventually do it. But it is going to take from one-third to one-half of your attacking force to do it." Slapping his legs against his horse, Jameson rode back toward the fort. Juan watched him go. He said nothing else, because he didn't want to give the Texian the satisfaction of knowing that Juan agreed with his estimate.

"He did what?" Travis exploded in anger.

"He sent me, with a message for Santa Anna, offering to surrender," Jameson said.

"How dare he?" Travis said. "Where is Bowie now? Lieutenant Dickerson, find him and bring him to me. Under guard if necessary. By God, this is treason!"

"Colonel, if I brought him here to you now, he wouldn't even know what you are saying to him."

"Drunk again?"

"No, sir. He's had another attack of the fever, worse than any time before. He's pretty near delirious."

"Dickerson, assign two men to keep an eye on Mr. James Bowie. If he tries to leave this place, shoot him. The same goes for anyone else who tries, again, to make contact with the enemy. I, and I alone, will decide when and if any contact is to be made."

"Yes, sir."

Suddenly there was a sound, like that of thunder. For a moment everyone looked at each other in curiosity, then there was a whistling sound as several balls fell inside the Alamo. They hit the plaza, raising dust, then rolling quickly across the ground until their motion was sharply arrested by the walls which contained the plaza.

"Artillery!" someone called from the fortress walls. "Colonel! The Mexicans have begun firing at us!"

"Shall we return fire, Colonel?" Dickerson asked.

There was another rumble of thunder, and again a barrage of cannonballs fell inside the Alamo, these doing no more damage than the first.

"No," Travis finally said. "Their fire now has no effect. We will save our ammunition until we can use it with more positive consequence."

THURSDAY, FEBRUARY 25, 1836, THE ALAMO

"Officer of the guard, post number two!" the guard at post number two shouted. His call was carried by the other guards, until it reached Hunter Grant, who, with Captain Jameson and Lieutenant Simmons, was leaning over a table, looking at a chart Jameson had drawn, to determine the best defensive positions to take, should the walls be breached.

"I wonder what's up?" Jameson asked, raising up from the chart.

"I'm the officer of the guard today," Hunter said, reaching for his hat. "I'll go see."

Hunter left Jameson's quarters and hurried across the quadrangle toward the west wall and post number two. When he climbed the ladder the guard waved him over.

"What is it, Private Day?"

"Sir, they's a bunch of Mexicans sneakin' up the gully there," Day said.

Hunter stepped over to the wall, then looked in the direction pointed out by Private Day. There he saw what Day was talking about. From two to three hundred Mexican soldiers had crossed the river, and were moving, bent over to take advantage of what cover and concealment there was, toward a group of houses that were very close to the wall of the Alamo.

"Good job, Private," Hunter said. He moved away from the wall to the back edge of the parapet, cupped his hands around his mouth, and shouted, "Colonel Travis!"

Travis appeared.

"We need riflemen to the west wall!"

"Mr. Crockett!" Travis shouted. "Would you bring your Tennesseeans to the west wall, please?"

Within moments Crockett and a score of his riflemen were climbing the ladders and moving to the edge of the wall. Jameson and Dickerson came up as well, and began loading the cannon.

Travis strode up and down the parapet, looking over the wall toward the approaching Mexicans.

"All right, men, we'll give them a load of canister," he said. "Then you fellows can fire at will. But make your shots count!"

"Cannons loaded, sir!" Dickerson called back.

"Fire the cannons!"

There were four flashes and puffs of smoke, followed immediately by heavy, stomach-shaking booms. A cloud of grape and canister hit the little houses where the Mexican soldiers were taking cover, and the effect was immediately noticeable by the cries of fear and pain from those who were wounded.

"Now, Mr. Crockett, if you please!" Travis shouted, and there was a ripple of fire as the riflemen, most of whom had already picked out targets and were just awaiting the order to do so, fired.

The Mexican soldiers fired back, though as their weapons were inferior to the weapons of the defenders, and their position was weaker, defensively, they had little effect.

The firing continued back and forth for nearly two hours, then the Mexicans began to withdraw.

"We whupped 'em, boys!" someone shouted. "They're goin' back to Mexico!"

There was a loud cheer, until Travis restored order by shouting at them.

"It is only a temporary withdrawal!" he told them. "They're just going back to town."

"Yeah, like whipped pups," another said. "They're takin' their dead and wounded with 'em."

Hunter looked toward the retreating Mexicans and saw that they were, indeed, carrying several men back with them. The defensive fire of the Texians had been very effective.

"Anyone wounded?" Travis shouted up the line.

"Hawkins and Lynn," somebody shouted back.

"How badly?"

"Ain't nothin', sir," Hawkins called back. "A ball hit right betwixt us and we was cut up some by flyin' pieces of rock, that's all."

"Have your wounds attended to," Travis ordered. "Guards, remain at your posts. The rest of you have my congratulations on a job well-done."

"Colonel, might I make a recommendation?" a captain named Carey said.

"You may."

"I think it might be a good idea if some of us went out there to set fire to those houses. That way the Mexicans can't use them as cover when they come up again."

Travis stroked his chin. "I hate destroying private citizens' houses," he said. Then he nodded. "But I think you are right. It has to be done. Very well, call for volunteers."

Hunter was the first to volunteer. Sam McCord was second.

"Get mounted and meet me here in one hour," Carey ordered.

"Sam, you've got no business volunteering for something like this," Hunter said, as he and Sam were saddling their horses.

"What do you mean?"

"Marie has a child on the way."

Sam looked across the top of his horse toward Hunter.

"Hunter," he said quietly. "You let me worry about that. She is my wife, not yours."

"Sorry," Hunter replied.

"Besides," Sam went on. Saddled now, he swung up onto his horse. "There aren't any of us going to get out alive anyway. Our only hope is that Santa Anna will have mercy on the women."

"I think you may be right," Hunter replied, mounting his own animal.

After the brisk firefight in the morning, the mission to burn the houses proved to be somewhat anticlimactic. What fire there was from the Mexicans was weak and ineffective. The band of Texians, their actions covered by well-aimed fire from the riflemen who were back on the wall of the Alamo, roamed swiftly from house to house, setting them ablaze. When they rode back to the safety of the Alamo an hour later, a dozen houses were burning furiously behind them.

At noon, Travis ordered Dickerson to assemble the garrison so that he might read them the letter he was about to send out.

Marie was looking after Angelina while Susanna was doing a wash, when Almeron stuck his head into the tiny quarters. "Sue, Marie, Colonel Travis is going to read a letter that he is sending out. He wants everyone to assemble in front of the church."

"Civilians, too?" Susanna asked.

"He didn't say so, but I'm rounding them up," Dickerson replied. "After all, what happens to one of us, happens to us all."

"All right, Almeron," Susanna said. "Just let me get a wrap for the baby."

A few moments later Marie walked with Susanna to stand with the group of men and women to listen to Colonel Travis read his letter. Travis cleared his throat, then began, reading in a loud, clear voice.

"On the twenty-third of February, the enemy, in large force, entered the city of Bexar, which could not be prevented, as I had not sufficient forces to occupy both positions. Colonel Batres, the Adjutant-Major of the President-General Santa Anna, demanded a surrender at discretion, calling us foreign rebels. I answered them with a cannon shot, upon which the enemy commenced a bombardment with a five-inch howitzer, which together with a heavy cannonade, has been kept up incessantly ever since. I instantly sent express to Colonel Fannin, at Goliad, and to the people of Gonzales and San Felipe. Today at ten o'clock A.M. some two or three hundred Mexicans crossed the river below and came up under cover of the houses until they arrived within point blank shot, when we opened a heavy discharge of grape and canister on them, together with a well-directed fire from small arms which forced them to halt and take shelter in the houses ninety or one hundred yards from our batteries. The action continued to rage about two hours, when the enemy retreated in confusion, dragging off many of their dead and wounded.

"During the action the enemy kept up a constant bombardment and discharge of balls, grape, and canister. We knew from actual observation that many of the enemy were wounded . . . while we, on our part, have lost not a man. Two or three of our men have been slightly scratched by pieces of rock, but have not been disabled. I take great pleasure in stating that both officers and men conducted themselves with firmness and bravery. Captains Carey, Dickerson, McCord, and Blair, Lieutenant Simmons and Cornet Grant rendered essential service, and Charles Despallier and Robert Brown gallantly sallied out to set fire to houses which afforded the enemy shelter, in the face of enemy fire. Indeed, the whole of the men who were brought into action conducted themselves with such undaunted heroism that it would be injustice to discriminate. The Hon. David Crockett was seen at all points animating the men to do their duty. Our numbers are few and the enemy still continues to approximate his works to ours. I have every reason to apprehend an attack from his whole force very soon; but I shall hold out to the last extremity, hoping to secure reinforcements in a day or two. Do hasten on aid to me as rapidly as possible, as from the superior number of the enemy, it will be impossible for us to keep them out much longer. If they overpower us, we fall a sacrifice at the shrine of our country, and we hope posterity and our country will do our memory justice. Give me help, oh my country! Victory or death!"

Travis literally shouted the last three words, and his words were echoed again and again by the men of the Alamo. Marie felt tears streaking down her face, but she didn't know if they were tears of fear, sorrow, or pride.

Nineteen

On March 1, a company of thirty-two men arrived from Gonzales, bringing the garrison's strength up to just over one hundred and eighty men. The new arrivals were welcomed with mixed feelings, for while any assistance was appreciated, the addition of thirty-two men did nothing toward improving the chances for survival. In fact, it only added thirty-two more souls who would, eventually, perish in the conflict. Nevertheless, the thirty-two men took up their positions, and within a few hours were as adept at dodging the shot, shell, and shower of rocks raised by the constant cannonading, as those who had been there long before them.

Hunter Grant was standing with Davy Crockett on the parapet above the church. Of all the men in the Alamo, Hunter had grown the closest with Davy. Davy was clearly the most famous of all the defenders and had the most to be arrogant about, but was the most unassuming. He also had a wisdom, born not only of his years, but of the life he had experienced.

"I know it's been hard on you, Hunter," Davy said. "But you did the right thing."

"I beg your pardon?"

"Turnin' your woman over to McCord like you did. It's his baby she's carrying, isn't it?"

"How did . . . ?"

Davy chuckled. "How did I know? Hell, son, I been readin' signs since I was six years old. And not all sign is left on the ground." Davy had been loading his rifle as he talked, now he turned and looked out across the wall. The Mexicans were about three hundred yards away, milling around in plain sight, confident that they were well out of rifle range.

"Hey, now," Davy said. "Look at that fancy-dressed fella. He's got more geegaws and doodads than any of 'em. You reckon he's a general?"

"Which one?" Hunter asked.

"That one standin' well back from the rest, leanin' on the wheel of that wagon."

Hunter looked. "I don't know if he's a general or not, but he has to be some high-ranking officer. See how he's standing back out of danger while the rest of them are up on the line?"

Davy chuckled. "He just *thinks* he's out of danger."

Davy wet his finger and held it up to gage the direction of the wind. Then he steadied the barrel of his rifle on the palisade and took careful aim. A moment later smoke and fire belched from his roaring rifle, and the recoil shook him. Hunter kept his eyes on the distant figure and saw the Mexican officer suddenly grab his chest, stagger back against the side of the wagon, then slip down.

"Got 'im," Davy said simply.

"Juan?" Major Quinterra said as he felt himself slammed back against the wagon by the impact of the ball. He put his hands to his chest, then looked down in disbelief as blood began spilling through his fingers, staining his tunic. He slid down to the ground.

Juan Montoya was studying a map of the Alamo, which was spread on the ground on the opposite side of the wagon. He had heard the thudding sound of the bullet striking his friend, but he had not heard the report of a rifle.

"Manuel?" Juan shouted. He looked toward the Alamo, far in the distance, and saw a little puff of white smoke drifting away from the southwest corner of the wall.

"You were right, Juan," Manuel gasped. "They are devils, those men with their long rifles. Never would I have thought they could shoot this far."

Juan began tearing open Manuel's tunic. "Hold on, my friend," he said.

"Juan?" Manuel said. He reached and grabbed Juan's wrist, squeezed it hard, then all the strength left and his hand dropped.

"Manuel? Manuel?" Juan called to his friend.

"He is dead, Senor Colonel," one of Juan's sergeants said to him.

Juan crossed himself, then breathed a quick prayer over his friend's body.

"It was the tall one, in the coonskin cap," the sergeant said. He gave Juan his spyglass, and Juan looked toward the Alamo. He saw a tall man with flowing hair. The man was wearing a buckskin suit and a coonskin cap, and he was standing up boldly, calmly reloading his rifle. More than a hundred Mexican infantrymen returned his fire, but their shots were falling far short of the wall, and the tall man made no effort to duck. "I don't know who that is, Colonel," The sergeant continued. "I know only that he never misses. Never has there been a marksman like that one."

"You are wrong, Sergeant. There are more than one hundred just like him inside the Alamo. But that one," he recalled the shooting exhibition he had witnessed. "That one is the best. *Dios!*" he suddenly swore.

"What is it, Colonel?"

"The man standing beside him! I know him!" Juan stared at him for a moment longer. "So, Senor Grant," he said under his breath. "I am responsible for the death of your friend, and now you are responsible for the death of mine. We start over, but we are even this time."

"*Que?*" the sergeant asked.

"*Nada,* Sergeant. *Nada.*"

Hunter lowered his spyglass, then smiled wryly. He had been watching Montoya watching him, and he knew, by Montoya's reaction, that Montoya had recognized him.

"Mr. Grant! Mr. Grant!" someone called up from below.

"Yes," Hunter said, turning away from the wall and walking back to the edge of the parapet. "What is it?"

"Colonel Travis's compliments, sir, and he asks that you report to him."

"Hunter," Davy said.

"Yes?"

"That Mexican officer who was lookin' at us through his spyglass. Do you know him?"

"Yes."

"A friend of yours?"

"I wouldn't say that."

"The reason I asked, I can pick him off as easy as I did the other one."

"No," Hunter said. "I want him for myself."

Davy laughed. "Son, you ever stuck your hand down into a whole bowl of pecans, trying to find one special? 'Cause that's what you're saying. There's four or five thousand of 'em out there, and you want one of 'em for yourself."

"That's right," Hunter answered as he started down the ladder.

"Mr. Grant, I am sending another letter out, and I want to read it to you."

"You want to read it to me, sir?" Hunter asked, curious as to why Travis would single him out.

"Yes. If, by chance, you would happen to lose the letter in transit, I want you to be aware of its contents."

"I beg your pardon, sir. Are you suggesting that I be a courier?"

"I am not suggesting, Mr. Grant, I am ordering," Travis replied.

"Sir, if it is all the same to you, I'd rather you select someone else."

"It is not all the same to me," Travis replied.

"But, Colonel—"

Travis held up his hand to interrupt Hunter. "Mr. Grant, there is no time for empty bravado. I know that you want to stay here to share our fate. All of our couriers have expressed the same desire. But what you must understand is that our fate may well depend upon men like you, couriers who will brave the Mexican army to deliver these messages. Now, sir, have I made myself clear?"

"Yes, Colonel."

"Then please, be silent while I read this."

Travis picked up the letter and began to read:

"Do me the favor to send the enclosed to its proper destination instantly. I am still here, in fine spirits and well to do. With one hundred and forty men I have held this place ten days against a force variously estimated from one thousand five hundred to six thousand, and I shall continue to hold it till I get relief from my countrymen, or I will perish in its defense. We have had a shower of bombs and cannonballs continually falling among us the whole time, yet none of us have fallen. We have been miraculously preserved. You have no doubt seen my official report of the action of the twenty-fifth ultimate, in which we repulsed the enemy with considerable loss; on the night of the twenty-fifth, they made another attempt to charge us in the rear of the fort; but we received them gallantly by a discharge of grapeshot and musketry and they took to their scrapers immediately. They are now encamped under entrenchments, on all sides of us.

"All our couriers have gotten out without being caught, and a company of thirty-two men from Gonzales got in two nights ago, and Colonel Bonham got in today by coming between the powder house and the enemy's upper encampment. Let the Convention go on and make a declaration of independence and we will then understand, and the world will understand what we are fighting for. If independence is not declared, I shall lay down my arms, and so will the men under my command. But under the flag of independence, we are ready to peril our lives a hundred times a day, and dare the monster who is fighting us under a bloodred flag, threatening to murder all prisoners and make Texas a waste desert. I shall have to fight the enemy on his own terms yet I am ready to do it, and if my countrymen do not rally to my relief, I am determined to perish in the defense of this place, and my bones shall reproach my country for her neglect. With five hundred men more, I will drive the invaders beyond the Rio Grande, and I will visit my vengeance on the enemy of Texas whether invaders or resident Mexican enemies. All the citizens of this place that have not joined us are with the enemy fighting against us. Let the government declare them public enemies, otherwise she is acting a suicidal part. I shall treat them as such, unless I have superior orders to the con-

trary. My respects to all friends, confusion to all enemies. God bless you.

"William B. Travis"

"Hunter?"

Hunter was in the process of saddling his mount when he
heard Marie's voice from behind him. It was the first time
she had spoken directly to him since she married Sam. Hunter
stopped work, but he didn't turn around.

"Sam said you were going to take a message out of the
garrison."

"Yes," Hunter replied. He turned around and, seeing her,
felt his heart leap. How desperately he wanted to go to her
now, to put his arms around her and beg her to come with
him so that she, and the child she carried, might live. Instead,
he managed only a weak, "You shouldn't be here, Marie."

"I had to come," Marie said. "I had to let you know
that—"

Hunter held up his hand. "No, don't say it. No explana-
tions are necessary."

"I love you, Hunter, but you know I could do naught but
what I did."

"I know," Hunter agreed.

"I want you to take Prince."

"Marie, I can't take your horse."

"He is the best horse in the garrison, is he not?"

"Yes, but—"

"Then you must take him. I'll get him from the paddock."

Hunter sighed, then nodded. "All right," he said. He
turned back to his horse and removed the saddle. When he
turned back around, Marie was leading Prince toward him.
Then she stood by Prince, laying her cheek against his neck,
as Hunter saddled him. "Thanks," Hunter said, when Prince
was saddled.

"Hunter, I know we are all going to die in this place," she
said. "But I must know if you love me as I do you."

"Marie, this is no good for either one of us," Hunter said.
"I know."

Hunter started to mount but he stopped and turned toward
her. Then, with an anguished sigh, he took her in his arms,
kissing her deeply, holding her full-length against him.

"Yes," he said in a throaty voice. "Yes, I love you so much that a few moments ago I would have willingly thrown aside honor and loyalty to take you with me, away from Sam McCord, away from this place. But I can't do that, for if I did, it would destroy my soul, and yours, and then there would be nothing left of either of us."

"I am glad that you did not ask me," Marie replied. "For I cannot, and I will not leave Sam. But I will take comfort in knowing that you are safely away from here. Go now, Hunter. Go with God."

Hunter swung into the saddle, then looked down at her. For a long moment their eyes held, exchanging communication on a level far deeper than either of them had ever gone before. Then, with a slight nod, Hunter rode Prince out of the stable.

A moment later Hunter waited just inside the gate while on the parapet above, a guard was looking out over the Mexican soldiers, trying to determine when would be the best time for Hunter to leave.

"Get ready to open the gate," the guard called down.

The crossbar was already removed, and a soldier stood at the gate, waiting.

"Now!"

The gate was opened just wide enough for Hunter to slip through. He spurred his mount and Prince, responding to the urging, took off like a cannonball. At full gallop, he passed right through the Mexican lines, and was well on his way before any of them could react quickly enough to do anything to attempt to stop him.

Thursday, March 3

Colonel Fannin read the letter, then, shaking his head, put it down. "I'll give this to Travis," he said. "The man does know how to write inspiring letters."

"Yes, sir," Hunter agreed. "The question is, Colonel, are they inspiring enough to get you to come to our aid?"

"We started out a few days ago," Fannin said. "I had the relief column all formed up and ready to go, but we no more than got started than we broke a wagon wheel. Then a terrible thunderstorm came up and the river rose so that we couldn't get the rest of our wagons across. We were twenty-four hours underway, Mr. Grant," Fannin said. "Twenty-four hours, and we traveled but one-quarter of a mile." Fannin ran his hand through his hair. "So, we came back here," he concluded.

"Is the wagon wheel repaired?" Hunter asked.

"Beg your pardon?"

"I'm talking about the wagon wheel that was broken. Has it been repaired?"

"Oh, yes."

"And the river has receded?"

"What are you getting at, Mr. Grant?"

"I'm trying to talk you into taking your army to the Alamo to relieve those brave men who are there."

"Are you a military man, Mr. Grant?" Fannin suddenly asked.

"No, sir. Not really."

"Well, I am, Mr. Grant, I am. And, as a military man, I do not intend to commit my forces in too hasty a manner. I mean, think about it, man! It is too great a distance. We have inadequate transport. Our cannons are too heavy for the roads between here and there, and even food and water might be a problem for us. I am only doing what caution dictates."

"Yes, Colonel Fannin," Hunter replied. "But are you doing what honor requires?"

Colonel Fannin was so shocked by the answer that all he could do was stare as Hunter turned and walked out.

"Where are you going, Mr. Grant?" Fannin called to him.

"I *am* doing what honor requires," Hunter tossed back over his shoulder. "I am returning to the Alamo."

FRIDAY, MARCH 4

Back at the Alamo, the defenders were working hard to shore up fortifications that had been damaged by the cannonade and to reposition guns that the cannonballs knocked from their mounts. They dug trenches within the plaza itself in the event the walls were breached, and they positioned ammunition, water, and food at various places in case they were besieged within the fort.

By now, Jim Bowie's illness had almost totally incapacitated him, though there were times when he was able to take part in the defense preparations. He had his men carry his cot from one part of the fort to another in order to allow him to give instructions and encouragement.

Colonel Travis had one last ace to play. There was under his command a Mexican named Juan Seguin, who had chosen to fight on the side of the Texians.

The Mexicans had made several unsuccessful assaults on the fort over the last few days, and had been turned back each time, often after losing several men. On one such foray a Mexican officer was killed close enough to the fort to allow the Texians to recover his body, and Juan Seguin was given his uniform to wear. It was Travis's intention to let Seguin slip out during the night, carrying one last desperate appeal for help. Because he was Mexican and because he wore a Mexican uniform, Seguin had a good chance of getting through.

Travis authorized the married men to write one last letter to their wives. A man named Isaac Millsaps approached Marie and asked her to write a letter for him. She couldn't turn down his request, though she dreaded the task of writing what might very well be his last words to his wife. Nevertheless, she located pen and paper and wrote the letter Millsaps dictated:

My dear, dear ones,

 We are in the fortress of the Alamo, a ruined church that has most fell down. The Mexicans are here in large numbers. They have kept up a constant fire since they got here. All of our boys are well and Captain Martin is in good spirits. Early this morning I watched the Mexicans drilling just out of range. They was marching up and down with such order. They have bright red and blue uniforms and many cannons. Some here at this place believe that the main army has not come up yet. I think they is all here, even Santa Anna. Colonel Bowie is down sick and had to be to bed. I

saw him yesterday and he is still ready to fight. He
didn't know me from last spring but he did remember
Washington. He tells us all that help will be here soon
and it makes us feel good. We have beef and corn to
eat but no coffee. The bag I had fell off on the way
here so it was all spilt. I have not seen Travis but two
times since he told us that Fannin was going to be
here with many men and there would be a good fight.
He stays on the wall some but mostly to his room. I
hope help comes soon 'cause we can't fight them all. •
Some says he is going to talk some tonight, and group
us better for defense. If we fail here get to the river
with the children. All Texas will be before the enemy.
We get so little news; we know nothing. There is no
discontent in our boys. Some are tired from lack of
sleep and rest. The Mexicans are shooting every four
minutes but most of the shots fall inside and do no
harm. I don't know what else to say. They is calling
for all letters. Kiss the dear children for me and believe as I do that all will be well and God protects us
all.

Isaac.

If any men come through there tell them to hurry
with the powder for it is short. I hope you get this and
know I love you all.

Colonel Seguin carried the letters out that night with god-
speed from everyone in the fort. There was very little sleeping
that night, because the Mexican cannon kept up its firing all
night long. Most of the men of the Alamo remained at their
posts, while the women moved into the sacristy of the church.

Marie helped Susanna put Angelina to bed, then the two
women sat on the floor with their backs to the wall and talked.
It was dark in the room; they dared not light a candle lest the
light attract the Mexican artillery fire. Occasionally one of the
Texas guns would answer the Mexican fire, and when a gun
inside the fort fired, it would send out a flash of light a little
like lightning, followed immediately by its own thunder. That
flash of light was the only illumination in the room.

"Susanna, why are you in here?" Marie asked. "Why

didn't you leave when you had the opportunity?''

"I don't know, really," Susanna answered. "I guess Almeron and I never thought it would come down to this. Besides, where would I go? San Antonio is our home. Almeron has a good business as a blacksmith there."

"But to put yourself inside a fort during a siege?" Marie said.

Susanna laughed, and though Marie couldn't see it, she could imagine the pretty young woman pushing her blond hair back from her face, as was her habit.

"Listen to you!" Susanna said. "When I came to San Antonio I didn't know we would undergo a siege. You came here knowing it."

"Yes," Marie said. "I guess you are right."

"We are both in here for the same reason, I suppose," Susanna said. "We are here to be with the men we love."

"Yes," Marie said. "The men we love." The word had a double meaning for her, but Susanna didn't pick up on it.

There was a whistling sound as a Mexican shell came in. It crashed into the wall of the church with a loud noise, sending pieces of rock scattering throughout. Marie and Susanna cried out in alarm and held each other until the noise subsided.

"That one was close," Susanna said.

"Yes, it was. Susanna, do you believe in the survival of the soul?"

"Yes, of course. Don't you?"

"I . . . I suppose I do," Marie said. "But it was easy to say in the past. I've never had to come face-to-face with death before now."

"Now is when the truth of it is most evident to me," Susanna said.

The two women talked a little longer, but after a while they grew quiet and, despite the cannonade, managed to drift off to sleep.

Saturday, March 5

The next morning the defenders of the Alamo saw that, during the night, the Mexicans had moved their cannon to within two-hundred-fifty yards of the Alamo. Now the guns were so close that when they fired against the walls, the stone chips flew like hail across the plaza.

The Mexicans kept up their firing all day long. Marie and the other women carried water to the Texians at their stations, but they had to be alert to dodge the shells. Also, the guns were beginning to do some serious damage to the walls, and the defenders were hard-pressed to make the necessary repairs.

Sam was at the artillery command post at the south end of the west wall. He smiled as Marie handed him a dipper full of water, and he reached out and put his hand on her hair.

"Marie, how I wish I had never even met you."

"Why, Sam McCord, why would you say such a thing?" Marie gasped.

"Because my knowing you . . . and loving you, is what got you mixed up in all of this. I am going to meet my Maker, knowing that it is my fault that you are here in the Alamo when you could be somewhere else, safe."

"No, Sam, there is no fault," Marie replied. "Neither yours, nor mine. There is only what is."

"Miz McCord?" someone farther down the line called. "Could we have some water down here, please?"

Sam let his hand drop from her hair to the junction of her neck and shoulder, and he squeezed it lightly. "Go," he said. "Tend to the others. I don't think we have much time left. Those cannons can't get any closer without the Mexicans staging an all-out attack."

"I'll come back as soon as I can," Marie promised. Then she moved along the parapet to give water to the others.

"Marie?" Susanna called up to her about half an hour later. "Won't you help me fix lunch for the men?"

"Yes, of course," Marie said, passing the water bucket off to someone else, then climbing down the ladder.

"Listen," Susanna said brightening, as the two women began cooking. "I have spoken with Colonel Travis and he said it would be all right for my Almeron and your Sam to leave the wall for a while tonight."

"Leave the wall? What for?"

Susanna looked at Marie and smiled. "Why, you're the

bride, not I," she said. "I shouldn't think you would have to even ask such a question."

"Oh," Marie said, blushing mightily. "I just wasn't thinking."

"Understandable. You've certainly had other things to think about. But Almeron believes the main attack will come tomorrow and he doesn't know when we will be able to, uh . . ." This time Susanna blushed as she found she couldn't finish the statement.

"Oh, Sue, do you really think the attack will come tomorrow?"

"Yes," Susanna said. "Yes, I do."

Marie blinked several times, and tears began to roll down her cheeks. Susanna put her hand on Marie's cheek.

"We've all known it was coming," she said.

"Yes, I know." Marie wiped her eyes, then smiled. "Please forgive me."

"There is nothing to forgive," Susanna said. "I guess I have just cried so much that I have no tears left."

"Susanna, I have never met a braver woman than you."

"Oh, I don't know about that. You are facing the same dangers, just as bravely."

"Yes," Marie teased. "Yes, we are both brave, aren't we?"

"Oh, Marie, I have a wonderful idea," Susanna said. "Let's have supper together tonight, you and Sam, Almeron and me. It'll be ever so nice, just as if the two of you had come to our house in normal times."

"Yes," Marie said, and though she tried to stop them, the tears began to flow again. This time the tears were for the sense of loss she felt at never having lived a married life in normal times and realizing that now she never would.

Marie and Susanna took the noon meal around to the men on their posts, dodging the shot and shell that continued to rain down on the plaza. After the noon meal was served to everyone the two women planned their evening. They gathered bone china and German crystal and silverware, and they even found a linen tablecloth in order to be able to set an elegant table.

"I have two party dresses," Susanna said, as they put the

last touches on the table. "You may have the first choice."

"I couldn't do that," Marie said. "They are yours."

"I won't enjoy dressing up for the party unless you dress up as well."

"Very well, but you must have first choice," Marie insisted.

"Let's pick them out now," Susanna suggested.

One of the dresses was red, the other blue. Susanna spread them out on the bed in the room she had shared with Almeron until the shelling had started in earnest. She stood there with her finger on her chin, looking at them. "You know the only thing I don't like about them?" she asked.

"What?"

"They are the color of the accursed Mexican uniforms."

"They are, aren't they?" Marie replied. "But I refuse to let the Mexicans take away those lovely colors. Susanna, you must wear the blue. It will really bring out the color of your eyes."

"And the red will look lovely on you," Susanna said.

Marie picked up the dress and held it to her. It was so pretty, and she closed her eyes and recalled the last time she had dressed up for a party. It had been the party at which the engagement of Lucinda Meechum and Hunter Grant had been announced.

"I have never had a better friend in my life than you," she said, and she put her arms around Susanna and embraced her.

"We are going to have such a fine time tonight that Santa Anna can just go to blazes," Susanna said, and she and Marie both laughed.

Twenty

Hunter surveyed the scene before him. In the distance he could see the Alamo, a great bastion spread out over several acres of ground. Flags waved from all four corners of the fort, and he could see the defenders moving along the top of the walls.

Surrounding the Alamo was an even larger assembly of troops than had been there before Hunter left. Tents, wagons, horses, cannons, and brightly uniformed soldiers were everywhere. Bursts of smoke drifted across the field, followed by a distant thunder. From his position, Hunter could see the black balls flying swiftly toward the fort. Some disappeared over the walls to land inside, but many hit the walls, sending showers of splinters from their impact.

Hunter tried to figure out a way to get inside the Alamo. No matter which way he went, he would have to pass through the Mexican army, and he would have to cover more than three hundred yards of open territory. Finally, he decided that the only way to get inside would be to approach the fort at full gallop and hope that the guards recognized him in time to open the gates. He took a deep breath, then slapped his heels against Prince's sides.

The horse broke out of the thicket at full gallop. Unfortunately for Hunter, a nearby defilade concealed an entire company of Mexican troops, and he suddenly found himself in their midst. At that, he might have made it through had not one quick-thinking Mexican soldier waved a blanket in front of Hunter's horse. Prince, already nervous from the cannonade, reared wildly, unseating Hunter. A dozen soldiers were on him in an instant.

"I know who you are," the Mexican officer to whom Hunter was taken said. "You are the brave one who rescued the senorita in distress."

"This is quite a change for you, isn't it, Lopez?" Hunter

asked. "These men are real soldiers, preparing for real battle. I thought you conducted all your battles against women."

Lopez chuckled. "I must confess that there was a time when I was in dishonor among my countrymen," he said. "But after this victory, my honor and the honor of my country will be redeemed."

"There will be no honor in this victory, believe me," Hunter said. "The entire world is watching what is going on here. You can't win. Even if you kill everyone inside, you can't win."

"We shall see about that," Lopez replied. "And we do intend to kill everyone inside."

"Women and children as well?"

Lopez took in the town with a wave of his hand. "The women and the children of Bexar, we will not harm," he said. "Those who went inside did so of their own free will. The responsibility of their death will lie with the defenders, for they had the opportunity to abandon the fort before we arrived."

"They couldn't do that," Hunter said. "They are honorable men. But of course, you would know nothing about honor."

"How about you, senor? Do you know anything about honor?"

"I think I do."

"And yet, you are out here while the others are inside. Were you trying to run away?"

"I was trying to get back in."

"So you say."

"I don't have to explain my actions to you."

"No, senor, you do not," Lopez admitted. "But, I will be interested, none the less, to see if you can die with honor and dignity." Lopez barked an order in Spanish, then he smiled at Hunter. "I have just given the order to have you shot," he said. "You have your choice as to whether or not you will wear a blindfold."

"He will not be shot!" another voice said, and, looking toward the speaker, Hunter saw Juan Montoya coming toward him.

"I beg your pardon, Colonel, but the orders of the *presi-*

dente are that everyone will be shot.''

"Those orders pertain only to those who are captured inside the Alamo, after the battle," Juan said. "They do not apply in this case."

"I believe they do, Colonel," Lopez said.

"And I say they do not! Are you going to question me, *Capitano?*" Juan snapped angrily.

"No, senor," Lopez replied.

Juan pointed to Hunter. "Tie his hands," he ordered. "And bring him into my quarters."

"*Si*, Colonel," a sergeant said. He pulled Hunter's hands around behind him.

"No," Juan corrected. "I do not wish to make him uncomfortable. Tie them in front."

"*Si*, Colonel."

A moment later, Hunter, with his hands tied in front of him, was led into one of the nearby houses, where Juan had established his headquarters. A guard was on either side of Hunter.

Juan looked up at the guards. "Leave," he ordered.

"But, senor, he is a prisoner and should be guarded," one of the guards complained.

"I said leave," Juan said again.

Both guards saluted, then left.

"Sit down, Señor Grant," Juan said, indicating a chair that was pulled up to a table. Juan got a bottle of wine and two glasses, then sat across the table from Hunter. He filled the two glasses, then slid one across to Hunter.

"I don't exactly regard this as a social occasion," Hunter said.

"*Por favor,*" Juan said. "Please."

Hunter hesitated for a minute, then he drank the wine.

"I know what you must think of me," Juan said. "But I want you to know that I didn't know anything about what happened to your friend until recently." Juan tossed his drink down, then wiped his mouth with the back of his hand. "Tell me, senor, what sort of men fight duels, even if one of the parties to the duel is not present?"

Hunter didn't answer.

Juan sighed. "It was not cowardice which made me leave," he said.

"Do you expect me to believe that?" Hunter asked.

Juan shook his head. "No, senor, I do not expect you to believe it for, indeed, I would not believe it either. But it is true. You see, I began thinking about the duel and I realized that it had been I who pressed the issue. Therefore, any blood that would have been shed the next morning . . . whether it had been your blood or mine, would have been on my hands."

Hunter continued to stare across the table, saying nothing.

"I did not want that," Juan continued. "I did not want to be killed, and I did not want to kill an innocent man. I thought if I left, that would be the end of it. Instead, in the . . . insane . . . code of honor by which fools live in Louisiana, you, senor, were forced to shoot your best friend. And for that, senor, I am truly, truly, remorseful."

"Yes, well, being sorry doesn't bring Johnny back, does it?"

"No, senor, it does not," Juan admitted. He poured each of them another drink. "And I know what it is like to lose a very good friend, for I lost one myself a few days ago."

"You are talking about the officer by the wagon," Hunter said. "The one Davy Crockett shot."

"Manuel Tomas Quinterra," Juan said. He took a drink, then nodded. "Manuel and I had been friends for a long time," he said. "We were cadets together, lieutenants, commanders. I was best man at his wedding, I am godfather to his firstborn." He shrugged. "We were both prepared to die in battle. But to die as Manuel did . . . with a bullet fired from so far away that one could not even hear the report of the rifle?" Again, Juan shook his head. "That is no way for a soldier to die, senor. It is not battle, it is murder."

"How does that differ from all the cannonballs you are shooting into the fort?" Hunter replied.

"I do not agree with that either. If it were me, I would shoot the cannons only at the walls, to break them down," Juan said. He paused for a moment, then continued. "Soon now, General Santa Anna will order an all-out attack and the garrison will surely fall. The question now is, what shall I do with you?''

"Looks to me as if you don't have any choice," Hunter said. "Your general wants us all shot."

"Then I won't turn you over to my general. I shall keep you for myself."

"Why would you want to do that?"

"Because, Senor Grant, after the Alamo has fallen, I intend to give you the opportunity to finish what we started in New Orleans."

"Do you mean the duel?"

"*Si*, senor. I mean the duel."

6:00 P.M.

The afternoon passed quickly as Susanna and Marie prepared a special supper to share with their husbands. Before supper, however, Travis called another meeting of his men, and Sam and Almeron had to attend. Marie and Susanna stood under the sally port and listened as Travis spoke in a quiet, but determined voice. Then he unsheathed his sword and drew a line in the dirt.

"Gentlemen, it is clear that Fannin cannot"—he paused for a long moment before he went on—"or will not come to our aid. As I see it, there are now three options open to us. We can surrender to the Mexicans, we can try to get away by sneaking out in the middle of the night, or we can stay and fight.

"For myself, honor dictates but one course. I am going to stay and fight. If I fall, I fall a sacrifice to the shrine of our country, and I hope posterity and our country will do our memory justice. I offer you the opportunity to stay with me, but if you choose to do so, you must know that all who remain here can have but one hope . . . and that is to realize a valiant death. With that as my only promise to you, I ask now that those of you who wish to stand by me to cross this line." Travis shouted the last three words. "Victory or death!"

"Well, hell, boys, I can't get across it by myself," Bowie

called from his cot. "So somebody better carry me."

With a hurrah, two men grabbed Bowie's cot, then everyone but one stepped across the line. The one man who remained behind was Louis Rose.

"I'm sorry," Rose apologized to the others. "I am just not ready to die. Come full dark, I'm going to slip out of here."

"Look here, Rose," someone started to say, but Travis held up his hand to stop him.

"No," Travis said. "Let no man here find fault with Louis Rose. For to fault him would be to decrease the valor of those who will stay." Travis turned toward Rose without rancor. "Mr. Rose, you have my permission to leave the post at your convenience," Travis said. "And may God go with you."

Rose looked at all the men. He started to say something, but he found that he couldn't speak. Instead, he turned and walked away.

No one spoke to him. They weren't purposely giving him the silent treatment . . . rather it was as if he no longer existed for them. They had already crossed over into another plane, no longer with the living, but not yet with the dead.

Later, as Marie and Sam shared their supper with Susanna and Almeron, the gaiety of their conversation belied the situation. The gaiety may have been forced, but it was there, nonetheless.

Angelina cried for attention once, and her mother picked her up and played with her. The little girl laughed, and Marie reached over to touch her.

"I think what I regret most," Marie said, "is that I will never see the child I am carrying."

Susanna looked up in surprise, for she didn't know until that moment that Marie was expecting. Then she picked up Angelina and handed the baby over to Marie. "We will share this child," she said.

Angelina sat on Marie's lap. For a moment, the baby just looked at her with large, curious blue eyes, then she reached up and grabbed a handful of Marie's hair. Marie laughed.

"Don't I get to play daddy?" Sam asked quietly.

"Of course you do," Marie answered, handing Angelina to her husband.

Sam held the little girl with exceptional tenderness, then he kissed her on the cheek and passed her back to her father.

"It is getting late," Susanna said a few moments later.

"It isn't late," Almeron said, puzzled by his wife's statement. "Why it can't be more than—"

"Yes, it is getting late," Susanna said pointedly. Suddenly Almeron realized what she was saying, and he smiled.

"Ah," he said. "Yes, I think you are right."

"What are you talking about?" Sam asked, not yet catching on.

"Sam McCord, I know you haven't been married very long, but you certainly ought to have sense enough to know when a husband and wife want to be alone," Marie teased.

"Oh," Sam said. "Oh, I'm sorry, I wasn't, uh . . ." His sentence trailed off in embarrassment.

"Don't worry about it, Sam," Almeron said. "I've been married a lot longer than you, and I didn't catch on myself for a while. But I expect we'd both like a little time alone with our wives."

"Yes," Sam said.

"Poor Sam," Susanna said. "You'll have so little time with your wife, and she is such a wonderful woman."

Sam smiled and put his hand on Marie's neck. "You're right," he said. "She is a wonderful woman. You know, I've heard that the Indians believe there is no difference between the soul of a tree that lives a hundred years and that of a flower that blooms and dies in a day. They figure that the flower gets as much out of life as the tree."

Hand in hand, Sam and Marie walked toward their own room to spend their last night together.

"Marie," Sam said in a husky voice. "On the night we were wed, you asked me to give you a little more time, and I have done that. But we're like the flower I told you about, darlin'. Time has about run out on us."

"I know," Marie answered. She leaned into Sam. "So we'll be like that flower, Sam. We'll get as much out of the time we have remaining as we possibly can."

8:00 P.M.

Outside in the plaza, some men were singing. At first the music was raucous and off-key, with a great deal of laughing and several loud criticisms thrown in. But the efforts continued until, at last, three or four men found a song that they all knew. They began singing and their voices suddenly blended into sweet harmony, with one clear tenor voice carrying the lead. The ballad was of a young man, parting from his true love, and the entire garrison grew quiet to listen to the music. The melody and the words drifted across the plaza to strike resonant chords in the hearts of all who were thinking of their own loves, and the insurmountable gulf that now separated them.

"Marie," Sam started, but Marie hushed him, and put her fingers on his lips.

"No," she said. "Don't speak now, Sam. We've said all the words that need to be said. We've other ways to communicate now."

Sam's breath quickened, then he took her into his arms and kissed her. They moved to the bed and Sam's hands went to her clothes, helping release a catch here and untie a bow there, until, finally, Marie was totally nude and caught up in a rising tide of pleasure.

While Sam removed his own clothes, Marie lay on the bed, silent and unprotesting, listening to the beautiful music from outside. It seemed, somehow, as if the music were just for them, and when they began their lovemaking, it was rich and fulfilling, strongly physical and immensely satisfying. It was as if all their emotions were perfectly orchestrated to move in harmony, so that there was a tremendous sense of mutual need and attainment.

Sam was amazingly tender with her, taking her slowly, causing her to arch her body up to him, holding himself in her for as long as possible, then feeling him join her as he spent himself in her.

A last shudder of ecstasy convulsed both of them, and they collapsed back onto the bed, lying in each other's arms for a long moment before Sam rolled away from her. Marie lay with her eyes closed until, gradually, sounds from outside began to penetrate.

The music was gone, to be replaced by the occasional crump of artillery, a sergeant shouting impatient orders, and a group of men laughing over some joke, shared in the very face of death.

Then, they both slept.

Sam awoke once in the middle of the night. Marie was sleeping beside him, breathing softly. Sam reached over, gently, and put his hand on her naked hip. He could feel the sharpness of her hipbone and the soft yielding of her flesh. The contrasting textures were delightful to his sense of touch.

He knew, and accepted, the fact that this would be his last night with her. He let his hand rest there, enjoying a feeling of possession, until finally sleep claimed him once again.

11:00 P.M.

"Where is Major Quinterra?" Santa Anna asked. He had called a meeting of his senior officers and noticed that Quinterra wasn't with Juan.

"He is dead, General," Juan answered.

"Dead? How can that be? We have not yet made an assault against the walls."

"He was killed by Davy Crockett."

"Kwockey?"

"*Crockett*. He is quite famous in America. I understand he was once a member of Congress. And his shooting is legendary, as I told you in my report."

"Oh, yes, the long rifle you were telling me about," Santa Anna said.

"*Si*. He, alone, has already killed more than a score of our men from over three hundred yards away."

"Well, we shall see how effective his one gun is against my entire army. Gentlemen, tomorrow morning, just at dawn, we will attack. Here is a map of the citadel. I suggest you study it."

Santa Anna spread the map out on a small field table and
his officers gathered around.

"I shall divide my infantry into four columns, each of
which shall contain eight hundred men. Two columns will
attack the north wall, one from the east and the other from
the west. A third column will attack the east wall, and the
fourth column, led by you, Colonel Montoya, will attack the
palisade from the south, here, nearest the church."

"That is where Crockett is most often seen," Juan said.
"I will be pleased to attack there."

"I will direct the attack from here," Santa Anna said,
pointing to a spot about five hundred yards from the wall. "I
will keep four hundred men in reserve."

The cavalry commander spoke: "You have given no position for the cavalry, Excellency."

"The cavalry will be held at the ready," Santa Anna said.
"If the rebels try to break out, you will run them down." He
took a deep breath. "And you will kill them," he added.

"When will the attack begin?" Juan asked.

"We will move into position at one o'clock in the morning," Santa Anna answered. "We will crawl forward, silently, on our bellies, and at the break of dawn we will
strike."

"That's a very good plan, General," several of the officers
said, and Santa Anna smiled and nodded in response to their
servile compliments.

"I have conceived the master plan," Santa Anna said.
"Now, I call upon you, Colonel Montoya, to work out the
details."

"But, General," Juan protested. "I have just learned of the
attack."

"The attack is already carefully planned. It is the other
things, the details of supply and movement, which I ask you
to arrange. If you are not capable, tell me, and I will find
someone who is."

Juan cleared his throat. "General, I will do as you ask."

Juan studied the map as the other commanders stared at
him. He knew that they were secretly enjoying his discomfort,
and he knew also that they were glad Santa Anna hadn't put
them on the spot.

"Issue each musket-bearer ten rounds of ammunition," Juan said. "And give every fiftieth man a scaling ladder and some picks and spikes."

"Very good, Colonel," Santa Anna said. The other commanders brooded over the fact that Juan had successfully risen to the challenge thrown him by Santa Anna.

"See that the men are fed and let them get as much rest as possible between now and the time we attack," Juan went on. "And end the cannonade."

"Why would you wish to do that, Colonel Montoya?" Captain Lopez asked.

"For eleven days we have been shelling the Texians. It has done nothing except unnerve them. If we end it suddenly, they will be even more unnerved."

Santa Anna smiled. "A good idea, Colonel. Ricardo, you should listen to him. Perhaps you could learn something. Very well, I will stop the barrage."

"General, we are flying the red flag," Lopez said. "That means that any rebel we capture is to be put to the sword. Am I correct?"

"That is correct," Santa Anna said. "We will take no prisoners. All will be put to the sword. These perfidious foreigners must be taught a lesson."

"And if we capture any prisoners before the battle?" Lopez asked.

"Before the battle? How would we capture any prisoners before the battle?" Santa Anna replied.

Juan glared menacingly at Lopez, as if warning him against saying anything else, and Lopez blinked a couple of times, then, thinking better of challenging Juan, cleared his throat. "*Nada,* General. Just an idle question," he said.

"We have no time for idle questions," Santa Anna said, dismissing him.

"General, I think tomorrow morning, as we attack, the buglers should again play the *Deguello,* as they did when the red flag was raised," Juan continued.

"*Si,*" Santa Anna agreed. "Only"—he held up his finger—"have the buglers begin now. They should play in relays so that it will be heard by the defenders throughout the night."

"*Si,* General."

"And now," Santa Anna said, "we must get some rest. Tomorrow, we shall have a great victory." He held up a wineglass. "For Mexico!" he shouted.

"For Mexico!" All the officers returned.

"For his Excellency, *El Presidente,* General Santa Anna!" someone shouted, and, as Santa Anna beamed, the others repeated the toast.

Juan returned to his own command, then sent word by courier to all the subordinate commanders within his area of responsibility. The word traveled fast, and the artillery bombardment ceased as the men lay down to get what rest they could. By nightfall, an uneasy quiet had descended over the land, except for the buglers. The buglers, as instructed, were playing the *Deguello,* and the plaintive notes drifted out loud and clear, then returned in a haunting echo from the walls of the Alamo.

Back in the house he had commandeered as his headquarters, Juan paced about nervously. Finally he mounted his horse and rode among the commanders to make certain that all was in readiness. Hunter called out to Juan when he returned just after midnight from his final inspection ride. Hunter was chained to the bedstead.

"Is it to be this morning?" Hunter asked.

"*Si,*" Juan replied.

"And you are to give no quarter?"

Juan nodded. "I am sorry. Santa Anna has given the order that we are to take no prisoners."

"In the name of God, Montoya, do you intend to murder them all?"

"Murder, Senor Grant?" Juan replied. "What will take place will not be murder, it will be an act of war. And those who are killed will fall, honorably, in battle. Unlike the coldblooded slaying of my friend from three hundred yards away!"

Hunter pulled at the cuffs and chain that restrained him, but he couldn't get loose.

"Free me, Montoya," he said. "Free me and let me go into the Alamo to die with brave men."

Juan shook his head. "I'm sorry. It is too late for that."

Juan walked away from Hunter and then, along with his officers, began waking the troops who had managed to go to sleep. Armed with muskets and ten rounds of ammunition apiece, the men began moving forward, quietly.

The moon and stars were hidden by clouds, and the night was cold. The men shivered convulsively, though perhaps as much from fear as from the chill night air.

By four o'clock, nearly every man was in position, lying on the cold ground, quietly waiting. Near the position Juan had taken, an owl hooted, and, in the distance, a coyote howled.

Twenty-one

4:00 A.M., SUNDAY, MARCH 6

The cry of the coyote awakened Marie. Or had she been aroused by the sound of her husband leaving their bed?

"Sam?" she called quietly.

Sam was standing in the doorway of their room, looking out over the plaza. Just beyond him was the final defensive line erected by the engineers. This was a circular palisade, made of dirt and cowhide, forming small fortresses outside each room. If the walls were breached the defenders would fall back to the low barracks and fight from inside the rooms. The thought of a battle occurring right here in the very room she had shared with Sam frightened Marie.

Sam turned at the sound of his name, and she knew he was smiling at her even though she couldn't see his face clearly in the shadows.

"Listen," Sam said.

"Listen to what? I don't hear anything except the bugler," she replied.

"That's just it," Sam said. "The bombardment stopped before midnight last night. That can only mean the Mexicans are about to attack."

"Oh, Sam, do you really think so?"

Sam heard the anxiety in Marie's voice and walked over

to sit on the bed and hold her in his arms.

"I want to say thank you, Marie," he said.

"For what?"

"For making these last few days of my life happier than all the rest put together."

"Sam, I know I disrupted your life," Marie started, but Sam put his finger to her lips to silence her.

"Let me talk," he said. "I don't have much time left."

"All right."

"I did you wrong—"

"Sam . . ."

"Please, Marie."

Marie grew silent.

"I sinned against God and against you by leaving you as I did . . . and by not having the strength to accept you for what you are."

"For what I am?" Marie asked, her face twisted in confusion.

"I know now that it doesn't really matter what a person is . . . it is *who* they are that counts. I love you now, and I loved you then. I should have had the courage to take you out of Louisiana so I could marry you."

"I don't understand, Sam. Why would you have to take me out of Louisiana to marry me?"

"Then you don't know? You really don't know, do you?"

"Sam, what are you talking about?"

Sam put his arms around her and pulled her to him. "It doesn't matter anymore, Marie. It doesn't matter at all."

"Sam, please. What are you talking about?"

Sam took a deep breath, then let out a long sigh. "Marie, in the eyes of the law, at least, in the eyes of Louisiana law, you are colored."

Marie stiffened in his arms, then jerked back and looked into Sam's face.

"I am what?" she asked.

"You are colored, Marie. Your mama is a quadroon."

Marie felt as if the breath had suddenly been knocked from her, and she took several steps back, then sat on the bed.

"I'm colored?" she asked in a small voice.

"Yes. But it means nothing, Marie. I can see that now. I

only wish that I could have seen it before all this . . . before it was too late for us.''

"Then that . . . that must explain why I never met any of my mother's people," Marie said. "I always thought it was because she was an orphan."

"I know she was just trying to protect you. I'm sorry that I'm the one to have to tell you now. But if . . . if the Mexicans spare you, I don't want you to ever be hurt by something hidden in your past."

Marie held out her hands and studied them.

"I know," Sam said. "You are just as white as I am. It isn't fair that you should be counted as all-colored, when your blood is only one-eighth colored. By rights, you should be counted as all-white."

"No, Sam," Marie said. "I don't want to be protected. And I don't want to be all-white."

Sam looked at her in confusion. "What do you mean?"

"Sam, I am who I am. To deny the part of me that is colored would be to deny my mother, and her mother, and her mother before her. I won't do that. I feel no different this morning than I did last night. I am still Marie Doucette. And if our marriage is legal—''

"It is legal, darling, it is!" Sam said. "We were married in Texas, by Mexican law."

"Then I am Marie Doucette McCord, through and through, no less that one-eighth part of me than any other."

"I love you, Marie," Sam said. He smiled. "All eight-eighths of you."

"And I love you," Marie replied, knowing that she did, even without denying her love for Hunter Grant. They embraced for a long moment, then Marie asked, "What's going to happen, Sam? I mean, when the Mexicans come, what should I do?"

"Go to the sacristy and stay there," Sam said. "Don't come out for any reason until the shooting has completely stopped. The Mexicans have declared that they will show no quarter, but I believe they will spare the women and the children."

Marie shuddered.

"Tell me you will do it," Sam said. "I'll feel much easier

if I know you have a chance.''

"I'll go to the sacristy," Marie promised.

Sam squeezed her one last time, then kissed her on the lips. He let his hand linger on her neck for just a second, then he turned and walked out into the chill night air.

5:00 A.M.

In the east, a faint streak of pink began to lighten the sky. Soon it would be dawn, and the attack would begin. Juan felt an uneasiness in the pit of his stomach, and he knew that if he held his hand before his eyes he would be able to detect a quiver. He was growing anxious for the attack to begin. Once the fighting was underway, he knew he would be all right.

The troops were also growing anxious, for they were beginning to fidget and whisper among themselves. Finally, one of the soldiers could keep quiet no longer. He rose to his feet and shouted at the top of his voice, *"Viva Santa Anna!"*

"Viva Santa Anna!" a hundred voices echoed. Then the shout was taken up by thousands, and the lone bugler was joined by a score of others, all sounding the attack. The troops surged forward, and the darkness of the morning was filled with the rolling thunder of thousands of running feet as the Mexican soldiers rushed toward the Alamo.

"Viva Santa Anna!"

There was only a tiny amount of coffee left, and the defenders of the Alamo had saved it for this very hour. Sam, Almeron, and Colonel Travis's adjutant, Captain John Baugh, stood on the wall nursing their coffee and wondering when the attack would begin. When they heard the shouts and the bugles and the rumble of running feet, they knew that this was the moment.

"Say a prayer, boys," Sam said quietly. "This is it!"

"I'll inform Colonel Travis," Captain Baugh said. He scrambled down the ladder and ran across the plaza to the room where Travis lay sleeping.

"Colonel Travis!" he shouted. "The Mexicans are coming!"

Travis leaped up from his bed, grabbed his sword and shotgun, then raced across the plaza toward the ladder on the north wall.

"Here they come, Colonel!" Sam said, as Travis and Baugh joined him.

Out of the morning darkness came the shadowy figures of hundreds and hundreds of Mexican soldiers. They were all shouting now. Some were issuing challenges; others were just shouting to keep up their own courage.

"We're loaded and ready, Colonel," one of the artillerymen said to Travis.

"As soon as you have them within range, blast away!" Travis said. "Then reload and fire again as quickly as you can!"

"They're in range, Colonel!" one of the riflemen shouted.

"Open fire!" Travis replied.

The Texas riflemen opened fire from their position atop the walls, and the cannon raked the charging mass of Mexicans with the cut bits of horseshoe that Almeron had prepared for them. The Mexican attackers fell in waves.

"Hurrah, m'boys, hurrah!" Travis shouted.

The Texians were cool and collected, and they took careful aim before firing. Every volley felled as many Mexicans as there were shots fired. Many of the Texians had three or four rifles loaded and at the ready. As soon as they fired one, they picked up another and aimed at a new target.

The column of Mexicans attacking the north wall stopped advancing. The attackers began to mill around, dazed and disoriented by the murderous fire that the Texians poured down on them.

Colonel Travis walked up and down the wall, shouting encouragement to his troops. He fired both barrels of his shotgun down into the mass of Mexican soldiers below him.

"Well, Sam, how do you think they liked that?" he asked with a smile.

As Sam turned to answer him, he heard an angry buzzing sound. Then, to his horror, a hole appeared in the middle of Travis's forehead. Blood spurted, and Travis's eyes rolled up-

ward as he dropped the shotgun over the edge of the wall and
staggered backward.

Sam reached for him, but Travis tumbled over the edge of
the parapet and fell heavily to the ground below. Sam ran to
the edge and looked down. Amazingly, Travis was sitting up.
He turned his head from side to side, as if trying to figure
out where he was.

"Colonel, sit still. Someone will help you!" Sam shouted
down at him, but even as he called out, Travis fell back and
his head rolled to one side. His eyes remained open but un-
seeing.

"How's Travis?" Almeron asked Sam, as Sam returned to
his position.

"He's dead," Sam said.

"He's one of the lucky ones. He went early." Almeron
raised his rifle to his shoulder and fired again, dropping another Mexican attacker.

Sam could see the Mexican officers running behind their
men, urging them forward by hitting them with the flat sur-
faces of their saber blades. The Mexican soldiers came forward again and again, only to be beaten back by deadly
accurate rifle fire and murderous grapeshot.

"You've got to hand it to the sons of bitches, charging
right into our fire like that," Sam said grudgingly.

On the third wave, the column that was striking the north-
west corner began to drift east. The eastern column, which
had been beaten back by the defenders, started moving to the
north, and both columns merged with the northeast column.
Now, all three columns formed one solid mass of men, and
that mass surged toward the walls of the Alamo, only to have
the front ranks cut down like grass before a scythe.

The Mexicans who had been scaling ladders, spikes, and
picks were all gone now, dropped and trampled to useless
sticks under the mad rush. The column reached the fort, but
without ladders they had no way to scale the walls. They
milled around in frustration for a quarter of an hour, while
the defenders poured down murderous fire from point-blank
range.

Juan was attacking the south wall, and, because most of the Texians had rallied to the larger attack, he was meeting with less resistance. He rushed ahead of his men and began to scale the wall. His soldiers, inspired by his courage, climbed the wall behind him.

Juan seemed to be leading a charmed life. Bullets were whizzing all around him, and to each side of him his men were dropping, mortally wounded, while he remained unscathed.

Behind him, a military band had taken up the *Deguello*, and Juan realized that Santa Anna had committed his final reserves to the battle. The fresh troops began firing so excitedly that their bullets started hitting Juan's men. Now, Juan was sustaining as much damage from his own troops as he was from the defenders.

"Inside!" Juan shouted. "We must get inside!"

Juan managed to tumble over the top of the wall, and several of his men followed him. The Mexicans were now inside the Alamo!

Juan ran down to the gate and opened it. Then the Mexicans came pouring through in a solid stream, shouting challenges at the Texians, who answered with their own calls of defiance.

Sam and Almeron came running across the plaza to meet the new threat. Almeron stuck his head in through the door of the sacristy, where he saw Sue, Marie, Angelina, and a handful of children, clutched together.

"Sue! The Mexicans are inside the walls!" he shouted. "If they spare you, save my child!"

"Almeron!" Susanna called, but already Almeron had closed the door and was heading back toward the melee.

The Mexicans and Texians met in the plaza. They managed to fire only one round from their rifles before resorting to pistols, and finally to knives, bayonets, swords, clubs, and even their bare hands.

"Sam! Behind you!" Almeron shouted.

Sam turned, just as a Mexican officer lunged toward him with his sword. Sam knocked the thrust away with his rifle, then brought the butt of his rifle up in a vertical stroke that snapped the Mexican's head back, breaking his jaw at the same moment it broke his neck.

Out of the corner of his eye, Juan saw Lopez go down from the vertical butt stroke and he knew, without having to look more closely, that he was dead. Then he sensed, rather than saw, someone lunging at him and, with a charge left in his pistol, he turned and shot his attacker, watching as a big hole appeared in the Texian's forehead.

In command now, Captain Baugh shouted for the Texians to withdraw to their final defensive line, the semicircle of parapets built around the doors of the rooms in the low barracks.

Sam looked toward the plaza and saw that, already, three-fourths of the Texians were dead. He looked toward the church, hoping that the women and children inside were safe. The church had not yet come under direct attack, though it had been struck by several cannonballs. Davy Crockett and his Tennesseeans were close to the church, trying to fight their way to the low barracks to join in the final defensive battle.

The Mexicans had poured into the Alamo in numbers that gave them almost a twenty-to-one superiority over the Texians. They surrounded Davy Crockett and the six men who remained with him. The Tennesseeans fought hard, loading and firing, then stabbing with their knives and bayonets as the enemy soldiers rushed them.

Many of the Mexicans recognized Davy Crockett as the "devil with the long gun" who had shot so many of them over the last few days, and they were anxious to avenge the deaths of their comrades. They took careful aim and fired, but not one of their bullets found its mark. Then Sam saw a Mexican lieutenant come up behind Crockett and slash him just above the eye with a ferocious blow from his sword. Davy Crockett fell to the ground, and within moments, more than twenty Mexicans were attacking him with bayonets.

Sam looked again toward the church. As he turned, he felt a blow to the back of his neck, and he pitched forward. A second later there was an explosion inside his head as a bullet crashed into his brain.

* * *

Marie crept through the church to peer through a crack in the
door. She turned her head away from the sight of her husband
and Almeron lying dead in the plaza. When she looked back,
she saw a cannonball blow away another parapet; then she
realized that the Mexicans had captured all the defenders'
cannons, and had turned them on the low barracks. One by
one, they began blowing away all of the parapets.

One of the Texas artillerymen suddenly appeared near the
church. His face was blackened with powder from the gun
blasts, and his eyes were wide in shock and horror.

"Miss, you'd best get away from the door," he shouted.
He'd barely got his warning out when he was felled by a
bullet. Marie ran back to the sacristy. She saw Robert Evans,
the man who had been carrying powder from the magazine
to the defenders. He had been grievously wounded and was
crawling toward the powder magazine, carrying a torch.

There were nearly two dozen people inside the sacristy
now, including women, children, and one slave.

"Listen . . ." Marie finally said, and the others realized that
it had suddenly grown quiet. After an hour and a half of cries
of anger and terror, and deafening explosions, there was now
only silence.

The battle of the Alamo was over.

Twenty-two

6:30 A.M.

The sun was well up now and the sky was light. It was only
ninety minutes after the first alarm had been sounded. Just
moments before there had been the explosion of cannons and
the crash of balls against the barricades, punctuated by the
sharper sound of musketry and the screams of dying and
wounded men. Now an eerie silence had descended over the
fort, interrupted here and there by a few solitary shots as the
Mexicans dispatched the wounded with grim efficiency.

Susanna and Marie stood together, their hearts in their
throats. They knew what the silence meant for their men, and

they were preparing themselves now, for what was about to happen to them.

The door to the sacristy opened and a bar of sunlight streamed in through the dense pall of gun smoke. Emerging from a cloud, a Mexican officer stepped inside, his face wreathed in a ghostlike haze as his piercing black eyes surveyed the room.

"Mrs. Dickerson?" he asked.

Marie felt Susanna tremble, and she squeezed her hand.

"If you value your life, woman, speak up!" the Mexican officer said sharply. As he stepped forward, Marie could see blood on his tunic. Was it his blood or the blood of an American he had killed? Was it Sam's blood?

Susanna took a deep breath and stepped forward, carrying Angelina.

"I am Susanna Dickerson," she said. She closed her eyes and prepared herself for whatever fate awaited her. Two Mexican soldiers started to seize her, but the officer who had summoned her spoke sharply to them, and they stepped back.

"What are you going to do with her?" Marie demanded.

"Who are you?"

"I am Marie Douc . . . I am Mrs. McCord," she said.

"Your husband was here?"

"Yes."

"You come, too, please."

The two women followed the officer outside. They saw hundreds and hundreds of Mexican bodies lying in the plaza. When Marie saw how each dead Texian was surrounded by many Mexicans, she realized how fiercely their men had fought.

She saw Davy Crockett's body lying between the church and the barracks, his cap by his side.

Suddenly a shot rang out. Susanna screamed and fell, bleeding profusely, still cradling her baby daughter in her arms.

"Who fired that shot?" the officer demanded angrily.

No one answered.

"The next man to fire a shot will be summarily executed!" the officer promised. "These ladies are under the protection of the Mexican army!"

A surgeon was summoned quickly, and he began to dress the wound in Susanna's leg.

"May I introduce myself?" the officer asked. "I am Colonel Don Juan Esteban Montoya."

"Montoya?" Marie said, recognizing the name. She well knew Sam's story.

Juan looked puzzled. "Do you know me, senorita?"

"It is senora, and I know of you, Colonel."

"May I ask how?"

Marie started to tell him that she had heard how his cowardice caused Hunter Grant to have to fight a duel with his best friend. But she checked the words before she could give them voice, for fear that he might be so angered by them that he would kill them now.

"I don't know. Maybe I am mistaken," Marie said. She looked around the plaza, trying to find Sam's body, though not really wanting to see it. "So many dead," she said.

"*Si*, but it was an honorable battle," Juan said.

"It looks as if it was an expensive battle for you," Marie said.

"I agree. Over one thousand five hundred of our brave men were killed, along with one hundred and eighty of your brave men. But, perhaps, it will serve its purpose. Perhaps a valuable lesson has now been taught to those who would make a revolution. We have shown them that they cannot win."

"Is that what this battle was? A lesson?" Marie asked.

"*Si*," Juan said. "And that is the message I want you and Mrs. Dickerson to take to the rest of the world."

"Why should we?" Marie asked.

"Because that is the price you must pay for your life," another officer said. He was a tall, handsome, impressive-looking man.

"Senoras, allow me to present his Excellency General Santa Anna," Juan said.

Santa Anna bowed slightly.

"I trust the wound is not serious?" Santa Anna said.

"It hurts," Susanna replied.

Santa Anna nodded. "*Si, si*, I'm certain it does. You have my most sincere apologies for that, Senora Dickerson," Santa Anna said. He ran his hand through his hair and studied her for a moment. "What will you do?"

"I beg your pardon?"

"Now that your husband is dead, you have no man, no one to support you. What will you do?"

"I will support myself and my child," Susanna replied.

A black man, who Marie recognized as Colonel Travis's slave, Joe, was brought out into the plaza.

"You," Santa Anna said to him. "If you want to live, identify the bodies of Travis and Bowie for us."

Joe pointed toward the north wall.

"Colonel Travis, he lie up there," Joe said. He pointed to a room. "Colonel Bowie, he be in there on his sick bed with eight or ten dead Mexicans lyin' around him."

"Bring all the Texians out here," Santa Anna commanded. "Make a stack here of bodies and wood."

"*Excellente,* what are you going to do?" Juan asked.

"I am going to burn the bodies," Santa Anna said.

"Burn the bodies? But no! You aren't even going to bury them?" Marie gasped.

"Is it necessary that we do that, General?" Juan said. "These men fought well, and honorably. Do they not, at least, deserve an honorable burial?"

"I will teach these rebels to fear the name of Santa Anna," Santa Anna said, holding his finger aloft. "Burn them. Burn them all."

"And the women and the children?"

"By the generosity of the *Presidente de Mexico,* the women and children may live," Santa Anna said magnanimously. "Also, any Negroes who are in here." He looked again at Susanna. "You are a very beautiful woman, senora."

Susanna said nothing.

"If you would like, you may come and live with me."

"Live with you?" Susanna asked, shocked by the offer.

"*Si.* As one of my courtesans. It will be a good life. I will see that you are well cared for, and the little girl is looked after and educated. Would you like that?"

"No!" Susanna gasped. "No, I would not!"

Santa Anna shrugged. "Such is the pity," he said. He waved his hand. "See that the woman's wound is well cared for, then find a wagon for them," he said. "Give them food and water, then send the women and the children . . . and the Negro, away.''

Back in San Antonio de Bexar, Hunter Grant had been able to follow the course of the battle by listening to the sounds. When it grew quiet, he knew that the Alamo had fallen, and now he could see the Mexican tricolors fluttering in the breeze atop the walls.

It was nearly eight o'clock when Juan came back into the room. He walked over to his trunk, then pulled out a quart of tequila and turned it up to his lips, drinking several swallows right from the bottle. His face was blackened with powder and his eyes were haunted-looking.

"The battle is over, senor," he said.

"It sounded to me as if the Texians gave a pretty good accounting of themselves."

"*Si,*" Juan replied. "They sold their lives most dearly." He took another drink of tequila. "They are dead now. All of them . . . the magnificent bastards!"

"All dead? Mrs. McCord? Mrs. Dickerson, too?"

Juan looked at Hunter. "No, they are not dead. We killed no women."

From the church, Marie could see the Mexican soldiers at work in the plaza, loading the bodies of their own dead into wagons and taking them away. Marie watched as wagon after wagon drove away, laden with bodies piled high like firewood.

It was late in the afternoon before the last Mexican body was removed. After that, the soldiers dragged the Texians to the center of the plaza. They piled dry branches and dead men, layer upon layer until the pile of bodies and firewood reached twelve feet high. Then a Mexican officer tossed a torch onto the pile. A few moments later a tremendous blaze cracked and danced over the funeral pyre as the bodies of all the dead Texians went up in flames. She closed her eyes tightly to hold back her tears as she mourned for all the brave men who had, so recently, been a part of her life.

After watching the flames burn for a while, she turned and went back inside the church.

"What are they doing now?" Susanna asked. She had been in pain most of the afternoon, and now she held her throbbing leg.

"Just some cleaning up," Marie answered. She didn't want to tell Susanna that all the bodies were being burned.

About an hour later, Colonel Montoya came to the door again.

"Mrs. McCord, do you think Mrs. Dickerson can travel?" he asked.

"I don't know," Marie started, but Susanna interrupted her.

"Marie, I want to leave this place. Even if it kills me, I want to get out of here, away from the smell of death."

Marie smiled wanly. She could well understand the young woman's determination to leave in spite of her injury. In her place, Marie would have felt the same way.

"Yes," Marie said. "She can travel. I'll help her."

"I have decided to send someone with you," Colonel Montoya said.

"One of your soldiers?"

"No, one of yours. Someone we captured before the battle." Montoya looked around him, then he stepped inside and spoke in a quiet voice. "I have taken it upon myself to give him an unconditional release."

"Is it someone you caught trying to flee the Alamo?" Marie asked. "Because if it is, I would rather travel by myself."

"On the contrary, senora. It is someone we caught trying to get into the Alamo. Can you imagine someone trying to go to his death?"

"Who is it?" Marie asked.

"It doesn't matter," Susanna said. "If he was trying to come inside to help us, then he is a good man."

"Yes," Marie said. "I suppose are right."

Montoya disappeared, then returned a short time later. "Here he is," he said.

A man stepped inside the sacristy. "Hello, Marie," he said quietly.

"Oh, Hunter!" Marie said, the sudden joy of seeing him almost overwhelming the grief she had been feeling. Unable to control herself any longer she ran to his arms and began sobbing.

Hunter comforted Marie for a long moment, then he looked over at Susanna. "Are you sure you can travel?"

"Yes," Susanna said, though pain strained her features. "Please, let us leave as quickly as we can."

"All right," Hunter said. He walked over to Susanna and picked her up in his arms. Then he indicated the baby with a nod. "Marie, carry the baby, and let's go," he said.

Marie picked up Angelina, who cooed and smiled and reached up to play with her hair.

Outside, Juan Montoya had a wagon waiting for them. He helped Susanna onto the seat. Marie, the baby, and the slave, Joe, got into the back. Hunter got onto the seat and took the reins.

"Here is a pistol for you," Juan said. "You may need it against marauding bandits."

Hunter looked at the pistol. "It is a revolver," he said.

"See, you can load all of the chambers and fire six times before you must reload again. It was the pistol of my friend Manuel."

"Thank you, Colonel. That is most kind of you," Hunter said.

"Senor Grant," Juan called.

Hunter looked toward him.

"This in no way changes things between us. There is still a debt to be repaid. But a place like this"—Juan held out his hand to take in the rubble and dead of the Alamo—"is no place to settle it. When the time is right, you and I will meet upon a field of honor."

Hunter nodded.

"Now, leave, please, while I am still the senior commander on the field," Juan said.

Hunter slapped the reins against the back of the team, and the wagon began to move. As soon as they were outside the Alamo, Hunter urged the team into a trot, the more quickly to leave the place behind them.

Susanna said that she had friends in Gonzales, so it was to that settlement that they headed.

They were no more than five or six miles away from San

Antonio, when Susanna's leg wound opened up and they had to stop. By then it was quite late, so Hunter suggested that they make camp for the night. The women, though still too close to the Alamo to be free from all their fears, agreed that it was necessary to stop.

"If it be all the same to you folks, I'd like to keep on goin'," Joe said.

"Where will you go?" Hunter asked.

Joe shook his head. "Don't rightly know," he said. "Now that Colonel Travis is dead, I don't know who owns me. I reckon I may just wander around on my own."

Hunter stuck out his hand. "Good luck to you, Joe," he said.

"Yes, suh, thank you," Joe said. "Good luck to you folks as well." Joe started to walk away, then he stopped and turned back toward them. "You know, someday folks is going to tell stories an' sing songs 'bout what went on in that place. And when they do, I hopes they all know that there was a gentleman of color inside them walls, fighting right alongside the others."

"Joe, I will make certain that the world knows that," Marie said, feeling an unexpected sense of poignancy for the moment.

"Are you ladies hungry?" Hunter asked, after Joe left.

"No," Marie answered. "The events of the day have taken away my appetite."

"I'm not hungry either," Susanna said, rocking her baby in her arms. "But I know Angelina must be. She hasn't eaten since last night."

Tears came to her eyes, and Marie realized that she must be thinking of the dinner they had shared. It was only twenty-four hours ago, yet it seemed like days, weeks, even months. It was, in fact, a lifetime ago, for Sam and Almeron, and hundreds upon hundreds of others who were dead now.

"Here," Hunter said, handing a piece of beef jerky to Susanna. "Give this to the baby."

"She can't eat this," Susanna protested.

"Do what the birds do," Hunter said. "Chew it up for her."

Susanna began to chew on the tough meat. After a while

she transferred the chewed-up jerky to the baby's mouth, and
Angelina ate it hungrily.

"Look at her," Susanna said. "Bless her little heart. She
was starving, and yet, she has scarcely cried all day."

"She's too young to understand everything that has happened," Hunter said. "But she realizes that something has."

While Susanna was feeding the baby, Hunter took a couple
of blankets out of the wagon. He spread one on the ground,
then set the other aside.

"We'll have to share the same blankets," he said. "It will
be too cold, otherwise."

The women made no comment. Later, the three of them
crawled under the blankets and went to sleep. Angelina slept
quietly in her mother's arms.

Marie awoke some time later and turned to see Hunter staring straight up into the night sky. She, too, looked up at the
stars.

"When I was a little girl," she said, "my father told me
that every time someone died, a new star was born in
heaven," she said. "Do you think that's true?"

"It could be," Hunter agreed. "Who is to say?"

"Sam is up there tonight," Marie said. "And so is Almeron, and a lot of other good men."

Hunter was silent for a long moment. "Did you love him?"
he finally asked.

"Yes," Marie said.

When Hunter said nothing, Marie had to speak again to fill
the silence.

"Hunter Grant, I am not going to apologize for marrying
Sam McCord," she said. "Not now, not ever. He was a wonderful man. I hope I was able to make his last days happier."

"I understand," Hunter said.

"I'm not sure you do," Marie replied. "But I want you to
know that I didn't just marry him for convenience. I married
him for love, and I would have been a good wife to him."
She was quiet for a moment, then she added, "Even though
I loved you."

Marie felt Hunter's arm move under her shoulder, then pull
her against him so that her head was resting on his shoulder.
Hunter squeezed her, and she kissed him.

"We can get married as soon as we reach Gonzales," he said. "If you will have me."

"Don't you think people might talk?" Marie asked.

"Let them talk. As big as Texas is, we'll just go someplace where we can't hear them."

Susanna's leg was somewhat better the next day, and they covered several miles. Early in the afternoon, however, three armed men stopped them. They were Mexicans, but they didn't appear to be members of any organized military unit. One of them held a pistol leveled at Hunter.

"So," the gunman said, smiling broadly. "We have some stinking rebels here."

The other two Mexicans laughed.

"Where are you going?" the leader asked.

"We are on a mission for General Santa Anna," Hunter said.

The Mexican laughed. "You are on a mission for *El Presidente*, eh? I see. And did he ask you to bring along two women and a baby?"

"Yes."

"That is very unusual, senor," the Mexican said. "I tell you what. I will take the two women and finish your mission for you."

The Mexican cocked his pistol and fired. A great puff of smoke issued from the pistol, and Marie saw the ball deflect off an iron fitting on the wagon seat, right in front of Hunter's leg. Miraculously, Hunter wasn't hit, and, quick as a flash he had his own pistol in his hand. His gun roared and the Mexican pitched from his saddle.

"Get him," one of the other two shouted. "He cannot reload quickly enough!"

"I have more bullets in this gun," Hunter warned, swinging his gun toward the other two.

The one who had spoken laughed and pulled his own pistol. He pointed it toward Hunter and took slow, deliberate aim.

"No!" Hunter said, but even as he spoke, he saw the Mexican pulling the hammer back, and he had no choice. He pulled the trigger and his gun roared a second time.

Now the one remaining Mexican realized he was not dealing with an ordinary man with an ordinary pistol, and he turned and dug his heels into his horse's sides to urge the animal to run.

Despite all the killing and destruction, despite their own grievous losses, Marie and Susanna were able to laugh at the spectacle of the Mexican fleeing for his life before the "devil gun" got him as well.

The laughter, the first since the Alamo, felt good.

Twenty-three

FRIDAY, MARCH 11, GONZALES

When the little party reached Gonzales, they were greeted by Major General Sam Houston. Three-inch rowels, shaped like daisies, jingled from Houston's spurs, and a long red feather fluttered over his white hat. Several men helped the women dismount, and Houston invited them into the tavern he was using as his temporary headquarters.

"We heard yesterday that the Alamo had fallen," Houston said anxiously. "Is that true?"

"Yes," Hunter replied. "It's true."

"How many of our men were lost?"

Nearly everyone in Gonzales had gathered around to hear the news. Many were women, and Hunter could tell by their anxious faces that they had loved ones in the Alamo.

"All of our men were lost," he said.

"Prisoners?"

"None," Hunter said. "They were all killed."

"No!" one of the women screamed.

"The volunteers from Gonzales, too?" another asked.

"All of them," Hunter said. "One hundred and eighty-three men. Only the women and children were spared."

"I don't ask this by way of criticism, you understand," Houston said. "But how is it you were spared?"

"He was captured as he tried to get into the Alamo before the battle," Marie spoke up quickly.

"You were going to help a little late, weren't you?"

"No, General, I was returning," Hunter said. "I had left the Alamo a few days earlier as a courier. I tried to get Colonel Fannin to commit his troops to the battle."

"It's probably just as well. They would have been killed as well."

"I don't think so, General," Hunter said. "If we had had three hundred more men . . . or even another one hundred and fifty, we would have stopped the Mexicans cold."

"That's quite a statement, isn't it, young man?" Houston asked.

"A statement of fact, General. Santa Anna brought five thousand men to the Alamo with him. Fifteen hundred of his men were killed in the siege."

Houston looked surprised. "Fifteen hundred killed by one hundred and eighty-three of ours?"

"Yes, sir," Hunter said. "I saw scores upon scores of wagons departing the Alamo, all of them loaded to overflowing with dead Mexican soldiers."

"Hurrah, boys, hurrah!" Houston suddenly shouted. "Hurrah for the brave men of the Alamo!"

Houston's shout was echoed by everyone in the room, including those women who had lost men there. With eyes wet and shining, and with tear tracks on their faces, they shouted with pride at the news of the terrible price their men had extracted from Santa Anna before their own voices were forever silenced.

"General Houston," Hunter went on. "Colonel Montoya will be headed this way now, with about seven hundred men under his command. How many men do you have here?"

"A little over three hundred," Houston said.

"Remember the Alamo!" someone shouted. "If one hundred and eighty-three can kill fifteen hundred Mexicans, then how many do you think we can kill?"

"Yeah!" another shouted. "Let's go get 'em, General!"

Houston looked at the ragtag assortment of men who formed his "army." They had been together for only a few days, and there had been no opportunity to drill or even to organize them into commands. The defenders of the Alamo had enjoyed several weeks of preparation before the battle commenced, and they were in a well-fortified position. The town of Gonzales, Houston realized, was not defendable.

"No!" Houston finally said. "We won't fight them here. We'll abandon Gonzales and fight them somewhere else."

"What?" someone shouted in dismay. "You mean we are runnin'?"

"What if the men of the Alamo had run?" another called.

"If they had obeyed my orders and abandoned the Alamo, they would be alive today, and our army would be the stronger for it," Houston said.

There were a few angry mutterings, and Houston held up his hands to implore the crowd to be quiet.

"Listen to me," he said. "If we vent our anger on the Mexicans in a few valiant, but foolhardy battles, we will accomplish nothing. I admire the courage and patriotism of the defenders of the Alamo. But how much better would it have been for all of us if they were here with us now? I say, let the Mexicans come to Gonzales. Let them find deserted houses and empty larders. Let them come on farther and deeper in Texas. The closer they come, the more vulnerable they will be."

"Why do you say that?" someone shouted.

"They will outdistance their supply lines," Hunter spoke up. The others looked toward him. "You all know there is not much grass on the muddy prairies at this time of year. That means the Mexicans will have to use wagons to haul grain for their horses. We won't leave any food for the men, so they will have to bring their own. Soon they will be low on food, low on grain, low on everything. We will be with friends who will keep us supplied. We will have the advantage."

"Listen to Mr. Grant," Marie urged. "What he is saying is true."

"That woman was inside the Alamo during the siege," one of the others said. "If she is willing to go along with General Houston's idea, then I reckon I am, too."

After that, there was a general agreement that the townspeople would evacuate.

By the time the meeting was over it was dark. The people hurried toward their homes. Marie stood in front of the tavern and looked up and down the street. She could see the candles flickering in all the houses as the people hurried to pack their belongings. When Houston rode away from Gonzales, he would leave nothing behind.

Houston wanted to take his two six-pound cannons with him, but he was afraid that they would slow down the column. Reluctantly, he ordered his men to take the guns to the middle of the Guadalupe River and push them in.

It was nearly midnight by the time the townspeople were ready to leave. Houston had only four baggage wagons, but he assigned three of them to transport civilians who had no other means of transportation. The wagon Hunter had brought from the Alamo was also pressed into service and Susanna and the baby rode in it. Marie and Hunter rode horseback.

The night was cloudy and damp as the band of refugees began pouring out of Gonzales. Hunter and Marie sat astride their horses next to the road and watched the small train leave. Houston rode out of the shadows of the night and stopped beside them for a moment.

"It pains me to have to retreat," he told them. "But I will do whatever is necessary to prevent all future murders."

"I know it is a difficult thing to do, General," Hunter said. "But I agree with you. It is necessary."

It began to rain shortly after they left Gonzales, and it rained unceasingly for the rest of the night and throughout the next day. The dampness made the journey miserable for soldiers and civilians alike. Houston responded to the people's complaints with blistering curses, but he managed to maintain control of the crowd.

Four days after they left Gonzales, the refugees reached the Colorado River. By now their ranks had been swollen by new recruits to some six hundred in number. The river was at flood stage, but they were able to get across. Once they had safely reached the other side, Houston decided that the river and his army would provide enough of a barrier to help him stand against the Mexican army, so he sent the civilians on ahead while his army made camp on the east bank of the river.

"Are you certain you don't want to go on with Susanna?" Hunter asked, as the civilians prepared to move on. Marie had announced that she intended to stay with the army.

"I am certain," Marie said.

She put her hand on Hunter's shoulder and looked into his eyes. "Hunter, I learned from Sam that it is not the amount of time you have together that is important. It is how you use that time. Whatever time you and I have left, I want us to spend it together. Please say you will not force me to go on."

Hunter embraced Marie and held her close for a long moment.

"I will not force you to go on," he said. "You may stay."

"Even if General Houston says I must go on?"

Hunter smiled. "If Houston says you must go on, then you will go," he said.

"But—" Marie started to protest, and Hunter put his finger on her lips to shush her.

"But," he went on. "If you must go on, then I will go with you."

Houston was not pleased that Marie would be staying with them, but he had no choice. He wanted Hunter as one of his commanders, and Hunter informed Houston that he would stay only if Houston would allow Marie to stay as well. Houston had to give in.

On March 21, the seven hundred men under the command of Colonel Juan Montoya arrived on the west bank of the Colorado River. The river, as Houston knew it would, provided an uncrossable barrier, for Houston's men would be able to pick off the Mexican soldiers as they attempted to cross. Juan, who well knew the deadly accuracy of the long rifles, had no choice but to hold his ground on one side of the river, staring in frustration at the Texians on the other side.

Then Houston received some distressing news.

Colonel Fannin, the commander at Goliad who had refused to go to Travis's aid at the Alamo, had been attacked by two divisions of Mexicans. Fourteen hundred Mexicans against four hundred Texians, and the Texians were poorly led.

Hunter watched Houston's face grow ashen as he read the message.

"General," Hunter said, walking over to Houston. "General, what is it? What is wrong?"

"Captain Grant," Houston said, referring to Hunter by his

restored rank. "These men you see before you now are the
last hope of Texas. We will never see Fannin or his men
again. They surrendered, and then they were murdered."

Houston sighed. "Now I must do something else that is
unpleasant. I had hoped to make a stand here and do battle
against the Mexicans, but I dare not. This is the only force
left to defend Texas. If we lose this battle, Texas will lose
the war."

"General, I don't think we will lose this battle," Hunter
said.

"Perhaps not," Houston said. "But even if we win, what
will we have accomplished? Santa Anna is not with this army.
We might inflict damage on this force, but until we defeat
Santa Anna, the war will go on."

Over the next six weeks, Houston divided his army into three
regiments. Hunter took command of a company attached to
Colonel Burleson's regiment. Then they began training. The
men were drilled unceasingly, and they maintained patrols,
scouting for several miles in all directions around their position to make certain the Mexican army didn't catch them
unaware.

Rifles were oiled, knives were sharpened, wagons were repaired, and cannon were assembled. There was no shortage
of food. The men slaughtered cattle from the pastures and
took corn from the cribs of a nearby plantation. The army
was divided into mess units, and each unit was provided with
a packhorse to carry its provisions. There was a shortage of
coffee, but there was plenty of tobacco.

At first Houston had lamented the fact that his soldiers were
without uniforms, but he soon discovered that his men wore
their ragtag clothing like a badge of honor.

"Rags are our uniforms, sir!" one of the men said proudly.
"Nine out of ten of our men are in rags. And it is a fighting
uniform!"

The two cannon that Houston had pushed into the river
back at Gonzales were replaced by two guns supplied by the
citizens of Cincinnati. The six-pounders were a matched pair,
so the men quickly named them the Twin Sisters.

Houston worked longer and harder than anyone else in the

entire army. Often he dozed in his saddle, so tired was he
from the long hours, and he claimed that those catnaps provided him with all the rest he needed.

Houston carried several ears of corn in his saddlebags, and
many times, instead of taking the time to prepare a meal, he
would simply gnaw on the raw corn. He also had two books
with him. *Gulliver's Travels,* and *Caesar's Commentaries.*
When he did find a few spare moments, he used them to read
his books or study his maps.

Houston didn't have any liquor with him, because he
wanted to keep his wits about him. It was necessary that he
be on his toes all the time, because Santa Anna was not his
only enemy. There was, brewing within his own camp, a per-
sistent rumor of mutiny. The men, and many of the officers,
were growing tired of the constant drilling and retreating.
They wanted action and they wanted it right away. They felt
that Houston's lengthy delay might be the result of a lack of
courage.

Finally, Houston decided that the only way to deal with
incipient mutiny was to meet it head-on. He had several
graves dug. Then he assembled the men and had them walk
by in ranks and look down into the graves he had just opened.

"Look into them, gentlemen," he said. "For the next person who suggests a course of action contrary to the one I
have laid out will be shot and buried, right here!"

Houston's forceful action paid off, and, though the grumbling continued, it was merely the grumbling of men who had
grown tired of drilling, and it had been heard from every
soldier in every army that had ever drilled. Talk and plans
for a mutiny were never mentioned again.

When Juan Montoya saw that the Texas army had withdrawn
from the opposite side of the river, he made ready to go after
them. Before he could cross, however, a courier arrived from
Santa Anna.

"I am attaching my headquarters to your division, Colonel," the message read. "Wait for me."

Santa Anna arrived in grand style in the luxurious comfort
of a liveried coach. The six prancing white horses stopped
near Juan's field headquarters, and Santa Anna's face ap-

peared in the window. As Juan walked toward the coach, he heard a giggle from inside. He saw a girl busily adjusting the bodice of her dress. The nipple of one of her breasts gleamed wetly, winking at Juan as she covered it. Then she sat quietly, with her hands folded in her lap, trying to regain her dignity.

"Juan, how are you?" Santa Anna greeted.

"Well, *Excellente*," Juan replied, saluting. "Welcome to my headquarters."

"They are my headquarters now, Colonel," Santa Anna said. The coachman opened the door, and Santa Anna got out. He had to reach for the door frame of the coach to keep from falling over. Juan could tell by Santa Anna's eyes that he had been using opium.

"Yes, General," Juan said easily. "This is your headquarters."

"Let us cross the river," Santa Anna said. "We must catch the enemy."

"Yes, General," Juan replied. On that, he was in complete agreement. He would have crossed the river earlier, had he not been ordered to wait for the president.

It took more than an hour for the army to cross the river. When they reached the other side, they went at once to San Felipe, reaching the village on April 7. But when they arrived, they discovered that the town no longer existed. It had been abandoned and burned to the ground.

Captain Baker's company had burned the town and he and his men were waiting for the Mexicans on the opposite side of the Brazos River. They had taken every boat with them to delay the Mexicans' crossing. Santa Anna ordered that rafts be built.

Baker's riflemen were well dug in, and their deadly accurate fire kept the Mexicans from crossing the Brazos for four days.

Santa Anna grew impatient with the drawn-out fight, so he ordered Juan and seven hundred and fifty of his men to come south with him to the crossing at Fort Bend. The fort, the scouts had reported, was abandoned, and they could cross there quickly and easily.

There was a tavern in Fort Bend owned by a woman named Elizabeth Powell. She had refused to abandon her tavern for fear it would be destroyed. As a result, she was standing in the doorway when Santa Anna arrived on horseback. Santa Anna took over the tavern for himself and his officers and ordered Mrs. Powell to serve them dinner.

That night, as Mrs. Powell and her son served the meal, Santa Anna and his officers sat around the table eating and discussing strategy.

"General, do you not think it would be wise to save our discussion until after our meal?" Juan asked. "Suppose this woman and her son overhear us and send word of our plans?"

"Nonsense," Santa Anna answered. "This woman speaks no Spanish." He turned to the woman, who was at that moment serving beans. "Tell me, woman, do you speak Spanish?" he demanded in Spanish.

"I'm sorry, sir, but if you want something you will have to speak in English," the woman answered.

Santa Anna smiled and held out his glass. "Tell me, do all Texian women sleep with dogs?" he asked, again in Spanish.

"More wine?" the woman said. "Yes, of course." She filled his glass.

"You see? She understands nothing," Santa Anna said.

The woman returned to the kitchen, but she left the door open just a crack.

"Now, gentlemen," Santa Anna went on "My scouts have told me that Sam Houston is just upriver from San Felipe. I understand he is teaching his Texians how to be an army . . . as if these backwoodsmen could be taught such a skill."

Santa Anna laughed at the statement.

"Forgive me, General, but the backwoodsmen who defended the Alamo did quite well for themselves," Juan reminded Santa.

"Ah, but they were desperate men, driven to desperate acts," Santa Anna said. "On an open field of battle, we would have dispatched them even more quickly."

"General, is it your intention to strike at Houston?" one of the officers asked.

"We could attack Houston, yes, but I have a better idea," Santa Anna said. He leaned forward on the table and smiled. "While Houston trains his men, we will proceed to Harrisburg."

"What is at Harrisburg?"

Santa Anna smiled again. "The so-called government of Texas. We will strike there, capture the leaders of this rebel force, then turn north to crush Sam Houston."

"A brilliant plan." .

"Yes," Santa Anna said. "We will proceed at first light."

"General, wouldn't it be better to move the troops up tonight?" Lopez asked.

"No," Santa Anna said. "I have other plans for tonight, and her name is Emily."

There was a ripple of ribald laughter around the table. As the officers reached for more food, they didn't notice the door to the kitchen being softly closed.

"Joe," Mrs. Powell called softly to her son.

"Yes, Mama?"

"Go out the back way. Get word to Sam Houston that Santa Anna is planning to seize the government at Harrisburg."

"Yes, Mama," Joe said.

"Here," Mrs. Powell said, giving him a bucket. "Act as if you are going for water. When you are out of sight, slip away."

Joe walked nonchalantly through the Mexican troops and down to the riverbank. When he was out of sight, he began to run along the river. He reached Houston's camp at dawn, the next day.

When Joe was taken to Houston's tent, the general was talking to a civilian named Donoho, who had complained that Houston's men were stripping his timber for firewood.

"Mr. Donoho, so far nearly one thousand men have given their lives, thousands more have given their time, and many have donated money, arms, food, and equipment to this war. Is it too much to ask that you allow a few hundred men to use some of your firewood?"

"The wood belongs to me," Donoho insisted. "You and your men have no right to it."

"Sergeant Collins," Houston called.

"Yes, sir?"

"Is it true that our men are cutting firewood from Mr. Donoho's land?"

"Yes, sir," the sergeant replied. He spit out a stream of tobacco juice. "General, we got to get it somewhere."

"Why are you cutting his timber?" Houston asked, "when he has already split rails for his fence? Wouldn't that be a lot easier?"

"What?" Donoho gasped.

Sergeant Collins smiled broadly.

"Yes, sir, General, I reckon that would be a whole heap easier," he said.

"No!" Donoho shouted. "Tell your men they can cut from my timber. As much as they want."

"I thought you might see things my way," Houston said.

Shaking his head in frustration, Donoho left the area. Houston turned toward young Joe Powell, who was bathed in sweat from his long run.

"What is this?" he asked.

"This boy run all the way here from Fort Bend," a soldier explained.

"You must have important news," Houston said.

"Yes, sir," Joe replied. "At least, my mama thinks so. Santa Anna and his army spent the night at our place. Mama, she speaks Spanish, only she let on like she didn't, and she heard 'em makin' their plans. General Houston, Santa Anna is gonna move north and try to capture our government."

Houston grinned broadly and slammed his fist into his hand.

"All right," he said. "This is what we have been waiting for! Joe, you did well."

Twenty-four

The Mexican army discovered that the Texas government had fled town. Everyone had left except the staff of *The Telegraph and Texas Register,* the local newspaper.

The newspapermen told Juan that President Burnet and the other officials of the Texas government had escaped to New Washington aboard the steamer *Cayuga.*

Juan took the news to Santa Anna. At first the general was

angry, then they looked at a map. It would take the steamer some time to reach New Washington, because of the meandering of the river. But, by land, New Washington was only twenty miles away.

Santa Anna made plans to take his entire army there, when he learned that Houston was going to defend Lynch's Ferry, a point about fifteen miles east of Harrisburg. The information pleased Santa Anna, because now he believed he could capture the Texas government and deal with Houston's army all at the same time.

"Now, we will put an end to this foolishness, once and for all," he said. He looked around the town of Harrisburg. Like the other towns, it was deserted. But, unlike the other others, it had not been burned to the ground.

"It looks to me as if the rebels were careless," Santa Anna said. "They forgot to burn their town."

"There was no need," Juan said. "I've already had my men search. There is nothing here we can use."

"Burn it," Santa Anna said. "Burn every last stick."

Juan delivered the order and within a short while every building in town blazed brightly, and smoke boiled into the sky.

"What is that smoke?" Marie asked, as she rode beside Hunter.

Hunter looked in the direction indicated by Marie and saw a wisp of smoke on the horizon. The wisp was small, but it was so far away that Hunter realized it must be a big fire.

"Harrisburg," he said. "Harrisburg is burning."

"Who burned it?" Marie asked. "Texians or Mexicans?"

"Ah," Hunter said, holding his finger up. "That is, indeed, the question."

For the rest of the day, Houston's troops continued to march toward Harrisburg. Their spirits were high, because they were certain they would soon meet Santa Anna.

Juan was at the head of the dragoons, the advance party of Santa Anna's troops. As they approached New Washington, where he hoped to capture President Burnet and the other government officials, Juan spotted an American scout. The scout saw the Mexicans and turned back toward the town at a gallop.

"Stop him!" Juan shouted. "Catch him before he can give a warning!"

Three of the fastest riders broke out of the ranks and gave chase, but Juan knew the American was going to get away. He had too much of a head start. There was one thing he could do, however. He could move the entire company at a gallop. Perhaps they could arrive so closely on the scout's heels that no one would have time to react to his warning. Juan stood in his stirrups and urged his men forward at a gallop.

The trees along each side of the road echoed the thunder of the hoofbeats as the fifty horsemen pounded toward the town of New Washington. They entered the town without breaking stride, and Juan led them to the docks. There was a schooner in the harbor, and Juan saw a rowboat approaching it. President Burnet sat in the rowboat, along with several others. Some of the Mexicans raised their rifles and took aim, but then Juan saw a woman in the boat with the men.

"No!" he shouted. "Don't fire! There's a woman in the boat!"

Juan's men lowered their weapons, and the boat continued to row out to the schooner. Once on board the schooner, the Texas government was safe.

Santa Anna arrived in New Washington a while later. He was annoyed by the escape of President Burnet, but not too concerned about it. His primary mission, he believed, was to defeat Sam Houston. Once Houston was taken care of, the government of Texas would fall into his hands like a ripe plum.

"General, perhaps we should leave now," Juan suggested. "If we make haste, we might reach Lynch's Ferry ahead of Houston. We could ambush him there."

"There is no need to hurry," Santa Anna insisted. "Victory is now within our grasp, and I desire a short rest. I saw a plantation near here. Does anyone know what it is called?"

"It is called Morgan's plantation, General," one of his staff officers informed him.

"Does this plantation have slaves?" Santa Anna asked.

"Yes, General."

Santa Anna smiled. "Ah, good. I have grown tired of the women who are with us. I shall require someone new for a small diversion. As soon as we are there, you will bring me the loveliest slave girls. I will make my choice. Oh, and see to it that my opium box is well-filled."

"Yes, General," the staff officer said.

Juan stood quietly until Santa Anna moved on.

"That hedonistic fool is going to lose this war," Juan said quietly. "And this is a war that could be lost only by someone with Santa Anna's genius for catastrophe."

After two and a half days of forced marching, Marie, Hunter, and the others with General Houston reached Buffalo Bayou, just across from Harrisburg.

Marie looked across the water. "You were right," she said. "It was Harrisburg that burned."

The town lay in heaps and piles of black and gray ashes. A dog, lonely and afraid, picked its way among the ash piles, as if trying to find its former home.

"Damn!" Houston swore. He had ridden his horse over to stand beside Marie and Hunter, as they stared at the remains of the town. "We missed Santa Anna. Where is he?"

"General, look what we've got!" someone shouted.

Houston, Hunter, and Marie turned toward the voice. A dozen men were shoving a Mexican along in front of them. The Mexican was in uniform, and he was shaking with fear.

"This here fella is a courier," one of the men said.

"A courier you say?" Houston replied. "Well, now, maybe we're about to get a break." Houston swung down from his horse and confronted the courier. "What messages are you carrying?"

"Here's his saddlebags," one of the men shouted. He started to pass them over to Houston, then suddenly stopped and stared at them.

"You son-of-a-bitch!" he shouted at the courier. "You bastard! I ought to kill you myself!"

"What is it?" someone asked.

"Look at the name on these saddlebags! William Barret Travis!"

"Kill him!" someone else shouted. "Kill the Mexican son-of-a-bitch!"

"No!" Houston said, holding up his hands. "Let us not descend to the level of the people we are fighting."

"But he was at the Alamo!" someone protested.

"They were all at the Alamo," Houston reminded them. "We will not kill him. Give me the message. Let's see what we can find out."

The messages were from Fort Bend, and they were directed to Santa Anna. From them, Houston learned that Santa Anna had split his forces into three divisions and that he was in New Washington with only seven hundred and fifty men, not many more than Houston had with him. For the first time in this war the Texians were to meet the Mexicans in equal numbers.

Houston also learned from the messages, however, that five hundred reinforcements would soon join Santa Anna at Lynch's Ferry, about eight miles away from New Washington on the plain of San Jacinto.

After Houston digested all the information, he climbed back onto his big white stallion and called for his army around him.

"The time has come!" he said. "You have been waiting for battle, and it is about to be thrust upon us. Victory is certain! Trust in God and fear not! The victims of the Alamo and those who were murdered at Goliad cry out for vengeance. Remember the Alamo! Remember Goliad!"

"Remember the Alamo!" someone called back, and his shout was echoed by everyone present.

"Remember Goliad!"

Again, the stirring call to battle was answered.

"They are ready to fight, General," Hunter said, as the formation broke up.

At Morgan's plantation, Juan Montoya stepped out onto the front porch of the little cabin he had commandeered for the night. The great house was about fifty yards away, on the other side of an open ditch. There were hundreds of tents pitched about on the plantation grounds, and the occupants of the tents were just awakening, testing gingerly the world they had abandoned the night before.

It was very early in the morning, and though there was light, the sun had not yet risen above the surrounding trees. The men went about their morning routine, shaving, relieving themselves in the ditch, starting their breakfast fires. Here and there Juan saw young slave girls slipping out of the tents, and he realized that the men had taken full advantage of the sexual opportunities offered them last night.

A rooster crowed.

Juan left the porch and walked among the tents to the big house. A guard came to attention as he pushed the door open to go inside.

A Norteamericano and his wife sat fearfully on a sofa in the parlor as Juan went in, and they looked at him with frightened eyes. Juan knew that the Morgans feared for their lives. He wanted to tell them not to be afraid, but he honestly didn't know what whim would dictate Santa Anna's behavior. He would not have thought the survivors of Goliad would be murdered, but Santa Anna had done just that.

There was a burst of laughter from the dining room, and Juan went toward the sound.

"Ah, Juan," Santa Anna greeted. A young black girl was sitting next to him. She was completely nude, and Santa Anna had one arm draped carelessly around her shoulder. His fingers were gently kneading her nipple. "I hoped you would join us for breakfast."

There were half-a-dozen other senior officers with Santa Anna, though only the general had a girl with him.

"We are having quail and eggs. A wonderful breakfast for the day of a battle, don't you think?"

"Do you believe we will do battle today, General?" Juan asked. He sat down and, almost instantly, food appeared before him.

"Yes," Santa Anna said. "I think this will be our lucky day. We will be at Lynch's Ferry when Houston arrives, and we will give him a surprise welcome."

"What if he is already there when we arrive?" Juan asked.

"That is impossible," Santa Anna answered. "His *army* . . ." Santa Anna slurred the word, " . . . is on foot. They couldn't possibly be at Lynch's Ferry yet."

"I wish I had your confidence, Your Excellency," Juan said.

"We will be victorious this day," Santa Anna said, smiling patronizingly at Juan. "I am willing to stake my position on it."

"Mr. President, you are doing just that," Juan reminded him.

The bulk of Houston's army had spent what was left of the night in a protective copse south of Buffalo Bayou. They had arrived just before dawn, taken control of Lynch's Ferry, then moved across the bayou to rest and wait. They didn't rest unprotected, however. Houston had sent out a patrol.

The patrol returned and informed Houston that Santa Anna and his men were bivouacked on the Morgan plantation just outside New Washington. Santa Anna had burned New Washington, they said, and their report was confirmed by the smoke that curled into the sky from the little town eight miles away.

Hunter tried to persuade Marie to wait for him across the San Jacinto River in the little village of Lynchburg, but she insisted on coming across with him.

"I survived the Alamo," she told him. "What could be worse than that?"

"You were spared at the Alamo," Hunter said. "If we lose this battle, you may not be spared a second time."

"Hunter, for a while, those of us who were left alive at the Alamo envied the dead. I will stay with you."

"Then you must promise me that when the battle begins you will stay back in the woods, out of danger, Marie. Without the assurance of your safety, I will not be able to fight."

"I promise I'll stay out of harm's way."

The woods in which the Texians were now resting, and in which Marie promised to stay out of danger, were thick with live oak trees, from which hung tangled strands of Spanish moss. These woods lined Buffalo Bayou, which the Texians had crossed before capturing Lynch's Ferry. The ferry itself crossed the San Jacinto River. Alongside the river ran woods and marshlands. About a mile downstream, the river formed a small backwater basin known as Peggy Lake. The lake protruded at a right angle from the river, and it, too, was surrounded by marsh and woods. The result was a great plain almost completely encircled by woods. The field was called the San Jacinto Plain.

Houston's army rested and waited as the Mexicans moved toward them. Santa Anna was determined to arrive there first, establish a strong position, and ambush Houston when the Texians arrived. He was surprised and dismayed when his scouts told him they had already spotted the Texians.

"Surely they must be long-range patrols," Santa Anna mused.

"I don't think so," Juan said. "I think Houston has beaten us to the ferry."

"Quickly," Santa Anna ordered. "Have your men take up positions in the wood line on this side of the field. The Texians won't come across the plain after us. As soon as General Cos gets here with his division, we shall have enough strength to go after the devil."

Santa Anna moved his soldiers into the woods. Then he ordered them to haul the lone cannon into position.

"We'll show the rebels that even the woods are not safe from our artillery," he said to the battery commander.

The men set up the gun, loaded it, and then fired. Santa Anna pranced forward on his white stallion, ordering his gunners to load and fire again. Suddenly there was a whistling noise; then a cannonball crashed through the trees. It felled half-a-dozen Mexican dragoons, and the thunder of artillery fire rolled across the plains.

The rebels had artillery, too! That realization surprised and unnerved Santa Anna, and, quickly, he retired from the scene.

"Ha! You got a bunch of 'em!" a soldier shouted from his post high in one of the trees near the Texas cannons known as the Twin Sisters.

The lookout clung precariously to his perch with one hand, while holding a spyglass to his eye with the other. He called down to the gun crews. "I see five, no six! There are six Mexicans down."

The men around the guns cheered.

"That was a lucky shot," Hunter suggested.

"Luck?" the battery commander answered. He patted the

breech of the gun. "Captain, luck has nothing to do with it.
That was pure skill. We are an army now. A real army."

Hunter smiled. "I see. And you believe that artillery makes
us an army?"

"Certainly. Artillery lends dignity to what would otherwise
be a bloody brawl," the gun commander said.

The heavy guns exchanged fire a few more times. Then
Houston ordered the Twin Sisters to stop firing, in order to
preserve powder. The Mexicans stopped firing their cannon,
too, but they kept up a brisk musket fire throughout the rest
of the day. They were far out of range, however, and not one
ball reached the Texas lines.

The Texians began complaining again. They had been prepared for battle, but as the day wore on, it began to look as
if Houston had no intention of engaging Santa Anna. They
satisfied themselves by saying that there would be an attack
at first light, and they made all preparations for battle before
they went to sleep that night.

Santa Anna also believed that Houston would attack with
first light, and he spent the entire night fortifying his position.
While the Texians slept, the Mexicans worked, erecting barricades, packing supplies, and digging trenches. Even Santa
Anna stayed awake, hurrying from one position to another,
giving contradictory orders as to how he wanted the barricades to be built. He grew more and more irritable as the
night wore on, and more than once he threatened to have men
shot for not responding quickly enough to his orders.

When the sun came up the next morning, the Texians
awoke, anxious to attack. They soon learned, however, that
Houston had left word not to be awakened until eight o'clock.
It was his first sound sleep in many days.

The Texians looked at one another dejectedly and grumbled
among themselves. Some wondered if Houston was ever going to fight.

Hunter had led a morning scouting patrol, and now he returned to the Texas camp with news. He had seen General
Cos's men coming from the direction of Harrisburg. Cos had
moved up during the night, and within the hour he would join
Santa Anna.

Houston took the news without comment. Then he ate his

breakfast in a surprisingly good mood.

"That's good news about General Cos," he said to Hunter and the others.

"Good news? But it nearly doubles Santa Anna's strength."

"It is better for Cos to arrive now, before the battle, than to get here in the middle of the fighting. At least there will be no unpleasant surprises for us."

"General, for a cautious man, you seem in excellent spirits this morning," Hunter observed.

Houston chuckled. "And so I am, Captain Grant. I saw an eagle this morning. That's always a good sign, you know."

"No, I didn't know," Hunter answered with a smile.

"Come," Houston said. "Let's move among the men."

Hunter followed Houston through the Texas camp. The men rested around several campfires, and the smoke from the fires hung low in the air. Sunshine stabbed down through the twisted growth of trees, and the rays of light were alive with drifting smoke.

"Boys," Houston called out to them. "Are you ready for a fight?"

"Yes!" the men shouted back.

"Well, enjoy your dinners, boys. Eat hearty, and then I will lead you into a fight. And if you whip them, every one of you shall be a captain!"

"Hurrah, boys, hurrah!" someone shouted, and the shout traveled as an echo through the woods.

"Captain Grant, I want you to take some men with you and destroy Vince's Bridge."

"Destroy it, General?" one of the other officers asked.

"Yes," Houston replied. "I don't want any more Mexican reinforcements to arrive during the battle."

"But, General, if we do that, we won't have any means of escape, should retreat become necessary."

"True," Houston answered. "That leaves us only two alternatives: victory or death."

"I'll take care of the bridge, General," Hunter said.

"Captain Grant," Houston called after him. "Unless you hasten back, you will find this prairie changed from green to red by the time you return."

Shortly after the noon meal, Houston assembled all his officers. He looked around at the men who had been grumbling for the last several weeks because he had not chosen to fight.

"The time has come," Houston said. "I have delayed fighting so long that some of you have questioned my courage. Despite your accusations, I put off fighting because I was waiting for the right moment. Well, gentlemen, the moment has come. The history of Texas hinges upon what we do here today. Shall this great territory become a vassal state to the Mexicans? Or shall we take control of our own destiny and breathe the air of free men? That question will be resolved here, today. This is not just a battle, gentlemen; this is the entire war! The only question remaining is this: Shall we attack the enemy, or wait to receive their attack?"

When Houston posed that question, the officers began arguing among themselves, trying to arrive at the best answer. The consensus was that it would be too risky to attack across an open field. The Texians would dig in and wait for the Mexicans to attack them.

Houston laughed. "Thank you, gentlemen, for your words of wisdom . . . and *courage*," he teased.

At a little after three o'clock that afternoon, Hunter returned with word that the bridge had been destroyed.

"Excellent," Houston said. He looked up at the sky. The sun was high and warm, though there was a light breeze. "Hunter, do you feel like fighting?"

"That I do, General."

"Well then, let us go."

Word was passed to all the officers, and the army was soon under arms and ready to go. They spread out in two rows over the field, nearly a thousand yards across. Hunter was in the middle of the first row.

A mile away, across the knee-high grass, the Mexicans waited in their camp. Texian lookouts, high in the trees, had already reported that the Mexicans had no patrols working and no sentries in sight. In fact, most of the Mexicans, exhausted from their all-night activity, were asleep. Their rifles were neatly stacked, while the soldiers dozed in the warm afternoon sun.

Santa Anna was himself asleep, and though he, too, had

worked during the night, his sleep was deepened by opium as well as fatigue.

On the Texas side of the field, Houston rode silently along the two rows of men. When he reached the center, he stopped in front of Hunter, then rode thirty yards forward.

"The general's not gonna stay up there durin' the attack, is he?" someone asked.

"Lord, I hope not. Why, he's the first one them Mex riflemen would shoot at."

"And he'd make a dandy target on that big white stallion," another added.

"Port arms!" Houston called in a firm voice.

The soldiers lifted their rifles.

"Forward!"

Marie watched the Texians start across the field. She waited until they were some distance away, then turned to go into the woods behind her.

A big hospital tent stood nearby. Inside it, several men were working diligently, preparing to receive the wounded. Marie recognized one officer as the division surgeon. Behind him stood three sturdy tables. On each table the men had placed a knife and a saw. Soldiers were busily rolling bandages and stocking them near the tables. Marie knew they were preparing for amputations, and the sight made her feel queasy. She leaned against a tree and looked away.

"We have to get ready for 'em, Marie," the surgeon explained, noticing her dismay.

"I know," Marie answered. "Forgive me. I was just being weak."

"I reckon we all are at one time or another," the surgeon replied.

Marie turned back toward the open field. The men who were marching across it had grown small in the distance. The ground was soft from the heavy rain, and deep furrows stretched out in long lines, pointing to the cannon that were being pulled toward the battleground. There was absolute silence, and now, even the jangle of equipment and tramp of feet was muffled.

Somewhere a woodpecker drummed impatiently, the only sound heard.

"Why aren't they playing the fife and drums?" Marie asked.

"When you hear that, you'll know they've been discovered," the surgeon said. "The sound of gunfire will come soon after that."

The sound of drums and fife reached them a moment later, and Marie took a deep breath and said a short prayer.

"Bring the cannons forward," Houston ordered, and the men rolled the Twin Sisters ahead of the line and into position. The gun crews poured in powder, then wadding, and then cannonballs. They looked at Houston, and he brought down his battered campaign hat in a grand, sweeping gesture. Both guns roared as one, and the deathly silence was ended.

As soon as the men fired the guns, the Texians started running toward the barricades.

"Remember the Alamo!" someone shouted.

"Remember Goliad!" another returned.

"Remember the Alamo!" still another said, and that became the battle cry on every Texian's tongue as the angry men surged forward: *"Remember the Alamo!"*

"My God!" Juan shouted, when he saw the Texians charging toward them. "Bugler, sound the alarm!"

The bugler stood up and looked toward the Texians. His lips were trembling so that he could scarcely blow a clear note.

"Sound it, damn you!" Juan ordered angrily. "You were willing enough to sound the death knell at the Alamo. Now blow the alarm!"

The bugler finally sounded his call, and the Mexican soldiers who had been taking their afternoon siesta awoke from their dreams in total confusion.

Houston tried to get the Texians to halt and fire, but they were too angry and too intent on closing with the enemy. They continued to charge toward the Mexican lines, shouting "Alamo" over and over again. Finally, when the Texians were no more than sixty yards from the Mexicans, they loosed their first volley of musket fire. They reloaded immediately and pressed on with the attack.

The men of the second line had moved forward to merge with the first, and now the single rank of attackers was fifteen hundred yards long. The orderly precision had ended, and the Texians were charging the Mexicans at a dead run.

Houston's horse was shot out from under him, and he stepped off skillfully as it went down. There were, however, many riderless horses running panic-stricken across the battlefield, and Houston managed to catch one of them and swing into the saddle.

Juan saw Houston mount a second time, and, believing that if he could stop Houston he could stop the attack, Juan fired at him. He saw his bullet hit Houston in the ankle, and, again, the horse went down. Undaunted, however, Houston mounted a third horse and galloped forward to join his men.

"Stand and fight!" Juan shouted to his men, but no one listened to him. In a total panic now, the Mexicans broke and ran, many of them not even trying to retrieve their weapons.

The attackers shot, clubbed, and knifed the Mexicans at will. Every Texian seemed to feel a blood-lust, and no one thought of his personal safety, but only of avenging those who had died at the Alamo and Goliad. Hatred for the Mexicans poured forth in the slaughter that ensued. Even Houston joined in. His boot was filled with blood from his wound, but despite his pain, he rode forward, slashing Mexican soldiers with his saber.

One group of Mexicans put up a spirited defense, and Hunter suddenly found himself surrounded by four of them. He shot one man and saw the others smile, thinking he had exhausted his one charge. They didn't know that Hunter had a revolver, and he squeezed off three more rounds, killing all four of them.

Juan was still fighting for his life, when he saw Santa Anna running away. "Come back here, you coward!" he shouted at his president.

Santa Anna didn't react to Juan's shout. He leaped on the back of a horse and rode away, leaving his men to die under the vengeful wrath of the Texians.

The actual battle was decided less than twenty minutes after the Twin Sisters loosed their first barrage. Then the killing came to an end, and the Texians stood in silence, surveying the carnage.

A small bayou ran behind the enemy camp, and the Mexican soldiers who had tried to cross it had been trapped there. The bayou was choked with their bodies, and the water, red with blood, began to surge through the grisly dam.

With the battle won, Houston turned and rode back across the plain to his headquarters. Hunter, who had led the attack on foot, now commandeered a Mexican horse and rode back with General Houston, steadying his commander in the saddle. Houston's wound was painful and had cost him a great loss of blood, which had weakened him considerably.

Marie was waiting anxiously for the men to return, and she recognized Hunter long before he was close. She let out a cry of joy and ran to meet him. She walked alongside him, holding onto the saddle pommel.

"For God's sake, man," Houston said, his voice racked with pain. "Pick her up and let her ride with you. That's no way for a gentleman to treat a lady."

Hunter laughed and stretched out his arm. Marie swung up onto the horse behind him, put her arms around him, and squeezed him tightly. He had come back to her! The battle was over, and Hunter was unharmed.

When they reached the Texas camp, Hunter had the doctor look at Houston. The wound was very deep, and for a while, the doctor contemplated amputating his foot. Houston refused to let them do it, insisting that they bandage the wound and let him rest. Reluctantly, the doctor did so, expressing his concern that it might develop gangrene.

After Houston received treatment, he lay beneath a tree and listened to the final report of the fighting. The battle had succeeded beyond Houston's expectations.

Eight Texians had been killed, and twenty-three wounded. Six hundred Mexicans had died, and the Texians had taken six hundred and fifty prisoners.

But Santa Anna had escaped.

It had all been for nothing.

Twenty-five

Juan had fought until there was nothing left for him to do but try to get away. The killing was still going on when he managed to slip through the wood line and make his escape. He mounted a riderless horse and rode quickly until the battlefield was far behind him. When he was far enough away, he walked the horse to let it rest. That was when he recognized Santa Anna's horse, tied to a tree. Slowly, he walked over toward the horse.

"Who is there?" a frightened voice called from the tall grass next to a bayou. Juan recognized Santa Anna's voice.

"So, my general, you are here," Juan said.

Santa Anna rose up, and Juan saw that he was covered with mud from hiding. He had discarded his grand tunic.

"Juan! Thank God, one of my commanders has had the sense to join me. Come, Gaona's division is at Fort Bend."

"Night will soon fall," Juan announced. "Can you find your way in the dark?"

"No," Santa Anna admitted.

"Neither can I," Juan said. "I think we should rest through the night. We can leave at first light."

Juan and Santa Anna spent the night in a deserted house. Juan slept lightly, while Santa Anna whimpered and complained that, without his opium, he couldn't sleep well.

The next morning, just after they got underway, they discovered a dead Mexican private.

"Good!" Santa Anna said excitedly.

"Good? This is one of our men!" Juan replied.

"Yes, and even in death he shall serve his president." Santa Anna removed the soldier's tunic and put it on over his own expensive linen shirt.

"General, if you are going to wear a private's tunic, then you should wear a private's shirt as well," Juan suggested.

"They won't look beneath the tunic," Santa Anna said. "To anyone who sees me now, I am merely a private, of no consequence."

Juan looked at the dead private from whom Santa Anna had stripped the tunic. "Every man is of some consequence to someone," he said. "Even if only to himself."

"Come, let's go," Santa Anna ordered impatiently.

"General, if we go that way, we will encounter the Texians once more."

"No," Santa Anna insisted. "Do you think I don't know where to go? I am, remember, the hero of Tampico."

"Yes," Juan said. "I remember."

"We will go this way," Santa Anna insisted.

Juan knew it was the wrong way, but he was suddenly very tired. Let the Texians capture them. Maybe it would end the war, the killing, and the despotic rule of this madman.

Juan followed Santa Anna, and they were soon captured by a Texas patrol.

The Texians could tell immediately that Santa Anna, despite his private's tunic, was a man of high rank. They knew that by the way he treated Juan, who made no attempt to conceal his rank. Then, when the soldiers took their captives to the compound where the other prisoners were being held, the Mexicans rose to their feet and cried out: *"El Presidente!"*

"My God," one of the captors said. "This here son of a bitch is Santa Anna hisself."

They took their prisoner to Houston.

Marie was tending to the fire when she saw the men leading Santa Anna. She had seen him inside the Alamo after the battle, so she recognized him and she called out to Hunter, who was resting inside the tent. "Hunter, they have Santa Anna!"

"What did you say?" Hunter asked, coming quickly to the tent opening.

"They have Santa Anna," Marie said. "I just saw him go by."

Hunter came out of the tent and embraced Marie. "This is what Houston wanted. With Santa Anna, we can sue for peace!"

"They got Santa Anna!" someone shouted. "They're takin' 'im to see the general!"

"Kill the bastard!"

"Yeah, murder the son of a bitch! What's he doin' still alive?"

"No!" Hunter yelled. "He must be kept alive! If he is killed, all our fighting will have been for nothing!" Hunter decided to walk along with Santa Anna to protect him. As he caught up with the patrol, he recognized the Mexican officer who was with Santa Anna.

"So, Senor Grant, we meet again," Juan said. "And under circumstances decidedly more advantageous to you."

"Colonel Montoya," Hunter said, "I see you have survived."

"Thus far," Juan said. "I have no idea what fate awaits me. I don't suppose you do?"

"I'm afraid not," Hunter said.

The men walked over to the shady spot where Houston lay resting. His leg was bandaged and slightly elevated.

Santa Anna stopped; clicked his heels, and bowed his head slightly. "Senor Houston, I am General Santa Anna, president of the Republic of Mexico. I am your prisoner, sir."

"I've got a rope here, General! You give the word 'n' I'll stretch his neck all the way back to Mexico!"

Santa Anna began to tremble. "Please," he said. "When I was captured, your men took my medicine box. I would like my medicine."

"Get his medicine," Houston ordered.

A moment later, a small, jewel-encrusted box was pressed into Santa Anna's hand, and he took a bit of opium. After that, he seemed a little better able to cope with the situation facing him.

"Have a seat," Houston said, pointing to an empty ammunition box.

Santa Anna sat down and looked at Houston. "May I tell you, sir, that a man may consider himself born to no common destiny who has conquered the Napoleon of the West?"

"Is that what you are?" Houston asked, unimpressed with the grandiloquence of the statement.

"Yes," Santa Anna answered. "And now it remains for you to be generous to the vanquished."

"You should have remembered that at the Alamo," Houston said quietly.

"You are a commander, sir, and a brilliant one," Santa Anna said. "You understand the rules of war. I was justified in my action at the Alamo, because the defenders refused to surrender."

"You have not the same excuse for the massacre of Colonel Fannin's command!" Houston roared angrily. "They surrendered on terms your general offered. And yet, after their defeat and surrender, they were all murdered."

Santa Anna began trembling again. "Tell me, General Houston, do you intend to exact the same revenge?"

"No," Houston answered.

"General, ain't you gonna kill this son of a bitch?" one of the Texians asked.

"Not if he does as I ask," Houston replied.

"And what is your demand?" Santa Anna asked.

"I want you to call an end to the fighting," Houston said. "And I want you to acknowledge our independence."

"I . . . I can't do that," Santa Anna protested.

"You will do it," Houston insisted. "Or I will allow my men to have their way with you."

"Let me have 'im!" someone shouted. "I lost a son-in-law in the Alamo!"

"I'll do it!" Santa Anna said quickly.

"Someone bring *El Presidente* a pen and paper," Houston ordered.

When the writing materials appeared, Santa Anna wrote the lines dictated by Houston. He concluded with the note: "I have agreed with General Houston upon an armistice which may put an end to the war forever."

"Now," Houston said. "I need someone to carry this note to the enemy."

"I will," Hunter said.

"You'll need a Mexican officer to go with you, to verify that the note is authentic."

Hunter looked at Juan. "Colonel Don Juan Esteban Montoya, would you go with me, please?"

Juan nodded. "*Si*, I will go," Juan said.

"General, I'd like to take another officer with me to bring you news of the Mexicans' compliance with your demand, because, with your permission, I will not return."

"You have my permission," Houston replied. "And the gratitude of Texas."

"No, General, it is you who shall have the gratitude of Texas. And Texas will never forget. As the United States named Washington after the general who led the new nation's fight for independence, so, I believe, will Texas name a town for you."

"Houston?" Houston replied. He laughed. "If Texas ever has a town named Houston, I predict that it won't amount to much."

Fort Bend, Texas

Upon reading the message from his president, General Gaona nodded, then gave his word that the terms of Santa Anna's surrender would be complied with. Later, as Hunter and Marie stood on the edge of the river, watching thousands of Mexican soldiers start the long trek back home, Juan came over to see them. He saluted Hunter.

"Senor Grant. Technically, I am still your prisoner," he said.

"In that case, consider yourself paroled," Hunter replied. "We have delivered Santa Anna's message to General Gaona. I have no further need for you."

"Then there remains only one piece of unfinished business between us," Juan suggested.

"Yes," Hunter said. "I suppose so."

"What?" Marie asked fearfully. "Hunter, what are you talking about?"

"Your choice of weapons?" Juan asked.

Hunter shook his head. "No, Colonel. This time the challenge is mine. The choice is yours."

"In that case, I choose . . . pistols," Juan said after a long pause.

"Pistols? But I thought you were proficient in swordsmanship."

"I am, senor. Perhaps the best in Mexico. But, as I dishonored myself before, I now wish to give you every opportunity for satisfaction."

"Stop this, both of you!" Marie said. "Hasn't there been enough killing? My God, Hunter, the Mexican dead covered the battlefield back at San Jacinto. And you, Colonel, wasn't the Alamo enough for you? My husband was killed there . . . and I'm sure you lost loved ones as well."

"*Si*," Juan said. "My brother, my best friend."

"And now, there has not been enough killing? There must be one more good man die before it is all over? For surely, whichever one of you lives, will have to live for the rest of your life with this senseless death on your conscience."

Juan and Hunter looked at each other for a long moment, then Hunter sighed.

"She is right," he said. "I am sick of killing."

"As am I, senor," Juan replied.

"Then let it end here," Hunter suggested.

"*Si.* Let it end here." Tentatively, Juan extended his hand. Hunter looked at it for a second, then he took it in his own. The two men clasped hands for a moment, then they let go.

"I will leave you now," Juan said, turning to go. From the small rise where they were standing, they could see the long line of Mexican soldiers, now leaving the field. Beyond that was the wide horizon of Texas. "We leave you this new country of yours," Juan continued. "I hope what it becomes is worthy of its noble founders."

THURSDAY, MAY 5, 1836, ROSECROWN PLANTATION, LAFOURCHE PARISH, LOUISIANA

Hunter and Marie were back in Louisiana, where Hunter was closing down his business, while Marie visited with her family. Tearfully, her mother and father confessed that what Sam had told her about her racial heritage was true.

"We didn't tell you, because we wanted to spare you the embarrassment and the pain," Cassandra said.

"Mama, don't you know that I am proud of the part of me that is you? Every part of me? I am neither pained nor embarrassed by it."

"And Mr. Grant knows about your, uh, background?" Phillipe Doucette asked his daughter.

"Yes, just as he knows about the child I am carrying."

"And he wants to marry you all the same?"

Marie laughed. "Yes, Papa. He wants to marry me all the same. And he will do so, as soon as we leave Louisiana."

Tears came to Phillipe Doucette's eyes. "He is a good man, this Hunter Grant."

"Yes, Papa, he is a very good man."

Two weeks later, after a tearful farewell, Marie and Hunter boarded a schooner in New Orleans for their trip back to Gonzales. It was dark by the time the schooner cleared the headwaters of the Mississippi and headed out into the Gulf. Marie stood at the rail in Hunter's arms, watching as the last strips of color faded from the western sky.

"You don't mind returning to Texas?" Hunter asked.

Marie smiled up at him. "You are my husband, Hunter Grant. Wherever you go, I will go; wherever you lodge, I will lodge. Wherever you die, there, too, I will die."

"We've seen enough dying to last us a lifetime, Marie," Hunter said. "Let's have no talk of it."

"There's a good way to keep me from talking," Marie teased.

"Oh? And how is that, my love?"

"Like this," she said, putting her arms around his neck and drawing his lips down to hers. The kiss grew deeper and they clung to each other passionately. Finally, Marie pulled away. "Do you understand now?"

"I know an even better way," Hunter suggested.

"And what would that be?"

"I would rather show you than tell you," Hunter said. Hunter picked Marie up and, with their lips once more locked in a kiss, carried her to their cabin and put her down on the bed. There, in a release of passion that rivaled the sunset, they made love as lovers who had clung to each other through the most tumultuous moments of history, and as husband and wife, who looked forward with easy assurance to the years of married bliss that lay before them.

Afterward they lay in each other's arms, enjoying the moment they knew was but one in an endless chain of moments that would stretch to eternity. Outside the cabin, the sounds of the ship reached them . . . the subdued rush of wind in the canvas, the creaking of ropes, the groaning of wood.

"You know where this ship be headed?" they heard someone on deck say.

"Sure I do," another answered. "We're goin' to Texas."

"Huh-uh. It ain't just Texas no more. It's the United States of Texas."

"Ain't no such thing. It's the Republic of Texas," someone else said.

"Well, whatever it is, there's goin' to be some exciting times there, I reckon," the first voice said.

"Lord, I hope not," Hunter mumbled with a chuckle. "I've got all the excitement I can handle right here in my arms."

Marie kissed him again, then snuggled into his arms.

"Hunter?"

"Yes?"

"Do you think that, years from now, people will remember what happened? Did the men of the Alamo buy anything more than a moment of glory?"

"Marie, a hundred years and more from now, no one will have ever heard of you or me. But men like Sam McCord, Almeron Dickerson, Jim Bowie, and William Barret Travis? They'll live forever. Don't you worry. As long as there is a Texas, people will remember the Alamo."